Heaven and Hell

Heaven and Hell

Kristen Ashley

First ebook edition: December, 2011
First print edition: June, 2015

ISBN: 0692455000
ISBN-13: 9780692455005

Discover other titles by Kristen Ashley at:
www.kristenashley.net

Commune with Kristen at:
www.facebook.com/kristenashleybooks
Twitter: KristenAshley68

DEDICATION

Once upon a time, I was a girl from a small town in Indiana who had big dreams of *everything*. Then, at university at Purdue, I met Kelly Brown who by that time had lived on four continents.

Then she introduced me to her parents, Pam and Neil.

They were chic, they were cosmopolitan, they were cultured, they were well traveled, they were unbelievably bright, and they were extraordinarily generous.

And they opened my world.

So I dedicate this book to Pam, Neil, and their daughter, my darling Kelly.

Thank you for sharing the world with me.

PROLOGUE

Hell

The television was on and I heard him. Like his voice was a magnet, even though I wanted to avoid that room, would do anything to avoid it unless ordered otherwise, my body floated from the kitchen to the living room.

Cooter was in his easy chair watching it, and automatically, my body stopped nowhere near his chair.

My gaze was riveted to the television screen, watching the gorgeous man, with his white smile and intelligent eyes, talking to the sports commentators.

They were probably talking about football, something I had absolutely no interest in whatsoever. But I knew a lot about it. This was because Cooter lived and breathed football during football season. He was the quarterback at our high school, popular, hot—God, I'd wanted him. So young, so fit, so talented, so cool, so beautiful.

And, dream of dreams, when I was a junior and he was a senior, he'd picked me.

I was in heaven.

Three years later, that heaven turned to hell.

I heard a yapping but ignored it. This was Cooter's dog, Memphis, saying hello to me.

When Cooter got Memphis, everyone in town was shocked. Cooter was definitely a pit bull or Rottweiler type of guy, and not because both those types of dogs were really cute but for other reasons. So when he came home with a brown and white King Charles spaniel, I was stunned. When he proceeded to dote on that dog like it was his child, I was freaked. I didn't think Cooter had an ounce of affection in him available to give to anyone, no human and certainly no dog.

But there you go. He did. He adored Memphis. Completely.

He'd named her Memphis with the declaration, "Fuck the redcoats," like the English were still our enemies and him naming a spaniel after an American city would offend them in some way that would cause nationwide distress.

Then again, Cooter had a full supply of animosity for a lot of people, places, and things, and he kept it stocked up.

Not to mention, Cooter was the quarterback of a winning team in a small town that lived football, and therefore, he hadn't had to worry too much about books. And not knowing this then, but definitely knowing it now, he was scary lazy; if he didn't have to do it, he didn't.

So he didn't. I wasn't certain he cracked open a book throughout high school. But I *was* certain he didn't do it in his very short tenure in college.

Therefore, Cooter was not the brightest bulb in the box.

"And there he is, folks, Sampson Cooper. Thanks for stoppin' in, Coop," the commentator said, and I watched Sampson Cooper smile.

My heart fluttered.

Sampson Cooper. Very tall. Very dark. Very beautiful.

I adored him. When Cooter was out of the house, I Internet-stalked Sampson Cooper. I knew everything about him.

Everything.

Well, everything you could learn on the Internet.

I knew his stats when he played college ball. I knew his stats when he played pro ball.

I knew the exact day he requested to be released from his contract playing for the Indianapolis Colts so he could join the Army. I knew he did this in memory of his brother, who had died in Iraq and he'd died a hero. I knew this upset Sampson Cooper greatly. I knew not long after he joined the Army, he'd disappeared "off the grid" for four years. I also knew when he came back.

And lastly, I, and everyone probably in the world, knew what he'd done when he was "off the grid," considering a tell-all (but anonymous) book was written about it and a big investigation was launched when it was. Therefore, I knew what he'd done was dangerous in a way people like me couldn't comprehend the level of danger. I knew it was also heroic. And lastly, I knew that he tried to keep a low profile, but when he found this impossible, he'd come out into the limelight and stayed there. I guessed he did this because, at least if it was his choice, he had some slim chance of controlling it.

"*Anytime, Frank,*" Sampson Cooper replied, his voice deep and weirdly rough—not rough like sandpaper, rough like velvet.

My stomach melted.

"*Babe!*" Cooter snapped. I jumped and my eyes shot to him.

Oh no.

He was getting out of his chair, and now, ten years later, he was no longer fit (in fact, he had a serious beer belly, which was only partly due to his copious consumption of beer; the other part was food, and the last part was being seriously lazy). I'd discovered he was not talented at all. He was definitely not cool. And he was anything but beautiful.

At the look on his face, my mind became consumed with what my next move would be. I knew one thing: I had a fifty-fifty shot at success. I could take a step back and piss him off more (for whatever reason he was pissed off), which would make it worse (but conversely, it could serve as a deterrent, snapping him out of whatever mood had hold of him), or I could stand my ground, which also led to both options.

Like often happened, I chose wrongly and my choice was to take a step back.

He advanced quickly, and no matter how much of a beer belly he had, my husband could move.

I didn't have a prayer to avoid it—I'd learned that—but still, I tried.

As usual, I wasn't fast enough.

He got close and backhanded me hard. With some experience, it was at the upper end of the scale of how hard he could hit me. I knew this because it hurt like a bitch and also because I flew to the side and landed hard on a hand and hip. I lost focus on the pain in my cheek when the pain radiating up my arm from my wrist took precedence.

Then he kicked me in the back. I bit back my cry at this new pain focus and thanked God he was only wearing a sock. When he kicked me, he did it no matter what footwear he was wearing, and since his job meant he had to wear steel-toed boots, I'd learned a sock was far, far better.

"I said," he snarled, and I sucked in a breath and stared at the carpet, "get me a fuckin' *beer*."

A beer.

I'd been watching Sampson Cooper, mesmerized by a beautiful man, a good man, a strong man, a loyal man, a loving man, and I'd missed my husband, who was none of those things, asking for a beer.

And he hit and kicked me because I hadn't jumped at his command.

God, *God*, I hated my fucking husband.

I stayed prone and kept my eyes from him. Again, it was a crapshoot how he would react to this.

Luckily, his presence retreated.

When it did, the beautiful Sampson Cooper was the last thing on my mind.

Getting my husband a beer was the only thing on it.

So I carefully but swiftly pulled myself to my feet and got Cooter a beer.

Two months, three days, four hours, and thirteen minutes later…

The doorbell rang.

Memphis yapped at it.

I moved toward it.

Then Memphis yapped at my heels.

I sighed.

I loved dogs. I loved all animals, actually, save snakes (they freaked me out). And lizards (they freaked me out too). And I wasn't really big on rodents of any kind. No, that wasn't true; hamsters were kind of cute.

But I could not pull up any affection for a dog Cooter loved. It wasn't that she wasn't cute, cuddly, and sweet, even to me.

It was just that anytime Memphis showed me any affection, it pissed Cooter off.

So I guessed that was it.

I did what I could not to piss Cooter off, including holding myself distant from our dog, even when he was not around.

Memphis, of course, had no idea what her being sweet to me meant. Memphis only knew Cooter's devotion and did not get why she didn't get the same from me. I had to give it to the dog; she never gave up. No matter how much I ignored her, she just got cuter, cuddlier, and sweeter.

I admired her for that.

I'd given up years ago.

I looked through the peephole and blinked.

Then my heart started racing.

And, in the expanse of about three seconds, my mind flew in a million different directions, finally settling on one.

It was after six o'clock.

Cooter was usually home by five fifteen.

That said, if he wanted to have a beer with the guys or whatever he did when he didn't come home, he did it and didn't bother to phone, text, or pop home to let me know. Lately, this happened more often than not. And the lately that included most recently, Cooter didn't come home until almost nine o'clock.

I wanted to enjoy these moments of reprieve but I couldn't, mostly because the time he was away and I was home I spent worrying about what mood he'd be in when he got home. He could be drunk and pissed, which did not bode well; he could be sober and pissed, which also did not bode well; or he could be either and horny, which was worst of all.

Lately, he came back smelling of beer (but not drunk) and always horny but in a way that made my skin crawl even *more* than it normally did at the thought of him touching me, and that was saying something. Nothing had really changed with our sex life except he got more into it (which also was not fun for me), and he lasted longer (again with the no-fun part), and it seemed he was getting off on it more, was more excited, and I did nothing, not one thing differently to cause *that.*

But right then, Ozzie was standing outside my door.

Barney "Ozzie" Oswald had been sheriff for as long as I could remember. He had to be older than dirt, but he still looked fit, spritely, and alert. (He'd always looked fit, spritely, and alert.)

And now, with him on my doorstep, he looked all those things but something else too.

I opened the door, smiled, and whispered, "Hey, Ozzie."

At my whisper, which was pretty much my normal tone (I was cautious with everything including the volume of my voice), Ozzie did a mini-flinch.

I had known Ozzie as sheriff for years, and Ozzie knew everyone in town for years too, including me, and he knew me pretty well considering he was a hunting buddy of my dad's. He'd known me since I was a little girl. He knew ten years ago I didn't whisper. And I suspected he knew why I did it now.

"Kia, darlin', can I come in?" he asked. His tone was also quiet, though not a whisper. And it was gentle. Then again, it was always a form of gentle. That was Ozzie. He was sheriff, but he was a gentle man.

I loved Ozzie. The whole town did.

"Sure," I replied, pushing out the screen door. Memphis moved instantly, yapping and jumping around Ozzie's ankles in a tizzy of excitement, but unless she was sleeping or snuggling, she was usually always in a tizzy of excitement.

This was because Memphis's world was golden. She loved her daddy. Her daddy got her the best food money could buy. Her daddy gave her table scraps. Her daddy showered her with affection. Her daddy bought her new toys and chews all the time. He liberally gave her treats and let her sleep in our bed, right in the middle, stretched sideways so I was nearly falling off my side. Her daddy also let her poo anywhere in the yard, knowing I'd clean it up. And her daddy often had his buds over and let them shower her with affection.

Memphis loved company as much as she generally loved life. So now Memphis was in throes of delight.

I thought this as my heart kept racing faster and faster. Soon my body would need to move, sprint through town to keep up, or it'd fly out of my chest.

"Is everything okay?" I asked Ozzie, and he studied me.

"Maybe we should go sit down in your living room," he suggested, and it was my turn to study him, but my heart only raced faster.

I nodded and moved, leading the way to the living room. I threw out an arm to the furniture there and Memphis did a little twirl, waiting for one of us to be seated so she could jump on one of our laps and be adorable.

"Please, Kia, sit," Ozzie muttered.

I studied him again, took in a deep breath, and sat on the edge of the couch.

Ozzie sat in an armchair facing me, also on the edge.

Memphis jumped onto his lap.

Ozzie started petting the dog, but he did this distractedly, his eyes never leaving mine.

"Ozzie," I whispered, my heart beating so fast I could feel it in my throat.

"You know Milo Cloverfield, darlin'?" he asked.

Oh God.

I knew where this was headed because I not only knew Milo Cloverfield (because everyone knew Milo), I knew who he was married to.

"Yes," I answered and it was less than a whisper. It was a breath.

Ozzie held my eyes. Then he closed his tight, turned his head away, and my gaze dropped at a movement I caught. I saw that he was petting Memphis with one hand; the other one had formed a fist.

My gaze shot back to his when I sensed his head turning again and I held my breath.

"Honey, I hate to tell you all this, but I'll go fast, get it done, all right?"

I nodded, let out my breath, then sucked it in again.

Memphis yapped, finally feeling the vibe slice into her cotton candy world.

Ozzie ignored the dog and got down to it.

"I'm sorry to say, darlin', that Coot was seein' Vanessa Cloverfield on the sly."

I *knew* it.

My husband was a sick bastard but now I knew just how sick. No wonder he got off on sex these days like he did. He was screwing Vanessa then coming home and screwing me.

The big man.

The head cheese.

He hadn't been that in *years* and he was loving it.

God, what a dick!

I let my breath out, clenched my teeth, and wondered when I would be able to walk out of high school.

Jeez, Cooter was an asshole. He was washed up. He was out of shape. And still, stupid, silly, jealous, grasping Vanessa Lockhart Cloverfield clearly stopped at nothing to get him.

Well, she could have him.

I just needed to figure out how to give him to her. I'd tried leaving six times. I'd failed. And the way I'd failed, Cooter finally taught me not to try again.

But fuck this shit.

"Kia," Ozzie called, and I focused on him.

"Yeah?" I asked.

"Honey, Milo found out."

Uh-oh.

Milo was a hothead. Everyone knew that.

"And?" I whispered.

"And he went to the Heartmeadow Motel with his shotgun and, Kia, honey…" He paused, pulled in breath, and finished, "He used it."

My body froze, every inch of it including my eyes, which were wide open.

"Coot's dead, darlin'," Ozzie whispered, and that was when I started hyperventilating.

Then I breathed, "What?"

"Coot's dead. Milo shot him, clocked Vanessa with the butt of his gun, and then called it in himself."

That was…

It was…

"That's *crazy*," I said softly. "Why would Milo do that?"

"'Cause he's got a short fuse, he loves his wife, he couldn't bear the idea of her steppin' out on him, and he lost it. He also ain't too smart, but he's smart enough to know he ain't, so he didn't bother runnin' 'cause he knew he'd be caught."

I had no reply to this. Any of it.

I couldn't think.

I could barely breathe.

Ozzie stared at me.

Then he called, "Kia?"

I blinked and my body started when it it hit me what he'd said.

Milo Cloverfield, who was normally a pretty fun-loving guy, good to have around, good for a laugh, but he definitely could lose it, had shot my husband dead with a shotgun.

"Where?" I suddenly blurted.

"Pardon?" Ozzie asked.

"Where did Milo shoot him?" I asked, and Ozzie's stare got more intense.

"At the motel," Ozzie answered, and I shook my head.

"No, I mean where on his body?"

That's when his face closed down and he said quietly, "Honey, not sure—"

"Where, Ozzie?"

Ozzie held my eyes. Then he sighed before he said, still talking quietly, "Got him one side of the head."

Closed casket, then.

"Kia, you all right?" Ozzie asked.

Was I all right?

I thought about it.

I sat in my living room with furniture Cooter picked and carpeting Cooter picked in a house Cooter picked in a subdivision Cooter picked with Ozzie sitting in an armchair, petting a strangely quiet but watchful (and her eyes were on me) dog that Cooter picked. None of which I liked (except the dog but only secretly). And I thought about this.

I thought that Cooter was never going to come home again.

I thought that I was never going to have to pretend I enjoyed sex with Cooter again. And I never had to fake another orgasm again, which, by the way, was exhausting but, fortunately, not difficult to achieve believability considering Cooter still (or did, not anymore) thought his shit didn't stink.

I thought that I'd never get backhanded, slapped, pushed, kicked or my arm twisted by Cooter again.

I thought that every morning, noon, and night I could eat what I wanted and not have to make exactly what Cooter wanted. I could go to bed when I wanted. I could wear what I wanted. I could watch on TV what I wanted. I could talk on the phone as long as I wanted.

And I could finally be nice to my own damn dog.

Then I thought, *Fuck yes, I'm all right.*

I did not say that.

I said, "I'm in shock," which wasn't a lie.

Ozzie didn't miss much and he wasn't missing much now. This must have been why he said super softly and very cautiously, his eyes never leaving mine, his body leaning in slightly, his hand stilling on Memphis, "You loved him once, darlin', and him passin', there'll come a time when you'll remember that and it'll hit you."

I was not surprised Ozzie knew I didn't love Cooter now. Like I said, Ozzie didn't miss much.

But I wasn't thinking about that.

I was thinking about loving Cooter.

And it wasn't the first time I'd thought on this over the years.

I already knew I'd never loved Cooter. Not in the beginning, not now. I loved the idea of him, the golden light that shone from his local fame, the promise he squandered. I was in love with that. I was young, I was stupid, and I was blinded by false glory.

But I'd never loved my husband. Marrying Cooter had been the worst mistake I'd made in my life.

I knew I did not at that moment, nor would I anytime in the future, mourn his passing. I also knew somewhere deep inside me that I would not go to hell for that.

Because I'd been in hell for the seven years I spent married to Cooter Clementine.

So I'd done my time.

Two weeks, one day, and sixteen hours later...

The phone rang.

How I heard it over the music, I did not know, but I did.

Cooter hated my music. He never let me play it. But he played his, and *loud.*

I turned down The Guess Who's kickass thirteen-plus-minutes live version of "American Woman" and strode to the phone.

Memphis yapped.

"Quiet, baby," I murmured.

Memphis wagged her tail.

I grinned at my dog.

She wagged her tail harder.

I grinned bigger.

Then I picked up the phone, beeped it on, put it to my ear, and greeted, "Hello?"

"Hello, may I please speak to a Mrs. Kia Clementine?"

My grin became a smile.

I was keeping Cooter's last name. His last name was awesome. It was the best thing he gave to me. Hell, it was the *only* decent thing he'd ever given me.

So I was keeping it.

"This is she," I replied.

"Hello, this is Stacy from Biller General Insurance."

My head cocked to the side in confusion and I said, "Hello."

"This is just a courtesy call to inform you we've received the information from his employer that your husband has passed. We've sent the forms to you to complete and you should receive them in the mail within the next week. As soon as you complete and return them, we'll process them as quickly as we can and you'll receive your check in four to six weeks."

I blinked at Memphis.

Memphis blinked back.

Then I asked, "What?"

"We're very sorry for your loss and we understand this is a difficult time for you. It's never easy handling paperwork in these times, but the forms aren't difficult to complete. The sooner they're done, the sooner we can pay Mr. Clementine's life insurance and you'll have the financial security he clearly wished you to have. In preparation for that, while you're waiting for the forms to arrive, you'll need to see to getting a notarized copy of his death certificate."

Say what?

Cooter wanted me to have financial security?

Heck, Cooter wanted me to have *any* security?

"I'm sorry, I'm not certain what you're referring to," I told her.

There was a moment of silence then, "Why, Mr. Clementine's five million dollar life insurance policy. Eight months ago, he took one out on himself and you."

I froze again, exactly like I did when I heard word Cooter was dead—head to toe, eyes huge.

Then I whispered, "Sorry?"

"Mr. Clementine's five million dollar life insurance policy," she answered.

I blinked at Memphis.

Memphis sat on her rump and blinked back.

Cooter didn't let me handle anything, not the household bills, not the bank accounts, nothing. He even took my paycheck and gave me an allowance. He wasn't just an asshole. He was a dominating, control-freak asshole.

"He took a policy out on me?" I asked my new best friend Stacy.

"Yes, at the same time he took his."

"Was mine for five million dollars?" I asked.

Another moment of hesitation before, "No, yours is for ten."

I blinked yet again at Memphis.

Memphis got up on all her paws and yapped.

That bastard!

Gossip had run rampant since Milo blew half of Cooter's head off, and it was so rampant, it was impossible to keep myself shielded from it.

Not that I cared. I just was trying to move on. Cooter was in the ground. Milo was in jail. Vanessa had sequestered herself behind closed curtains. And I was making plans for the future.

My house was already on the market. My salary didn't cover the mortgage, but upon Cooter's death (or not long after—his boss didn't mess around because his boss was a good guy), his pension was released to me, and even though the government took their chunk, Cooter's pension was still a whack. I was good until the house sold and we'd been living there for seven years. The market wasn't great, but his folks and my folks had given us a decent down payment. My friend Paula was my real estate agent, and she said I had equity in it and would make a tidy profit in order to downsize to a condo or something more within my budget.

I was already planning my yard sale. Everything must go. I was going to buy all new. I just hoped that the house sold relatively quickly before my living expenses bit into Cooter's pension too much because I wanted nice stuff. I also wanted a fabulous vacation (something Cooter never took me on). And, further, I wanted an entire new wardrobe that *I* picked.

These were my plans and I spent a goodly amount of time thinking on them. But I still heard the talk.

And with what I heard, I knew that Cooter had started his thing with Vanessa nine months ago.

Nine months.

One month shy of when Cooter took out a huge, crazy, probably insanely expensive life insurance policy on me for no good reason.

Holy crap, they were planning on offing me!

"Mrs. Clementine? Are you there?" Stacy called

My back straightened and I clipped into the phone, "Yes, I'm here. I'm alive, breathing, and very, very *here*."

"Uh…" she mumbled. "Good. So, um…the forms—"

"You bet your bippy that I'll be all over completing those puppies. Never fear, Stacy, I'll get the business of filling out forms out of the way so I can continue mourning the passing of my beloved, freaking husband."

This outburst bought me a moment of silence, then, "Uh…" she mumbled again. "Right. Okay."

"Okay," I replied. "Thanks for your call. I'm certain this part of your job description is no fun."

"No, actually, you're right. It's, um…not real fun."

"Well, tick me off your to-do list, sweetie, go to some fancy coffee cart, and get yourself a nice coffee. Spoil yourself. Life's short."

"Yes, right, Mrs. Clementine."

"Ms.," I corrected her.

"Pardon?"

"Ms.," I repeated. "I'm Ms. Clementine now."

Silence, then a whispered, "Right."

"Have a good day," I urged.

"Right, uh…you, um…too."

"Will do," I assured her, then beeped the phone off.

I walked straight to the phonebook and looked up the number to the Sheriff Department. I called it. I asked to speak to Ozzie. They transferred me to Ozzie and I told him about my boon and the timing. He was silent a long time.

Then he whistled.

He expressed his gratitude and got off the phone.

I looked at Memphis and stated, "First, we're searching every inch of this house to look for evidence those two *creeps* wanted to *knock me off* to collect the insurance. Then we're turning on the computer and calling up a map of the world. We're going to point at it, or I am, since you can't, and then we're planning my vacation to wherever my finger lands."

Memphis yapped her agreement to this plan.

"Unless I don't hit somewhere in The States," I warned. "If I pick Okinawa, you'll probably have to go stay with Mom and Dad while I go off and enjoy Cooter's wife-killing money."

Memphis yapped again and her cute, little, brown and white body shook with her tail wags.

She loved my mom.

Then again, she loved everyone.

So much, it didn't even seem like she noticed Cooter was gone. No staring at doors. No little doggie melancholy.

But I had taken over the affection, treats, feedings, and the like, so she wasn't missing out.

"You with me?" I asked, even though I knew. Memphis wasn't one for solitude. She'd be with me every step of the way.

She yapped anyway, just so I knew she had my back.

I nodded.

Then I searched.

I found the e-mails.

My husband was so fucking dumb.

His girlfriend wasn't much smarter.

I called Ozzie again.

He came over.

The next day, Vanessa came out of seclusion, mostly because she had no choice, and she did it in handcuffs.

While this was happening (though I didn't know it), I was on the phone with my friend Teri, who was a travel agent, booking my flights to Paris.

1

I KNOW YOU, YOU KNOW

I stood underneath it a long time, smack-dab in the middle of the vast, populated space, my head tilted way back, my back arched, looking up. So long, people probably thought I was crazy. So long, I got dizzy. But I did it. And while I did it, I memorized what I saw.

Then I righted my head, turned, and walked down the avenue.

I took my time.

This was because I had all the time in the world.

When I got a fair ways away, I pulled my camera out of my purse, did the head-tilting back-arched thing, aimed, and shot once—an adjustment—twice—another adjustment—then a third time.

I looked at the display and moved through the photos I took of a nighttime, lit up, cool-as-freaking-*shit* Eiffel Tower.

I grinned and muttered, "Memphis, baby, you're gonna like that one."

Then I turned off my camera, tucked it in my purse, and gave the Tower one last, lingering look before I moved back down the avenue to saunter the streets of Paris.

I stood in front of the full-length, freestanding mirror. It was oval. It had a lot of carving in the wood around it and black marks on the mirror, which meant it was old and the silver was fading, but it was fading in a supremely cool way.

Studying the wood, I was pretty impressed with the cleaning staff at this hotel, considering there wasn't any dust in all those grooves of the mirror. It was all glossy and gleaming. Someone had spent a serious amount of time polishing it.

My eyes moved from the wood to me.

It was summer. My reflection showed me what I knew: I was tan. This was because, for the last three weeks, I'd spent a lot of time outside wandering the streets of Paris, Rome, and Florence.

I'd also bought myself the new sundress I had on and I'd never owned anything so expensive or so exquisite.

A long time ago, Cooter decreed that all my apparel come from Target or Walmart, explaining that this was all we could afford within our budget and he kind of wasn't wrong. Except he didn't get all his clothing from those places. I really didn't mind. Target, especially, had some nice stuff.

What I minded was that Cooter also decreed anytime I bought something for me he would come along, and he didn't have a good eye to what suited me, style, fit, or color. Cooter had a taste for skank so he dressed his wife like one.

I hated it.

My sundress did not say skank. Not even close.

It was kind of a salmony-peach. It had a flimsy, flippy skirt that was not short, but it was also not long. Loads of pin-tuck pleats around the waistline. And at the bodice, thin straps led into a halter neck. It was really kind of simple, but the filmy fabric, unusual color (that went freaking *great* with my golden skin), and attention to detail made it superhot.

I loved it.

But I was wearing flip-flops.

They were cute flip-flops, with big, floppy flowers at the toes, and they matched the dress nearly perfectly. But as my eyes slid up and down my body in the mirror, I just didn't think they'd do.

My gaze shifted to the windows. I'd pulled open the wooden shutters practically upon waking and all you could see was the beauty of Lake Como.

Seriously. Did you wear flip-flops with an expensive sundress in a fancy hotel on Lake Como in Italy?

It was morning. I was heading to the dining room. In my world, breakfast was flip-flop territory.

But the dress wasn't.

In fact, inspecting myself top to toe, the whole gig was wrong.

I went to my cosmetics case and back to the mirror.

A dusting of face powder. Good.

A bit of shimmery, peach cream blusher. Better.

A bit of eye shadow, filling in my brows with pencil. A thin line of eyeliner pencil, softened with the tip of a brush. A swipe of mascara. And a touch of shimmery, peach lip gloss.

Much, much better.

I moved to the wardrobe, opened it, and pulled out the shoebox.

Then I pulled out the strappy sandals that cost way, *way* more than the dress.

I'd bought them in Paris. The straps were super thin. The heel was super high. It was also super thin. And they were bronze.

They would kick *ass* with this dress.

The women I'd seen in Paris, Rome, and Florence—attractive, even stunning beauties and very fashionable—would not blink at wearing those sandals with that dress to breakfast.

I strapped them on and walked to the mirror.

Yes. Perfect.

I stood in front of the mirror, put on three more coats of mascara at the very outside edges of my lashes, and *kapow*! My eyes looked *awesome*.

I pulled out the ponytail holder, fluffed out my hair, and stared at myself.

Yep, this was it. This said Lake Como. This said Europe. This said jet-setter.

I blinked.

Tears began to fill my eyes so I blinked again, quickly turned away, grabbed my cute, little, Italian leather purse I got in Florence and my room key, and I went to the dining room.

I knew very little Italian. My Italian language arsenal included pizza, *grazie*, *ciao*, and *capisce*, and I actually wasn't really certain what *capisce* meant, just that gangsters in the movies said it. Even though I'd been in Italy for two weeks, I wasn't picking much up, mostly because I was too shy to try.

So I did my communication with a lot of smiling and hand gestures. Which was how I greeted and thanked the maître d' when he saw me, smiled, and started babbling, nodding his head, snatching up a menu, and throwing out his arm to show me through the dining room.

It was packed and I could see why. This hotel cost a freaking fortune, but it was in an awesome location with spectacular views.

Looking around, I did the right thing with the dress and sandals. If I'd thrown on a tee and shorts with this crowd, I would be *way* underdressed.

I was so busy studying those around me and patting myself on the back for my wardrobe decisions, at the same time trying to look cool and aloof, like this was an everyday occurrence for me, I didn't pay attention to where the maître d' was taking me.

I paid attention and nearly passed out.

Seriously. I nearly *passed out.*

This was because every table was taken except one, which was in front of two doors opened to the elements, the view of the lake, the sun shining in. And at the table in the corner next to it, his back to the wall, sat Sampson Cooper.

Sampson Cooper!

Oh.

My.

Freaking.

God!

I couldn't sit one table over from Sampson Freaking Cooper!

What was he doing in Italy?

What was he doing sitting *alone* at a table in a beautiful, expensive hotel in Italy?

Where was the supermodel-esque hot chick that had to be his woman?

Perhaps she was in their room finishing up her makeup, seeing as, when I finally tore my eyes from him, I saw he didn't have any dirty dishes on his table, only a coffee cup and cafetière half full of coffee. Perhaps he was tired of waiting for her, he needed caffeine, he was a man on the go and didn't wait around for chicks, even hot ones that looked like supermodels, so off he went, telling her to meet him downstairs.

Yes, that made sense. That had to be it.

While we approached and I tried not to hyperventilate, my eyes went from his cafetière to his face to see he was still looking out his set of opened doors. In profile, his strong jaw was stronger in real life than in pictures or on TV. His high cheekbones were also higher and more defined. His straight nose was straighter and more attractive. His thick, black hair, clipped short to his head, had a healthy sheen to it that was healthier in real life. And the appealing dark tone to his skin he got from being half white, a quarter black, and a quarter Hispanic was far more appealing in person.

Oh man, I was *not* going to be able to do this.

Sure, I had about ten thousand, seven hundred and twenty-two fantastical, intense, and long-running fantasies about this guy—how we would meet, how he would fall in love with me instantly and sweep me away from the hell that was my life and make me blissfully happy forever. But now, faced with the possibility of sharing his air space, I wanted not one thing to do with him.

The maître d' stopped and said something in Italian to me, and when I stopped and turned dazedly to him, it hit me.

I knew how I would handle this.

Sampson Cooper didn't exist.

Not across the table. Only in a dreamworld.

I would ignore him, his hot chick would show, my fantasy would be crushed, but I'd get on with my day, my vacation, and then use him as a totally killer travel story when I got home.

Paula and Teri would eat this up. They loved him as much as I did.

Teri even had a life-size cardboard-standing thingy of him in his Indianapolis Colts uniform. She kept it in her bedroom. She also asked me once if I thought that was putting off the real life men she invited there (and there were a fair few), because many of them, more than seemed appropriate, found it difficult to perform.

I did not have within my mental hard drive statistics about how often or what percentage of men could not go the distance. I was also not a man and, therefore, could not know if a life-size cardboard cutout of a hot guy wearing football pads would affect performance. What I did know was that if there was a life-size cardboard cutout of Pamela Anderson in her *Baywatch* suit in the same room as me and a guy doing the nasty, I'd definitely find it, at the very least, distracting.

So I decided I'd use him as a cool-ass story, and they would never know I spent the entire breakfast ignoring his existence and staring at a lake.

I communicated in the universal language of smiling to the maître d'. His already big smile got enormous for some bizarre reason, which made me fear he was going to hug me and declare in Italian that I was his long-lost daughter, something I wouldn't understand since I didn't speak Italian, and thus, I'd probably freak out and do this in front of Sampson Cooper.

No, no. Repeat after me: Sampson Cooper did *not* exist.

It would be fine. *Everything* would be fine.

Still smiling weirdly maniacally, the maître d' went on the move. I had wanted to sit with my back to Cooper's table, but the maître d' was scooting me in on the side facing him in a way that was strangely paternal at the same time it was aggressive. I had no choice but to go with it or maybe end up in a smackdown with a maître d'hotel in an exclusive hotel on Lake Como with Sampson Cooper as one of my audience, and for obvious reasons, that wouldn't do. It would be harder to avoid Cooper when he was sitting in my direct line of sight, but I'd survived a very bad marriage, my husband had cheated on me, and with his girlfriend, he had plotted my demise.

If I could live through that, I could sit across from Sampson Cooper.

So I sat across from Sampson Cooper.

With a dramatic flourish that startled me so much I jumped a little, though it was kind of cool, but I couldn't exactly explain why, the maître d' flipped open my menu and plopped it in my upturned hands.

Then he spoke swiftly to me in Italian all the while my head was tipped back and I glued my eyes with fierce determination at his face, my lips curved in a small smile that I hoped didn't look stupid in the very unlikely event that Sampson Cooper was actually looking at me. He kept talking for some time and if he was describing the specials (did they do breakfast specials?), they had a lot of them.

He clapped his hands, fluttered them in the air for a second, and turned toward Sampson Cooper. I caught his wink at Cooper, something else I thought was weird, before he scurried away.

I turned my attention directly to the menu.

Perusing it, I did what I'd been doing the last two weeks in Italy; I called up my very limited (but increasingly less so) experience of looking at menus in Italian restaurants. Cooter was not one to take his wife on the town, and when he did, it was for pizza and not in the kind of pizza joints that printed their options in Italian.

Mozzarella I knew, but I didn't see that anywhere on the menu (alas). I saw something that ended with *di funghi*, which I was pretty certain meant mushrooms because other stuff I'd ordered with those words in it also had mushrooms. I hoped it was a mushroom omelet because that sounded really good, and I had hope since the word before it was *omelette* and I figured an *omelette* was an omelet the world over.

I'd made this decision when a cafetière was plonked on my table with a small, elegant pitcher of cream and matching sugar bowl and another Italian man, my waiter, started talking to me. He didn't talk long, but he did clap when he was done and move away without taking my order.

I watched him go, and as best I could without looking like a freak, I turned my attention to the lake without my eyes once hitting Sampson Cooper.

At this moment, it struck me I needed coffee and I needed it STAT.

So, as casually as I could muster, I turned my attention to the cafetière, did the press thing, upended the coffee cup at my place setting, and prepared my coffee.

Sipping carefully so as not to burn my tongue or choke, I turned my attention back to the lake.

Seriously, it was pretty. I'd never seen anything like it. It kind of sucked that Cooter and Vanessa wanting me dead was the reason why I had this gift but…whatever. It was a gift. I'd lived through hell; now it was my turn in heaven, and Lake Como not only looked but felt just like what heaven had to be.

The waiter came back, shot some Italian at me, and I made a stab in the dark and decided he was asking for my order. I didn't bother speaking, just did a lot of smiling and pointed to what I wanted on the menu. He nodded, snatched the menu out of my hand, did a dramatic flourish with it in the air that took slightly less space than the maître d's flourish (but even more compact, it was no less theatrical), before tucking it smartly under his armpit and he hurried away.

I was looking after him in preparation for the taxing effort of once again turning my head and not acknowledging Sampson Cooper's presence when I heard a deep, low, masculine chuckle, and it was so attractive, without my permission, my eyes went to him.

My heart stopped beating. Total stall. It would take paddles to get it pumping again.

He was no longer chuckling, but he was smiling.

At me.

"Do you speak English?" he asked, and I blinked.

Holy cow! He was talking to me!

"Yes," my mouth, fortunately, answered for me.

"These guys got it goin' on," he informed me, and I blinked again.

"What guys?" my mouth, luckily, kept speaking.

He tipped his head in the direction of where my waiter was last seen and my heart started beating again, hard and fast. I could feel it in my neck, my wrists, even at my temples.

"You think they train them in that shit?" he asked, and I blinked again.

Sampson Cooper just used a curse word in a swanky Italian hotel on Lake Como!

Why did I think that was so…*freaking…cool?*

"What…" I hesitated, then cautiously went on, "shit?"

He smiled again.

My heart stopped beating again.

Then he answered, "The menus." He shook his head and immediately proceeded to blaspheme in a swanky Italian hotel on Lake Como. "Jesus. The first time the head guy did it, thought he was gonna clock me."

"That would have been unfortunate," I observed and sucked in a sharp breath when he threw his beautiful head back and burst into deep, rough-like-velvet laughter.

I'd never heard him laugh. I'd never even *seen* him laugh. Smile? Lots. Chuckle? Sure. Grin? More than occasionally.

Full-on laughter?

Never.

He was the most beautiful man I'd ever seen in my life. By far. And that was before I saw him in real life, and in real life, he was more beautiful than ever.

But that deep, rough-like-velvet laughter glided right across every inch of my skin, leaving beauty in its wake that soaked through, and I swear to God, it felt like it settled into my soul.

He sobered, but his dark brown eyes were still dancing when he focused on me and agreed, "Yeah, that would have been unfortunate."

It was at this point I jumped at least six inches because the maître d' was suddenly there, talking fast, gesturing broadly, his head going back and forth between Sampson Cooper and me.

Then my waiter was there.

I had no idea what was going on, and further, I had no hope of finding out because he not once used the words mozzarella, *ciao, grazie, capisce,* or pizza, and if he did, that probably wouldn't have explained what was happening.

But before I could form any conclusions or, say, react *at all,* my entire body went rigid when I watched in sheer, unadulterated terror as the waiter moved my cafetière, creamer, sugar bowl, and coffee cup to Sampson Cooper's table.

What were they doing?

Cooper's deep, rough-like-velvet voice came to me, and my eyes shot to him when he asked, "Do you speak Italian?"

"Uh..." I was able to get out before...

No joke.

Seriously.

The maître d' grasped my elbow, forcibly yanked me out of my chair in that aggressive but paternal way he had, then guided me around the table, shuffling me between my old table and

Sampson Cooper's definitely current table at the same time the waiter scooched with me. The waiter pulled out the chair across from Cooper and the maître d' plonked my booty in it.

I was deep breathing and feeling acutely like I was in the preliminary stages of my first ever seizure when my head tipped back for some reason and I saw Sampson Cooper had stood. Not fully, just up a little from his seat, his eyes on me. I thought it was to protest, but when the waiter shoved my chair (with me in it, incidentally) under the table, he sat again and I realized it was because he was a man, I was a woman but mostly he was a gentleman who stood when a woman was seated at his table, and I was a woman who found herself, for inexplicable reasons, seated at his *freaking table.*

No man had ever done that when I'd been seated at his table, and there was a beauty to it that seemed to seep into my soul too.

My heart stopped again, and fortunately, because I didn't want Sampson Cooper to see me panting, so did my breath.

The maître d' and waiter whisked themselves away.

"You figure they needed your table?" Sampson Cooper asked dryly, and considering my present circumstances, I had no idea how I managed to loosen up enough to do it. Maybe because the situation was so bizarre, so extreme, so frightening, I had to let some tension go. But at his comment, it was my turn to burst out laughing.

And, God's honest truth, since Cooter died, I'd smiled more than I had in years, which might not say good things, but there it was.

But I hadn't laughed like that in so long I forgot how good it felt.

When I quit laughing, I focused on him to see him grinning at me, but there was a look on his face, a warmth in his eyes, an intensity, it almost felt—no kidding—like he found me fascinating.

Me.

Kia Clementine.

And seeing that look in his eyes aimed at me, no one but me, a look I had seen in…never (never had I seen a look like that directed at me), I wanted to run. And I wanted to run because I wanted that to be it, my last memory of Sampson Cooper. I wanted to go somewhere and burn it into my brain. I wanted to keep it with me forever.

But I couldn't do that so I forced myself to reply, "They *are* pretty busy."

His grin faded, but his lips still twitched when he agreed, "Yeah." He sat back, snagging his coffee cup as he did, and he asked, "Do you mind?"

"Mind?"

"Sitting with me," he explained before taking a sip.

Uh. *Yes!* I was pretty certain my body needed my blood to flow through its veins, and my heart was constantly stopping so I didn't figure that was good.

But obviously I couldn't tell him that, so instead, I said, "Not if you don't mind."

His eyes changed again. They dropped quickly down my torso then up, and he murmured, "Oh, I don't mind," in a sexy way that I was pretty certain made my nipples go hard.

Oh.

My.

God!

Did he just do that?

And if he did, what did it mean when a man did that? The last man to flirt with me was Cooter, and he did it by buying me extra Tater Tots at the local burger joint.

Did it mean what I thought it meant?

Oh.

My.

GOD!

He took another sip from his coffee, put it down, and extended his big hand my way. I stared at it, luckily not jumping ten feet. It was not my first time seeing his masculine, long-fingered, well-veined, strong-looking hand that I thought was immensely attractive in a way that, if I was just a shade on the sick side, I could create a religion based on it.

It was just the first time I saw it in real person.

"I'm Sam Cooper," he introduced, and I forced myself to lift my hand and put it in his. His fingers curled around instantly, warm and strong.

"Kia," I told him, my voice softer because I was freaking out because *he was holding my hand*! "Kia Clementine."

That got me another grin.

"Kia Clementine?" he asked.

I nodded.

He held my eyes.

He also kept hold of my hand.

My heart stopped again.

Then he murmured again in that sexy way, "Clementine."

"Yep," I said.

His head tipped to the side and he remarked, "Great name."

"It's my husband's," I told him stupid, stupid, *stupidly*.

His hand tightened in mine for a half a second before he released it.

Oh yes.

Stupid!

His face was still friendly but now somehow a shade remote when he noted, "You're married."

"Not anymore."

Luckily, this came out calmly, not quickly or desperately.

Thank God.

"Divorced?"

"He's dead."

His back straightened and his eyes again grew intense, this time in a different way. There was emotion there—compassion—and it, too, was knock your socks off beautiful.

"I'm sorry," he said gently.

And that was when, no joke, I blurted, "Four months ago, half his head was shot off in a motel room while he was boinking my high school arch-nemesis, who remained my arch-nemesis long after high school. Though I didn't know that until her husband burst in on them in the local motel with a shotgun he was prepared to use. My husband got dead. Her husband got five to ten for involuntary manslaughter."

Sampson Cooper blinked.

Okay, uh…what was *that*? Why did I tell him that?

Not only was I in imminent danger of having a heart attack, I was also clearly temporarily insane.

I needed to get out of there, like, yesterday.

"No shit?" he asked into my mental strategizing on how to beat my retreat.

I shook my head.

"Christ," he muttered.

"That about says it all," I muttered back, looking from him to the table and wondering if I should pretend to have a crying jag at the passing of my husband and ask to be excused, then promptly get the first taxi, rental car, bus, train, or plane out of Lake Como and go back to Heartmeadow, Indiana. A place Sampson Cooper had never been and one where he'd more than likely never go. Upon arrival, I would immediately enter what would probably be years of therapy to deal with this encounter.

But before I could fake tears, his deep, rough-like-velvet voice came back at me.

"Are you okay?"

I looked up at him and, again, there was intensity. This was curious, cautious, but also still warm.

So my mouth whispered for me, "Yeah."

"What happened to the arch-nemesis?"

"She got clocked with the butt of her hubby's shotgun," I answered, leaving out the fact that she was now awaiting trial for plotting my murder. I'd already instituted a major overshare. I didn't need to make the same mistake again.

"Off easy," he murmured.

"Kind of," I said softly. "She's the town pariah. No one liked her much before, but they openly don't like her now, and we live in a small town so you feel that kind of dislike in a small town, you know?"

"Not really," he replied. "I've never fucked another man's wife, setting him on a murdering rampage, or even fucked another man's wife and not setting that man on a murdering rampage. So I have no fuckin' clue."

At his honest, blunt, and, weirdly somewhat harsh, words, he became real to me like any normal person. Not a famous ex-football star national hero who had a past filled with doing dangerous things. And, suddenly, I relaxed. Not completely, but a little. Enough to smile before I recommended, "Well, my advice is, don't."

He smiled back and said, "Good advice."

"And also," I kept going, "I think in Lake Como, surrounded by swanky rich people, you're not allowed to drop the f-bomb or probably the s-bomb, for that matter."

He lifted his coffee cup, and before taking a sip, his eyes on me over the rim, he asked, "You read that somewhere?"

"Uh…no," I answered.

He sipped, dropped the cup, and noted, "So it's not a law."

"I wouldn't know. Maybe."

"If it is, then you wouldn't be able to do it in Italian. Since I don't know Italian, I think I'm good."

"Well, if you're wrong and they arrest you, I promise to post bond," I assured him.

He grinned. "Good to know you've got my back."

I shrugged. "We Americans have to look out for each other."

His grin got bigger and he murmured, "Right."

It was then our food was served. There were some flourishes whilst the waiter served it, which made Sampson Cooper catch my eyes, his smiling. When they did, I felt my mouth twitch and my heart flutter because I was sharing an in-joke with Sampson Freaking Cooper.

The waiter moved away, Sam picked up his cutlery, and so did I.

He tucked in.

I wondered if I could watch him consuming food across a table from me without having an orgasm.

And it was then I decided to come clean.

"I know you, you know," I whispered, and his eyes went from his plate to me.

Then, to my shock, my delight, my horror, and totally messing with my peace of mind and understanding of the world, he whispered back, "Baby, for ten minutes you made me invisible. Women who know who I am do one of three things: they get in my space, they do anything they can to get my attention but do it pretending badly that they don't know I exist, or I flat out cease to exist. I know you know who I am."

"I wasn't being rude," I quickly told him.

"I get that," he replied just as quickly. "For you, it's about bein' shy. But for me, it gives me privacy and I don't get that much. It also allows me to be the one to make the play. And in my life, serious as shit, Kia, that's rare and it's really fucking valued."

That was when I panicked and assured him, "Well, I wasn't making some whacked-out play either."

He put his fork on his plate, reached across the table, and took my hand.

My heart stopped again.

He squeezed my hand and looked in my eyes.

Then he whispered, "Relax, Kia, and just enjoy breakfast."

"Okay," I whispered back. It was breathy, but at least I didn't wheeze.

He let me go and focused back on his food.

It took some effort, and not a small amount of it, but I did too.

And there it was on my plate—proof an *omelette* was an omelet the world over.

Thus commenced me eating breakfast with Sampson Cooper, and I didn't think I could relax, but I didn't take into account how much he wanted me to.

So for the next forty-five minutes, we ate. We sipped coffee. We sometimes looked out the windows at the beauty of the lake. But mostly, we looked at each other and Sam asked me questions that weren't invasive or taxing, chiefly about what I was doing in Lake Como and how long I was staying. So I told him about my vacation, which started in Paris and would end in two weeks at a beach on Crete. And with his guiding questions, I went into some detail that was probably embarrassingly enthusiastic about what'd I'd done, what I'd seen, and what I was looking forward to doing and seeing.

For his part, when I asked, he told me vaguely he was in Italy "on business." He didn't elucidate and I didn't pry.

When we were done, the last drops of coffee consumed, our plates long since whisked away, Sam Cooper stood and rounded the table like the gentleman he was, helping me out of my chair.

No man had ever done this for me either. It was considerate and attentive in a way I liked a lot and it settled in my soul too.

He walked me through the dining room, the tips of his long fingers barely touching the small of my back to guide me through the room, another chivalrous gesture that also felt like something else, something I didn't quite get.

Outside the dining room in the lobby, with its beautiful tiled floors and sweeping staircase, his fingers moved to my elbow, curling around, and he stopped me. He turned to stand in front of me, a foot away.

I tipped my head back to look up at him.

It was over. I survived. I had breakfast with Sampson Cooper. I enjoyed it, and the knowledge that he was truly in real life what he was in my fantasy life—a decent, good, kind man as well as a gentleman—also settled in my soul.

Looking up at him, I memorized our morning like I'd been memorizing many of the gifts I'd received the last three weeks, but this one I burned deep in my brain in the hopes of never forgetting even a second.

"I need to go," he told me, his fingers still curled on my elbow.

"Okay," I replied and smiled. "Maybe I'll see you around."

My breath caught as his fingers on my elbow tightened and pulled me slightly toward him. I went forward three inches as he bent from his height of what I knew was six foot three, and in a barely there touch, he swept his lips against my cheek.

I closed my eyes and experienced the beautiful tingle.

In my ear, he whispered, "You'll see me around."

My heart stopped again, and his fingers gave me a squeeze then let me go. He straightened, smiled in my eyes, and then he was gone.

And, staring across the foyer that no longer held the tall, built, powerful body of Sampson Cooper, it belatedly hit me that he'd said, *It also allows me to be the one to make the play.*

That was when my heart stopped beating.

Again.

2

CAT AND MOUSE

I stood in front of the full-length, oval mirror in my hotel room, surveying my ensemble.

I was wearing a dark teal strapless dress shot liberally with silver. The top fit like a second skin all the way down to my hips, then flared out in a cute flippy but short skirt that exposed a whole lot of leg, more than my sundress. I wore this with a pair of strappy, silver, high-heeled sandals. My hair was swept back at the top and held in a pretty silver clip at my crown, but the sides were sleek and long, the tapered ends curling along my jaw and neck, the rest falling down my back. I had on a pair of earrings that were four dangling silver chains interspersed with teal beads.

It was an awesome outfit.

But really, I was being an idiot.

In Heartmeadow, Indiana I would have no occasion to wear a dress like this. Or the shoes. Or the sundress I'd bought. Or the bronze sandals. Or, really, almost everything I'd purchased on my trip.

I'd flown first-class because I could. This meant I could bring two suitcases, so I did, but there was barely anything in them since I intended to shop profusely, something I had done.

I had just not made smart choices.

Like the entirety of my outfit, which I bought that day with Celeste, my new Lake Como bud.

I had spent my first day in Lake Como touring around, riding the unbe-freaking-leivable high of breakfast with Sampson Cooper and riding the not as awesome but very close to it high of being in a stunningly beautiful place I'd never thought I'd be.

I'd also spent that day on tenterhooks, expecting Sam to jump out and whisk me away practically every second.

He didn't.

So, trembling with expectant excitement and, again, kitted out and made up, I'd wandered down to breakfast only to find him not there.

My matchmaking maître d' looked more devastated than I was that Sam was not waiting for me nor did he show while I had breakfast, and I gave him plenty of opportunity. So much, I was grateful when my waiter brought me another cafetière of coffee I could sip and not look stupid as I waited in vain.

It was at lunch, as I sat at a table with an umbrella (though I chose a seat in the sun, not the shade) on the wide sidewalk facing a flower- and fountain-bedecked square, when I met Celeste and her husband, Thomas.

They were old enough to be my mom and dad's much younger, cooler, and far, far richer sister and brother.

Celeste was French, but she spoke English and Italian. Thomas was American, but he spoke with a slight Australian accent, considering the fact that, while growing up, he'd lived there for ten years and they visited his family there regularly.

We'd been seated at tables next to each other and my table had no pepper shaker. I'd asked if I could use theirs and there it began—just like with Sam, I'd joined them. However, not like Sam, they invited me and I accepted.

Chatting with Celeste, I didn't know what people were talking about when it came to French folks. Cooter, being Cooter, had hated them. But Celeste was awesome, chatty, and friendly, all in this droll, sophisticated, cosmopolitan way that was way beyond cool.

Within two minutes of talking with her, I decided I wanted to be her when I grew up.

Fortunately, I kept my cool, and unlike blurting them out bluntly to Sam, I did not share my recent circumstances with Celeste and Thomas but informed them only I was on vacation.

Celeste cottoned on that I had no clue when it came to Italian. I also had a feeling Celeste further cottoned on to the fact that I had no clue when it came to a lot of things.

So she'd taken me under her wing.

She taught me "please" was *per favore,* "yes" was *sì,* "no" was just *no,* and "table for one, please" was *solo tavolo, per favore.*

Easy!

Thomas was taking his lunch with his wife but had to get back to work, so Celeste invited me to spend the afternoon with her. I accepted. After we wandered and she showed me some sights, she invited me to spend the next day with her. I accepted that too.

After another disappointing breakfast alone, Celeste had swung by my hotel in a sporty convertible, her hair (get this!) covered in a flowy chiffon scarf and she had huge sunglasses on her face, making her look straight from a movie. She'd whisked me to her favorite spa where we got facials, massages, manicures, and pedicures, then had our makeup done and our hair styled. Off we went to spend the afternoon shopping whereupon, at Celeste's insistence, since everything I tried on she declared effusively was "*Belle, ma chérie!*" I spent an enormous amount of money on clothes I'd probably never wear again.

And I was going out to dinner with them that night, all gussied up after spending three fun, relaxing days in Lake Como eating, sightseeing, shopping, and spa-ing (or whatever they called it). But, although fun, as he'd promised and I'd hoped, I'd not seen Sampson Cooper.

Therefore, I realized that when he said he'd see me around, he was being nice. In fact, I realized he'd only just been being nice throughout our time together.

And I had to admit, it was disappointing, definitely. Still, I met him, he was wonderful, I had a great story to tell, and therefore I decided I could live with that.

What I couldn't live with was making a stupid dent in my somewhat large, unexpected fortune by buying clothes I could not wear to the grocery store in Heartmeadow. I'd even bought a formal gown, mainly because it was beyond awesome too. In fact, it was so stunning, it was indescribable. I'd never owned anything near the like, never even tried anything on even close. My wedding gown, which I thought was beautiful, wasn't even as nice as that gown.

But I got caught up in the life. Celeste, my audience, sitting back with her feet crossed at the ankles, knees closed, slim fingers curled around a flute of champagne (yes, champagne—this was how exclusive the shop was; they served champagne while you tried on clothes), her entire face lit with delight when I'd walked out wearing that gown. The instant I did, she threw out a graceful hand, saying I simply *had to have it*, that it was *made for me*, and I forgot who I was, where I came from, where I would go when I went home, and bought it.

But it was ridiculous. I'd have nowhere to wear it.

Still, I liked the idea of just owning it and decided that, maybe, on occasion, I'd make myself a fabulous dinner, buy myself a good bottle of champagne, put it on, and share my dinner with Memphis, pretending I was back in this life. That this was me.

That might be a weird thing to do, but I figured it also would be fun.

There was no one to care so why the heck not?

And Memphis would get into it. Then again, she pretty much liked to do anything just as long as her human was around.

That said, I had to stop. Enough was enough.

My cell on the bed rang. I moved from the mirror to it, saw it was Celeste, took the call and put it to my ear.

"Hey, Celeste," I answered.

"*Allô, ma chérie.* We're downstairs. Are you ready?"

God, her voice was even awesome.

"I'll be right down," I told her.

We rang off. I grabbed my evening bag (an evening bag! Seriously, I was out of control) and headed downstairs.

I was dressed to the eights (my gown being definitely to the nines, or even tens), but upon seeing Celeste, I noted she still totally outclassed me. Even so, when she saw me, she did this cool thing where her head dipped to the side and her hand elegantly swept through the air, a nonverbal indication she thought I looked great.

And, coming from her especially, that *felt* great.

Jeez, totally, I liked her.

When we greeted, I reminded myself to grab her upper arms and touch cheek to cheek on both cheeks as she always did with me, with shop assistants, and her friend Gertrude, who we'd run into at the spa. It was really too bad Americans didn't do that. It wasn't only chic, it was sweet.

Then she swept me out of the hotel. I did the cheek thing with Thomas at the car, and off we went in Thomas's big burgundy Jaguar to dinner.

Celeste and Thomas lived on Lake Como and had for nearly a year. His business took him everywhere and Celeste had confided in me while shopping that it was likely they'd be moving again soon.

I hoped (but didn't share this with her) that maybe he'd be sent to Chicago or New York so I could visit and take all my fabulous clothes and shoes and pretend to be awesome like her again.

And also, I hoped this because I liked her.

They took me to an eatery that was off the beaten path, but they declared was the best in a fifty-mile radius. They would know, considering Celeste also confided to me that, though French and enjoying her food (even if, on her slim frame, it didn't show), she was a terrible cook, so they went out all the time.

They were not wrong about the restaurant and I decided this at first glance. It was fabulous.

But as we were shown to our table, I became enchanted. It had lots of Christmas lights strung everywhere and tables with small, compact arrangements of cream flowers set in the middle atop peach tablecloths draping low, which lined a balustrade of a long, stone terrace that faced the lake. The Christmas lights twinkled off the polished crystal and silver on the tables. And, to top that, there was soft music playing from a real live string quartet at the end of the terrace.

It was the most beautiful restaurant I'd ever been to in my life, and in the last three and a half weeks, I'd been to some lovely ones.

"This is gorgeous," I breathed, walking closely with Celeste, who had her hand snug in the crook of my elbow.

"What did I say?" she asked, grinning at me.

"You don't lie," I replied, grinning back at her.

"Oh yes I do, *ma chérie,*" she informed me. Lifting her other hand with her thumb and forefinger an inch apart, she leaned closer and whispered, "*Petites mensonges* to Thomas, after shopping."

My grin became a smile and I noticed Thomas and the maître d' had stopped, so I looked to him and our table.

That was when I saw Sampson Cooper three tables down, sitting facing me, and across from him was a brunette. Her back was to me, but I could still see she had on a fabulous dress. She also had unbelievably beautiful, glossy, long, thick, dark hair and an amazing figure if her shoulders, slim arms, and the line of her exposed back were anything to go by.

I stopped breathing again and this time it didn't feel so good.

Okay.

Shit.

Okay.

Shit!

There it was. I was an idiot. I'd totally misread the situation. Clearly, his supermodel-esque girlfriend slept in or skipped breakfast in order to do Pilates or something. And he *was* just being nice to me.

Shit.

Luckily, this time Thomas guided me to the side of the table where I'd have my back to Sam and his woman. Even more fortunately, he did this before Sam saw me.

The maître d' held my chair and pushed it in while Thomas moved to do the same with Celeste across from me.

I looked to the lake and my heart restarted, but my stomach felt funny and that didn't feel so good either.

It was late. They ate late here, or at least Celeste and Thomas did. They'd picked me up at eight thirty. The sun was beginning to set on the lake and the view was amazing.

I still wanted to cry.

"Kia, is everything all right?" Celeste's melodious, French-accented voice came at me and I looked to her.

I had to get myself together.

Okay, I was an idiot. Three days ago, I had breakfast with my fantasy man and stupidly thought that I'd see him again. I had not allowed myself to fantasize about what seeing him would mean. I was smart enough not to set myself up for that kind of disappointment. I just looked forward to doing it because he was a nice guy, and in the end, when he got me to relax, he was easy to talk to.

But I didn't think when I'd see him he would be with a beautiful woman.

That sucked.

But, whatever.

Right?

I was in a fabulous dress and fantastic shoes, sitting in a beautiful restaurant next to a world famous lake with people who were worldly yet kind.

And a year ago, I was in a rotten marriage with an abusive husband and I'd given up on life because I'd convinced myself there was no way out.

Sam probably barely remembered me, considering how many people he had to meet in his life. He certainly wouldn't recognize me from the back.

So, onward.

Onward!

This was my motto since Cooter took a shotgun blast to the head.

Freaking *onward.*

I smiled at Celeste and whispered, "Better than all right. Thank you so much for bringing me here. I don't even have to eat and it's my most favorite restaurant in the world."

Celeste smiled at me as she reached across the table, took my hand, and gave it a squeeze. I squeezed hers back. Then I smiled at Thomas.

After that, I took the menu I belatedly noticed the maître d' was holding out to me.

I was sitting on the balcony of my hotel with a snifter in my hand filled with one piece of ice and a healthy dose of amaretto.

I'd ordered a double.

Dinner was delicious. The company even better. And Sam hadn't noticed me.

He also hadn't left (not that I noticed, unless there was another exit) by the time we left. He would have to walk by our table and he didn't. I didn't want to be, but I was on edge all night, waiting for him to do it and hoping he didn't notice me.

But, even though we ate four seriously delicious courses and took our time, he did not walk by our table.

And when we left, I made certain to get up and walk out without looking back. I put everything into doing it casually, trying to appear natural so Sam wouldn't read the effort like he'd done at breakfast.

But it didn't matter if I pulled it off or not. Even if he'd noticed and recognized me, it was highly likely he wouldn't care. In fact, he told me himself such behavior would be a relief.

So there I was, having a nightcap, staring at the dark waters and the blinking lights dotting the sides of the lake. I was doing this because I was really full and would never sleep, even if it was way late, but also because, even if I was alone on the balcony and no one could see me, I really didn't want to take my fabulous outfit off yet.

I lifted my snifter and took a sip. I'd always liked amaretto. My mother drank amaretto sours everywhere she went. She made desserts with amaretto in them. Dad had bought her an expensive set of Waterford snifters for Christmas when I was ten years old so she could further enjoy her amaretto. She was an amaretto freak. We had a bottle in our house at all times.

This she had given to me. I loved amaretto too. Though, when Cooter was alive, the bottle I kept in the house I hid because it pissed Cooter off I spent so much on a bottle of liqueur I sipped on a very rare occasion when he wasn't around. Clearly, he didn't think me going through a bottle of amaretto once every year and a half and him going through a case of beer once a week was fair.

On this thought, my eyes welled with tears and I pulled in a deep breath, rethinking my solitude and my double of almond liqueur on top of three glasses of wine at dinner.

This had been happening unexpectedly, mysteriously, and with relative frequency since the day after my plane touched down in Paris. I had not shed one tear since Ozzie came to the house and broke the news. I hadn't even felt my nose sting. But since I started my vacation, it seemed to happen all the time.

I had no idea why, and I had, until that moment, been so busy I was able to power through it without giving any headspace to wondering why.

But now, alone, sated, a wee bit tipsy, and relaxed, my guard was down and my head flooded.

And it flooded with a memory, years ago, of having dinner at Mom and Dad's house. After dinner, Dad and Cooter had gone into the living room to watch something on TV and Mom and I had done the dishes. When we were finished, we sat down at the dining room table, which we were wont to do when Dad and Cooter were lapsing into food comas in front of the TV (Mom was a comfort food cook, as in, that was all she ever made) and it was time to right all the wrongs in the world.

It was just that, that night, Mom had a specific wrong she wanted to right.

At that time, I'd been married to Cooter for a year and a half. Looking back, I couldn't say Cooter treated me with love and affection in the three years we were together prior to getting hitched. He'd treated me being on his arm like it was his due. But he'd never been cruel. Then, for whatever reason it commenced, Cooter had started to tear me down three months after we got married. This started small, incidences I could easily sweep aside as bad moods or anxiety due to a change of life, marriage, mortgage, needing to grow up fast and hold down a job in order to take care of home and hearth.

But it quickly escalated.

So by that time, I'd had huge chunks torn from me.

And for some bizarre reason, I thought I was hiding it from the world. Even my mother.

I should have known that no way could I hide anything from Essie Rigsby. First, she was a mom with two kids and had been, at that time, for twenty-three years. Second, she was far from stupid. I'd never been able to pull one over on her.

Not ever.

And that night, when she sat at the foot of our dining room table, her back to the living room, and I'd sat at her side, the wall obstructing me from Dad and Cooter's view, Mom had not delayed.

Her eyes settled on me. They were troubled. I instantly clawed at the tattered edges of the personality that my husband was stripping from me, pulling them close in the hopes of using them to protect me from what I knew was to come.

But I didn't succeed before she leaned into me, her hand cupping my cheek, and she whispered, "You know, your dad and I are always there for you."

Tears had filled my eyes and I'd looked away.

Her other hand came up so she was holding me by both cheeks, and she made me look at her again.

"Kia," she kept whispering, "no matter what, no matter where, no matter anything, we're always there for you."

"Okay," I whispered back.

She said nothing more, just stared in my eyes.

I sat across from her and kept my mouth shut. I didn't know why then, and I didn't know why while sitting beside Lake Como, drinking my favorite drink, which was also my mother's favorite drink and therefore reminded me of her. Maybe it was pride that did not allow me to admit I'd made a huge mistake. Maybe I still had hope that Cooter would show me the glory he'd promised to me. Maybe I was in denial and didn't want to face what was happening to me.

But I said nothing.

And I never did. Not for seven years. Not one of the times I tried to escape him. I said nothing.

Seven years.

I'd lost seven years, and that was on me because help had been half a mile away.

A tear slid down my cheek and Lake Como went fuzzy.

"Not even a smile?"

My body jerked as the question came from close in a deep, rough-like-velvet voice tinged with something I didn't quite get—impatience or annoyance. I twisted in my wrought iron, comfily padded chair and tilted my head back to see Sam standing right beside me.

In the muted outside lights that lit the balcony but didn't take from the view, I saw his face shift as he whispered, "Jesus, Kia."

Oh God.

Shit!

I quickly lifted a hand and dashed it across my cheek, stupidly thinking maybe, even though his eyes were locked on my face, he'd miss it, and I casually said, "Hey, Sam."

"Are you okay?" he asked.

"Yeah, great. Just enjoying a nightcap," I answered, and his brows snapped together making him look slightly irritated.

"Are you okay?" he repeated.

"Yeah," I replied.

Suddenly, he bent at the waist, put one hand into the arm of my chair, and his face was three inches from mine.

I sucked in breath at this move and his sudden proximity and pressed into the back of the chair, but I didn't have far to go and only gained an inch before he spoke again.

"Okay is not sittin' alone, drinkin' with tears in your eyes," he stated.

Well, I had to admit, he was right about that.

"Uh…" I mumbled.

"Are you okay?" he repeated, this time gently, his eyes holding mine captive, and while they did, they were looking deep.

So deep, I was mesmerized and found myself whispering, "I don't know."

"That's a better answer," he decreed on a return whisper, then moved again, swiftly.

He bent to the side, reaching out a long arm. He tagged a chair and dragged it next to and facing the side of mine. He sat in it, leaned forward, put one elbow to his knee but reached out with the other hand, capturing mine and pulling it toward him. His other hand shifted and both of his hands held mine at his knees.

He did this so quickly, even when he settled, I hadn't come to terms with the fact that Sampson Cooper was holding my hand, sitting next to me, and completely focused on me in an intent way that made my entire body feel warm.

"Your man?" he asked.

"What?" I asked back.

"Are you thinkin' about your husband?"

I shook my head and answered, "No, my parents."

His hands gave mine a squeeze that felt convulsive before he asked, "Are they okay?"

I nodded. He waited. I didn't say anything.

His hands gave mine another squeeze, this one a clear prompt.

"It's a long story," I said softly, and it was. It was also one he would never, ever know.

He held my eyes.

Then he guessed accurately, "You don't wanna talk about it."

"No," I verified his accuracy.

"Right," he murmured, and asked, "You don't wanna talk about that, you wanna talk about why you sat three tables away from me for three hours tonight and didn't even smile at me, comin' or goin'?"

I blinked, but my heart started stuttering. I figured this was an improvement—at least it didn't stop.

Then I asked, "What?"

"Baby, you saw me."

Well, there it was. I didn't pull one over on him.

Shit.

"I, uh…didn't want to disturb you," I told him.

"Bullshit," he shot back instantly, and I blinked again at the same time my hand jerked in his, so his tightened around it.

"Bullshit?" I asked.

"Yeah, Kia, bullshit."

My shoulders straightened, and I didn't even tell them to do it, before my mouth accused, "Well, you didn't smile or come say hello to me either."

He stared at me and it occurred to me, even though I didn't know him, like, at all, that I could sense he had been being real, but now he was getting mad.

"So now we're playin' a game," he stated.

My shoulders got straighter and my torso turned more fully to him as I snapped, "I'm not playing a game."

"Breakfast, totally fuckin' transparent. Fuck me, seriously refreshing. And now it's cat and mouse." His hands squeezed mine. "Which one am I, Kia?"

Oh my God?

Did he just ask me that?

Seriously?

I yanked my hand from his and turned fully to him, declaring, "Neither, Sam. You were with another woman and I didn't want to disturb you."

"You came by to say hi, I could have introduced you to Luciana, who's the widow of a buddy of mine."

My stomach clutched.

Oh man.

Sam kept talking. "She's beautiful, she's sweet, but she's also not my type, and even if she was, she's my buddy's widow so I'd never fuckin' go there."

Oh man!

"Sam—" I started.

"So I can decide what I'm gonna do now, I gotta know, you want me to be the cat or the mouse?"

"Neither," I whispered.

"We done with this bullshit?" he asked practically before I finished my one-word reply.

"I…well, uh…" I stammered, then told him truthfully but hesitantly, since he seemed kind of pissed off and definitely impatient, and he was a very big guy so I didn't want to make him more of either, "we hadn't really started with the bullshit."

"Right," he muttered, still leaned forward, elbows to his knees, eyes on me.

"Right," I whispered.

He held my gaze.

Then he said, "Good. I'll call Luciana in the morning, tell her I'm bringin' someone to her thing tomorrow night. I'll come to your room, eight o'clock. Don't eat. She's gonna put on a spread. It's formal. Can you do that?"

I blinked before I whispered, "What?"

"Tomorrow, Luciana's party, formal. I'll be at your room at eight o'clock. Can you do formal on short notice, or should I call her and tell her I can't come and we'll go out to dinner?"

Oh my God.

Was he asking me out?

"Are you asking me out?"

The slightly pissed off and impatient look swept clean from his face, his lips twitched, and he answered, "Yeah."

"On a date?"

The last two words rose higher and higher and I was pretty certain my eyes were huge.

He grinned, scooted forward in his chair, and said quietly, "Yeah, Kia, on a date. But you gotta tell me where we're goin'. Luciana doesn't fuck around when it comes to her parties or her clothes. You can't swing that, let me know and we'll do something else."

"I can swing that," I said instantly and damnably enthusiastically.

That was when he smiled full-on, the white flash of his teeth nearly blinding in the semidarkness, and it was better than any smile I'd seen him smile before, in person or not. It was so much better, my entire body got warm again.

Then he murmured, "Transparent."

"Sorry?" I asked.

He didn't answer. Instead, he said, "Not surprised you can swing that."

I didn't know exactly why he thought that, but I didn't get the chance to ask because he was speaking again.

"I got shit to do early so I gotta hit it. I leave, you gonna be okay?"

At his open concern, I pressed my lips together and felt that allover body warmth start seeping into my soul.

"Yeah, Sam, I'll be okay."

His eyes moved over my face and he whispered, "Okay."

Before I could twitch, he was up, squatting over his chair, and his mouth was touching mine.

That's right, Sampson Cooper's *mouth* touched *mine.*

And it felt sweet. Unbelievably sweet.

My head got light and I blinked repeatedly when his head moved back. He was so close all I could see were his eyes.

"Sleep well and have good dreams, baby," he said softly.

Then he was gone.

3

UNLESS LIFE LED YOU TO THAT

I stood in front of the full-length, oval mirror in my hotel room, but I didn't see anything because I was blinded by anxiety.

Freaking out.

Totally wound up.

At nine o'clock sharp that morning, the morning after Sampson Cooper asked me out on a date, I'd called Celeste. I'd been awake for three hours by that time, waiting (not patiently) until a time it would not be rude to call.

When she answered, I didn't even say hello. I just launched into mile-a-minute speak about the night before—the amaretto, Sam, what he'd said, and the fact he'd asked me out. I also went into embarrassing detail about who he was and how much and how long I'd admired him.

At some point during my demented monologue, I even cried somewhat hysterically, "He's seen all my good shoes!"

When it finally occurred to me how much I was talking, and exactly how much I was exposing, I shut up.

When I shut up, Celeste had been silent for long, agonizing moments, and I feared I'd given it all away and she was rethinking her newfound friendship with a random American tourist.

Therefore, she shocked the crap out of me when she told me, "I'll be there in an hour, *ma chérie*. Be ready."

And she was, as was I.

Off we went to seven shoe shops—our mission: to find a pair that went with my gown. This took a lot less time than you would think visiting seven shoe shops and trying on a plethora of hair-raisingly expensive shoes would take, because Celeste did *not* mess around.

While I tried on shoes Celeste pointed out and asked the shop assistants to get me in my size, she was on the phone speaking Italian. To whom and saying what, I didn't know or ask, because firstly, it wasn't my business so that would be rude, and secondly, I was freaking out and consumed with finding the perfect shoes as if my life depended on this mission being successful.

We finally found the shoes that Celeste decreed would be perfect with my gown, and it was good that I agreed with her (wholeheartedly). Rounding out what was coming to be known (by me) as my "metal collection," they were gold, they were strappy, and the heel was thinner, more elegant, and way sexier even than my bronze sandals. And the awesomest of the awesome was that the ankle strap was unbelievably thin, and it wrapped around and around and around my ankle and tied at the back.

They were not perfect. They were *perfect.* So perfect, they could be displayed in a shoe museum that was how perfect they were.

But they also cost more than Cooter's and my monthly mortgage.

I bought them.

She then whisked me back to my hotel, ordering me to put on my bathing suit and sit by the pool, "Because, *ma chérie,* your glow is lovely, but with that dress, we need *gold.*"

She assured me she'd be back and she took off.

While I spent time deep breathing at the pool, she called me and told me I'd have a visitor, and I did. And (get this!) *right beside the pool* a woman showed up, sat beside the foot of my lounger on a low stool, and took off my bright, summery, berry-pink finger and toenail polish I'd had my nails adorned with just the day before. She then painted my fingers and toes a peachy-gold that was *gorgeous* and would go freaking *beautifully* with my dress and, better, my shoes.

I didn't even pick the color. Celeste did.

Seriously, she was the shit.

While lying in the sun, hoping I was going *gold*, I tried not to think about the fact that I was going out on a date with Sampson Cooper.

I tried hard to achieve this feat.

And failed.

I also tried to stop myself from calling and/or texting Paula, Teri, and my other friend, Missy (who was not a Sampson Cooper devotee, as such—she appreciated him, as any woman would, but she had a different stock of famous hot guys she obsessed about. Still, she was my friend), to tell them about this astonishing turn of events.

I tried hard with this too, and luckily, I succeeded.

I succeeded, mostly because part of me didn't think it would actually happen. He'd stand me up. Or something better would come along and he'd send a note to say he couldn't make it. I didn't want to tell them this was happening, have them freak in a good way—as in, I'd probably hear them scream all the way from Indiana, that kind of good way—and then have to tell them it didn't happen.

So I didn't call or text.

What I did was nurse my nerves until they became panic.

Luckily, before my panic escalated and I became paralyzed or did something equally stupid, like run away, Celeste showed and whisked me back to my room and into the shower. By the time I did my business in the shower, taking more care with every aspect of that daily occurrence than I ever had in my life, even on my wedding day, it was after six. I walked into my room folded in a robe with a towel wrapped around my hair and Celeste had a bottle of champagne in a bucket on ice and an enormous antipasti platter waiting.

I stared at the platter then moved my stare to Celeste. "Sam told me not to eat. There'd be a spread."

"Indeed." She inclined her head. "But a lady does not arrive at a party famished, and *chérie*, you've had no lunch," she reminded me and went on, "And then she commences in devouring every morsel available to her, all the while drinking and becoming intoxicated quickly because she has nothing in her stomach. She sips champagne, like its nothing more than water. She nibbles food she can take or leave. She is beautiful and enchanting because she's beautiful and enchanting. Gorging on hors d'oeuvres and guzzling champagne are *not* beautiful *or* enchanting." She tipped her head to the platter. "Eat, Kia, every bit."

I saw the wisdom in this and ate every bit while drinking champagne. This wasn't easy either, since my stomach was tied up in knots. But I knew one thing for certain…Celeste had it going on and she was sharing her worldly ways with me, so I did it.

The hairdresser and makeup artist showed when the hotel guy took away the empty plates. This Celeste also had arranged. I did not quibble, mainly because I had to admit I wasn't all that hot with doing either. I didn't look like a clown or skank when I was done with my makeup, and I could make my hair look decent, but I had one way to go—the blowout. Sam had seen that twice, and my dress was not a dress you wore with your hair blown straight. It was a dress you wore with your hair looking *hot.*

It took an hour but was worth every minute when the stylist curled every strand of hair, then pulled it softly back from my face and arranged it at my nape in a thick, wide, beautiful mess of tucked and pinned curls. The makeup artist went golden, more than likely at Celeste's command, including dusting a hint of gold powder along my collarbone. Her handiwork highlighted my tan in a way I never would have been able to pull off if I was doing it myself. I wouldn't have even thought to try.

They left. I put on my white lace panties (another Parisian purchase—they cost more than the contents of my whole underwear drawer at home and they weren't the only pair I bought) and Celeste instructed me on the proper use of perfume.

"Your scent does not precede you. It also doesn't define you. Any scent you wear is a discovery."

This made no sense to me so I asked, "A discovery?"

She smiled a small, very cool smile and said softly, "Yes, Kia, a discovery. The kind of discovery your partner, if he is very fortunate, makes when his nose *encounters* the flesh the scent adorns."

At her imparting this nugget of wisdom, a nugget I not only processed in my brain but three other parts of my body besides, I made not a peep and stared at her, so she went on.

"A touch behind the ears, at the wrists, behind the knees, and at the cleavage…a *touch.* Half a spray if it is spray or just a dab if it is not."

My mind became consumed with Sam's nose being in *any* of those places, so it took Celeste's rich, cultured laughter to snap me out of it.

I did the half the spray route for that was all that was available to me.

Then I pulled on my dress. It was white, one shoulder bare, and fit like it was made for me down my torso to the very tops of my thighs before dropping into a full skirt to my ankles. The clingy silk jersey hung and moved beautifully around my legs. But the best part was that it had a deep slit just to one side and up to the upper thigh that exposed my legs in an awesome way when I moved. And better, the inside hem was embroidered intricately and subtly with gold thread.

Told you it was awesome.

I strapped on my shoes and Celeste pulled a pristine white evening clutch with a gold clasp out of her bag and tossed it on the bed beside me. Then she lifted my right hand and slid a dozen very slim gold bangles on my wrist. She handed me a pair of tiered gold earrings sprinkled with tiny pearls.

After I put them in my ears, her hand came out and she gently touched my earlobe with the tip of her finger. My head went back, my eyes went to her, and she spoke softly.

"Nothing at your neck, your lovely collarbone is enough. A touch…only a hint…of everything. An intriguing woman does not share her secrets in *any* way. She does not speak of them. She does not give them away through her manner. And she *definitely* does not make the mistake of giving them away through her appearance."

Well, if that was the case, blurting the information about Cooter being murdered within a few minutes of knowing Sam was an even bigger mistake than I thought it was and I already thought it was a doozy.

I did not share this with Celeste.

Instead, I looked into her unusual eyes, eyes the like I'd never seen, a light brown with hints of blue, her perfect skin touched with sun but not brown, leathery and wrinkled, her dark hair worn casually in a stylish cut that suited her heart-shaped face, and I informed her quietly, "Sam doesn't like playing games. I've been around him twice and he's already made that pretty clear."

To this, Celeste's already warm, kind eyes got warmer and kinder. They also grew knowing, and she reached out and took my hand, holding it in both of hers between us.

When she spoke, she spoke gently.

"My darling Kia, behind your eyes you hold secrets, more than any woman I've ever seen. For any woman, but I suspect for you especially, a man must prove he deserves the honor of you sharing those secrets. No woman should ever make the mistake of sharing any of her secrets with a man who does not prove he deserves to have them. I think, *ma chérie*," her hand squeezed mine and her voice dropped lower, "you have already learned this."

Her words affected me so deeply, I felt my eyes fill with tears and I was speechless, staring up at her and holding her hand tightly.

Because she was right. She was *so* right and at that moment I wished I'd known her ten years ago, before I gave all my secrets away to Cooter.

"Make him work to unlock your secrets, my Kia," she whispered. "Do not accept another man in your life who does not rise to that challenge and do it gallantly."

Wow, she got me. She totally got me. She knew. I had no idea how, but she knew.

And she understood.

And in that moment, I fell in love with Celeste Masterson.

I also nodded.

She bent toward me and kept advising, "I caution you to understand, at the same time I tell you this, whatever you've been doing has brought you to this moment. So *be* yourself, just don't *give* yourself unless you're certain he deserves that gift. Do you understand me, *ma chérie*?"

I nodded again, even though I kind of didn't.

She smiled, squeezed my hand in hers, and straightened, letting me go.

"He's due in twenty minutes. We'll share another glass of champagne to help you relax," she announced. "I'll pour while you sort your evening bag."

I nodded again. She moved to the champagne. I twisted on the bed and started sorting my evening bag. She came back with the champagne flute and I stood, taking it from her.

Then I whispered, "Today, everything…the manicure, the girls, my jewelry…I don't…" I hesitated and forged on. "Thank you."

She smiled and tipped her head slightly to the side before she whispered back, "You cannot know, *ma chérie,* but some other time I will explain why, but being with you today, it has been my *deep* pleasure."

I held her eyes, concerned at her words but sensing she needed me to let them go for now. So I did.

I lifted my flute, she lifted hers, and we smiled at each other while we clinked.

Five minutes before Sam was due, after a long, close, warm hug, Celeste left.

And when she left, I felt certain I could do this.

That was fifteen minutes ago, and without Celeste, I was a wreck. First I was a wreck because the time was nigh. Then I was a wreck because the time was slightly past nigh. And now I was a wreck because he was ten minutes late and that was getting to the point of well past nigh.

I was stopping myself from spraying on more perfume just for something to do. I had just refreshed my lip gloss from the tube the makeup girl left me. And I was looking in the mirror not seeing me.

I was thinking that life had somehow brought me to this pass, and without Celeste with me, I forgot how to pretend that this was me. Instead, I remembered who I was and felt through to my bones that I was an imposter.

And maybe, as the seconds ticked by making ten minutes eleven, Sampson Cooper had figured that out.

I moved from the mirror to the window and stared at the view, forcing my mind to Celeste and the fact that I had not paid one penny for any of the things she'd arranged that day (except, of course, my shoes). I was making a mental note to phone her as soon as possible the next day to talk to her about paying her back when there was a knock on the door.

My head snapped to the door.

Holy cow, he'd showed.

Holy cow, *he was out there.*

Holy cow, I was going out on a date with Sampson Cooper!

Shit!

Okay, now I didn't want him to be out there. I didn't want to do this because I didn't want him to find out I actually *was* an imposter.

Shit!

I stared at the door. Then I realized I had to go open it.

Shit.

I moved across the room, deep breathing, and since there was no peephole in the door, I set the chain (you couldn't be too careful and you should never be stupid; I'd learned that the hard way), opened it, and looked out.

It was Sam.

"Hey," I said swiftly, shut the door, quickly slid off the chain, and opened it. "Sorry. Have to be safe."

He didn't answer and I didn't notice. I was a flurry of nervous energy.

Therefore, I turned from him and strode across the room so fast my skirt flew out behind me, doing this stating, "I'm ready. Just need to grab my bag."

I bent to the bed, picked up my bag, shoving in the lip gloss I noticed had rolled out, and clasped the gold clasp before straightening at the same time I turned.

And when I turned, my shoulder and arm brushed something very hard and very solid.

My head tipped back to see Sam in my room, right there as in *right there.*

I froze.

Sam did not.

One of his arms slid along my waist, pulled in, and it kept doing that until our hips and bellies were brushing. Once he accomplished this, and as I was focusing all my energies on not panting and having difficulty with this endeavor considering my brain was focusing all *its* energies on the exquisite feeling of my belly and hips brushing Sam's, his hand came up, fingers curling around my neck, thumb out and sweeping my jaw.

His head was tipped down, his eyes on me. They were warm like I'd noticed several times before. They were also intent, again like I'd noticed before. But they were something else, something that made my stomach pitch, my nipples tingle, and heat rush to my cheeks.

Oh my God. I was in danger of either passing out and/or having an orgasm just from this!

"Hi," he whispered a rough-like-velvet whisper on a jaw brush of his thumb, and my legs trembled so badly, my hands automatically lifted to hold on to his also very hard and very solid biceps to stop myself from going down.

"Hi," I whispered back.

"Sorry I'm late." He kept whispering, his thumb kept stroking, and my legs kept trembling.

"That's okay." I also was still whispering.

His eyes moved to my mouth, my neck, down to my chest then up, slow and lazy. He didn't release me and his thumb never quit moving. This meant my legs never quit trembling, my stomach pitched again, and I felt another tingle, this one lower and way, *way* better.

He murmured, "Fool."

I blinked.

Then I asked, "Sorry?"

Sam didn't hesitate with his answer. "Baby, I don't know what you're like in bed, but if it's even half the promise of you, your man was a fucking fool."

My fingers clutched his biceps, the ones still holding my bag digging painfully into the clasp, and I felt my lips part.

Holy cow! *Did he just say that?*

"Did you just say that?"

Yes, that was what came out of my mouth, and it was both lucky and unfortunate it did because it broke the spell. I didn't want the spell broken, but also, if I was going to keep my secrets and all my gifts, the spell had to be broken or I was in imminent danger of jumping his bones. I suspected doing something like that would give it all away and Celeste would be disappointed.

I didn't want to disappoint Celeste. But I also knew she was far from stupid, she got me, and even if this was Sampson Cooper and I was Kia Clementine, every word of advice she gave me was one hundred percent right, so I had to follow it.

To the letter.

The spell was broken when his lips twitched. His thumb stopped moving, but his fingers at the side of my neck gave a gentle squeeze before he answered, "Yeah, I just said that."

"Okey dokey," I muttered, and his lip twitch became a grin. For sanity's sake, and so I wouldn't fall back and give into the urge of ripping his clothes off, I asked, "Are we going to stand here all night, or are you going to take me someplace where I can show off my dress?"

To that, he replied, "We stand here much longer, we won't be standing. So yeah, I'm gonna take you someplace where you can show off that fuckin' gorgeous dress."

Before I could fully react to what his words implied or his compliment, he let me go, grabbed my hand, and pulled me to the door. He stopped us in the hall so he could test the handle to make certain it locked upon catching and he pulled me down the hall.

It was then I finally noticed what he was wearing.

He was in a tuxedo, which looked good on him and fit well. I was no expert, but it fit him so well, I figured it had to have been made for him. And I'd had my hands on his jacket. The material was not anything the like I'd ever touched before. It was nicer in a way I couldn't describe but definitely nicer, and I knew it had to be expensive.

The cool part was, he was wearing a black shirt, no tie at all, the shirt opened at his throat.

Still, even without that accoutrement, the suit and shirt were so well-made, he wore them with a natural confidence that was magnetic; they seemed more formal than if he'd had on a white shirt and bow tie.

I couldn't say in my past two times with him that I'd noticed his clothes at all. I also couldn't say I'd spent much time the years I obsessed and fantasized about him that I'd noticed them either. I was too busy noticing the beautiful male perfection of his features, the even more beautiful male perfection of his smile, and the rough-like-velvet beauty of his voice.

But striding beside him, with my hand engulfed in his big, strong one, I noticed that, even as a tall, very built man, the like who could seem ungainly due to their size, he totally rocked his clothes in a way that was super cool because he didn't look like he was trying to rock his clothes. In fact, even wearing a tuxedo, he didn't look like he cared at all.

And more, he had a masculine grace when he moved that probably had to do with him being an athlete and highly trained, skilled soldier. But even with these things, this was a surprise. Men of his build, again, often seemed lumbering.

Not Sam.

And let me just tell you, it was *hot.*

All of it.

While Sam guided me down the hall and stairs, he didn't speak. What I noticed he did do was walk slowly. A man his height, with legs as long as his, definitely could take twice the amount of ground with each stride than he was taking, and I knew he was doing this for me because of my shorter legs and my feet wearing delicate, high-heeled sandals.

This was another indication of his graciousness. Not a word, not a show. He just did it—thoughtful, sweet—and that settled in my soul too.

Out the door we went, across the front of the hotel. Down four cars, he turned us and stopped me at the passenger side of a bright yellow Lamborghini.

Yes, a *bright yellow* Lamborghini.

Seeing his car, for some reason, I deflated. Not totally, but I felt it.

This was not to say it was not a cool car; it definitely was. And this was not to say I didn't look forward to my first ever (and probably only) ride in a freaking Lamborghini. I did. I definitely did.

This was to say it was expensive and flashy to the point of being a shade off trashy and I did not see Sampson Cooper this way. This car screamed, "Look at me! I have money! I have fame! I am important! Bow to me, all you minions."

Okay, maybe it didn't say all that, but it said enough of it to make me, for the first time, wonder about a Sam who stayed at an expensive hotel, owned an expensive tuxedo that had been tailored for him, and ate at restaurants like the one he ate at last night. I didn't pay, Thomas did and refused to even discuss it (my debt to him and Celeste was growing by the day), but I knew it was expensive. And when I say that, I mean, if you think of the most expensive restaurant you've ever been to, it was more as in *a lot* more. One bottle of wine was more than a three-course meal at a normal expensive restaurant, so it was *that* expensive.

And the Sampson Cooper I had in my head from all I knew about him and his life before I met him, and the man I'd been in the presence of three times who'd been real, who cursed when he felt like it and held my hand when he saw tears in my eyes, that Sampson Cooper, or Sam, did not have a flashy car that screamed, "Look at me!"

He opened my door for me and, with his long fingers wrapped around my bicep, guided me gently into the car, making sure I cleared my skirt and was settled in before closing the door.

I glanced through the interior as he rounded the hood and vaguely wondered how he'd get his tall, sizeable frame in it. Then I looked out the windshield, weirdly despondent and suddenly not nervous or even excited about the evening.

Very weird. Very stupid. And also judgmental.

But there you go. Men were men, and just like Cooter, but for Sam in a bigger, showier way, they all found their ways to prove they had a big dick. Even Sam Cooper.

It wasn't until Sam burst out laughing that I realized he'd folded in beside me and he'd been there awhile.

I turned my head to look at him.

Okay, I was suddenly nervous and excited again. This was because he might want the world to know he had a big dick, but he was unbelievably gorgeous while he was doing it.

He stopped laughing but kept smiling at me when he declared, "It's Luci's."

"What?" I asked.

"The car," he answered, and I felt my lips part.

Jeez, was he in my head or what?

Sam kept speaking, "She has five cars and she insisted I use one and not rent one. She also insisted I stay with her. I won on having some privacy and not spending every minute I wasn't workin' having Luci in my face about all the things Luci gets in my face about. And baby, there's a lot of that shit. I gave in on the car. I see from your face I shouldn't have. Then again, I didn't know I'd meet a beautiful blonde who's the only beautiful blonde on five continents who would not get off on sittin' beside me in a car like this."

"I didn't—" I started to deny through a lie.

He kept smiling, though bigger, and interrupted through it, "You did."

"I—"

He leaned toward me. His hand reached out, his fingers curled around the side of my neck again and I shut up.

"You did," he said gently. "And I don't care because I agree. This car is not me and it's good it's not you either." The smile came back. "But wait 'til it goes. This ride screams Eurotrash, and anyone who's got a hint of class feels like an asshole sitting in it. But when it purrs, it makes it worth it."

"Okay," I whispered, and I whispered because I couldn't get my voice to go louder. There were three reasons for this. One, he was touching me again. Two, it hit me he called me a beautiful blonde. And three, I really wanted to feel that Lamborghini purr.

"Buckle up," he murmured, let me go and turned away.

I buckled up. Sam hit the ignition and the car came to life.

I sighed with deep content and I did this *audibly.*

Sam burst out laughing again.

I bit my lip to stop myself from doing anything (else) stupid as Sam backed out of the spot, still chuckling, and my mind turned to

Celeste's advice because I was getting the distinct feeling I was not holding *anything* secret.

I pulled myself back on track when we were away, and I did this by asking, hopefully casually, "Uh...Luci, that is, Luciana owns five cars?"

"You can call her Luci. I'll say it before she says it, and when she meets you, she'll definitely say it."

This was a somewhat weird comment, but I had no time to decipher it or ask because Sam kept talking.

"And yeah, she owns five cars. She's loaded. Her parents are loaded. She's a trust fund baby and, on top of that, before she hooked up with Gordo, she was a model. A successful one. You see her face, you'll probably recognize her."

Oh man. I wasn't sure that was good.

Sam went on.

"Sayin' that, about ten seconds after you get over it, you'll see she's not a Luciana. She's a Luci."

"How is she a Luci?" I asked.

"She's a Luci because, regardless if she's sittin' beside a catwalk at a fashion show in Milan or sittin' on your deck, drinkin' a beer, she always acts like she's sittin' on your deck, drinkin' a beer."

I felt my heart flutter because I liked that he liked that since I was the kind of girl who knew all about sitting on a deck, drinking a beer, and *not* the kind of girl who knew what it was like to sit beside a catwalk at a fashion show in Milan. And I felt slightly less nervous because I liked that Luci was like that. It was only then I realized that part of my anxiety was about meeting Luciana, going to her party, and being amongst her set, which was not my set.

But the way he described her, at least she was.

"So, uh," I started cautiously, "what does she get in your face about?"

"The better question is, what *doesn't* she get in my face about?"

I looked from the view of the road—the brilliant blue of the lake stretching out on one side, sharp rises of green mountains dotted with gray stone on the other—to Sam.

"Sorry?" I asked as a prompt.

He glanced at me, then back at the road.

"She's an only child. Gordo was like a brother so she thinks of me as her brother-in-law. Before we lost him, they didn't have kids. She loves kids, and since she can't have her own and won't be an aunt any other way, she's counting on me and she's impatient."

I found this open declaration intriguing for more reasons than the fact it was an open declaration.

Before I could say word one, not that I had any clue what to say, Sam kept going.

"She's desperate for me to hook up. I'm thirty-five. She's known me five years, and Gordo's been gone one of those. She's spent that time concentrating on me."

"I get this," I said softly, because I did but not for the reason Sam thought I did.

And I knew the reason he thought I got it because, at my words, there was an intense pulse coming from Sam that hit the air of the car. I powered through the pulse and continued.

"My friend Missy lost her husband in a car crash. Sudden. They'd been married less than a year." I looked out the side window and kept sharing, "I never saw her cry. That was a long time ago and I still have never seen her cry. But she had a full-time job, and still, she volunteered for, like, seven charities, went for every promotion going, and enrolled in night classes to get her MBA. All this time, she's never slowed down. She's done anything she could do to concentrate on anything other than losing Rich, what that meant, dealing with it, and moving on. Now she's a Deputy Director of one of those charities she volunteered for. It's her life. It's been years and she hasn't even dated."

I told Sam this, but what I didn't tell him was one of the charities she went all out for was me.

By this time, I'd been married to Cooter for five years and there wasn't much of me left. All my friends had said things, done things. I'd noticed the looks and they all avoided Cooter like the plague.

And not because he made it clear he didn't like my friends around the house or me spending time with them (both of which he'd made very clear), but because they hated him for what he was doing to me, and by that point, they hated him so much, they couldn't be responsible for their actions or their words if they had to spend too much time with him.

But after Rich died, Missy had approached me three times, each increasingly more assertive, to discuss what was happening to me. Or, more to the point, what Cooter was taking from me. Finally, I had to lay it out that Cooter and I were just fine, not perfect but happy, and I'd done this in a way that was not mean or ugly but *definitive.*

After that, none of my friends said things or did things (but I still noticed the looks). And sitting in that Lamborghini, it hit me that they didn't probably because Missy warned them I was living the dysfunction, and until I got my head out of my ass, there was nothing they could do.

And I got this too. I loved them all enough to know that, even if a man had stripped away most of what was them, I'd take what was left rather than pushing something that might mean she'd take away anything I could get.

I pressed my lips together and tried to force this new knowledge out of my brain. I was failing at this when Sam spoke again, taking my attention, and when he took it, the way he took it, he took *all* of it.

"So tell me, baby," he asked gently, his tone in his deep, rough-like-velvet voice gliding along my skin, coating it with a sheen that was like an invisible barrier that, if I had a lifetime of his voice stroking that soothing ointment along my skin, I knew nothing would ever harm me. My head turned to him. "You get this. What do I do?"

I was lost in his voice, so lost, his question confused me. "What do you do?"

"Gordo was my boy. We spent a lot of time together, good times. He also had my back in some serious situations and there was no one I trusted more than him. Knowin' Luci loves him like she does, witnessing her devotion even after he's gone, gotta admit, Kia, I dig that. Gordo deserves that. But time is passing. She's young and she's got a life she isn't livin' because she's dedicating hers to livin' mine. How do I stop that?"

There was something about this question—an intimacy, a trust—that threw me. I'd been in his presence three times and he was asking me a question the answer to which was beyond important. It was about friendship, and the wrong answer could lead to the wrong action and might result in the end of their friendship and that could mean me giving him an answer that would guide him to a loss of something that was unbearable.

And, for some insane reason, I found my mouth telling him that.

I did it like this: "I don't know, honey. I don't know Luci so I can't say, and I'd never give blind advice when something as important as friendship lies in the balance. Your friend, if he knew what would happen to him, would trust you to handle her with care. And I wouldn't be handling her with care if I pretended to know the answer just for the sake of giving you one."

Sam didn't reply, but the air in the car changed again. This wasn't an intense pulse. But whatever it was shifted in like it was going to stay a while. It was warm, languid, and it had the kind of feel you wanted to float in forever.

I faced forward, trying to ignore the air and what it was doing to my state of mind and understanding of the world.

"Kia," Sam called.

"Yeah," I answered the windshield.

"Your friends handle you with care?"

Oh man.

Shit.

I closed my eyes and opened them, trying to think fast of how to answer without giving away any secrets.

When I did this by not speaking at all, undeterred, Sam compounded his question.

"His boys?"

I pressed my lips together.

Then I gave away a secret. I didn't say much and hoped it wasn't too much.

"Yes," I answered his first question, paused, then answered his second question softly, "And no."

"Right," he murmured, that word quiet but heavy with an easily read edge of harsh.

This said he got me and he gave a shit. This said he understood and he knew exactly what kind of "boys" Cooter had. And being a man, this meant he could probably guess a variety of ways, some of them likely accurate, of just how Cooter's friends did not handle me with care not only after his death but prior to it.

And they hadn't.

Well, it appeared I'd said three words, and still, I said too much.

I looked out the side window. Sam drove without speaking. After some time, he turned into the forecourt of a rather large but weirdly not imposing pink villa.

He rolled the Lamborghini to a stop. A red-coated valet rushed to his door and another one rushed to mine as I undid my seatbelt and saw Sam turned to the valet but shaking his head.

When I'd released the seatbelt, he turned to me.

His hand shot out, caught me around the back of my neck, and pulled me across the short expanse of the car to within an inch of his face. When he had me in position and I was concentrating on breathing, he rocked my world.

"There are very few, *very* fuckin' few people, Kia, who get what's precious in this world. They work their asses off for pure shit and think they'd fight and die to keep it. You don't fight and die for shit. You fight and die for things that matter. You are the first woman I've met outside a life that leads you to understand that shit who gets that. And straight up, baby, you gotta know, I like that a fuckuva lot."

Oh…wow.

"Sam—"

He shook his head and his eyes dropped to my mouth. I kept consciously breathing in air and letting it out. His eyes came back to mine and he brought me half an inch closer, so I stopped breathing completely.

Then he whispered probingly, his eyes staring deep into mine, "Unless life led you to that."

At that moment, that close, with his hand on me, his eyes looking deep into mine, I wanted to hand him another secret.

But I didn't.

I couldn't.

He could never know.

Because I understood right then that I *was* an imposter. Sampson Cooper thought I was someone I wasn't.

Celeste had been wrong. I didn't need to find a man who proved his worth before I shared my secrets.

Sam needed to find a woman who proved hers before he shared his.

And I decided, staring in his eyes, I would live that night with Sam, live it to its fullest.

I'd need it because it would have to last a lifetime.

And that was why I answered, "Can we go in, Sam? I need champagne."

Sam said not a word. He also didn't let me go. And lastly, he didn't release my eyes.

Finally, he spoke, and when he did, he did it with a quiet warning that made my heart hurt.

"I see it, Kia, and I get this is gonna take effort. But what I'm sensin' is, you don't notice I'm makin' that effort. Don't fuck up, baby, and out of habit reinforce your shields to hold back a threat that doesn't exist. You get me?"

Okay, it was safe to say he was kind of freaking me out with how much he knew when I thought I was doing a bang-up job keeping it guarded.

Without a single clue as to how to reply, I licked my lips to buy time. His eyes dropped to them, I watched them heat, their heat made heat rise in certain areas of my body, and his fingers tensed at my neck.

Right, mental note: when Sam Cooper was an inch away, don't lick your lips to buy time.

His eyes came back to mine, and when they did, immediately I nodded.

He let me pull away two inches and he did this with his mouth twitching.

Then he said, "Fuck me, how a woman can be so transparent and so full of shit at the same time is beyond me. But, baby, you got it down to an art."

Well! I was so sure.

"I'm not full of shit," I informed him.

"Your eyes run through every play you can make before you even twitch. Don't know what I do or what shuts off in you when you forget that bullshit and be real, but I promise you, Kia, I'm gonna find out."

Uh-oh.

That didn't sound good.

I had no idea how to respond so I decided to go with annoyed bravado.

"Sam, I keep telling you, I'm not playing at anything."

"Then, baby, you are totally clueless but still an idiot savant with this shit, because I've had my fair share of experience and you're a master."

Seriously?

I mean, *seriously*?

"All right, Sam," I retorted acidly. "I'll tell you what's *not* a good play. What's *not* a good play is telling your date *on your first date* that you've had your fair share of experience."

He burst out laughing and jerked me forward the two inches I gained, and let me tell you, watching him laughing that close was *hot.*

Shit!

He was still smiling when he stopped laughing and asked, "Honest to God, you think you can convince me you didn't already know?"

"Didn't already know what?" I snapped.

"I played football, then I joined the Army. These are not the occupations of a man who does not like to get himself some and often. You know both. You also know I played pro ball so you know I had choices, and there is no way you can convince me you think I'm a man who wouldn't avail myself of that every chance I got."

Was he for real?

Suddenly, I was rethinking Sam needing a good, loving, decent woman working hard to prove she was worthy of his secrets. Suddenly, I was thinking Sam needed a woman, any woman, to kick him in the shin.

"You aren't making things better, Sam," I warned, pulling at his hand.

This was a mistake. That hand tightened. I got the message. *Do not pull away.*

I stopped pulling.

His hand told me one thing, but his face was smiling huge and in a way that did crazy things to my system. Crazy things that felt really good at the same time they scared the shit out of me.

Then his hand pulled me closer, but his head veered to the side, and at my ear, he whispered, "You cannot bullshit me. You know what kind of man I am. What you don't know is, I like to get me some, but everything you do, everything you wear, everything you say, every signal you give tells me I'm gonna *really* like gettin' some of you."

Oh.

My.

God.

Ohmigod!

Oh. My. *God!*

Before I could get my stalled systems (heart, lungs, brain) functioning again, he released me, and he did it in a way I'd never forget. In a way no woman would ever forget. In fact, I figured I should find some way to tell the world so his smooth move could hit history books.

And this was, his mouth left my ear and his lips trailed down my jaw at the same time his hand left the back of my neck, but his fingers also trailed down the other side of my jaw. Both touches were light. A tease. A dare. Making me want more and telling me I'd have to go for it to get it.

And when his presence was gone, because he was exiting the car and the valet opened the door at my side, I was left frozen, turned toward the empty driver's seat, probably looking like a love-struck idiot but thinking about nothing. Not one thing.

Except how damn badly I wanted to go for it.

4

FEARLESS

It was unfortunate I had not recovered from the crazily veering emotions I'd experienced on the ride there, particularly the last five minutes in the Lamborghini, by the time Sam, holding my hand again, walked me into the villa. Because, although there were a large number of people there, Luciana appeared out of nowhere and she did this shouting Italian.

Sam stopped us and I blinked because I was not the kind of girl who bought glossy fashion magazines (not that my husband would let me). But still, I recognized her, and if she was beautiful from behind, she was exquisite in a lush, smack you back, wish you were her with all your heart, Sophia Loren kind of way from the front.

She was also affectionate.

I knew this right off (though it was impossible to miss) because she threw herself in Sam's arms like she hadn't had dinner with him yesterday evening but instead hadn't seen him in two decades. And she didn't do the cheek touch, switch, cheek touch business. Instead, she kissed his cheeks back and forth and back and forth and back again, alternately babbling at him in Italian.

"Luci, girl, you know I do not understand one fuckin' word you're sayin'," Sam informed her, his arms having gone from a close hug to his hands at her waist. He set her firmly away with a practiced hand, which gave me a strong indication that this was a familiar dance.

She grinned up at him and admonished, "I'm always telling you, Sam, you need to learn Italian."

"Why?" he replied. "This is the second time in my life I've been here."

Sam had only been in Italy twice?

Hmm. Interesting.

"Because," she returned.

"That's a reason?" Sam asked when she said no more.

She rolled her eyes, wisely giving up before she lost to Sam, and I had a feeling not many people won with Sam, including stunning ex-models.

Then she turned to me and cried, "*Kia!*" very, *very* loudly and threw herself in my arms so forcefully, I went back on one of my delicate gold heels and my arms automatically folded around her, mostly so I wouldn't tumble backwards.

She kissed my cheeks back and forth and back again while babbling Italian, and I let her because she was my hostess so I figured pushing her off would be rude. Also, she was Sam's friend so pushing her off would definitely be rude.

She finally stopped, pulled back but grasped my upper arms, and shook me gently while her eyes went from top to toe, toe to top, and back again, and she cried, "*Bella!*" Then, not letting me go, her head jerked to Sam and she noted in her sexy, throaty, Italian-accented English, "Oh, Sam, *so* much better than the last one."

I blinked once again.

Sam's head tipped back and he scanned the ceiling.

Luci turned to look at me.

"*Cara*," she said low, "I did *not* like the last one." She leaned into me and whispered, "She wore Burberry." She paused, then said with deep meaning, "Obviously and *profusely*."

"I don't own any Burberry," I assured her with the God's honest truth.

"Oh, Burberry is delightful," she declared, letting me go but sliding an arm around my waist. She propelled me into a huge room with beautifully tiled floors. Lush, plush but comfortable-looking furniture scattered around that practically begged you to collapse on it and have a nap. And huge, arched open doors that led out to a flower-bedecked terrace with a view to the lake. "But *obvious* is bad any way you can be obvious, and profuse is *definitely* bad no matter how you're profuse, *no*?"

Clearly, Luciana went to the same How to Be a Sophisticated and Chic Woman class as Celeste but missed the day where they taught you not to accost people even in a friendly way. She also missed the day where they taught you not to blab about your friend's exes or, at the very least, former dates within seconds of meeting his current one.

"Well," I started, "profuse being bad as in, you're faced with a box of chocolates you really like, then eating so much of them it makes you sick so you never do something that idiotic again, then, no. Profuse as in, using a heavy hand while spritzing perfume, then, yes."

Luciana threw her dark mane back, laughed a throaty laugh, and I noted around fifteen men turn their heads to watch. Then I turned my head and looked over my shoulder to see Sam talking to a white-coated waiter.

I hoped that meant champagne. I was thinking I was going to need it.

She stopped us in a pocket of privacy and turned to me, dropping her arm and asking, "So, *Lago di Como*, how are you liking my home?"

"It's beautiful," I told her and meant it.

"*Sì, bella*," she murmured, her eyes moving over my face. I got the impression she was complimenting me, but I didn't have the opportunity to react to a stunningly beautiful woman implying I was the same.

No.

Instead, for the first time, I had the opportunity to take her in fully, and she was stunningly beautiful. But the rest was a complete and total farce.

She was kidding herself if she thought she was hiding the pain in her eyes.

I was learning a good deal about kidding yourself since I'd been doing it for years.

And for some reason I didn't know (and even later, thinking back, I didn't get), before I could think better of it, my hand shot out and caught hers. When it did, I gave it a firm, warm squeeze, and just as quickly, I let her go.

I realized my mistake and wished I could take back my gesture when the sorrow so close to the surface suffused her face. I watched her swallow, then she turned her head, buried it shallowly below the surface again, clapped, and cried, "*Bravo*! Champagne!" at an approaching Sam who was carrying two flutes filled with champagne.

I made a mental note to tread more cautiously with the effusive but clearly fragile Luci as Sam made it to us. He gave me mine, gave one to Luci, and then slid in beside me, his long arm curving at a slant down my back starting high at my side and ending with his fingers curled in at my hip. I felt funny standing there like that and I had three choices: pull away (which would be rude), put my arm around Sam (which, uh, no way in *hell* I was ready for that), or lean into him.

I chose door number three and when I did, Sam's arm curled tighter and the pads of his fingers dug in at my hipbone.

My knees went weak.

Luci spoke.

"Why don't you have a glass?" she asked Sam.

"Because I'm driving," Sam answered.

She waved a hand in front of her face even as she took a sip of champagne.

She lowered her glass and stated, "Drink, enjoy. I've plenty of bedrooms. You get tipsy, you and Kia can spend the night in one."

Unfortunately, at this announcement, I too was sipping champagne. Therefore, hearing her words, I choked on it.

Sam chuckled.

I tipped my head slightly to the side on a turn, giving him a look out of the corner of my eye.

Sam chuckled deeper and longer.

Whatever.

I looked to Luci and declared, "This Cinderella has a curfew."

Mistake.

Luci's brows snapped together with adorable confusion, but I didn't take much of that in before Sam's arm around me curled, taking me with it. So instead of my side leaning into his long, hard one, my front was pressed to it.

I tipped my head back to see his was tipped down and he asked, "What?"

"I have a pre-booked boat tour that takes off at seven. I have to be in bed early so I can be rested and enjoy my tour."

This, actually, was true.

"How early?" Sam asked.

"Ten o'clock," I tried, even though I probably could push it to eleven.

This time, Sam's brows drew together and it wasn't confused or adorable. It was scary.

"Baby, it's quarter to nine now and we just got here."

"Sorry. I'm seeing maybe I should have told you this before," I muttered.

"Don't worry," Luci butted in. "Drink, eat, enjoy, and miss your tour. Stay the night. I'll let you borrow some clothes tomorrow so you can sleep in. While you have breakfast with me, Sam can pop back to the hotel to get something to wear, then you two can use my boat and he can take you on a personal tour tomorrow."

Uh-oh.

There were so many things wrong with this suggestion, I didn't know where to start. First, she was at least two inches taller but still twenty pounds lighter than me so she had to be two sizes smaller than me. Second, I was *not* spending the night in her house with Sam under the same roof, in the same bed I was in (definitely!) or not. I could do a hotel. I could not do a home. Don't ask me why, that was just the way it was. Third, this was my only night with Sam. No way was I spending a day in a boat on a beautiful lake in romantic Italy alone with him.

No way.

"I—" I started.

"Works for me," Sam said over me. "My shit is done, got all day."

I looked back up at Sam and opened my mouth to say something when Luci again butted in.

"Perfect. I'll have Giuseppa pack you a lunch. Something gorgeous." She aimed a brilliant, perfect-teeth-against-kickass-cranberry-colored-lipstick lips-and-flawless-olive-skin smile at me and declared, "Done!"

Uh-oh!

"I—" I started again, but that time it was kind of me who interrupted me.

Or at least it was my cell phone ringing in my bag.

"Excuse me," I muttered, pushing back a bit from Sam (or as far as he'd let me go, which, frankly, wasn't very far). Juggling my drink while opening the clasp on my bag (or I did for the nanosecond it took Sam to slide the drink out of my fingers like the gentleman he was), I pulled out my phone. Shoving my bag under my arm, I looked at the display and saw it said Paula Calling.

"Sorry." I looked between Sam and Luci. "I have to take this."

"So take it," Sam invited, but I will note, he didn't let me go.

The phone kept ringing. I waited for him to let me go or Luci to wander away. He didn't and she didn't.

Damn.

I took the call and greeted, "Hey, girl."

"*There's a bidding war on your house!*" she shrieked so loudly, I had to jerk the phone away from my ear. And I knew, because *I* heard it, that Sam and Luci heard it and probably anyone in a ten-foot radius.

I put the phone back to my ear and began, "Paula—"

That was as far as I got before more screeching that forced me to take the phone away from my ear, which meant, again, Sam and Luciana could hear everything.

"*Ohmigod, ohmigod, OHMIGOD! It's been months and no nibbles. NOW THIS! My commission is gonna be KILLER, AND I just heard word there's a unit that's opened up at The Dorchester! EXACTLY WHERE YOU WANTED TO MOVE!*"

When she shut up, I quickly put my phone to my ear and told her, "Paula, honey, I'm at a party and everything you scream, everyone can hear."

Silence, then a whole lot quieter, "Oh shit, sorry." Pause, then, "You're at a party?"

"Yeah," I replied and said no more.

Paula, being Paula, didn't let it go at that. "You're on vacation. How are you at a party?"

"Uh…I'll explain later," I evaded.

"Okay, but cool. Parties are fun," she informed me.

This one, we would see.

"This is good news, though," I said softly, bringing the discussion back in hand, and it *was* good news.

Unloading the house I hated and restarting my life at The Dorchester, which was an absolutely awesome condo complex, was seriously good news. And even better, it was very rare a unit opened up for sale.

So this wasn't good news, it was *awesome.*

"Totally, babe," Paula told me. "This is *huge.* I *love* it. Now, I know you're vacationing with the rich and famous…" Jeez, she had no idea, and when she learned, I'd have to put cotton in my ears, she was going to scream so loud. "But I gotta move on this. I'll see if they have digital shots or a web listing set up. If not, I'll get in the unit and take some, e-mail them to you. Can you go somewhere, get on a computer and pick up your webmail?"

"Probably," I answered.

"Good. I'm gonna do that today and then tell the two couples I have on the hook that they gotta get their shit sorted by end of business. Get that nailed down, get your deposit. If you give the go-ahead on the photos, I'll move on The Dorchester. Do we have a plan?"

I couldn't believe this. This was amazing. This meant I got to go home, have my yard sale, and get on with my life. *My* life. My life with Memphis that had no nuance of Cooter in it except, of course, the existence of Memphis, but that wasn't her fault.

I loved this.

And that was why I smiled at the phone and whispered, "Yeah, honey. We have a plan."

"Killer, babe. Kill...*er.* I'm freaking out, I'm so happy. It's like... I know this is gonna sound totally unhinged and so far beyond bitchy, I may go straight to hell...but it's like Milo blew a hole in Cooter's head, and at the same time, he blew you a shitload of luck. Cooter's pension, five million dollars, the vacation of a lifetime, and now this."

At her words, I closed my eyes, my body got stiff, and I was so freaked, I didn't notice Sam's arm going tight or his body closing in on mine.

When I didn't speak, Paula whispered, "Oh shit, I took that too far, didn't I?"

She did.

She was right with what she said, of course. It sucked for Milo, who was a good guy driven to do a very bad thing, but there was no question his actions meant good things for me. Including getting my life back, getting a shitload of money, and dodging a bullet, literally, because Cooter and Vanessa were going to hire a hit man.

But still. I wasn't ready for it to be laid out like that, and certainly not when I was experiencing all that was Sam. I wasn't prepared. I was vulnerable and her words brought shit to the surface I didn't want to deal with unless I was in familiar surroundings and close to Memphis who would cuddle, give me doggie kisses and make me feel better.

I sucked in an unsteady breath but didn't open my eyes when I replied quietly, "No, honey, that's okay."

Silence, then, "No, it was too far."

"It's okay."

I heard her take in breath before she said cautiously, "I know we haven't gotten 'round to talking about this, babe, but you know we'll have to and—"

I shook my head, then tipped it down, opened my eyes, and looked at the floor, whispering, "I can't do this now."

More silence, then, "Oh God, I forgot. You're at a party."

Yes, I was.

Oh shit.

I was.

With ex-model Luciana, who had a villa, a Lamborghini, four other cars, and a boat, and Sampson Freaking Cooper, who I noticed belatedly was holding me front-to-front in one arm.

Shit!

I looked up at him. He was staring down at me with that intent look and, I knew, listening to every word.

"Yes," I answered Paula, my gaze sliding away. "I'm at a party."

"Right, well, okay then. Don't hate me, but I'm gonna take this shot."

Oh man.

Sneak attack!

Before I could intervene, she kept talking.

"I'm gonna get your house sorted for you and then me, Teri, and Missy are gonna get *you* sorted, babe. No." She said the last word swiftly, like she thought I'd refuse, which, totally, I would. That was,

I would if I didn't have an audience. "When he was alive, we got it. He was a threat. You don't see your girl with bruises on her face too often to count for seven years and not get that, babe. And also not get that that shit, dished out regularly, would put the fear of God in anybody. But he's gone and we're gonna sort out the shit he left behind. And, Kia, we all dig that you think you can just put it behind you, get rid of all that was him and move on, but that shit isn't gonna fly, and deep down, I know you know it, girl."

"Paula, *please,* now is *really* not the time," I whispered, and when I did, Sam's other arm slid around me.

Damn it!

"I know. I'm just saying, when you get home, we're *making* it the time."

And I was just thinking that maybe I'd find a place on Crete and never go home.

"Kia? Babe?" she called.

"Fine," I whispered, because at that moment I had no choice.

"Okay," she whispered back.

"I'll find a computer to pull up the pictures you send me, but it's late here so it won't be until morning."

"Right."

"Okay."

"Well then, have fun at your party."

Impossible.

"I will," I lied.

"*Ciao,* babe," she said, and I could hear her smile in her voice but could only guess it was relieved.

"*Ciao,* you big dork," I replied, and I could hear her laughter, which I knew was relieved. My words said I wasn't pissed at her and I'd given in on the talk.

Then she was gone and I knew at that moment, in Heartmeadow, Indiana, my friend Paula was dialing Missy or Teri, or if she was at a phone that had the option, she was conferencing.

Shit.

I pulled in a soft breath, tucking my phone into my bag, when Luci unsurprisingly immediately offered, "Tomorrow, when you wake up, you can use my computer."

God, seriously, it would be a lot better if she was a haughty über-bitch like all supermodels were supposed to be and not hyper-friendly.

I looked at her and noticed that Sam's arms hadn't moved, nor had his body, which was right in my space.

Still, even so, I ignored both.

"Thanks," I said softly.

"*Prego,*" she said softly back.

"Luci, give us a minute, yeah?" Sam said not softly but firmly, and there was only one answer to his "yeah?" This was the answer Luci gave him after throwing him a radiant, happy, certain-she-was-going-to-have-quasi-nieces-and-nephews-imminently-as-supplied-by Sam-and-me smile before she melted away.

My mind was stuck on giving Luci nieces and nephews as supplied on me by Sam when Sam called me.

"Baby."

Reluctantly, I tipped my head back to look up at him.

"You okay?" he asked softly.

"If I say yes, will you ask me repeatedly until I tell you the truth?" I asked back, and he grinned.

Then he answered, "Yeah."

"Then, no."

"Talk to me," he ordered gently.

I shook my head, put my hands to his biceps, and pushed back as I started, "Sam, I—"

His arms got tight and it was proved positive I was totally clueless because he was not a small man. He was a tall man. He was definitely a muscular man. And thus, I should have cottoned on to the fact that he was a very strong man.

I knew this in that instant because his arms separated, one going low at my waist, one going up to rest under my shoulder blades.

They got tight in a way I knew there was no escape, even without trying, and suddenly I found myself chest to chest, hips to hips, and thighs to thighs pressed deep to Sam Cooper.

His neck bent and his face was an inch from mine.

My stomach pitched, my knees wobbled, and my mouth clamped shut.

When he had my undivided attention, he said in a firm, unrelenting but still somehow gentle voice, "That was not a request."

"I need some space, Sam," I whispered and it was breathy, mostly because I was breathing so hard I was close to panting.

"You're not gonna get it."

Say what?

"Sam!" I snapped.

"Talk," he returned.

"I get to decide when I want to talk, not you," I retorted, and that was when it happened.

Right then.

Right there (nearly).

Within maybe ten minutes of showing up at his dead best friend's wealthy, gorgeous, famous wife's fabulous villa on *Lago di Como*, it happened.

Sam released me with one arm but only to twist, taking me with him and putting the champagne flute on a table within his reach. He repeated this maneuver when he divested me of my bag. Then he shuffled me backward out the door. Once there, he turned me to his side, his arm clamped around my waist, and he pulled me to the very end corner of the terrace balustrade, alone, no one close. There, he twisted me into the corner and caged me in.

And through this, I lost it. Completely. I forgot who he was, but I didn't forget who I was. I didn't forget what I'd learned at the hands of my husband. It had been months, but I remembered it in excruciating detail.

Sam's actions brought back Cooter's lessons and fear gripped me, extreme and paralyzing.

So when his hands came to either side of my neck, his thumbs at my jaws forcing my head back to look at him, his head jerked with his flinch so violently it was like I had struck him and I knew it was written all over my face.

"Baby," he whispered and his voice was not rough as velvet. It was just rough.

"Step back," I whispered and there was no way to miss the plea.

"Kia."

"Step back."

"Kia."

"Step *back*."

There it was.

A whimper.

Weak. Exposed.

Humiliated, I closed my eyes tight and tried to turn my face away. Sam allowed this, his thumbs gliding from my jaws, but he kept me pinned and he kept his hands at my neck.

Then he ground out, "He hurt you."

Oh man.

Oh God.

How did this happen?

Why couldn't I keep *anything* secret?

I kept my eyes closed and my face averted.

Sam kept going.

"He did it often."

I couldn't escape him, so I did the only thing I could—I twisted my neck deeper to turn my face further away in hopes he couldn't see it.

"He didn't check it. Not once. Not fuckin' once," Sam kept speaking, his voice now abrasive.

He wasn't pissed. He was *angry*.

Oh God!

Sam didn't relent.

"He broke you."

"Step back," I pleaded.

He didn't step back.

He did something entirely different.

Both his arms closed around me, one at my middle back, the other around my shoulder, his hand up and curled tight at the back of my neck. He pressed his fingers in to keep my head turned away, and his mouth was at my ear so close I could feel his nose brushing my hair.

"I didn't know." Now his voice was rough a different way. "I didn't know. If I had known—"

"Sam, don't," I cut him off. "Please just move away."

His arms got tighter and he ignored me. "I'd never hurt you."

I swallowed and stopped talking.

"I wanted your attention, Kia. That's it. I get where you are now, baby, and I'll never do that again. And I would never…no fuckin' joke, baby, please get this…I would never, *ever* hurt you."

I stayed silent.

Sam stayed close.

I didn't move.

He didn't let me go.

God, I needed him to *let me go*!

I swallowed again, hard, and I did it to swallow back tears, so my breath hitched and my chest jumped with the effort and his arms got tighter.

"My dad beat my ma."

My head snapped around as my eyes opened. His head jerked back at my movement and his hand at the back of my neck instantly moved to wrap around its side.

"You see that as a kid, you live it, you're powerless to stop it, it marks you. You got two choices: you keep that shit alive by givin' in and perpetrating it on your family, or you vow it'll end with him. My brother and me, we vowed it'd end with him and that's where it ended, Kia. We got older, taller, bigger, and that shit stopped. You want, I'll tell you how me and Ben made it stop, but it was us who made it stop. I haven't seen my dad in nineteen years, and this is because he knows I see his face, he won't be conscious long enough to blink at me. You get where I'm comin' from with this?"

Stunned speechless at his open, raw sharing, I nodded.

He watched me nod. Then his eyes moved over my face and they changed, filling with something that made my body tense so tight I thought tendons would snap. But he didn't seem to notice as the flame that lit in his eyes quickly built to an inferno.

And I would know why when he spoke again.

"Cheated on you and beat you."

Oh God.

"Sam—"

"You. Fuckin' *you*. Look at you. What the fuck?"

I pressed my lips together.

He wasn't done.

"Any woman, but fuck, *fuck*," he clipped. "You. *You*. Takin' a hand to you would be like takin' a razorblade to *La Scapigliata*."

His last two words jolted me out of our current drama and I blinked, then whispered, "What?"

"What?" he shot back, still pissed, definitely, and thus not following me.

"La Scapila-what?"

He stared at me a second before he repeated, "*La Scapigliata*."

I felt my brows draw together. "What's that?"

"*La Scapigliata*?"

"Yeah."

"*La Scapigliata. The Head of a Woman. The Lady with Disheveled Hair.* By da Vinci. It's unfinished, but it's still a masterpiece. It's in Parma. I've viewed it twice and it's the most beautiful thing I've ever seen."

My mouth dropped open and this wasn't only because Sampson Cooper, ex-pro football star, ex-dangerous commando, and current big, tall, powerful hot guy was talking about an unfinished masterpiece by da Vinci, but because he'd compared me to the most beautiful thing he'd ever seen.

He looked at my mouth, then he looked in my eyes, his arm and hand giving me a squeeze before he stated, "Now I think she finally fuckin' gets me."

"Sam—" I whispered.

"I'd never hurt you, Kia."

"Sam—" I tried again.

"Never. Don't give a shit what you said, what you did. I would not take a hand to you and I would not cut you down any way I could, verbally or mentally."

"Sam—" I tried yet again.

"I scared you just now. I get why, but I didn't mean to and I won't ever do it again, so I need to know you believe me."

"I don't."

Yes. That was what I said. It came right out of my mouth and it caused a flash of something I didn't like to see to score through Sam's eyes.

"Baby," he whispered.

"I barely know you," I whispered back.

He held my eyes.

Then he muttered, "Four months."

"Sorry?" I asked.

"You said he got whacked four months ago."

"Yes," I confirmed.

"You're sellin' your house, gettin' a new place and off on vacation, sitting on balconies, drinking alone, tears in your eyes. It's too early. You aren't ready to believe me."

You know, seriously, it was beginning to piss me off how often he figured me out.

So much so, I informed him of this fact.

"You know, Sam, it's beginning to piss me off how you figure me out. How the heck am I supposed to be intriguing and mysterious if you keep figuring me out?"

Yes. Again. That was what I said.

And I knew I didn't imagine my extreme idiocy when he suddenly burst out laughing, throwing his head back to do it, then bending his neck so he could bury his face in my neck and finish doing it as his hand slid down to become an arm tight around me.

"I can see that was amusing to you. The problem is, I wasn't being funny."

He lifted his head, his dark brown eyes still dancing with hilarity, and his arms gave me a squeeze. "Intriguing and mysterious?"

"I'm chic and cosmopolitan. Women like that are always intriguing and mysterious."

"Baby, I knew you all of two minutes when you told me your husband was murdered while doin' your high school arch-nemesis. That's intriguing, yeah. But it sure as fuck isn't mysterious."

He was right, which was also annoying, so I just glared at him.

"You also told me you knew me," he reminded me.

"I do," I again confirmed, then went for the gusto because, what the heck? In my efforts to get him to back off, nothing else was working. "In fact, I borderline Internet stalked you."

I thought he would let me go instantly, repulsed by this news, or at the very least it would creep him out, but instead he started chuckling.

Chuckling!

"That isn't funny either. That's creepy," I informed him.

"You aren't the first," he replied, which was definitely the truth. Teri was way into him before he even quit football and went into the Army. "And you won't be the last," he finished.

"It's still creepy."

"Paparazzi was in your business, a picture of you was in front of my face, Kia, baby, seriously, I would look. You were in that dress, I'd look for a while. You were in a bikini..." he trailed off.

I belatedly forced my arms between us but only succeeded in getting them trapped with my hands flat against the hard wall of his chest. This was another mistake. I'd already had a variety of opportunities to experience the hard parts of his body. I certainly didn't need another one. It was distracting.

"Okay, can we change the subject?" I requested, though, at that moment, pressed to him tight when he was accepting me even though I was laying out all my dark secrets, proving without a doubt he should take me back to the hotel, drop me off and never look back, I didn't know what subject to change it to.

It didn't matter. As I was becoming accustomed with Sam, I didn't get the chance.

"No," he answered.

I rolled my eyes.

"Gettin' back to the point," he started, and I rolled my eyes back to him. "You said you knew me."

"Yes."

"Well, you know what I did. If I didn't know how to figure people out, what I did, I'd be dead. I was taught to pay attention, close attention. I do it out of habit. I do it with you out of interest. And I'm gonna keep being straight..."

Great. He was going to keep being straight. Wonderful.

He kept being straight.

"I know you're freaked. I know you're scared. And I know you can come up with a million reasons why you're not ready, all of which will be excuses. But now that I know exactly what's behind those shields you got up, baby, and just how flimsy those shields are, you gotta know that knowin' that makes me no less into you."

My irritation leaked right out of me. I felt my body start to melt against his and I whispered, "Sam—"

"In fact, it makes me *more* into you."

Oh man.

"Sam—"

"And you'll learn," his arms got tighter, his face dipped closer, and his voice got sweet and gentle, "because I'll prove it to you, I'll *never* hurt you."

I stared into his eyes and I asked quietly, "Well, will you let me finish a sentence?"

His eyes flared with humor as he said, "Sure."

"Thanks," I said back, partially sarcastically, and his eyes flared with humor again. I got serious and laid it out. "You're right. I'm freaked, I'm scared, and there are a million reasons why I'm not ready and I'm not certain all those are excuses."

"Kia—"

I slid my hand up his chest and touched my fingers to his lips. He went quiet and I slid it back down.

I finished on a whisper, "But this isn't about me. This is about you. You're a good guy. You can be annoying, but I can tell you're a good guy. And seriously, please listen to me…men who are good men, they deserve better, Sam. They deserve the best. And you shouldn't settle for anything less."

I watched in the waning light as his eyes grew heated and felt as his arms stayed locked around me tight.

Then he whispered back, "Yeah, totally full of shit."

I blinked at his bizarre response to my heartfelt words, which I thought were very nice, and he went on.

"The thing I didn't get before is that you not only have no clue, you also have no clue you're full of shit."

"Sam, I'm not full of shit."

Suddenly, his head dipped down but to the side and his mouth was at my ear.

"You get that he took something precious from you. Your ability to trust. But, I hate to break this to you, honey, he took more. And whatever your girl was tellin' you on the phone that made you freak, and if you'd open your eyes to what's happenin' right now, you'd see what he took was more precious even than trust. You'd also see you got people around you who want to help you get it back. Do not fuck up and let that opportunity slide. He took that from you. Now's your time to fight and get it back."

"I don't know what you're talking about."

"You'll see."

"Sam—"

"Just live in the now, Kia. Keep livin' in the now, and when I say that, right now, I mean with me, and I promise you'll see."

"That doesn't make me any less scared, Sam," I whispered in his ear, and he lifted his head and looked down at me.

"He strapped you with that too, baby. Fight back and learn to be fearless."

Something about his words struck hard and it struck deep.

I had lived in fear a long time. I couldn't remember the last time I woke up and didn't spend every second of every day living in fear. Even now, even after Cooter was gone, I woke up filled with fear.

It had gone so long I had no clue how to be fearless.

"I don't think I can," I admitted.

"You can. Everyone can."

"I'm not sure that's me."

"Okay, when you can't, you learn how to be."

"Sam, I don't—"

I stopped speaking when he gave me a squeeze and asked, "Where are you?"

"Sorry?"

"Where are you right now, Kia?"

"In Lake Como."

He grinned before he bent close again and whispered, "You're in the arms of the man you borderline Internet stalked a day after he asked you out on a date. You didn't take today to run away. You didn't sit in your room, listen to me knock and not answer the door. You put on a dress, you walked with me to a Eurotrash car and you went out with me. If there's fear in there somewhere, I don't see it. What I see is, today you may have been nervous, but you didn't let that cripple you and right now, you're here with me. Baby, you're *already* fearless."

"But I've been terrified all day."

"Did you let it stop you?"

"No."

He said no more.

Ohmigod.

Was he right?

Ohmigod!

He was right!

"She sees the light," he muttered through a grin, watching me.

"Sam—"

He cut me off. "That's your first block, baby. Use it, step up on it and keep climbing. You'll get to the other side. You with me?"

"I'm not sure," I whispered.

"You not with me?"

"Um…well…"

"You might not be sure, but you are definitely with me," he stated and made his point by giving me another squeeze. "So how about you go with that for now. Yeah?"

I stared up at him.

Then I predicted, "You're going to get bored of this."

"Yeah?" he asked on another grin.

"Definitely."

"We'll see," he muttered.

"I'll bet you a thousand dollars you get bored of me," I told him.

His head tilted to the side and he burst out laughing.

"Seriously," I said through his laughter.

He sobered, but still smiling, he replied, "I'll take that bet, Kia. It'll serve me right to pay up, I'm stupid enough to get bored of you. And an example of why I know I'd be stupid to get bored of you is that you'd make me a fuckin' bet for one large that I'd get bored of you."

My heart fluttered and my fingers spasmodically pressed into his chest.

His smile got bigger.

"I'm back to thinking I need champagne," I informed him.

To which he murmured, "I bet you are."

"I'm serious," I pressed.

"I bet you're that too."

"Sam," I snapped, and he grinned again.

He moved back but curled an arm around me and moved me down the terrace toward the doors we went through to come out.

"Champagne, then I'll show you Luci's other cars," he declared, and I had to admit, after the Lamborghini, which also didn't fit her, I was intrigued.

"With a Eurotrash rating of first to last, where does the Lamborghini fit?" I asked.

"Number five," he answered instantly, and my head jerked around to look at him.

"You mean the others are worse?"

"She's got great taste in clothes, shit taste in cars. She let me pick which one I wanted and the one I have is the only one of her rides I'd even consider putting my ass in."

"What did Gordo think of this?"

He guided me in and immediately jerked up his chin to someone. I followed his eyes and saw a white-coated waiter nod and move away, then Sam looked back down to me.

"To forget she goes to bed alone, and until she sorts her shit out, she'll keep doin' it. First, she's up in my business, and next, she buys cars Gordo would lose his mind if he ever knew she'd even test-driven much less bought them and brought them home."

My eyes slid through the room trying to find her and not succeeding as I muttered, "Interesting."

"Yeah," Sam said distractedly. "I can read a lotta shit, baby, but that I do not get."

I had no reply and luckily didn't have to make one because the waiter came bearing a flute of champagne. I took it and sipped.

Then Sam took my hand and moved me through the people, muttering, "Cars."

We went and inspected Luciana's cars.

He was right. The Lamborghini was the least flashy. Even Vin Diesel would turn his nose up at that lot of them.

And, not able to stop myself from giggling at beautiful, sultry, sophisticated, sweet Luciana's very bad taste in automobiles, Sam did it again.

When I thought I could never relax, when I thought there was no way I could get over my latest life drama, I underestimated Sam's determination to make me do both.

So, without even noticing it, I relaxed and got over it.

5

SMART ENOUGH TO HOLD ON

I woke feeling warm, content, comfy, and something else. Something that felt strange. Something I knew didn't feel strange once upon a time in my life.

It was a feeling I registered and understood when I was six years old.

It was the feeling I used to have all the time, every second of every minute of my life. But I understood it when my dad took my brother, Kyle, and me to that haunted house.

I'd been terrified, completely, even though, looking back, it was meant for little kids like me so it was seriously tame. But I'd never experienced anything like it until then.

And as I wandered through that haunted house with Dad and Kyle, monsters popping out, the bloody bride and groom gruesomely murdered on their blessed day, I got more and more scared when, suddenly, my father took my hand and that feeling of fear evaporated completely.

Dad was with me. Dad was close.

I was safe.

Dad wouldn't allow anything to harm me. Not monsters. Not zombie brides.

Nothing.

And I felt that upon waking. I felt it again for the first time in *ages*.

I opened my eyes and saw the corded, dark-skinned column of a man's throat. I felt my legs tangled with long, heavy ones, my arm resting around a man's waist, my other hand pressed to a hard chest, and two strong arms around me, holding me close to a solid, steady heat.

I tipped my head back and saw Sam's head tipped slightly forward, his eyes closed, his handsome face relaxed, his power at rest. I stared, immobile, such was his beauty. His eyelashes were black, short, and spiky, but they were thick. So many of them, their fan seemed a unit, not individual lashes, and instantly I was transfixed.

Then, as they had a tendency to do, memories washed through my head, taking my mind away from feeling warm, comfy, safe and fascinated by Sam's eyelashes, forcing it to last night.

I tipped my head down, and I didn't know why, but automatically my body sought more contact with his by pressing forward.

When it did, Sam's arms convulsed, going tight and staying that way a moment before they partially released. My head tipped back again, thinking I woke him, but he was still asleep.

He was still asleep.

This meant Sampson Cooper hugged in his sleep.

Oh man.

I sighed.

Then I closed my eyes tight and sifted through my memories of last night.

After I giggled myself silly at Luci's cars while Sam watched and smiled, he took me back to the party. Thus commenced me meeting a variety of Luci's friends and acquaintances, very few who Sam knew, almost all of whom knew Sam. I did this while drinking, and several times Sam led us to the dining room where Luciana had indeed put out a spread.

Even though the food looked gorgeous, luckily Celeste had primed me for this, so I nibbled and enjoyed rather than gorged myself, which was probably what I would have done not having lunch or dinner.

Before my fifth glass of champagne, I realized a number of things.

One, I was having fun.

Two, Sam did not leave my side.

Three, he did this not in an overbearing way but in a way that simply said he liked being there.

Four, I liked this, like, *a lot.*

Five, Sam was funny in a dry, blunt, observational way.

Six, because of this, I laughed a lot.

Seven, Sam thought I was funny and I knew this because he also laughed a lot.

Eight, I liked it when Sam laughed, mostly because it sounded good, he looked beautiful doing it, but also because he was making a habit of touching me when he did. Either sweeping an arm around my waist and pulling me tight to his side, or sweeping an arm around my waist, his other arm joining it, pulling me tight to his front and holding me close.

Nine, Luci liked it that Sam and I were laughing and touching a lot. I knew this because, either when she was with us or she was across the room, any time I noticed her, she was smiling at us like a happy sister who, after years of putting up with her brother's girlfriends who she loathed, she'd finally met her soulmate who she could shop with, gossip with, and instigate regular margarita nights and get drunk with.

And ten, Luci's friends and acquaintances were awesome. I knew this because they were obviously rich, obviously well-traveled, obviously well educated, but they were also nice, welcoming, entertaining, and easy to talk to. I also knew this because I caught her friends openly and often glancing her way with concern on their faces. She wasn't hiding anything from them either and they were worried. I liked this too, even though I didn't like the reason they were feeling it.

But after glass of champagne number five, Sam handed me glass of champagne number six which, with the bottle I'd shared with Celeste, was actually glass of champagne number nine.

And I learned last night that was one glass too many.

This I learned when, three sips into glass number nine, Sam led me out to the balcony. There were others out there, but by that time it was dark, the lake was set in moonlight, and for those who wanted privacy (like, clearly, Sam), Luci had not turned on the outside lights, and thus it seemed romantically secluded.

Sam settled us at the stone balustrade, me facing front, Sam fitting his body into mine at the back, his arm stealing around my ribs, the other one around my chest. I felt his jaw come to rest at the side of my head.

Like his voice, like his laughter, and like the now gazillion times he'd demonstrated his gentlemanly behavior (for instance, I did not have to ask for a glass of champagne, Sam always procured them for me; I did not have to walk unguided or unprotected, Sam always was close with a hand at the small of my back or an arm curled around my waist; and I did not have to introduce myself to anyone and start conversation, Sam did it for me and was certain to lead any discourse so I never, not once, felt left out or ill at ease), the position he held me in settled in my soul, deep and warm.

And when he settled us, he didn't speak, he just held me and we both took in the view.

I found myself sighing.

And I sighed right before I panicked.

Because in that moment it came to me with drunken clarity that I wanted this, all of it. This life that led me to wearing beautiful gowns, meeting interesting, friendly people, giggling over silly but unbelievably expensive cars, eating delicious food while drinking dry, crisp champagne, and most especially, standing outside in the moonlight on the terrace of a beautiful home on an even more beautiful lake with a man who would hold me like Sam was holding me after treating me like Sam had been treating me.

In fact, the bottom-line truth of it was, I really liked all the other stuff, but it was Sam holding me like he was holding me and treating me like he was treating me—if it was in a fantastic villa in Italy or if it was getting bitten by mosquitoes and not caring even a little bit on a deck in Indiana—that was what I really wanted.

I wanted it then. I wanted it the next day. I wanted it forever.

And I couldn't have it.

This was Sam's world, not mine.

But he couldn't possibly know that. Not with me staying at our swanky hotel and wearing fabulous footwear every time I saw him.

And right then, into my sixth sip of glass of champagne number nine, I completely forgot all of Celeste's worldly advice and drunkenly decided he had to know who he held in his arms.

Full disclosure.

For the sake of my sanity because, if he found out later I was not a jet-set, high-heels-wearing socialite but instead a...well, *not* jet-set, flip-flop-wearing non-socialite, I knew he'd be angry. He'd think I'd duped him.

So he had to find out now so, if he chose, which I drunkenly decided he would, he could move on and could I too (maybe).

"My friend Teri has a life-size cardboard cutout of you."

Yes. That was me. That was what I said into the moonlight, breaking the comfortable, cozy, romantic silence Sam had guided us to.

His arms gave me a slight squeeze and he muttered, "What?"

"My friend Teri has a life-size cardboard cutout of you," I repeated.

No arm squeeze and also no reply.

"In her bedroom," I went on.

Again, no response whatsoever.

"You're in your Colts gear."

Nothing.

Hmm. I wasn't sure if this was working or not.

I took a sip of champagne.

Sam remained silent.

I drunkenly blathered on.

"At an average of thirty-five percent, we've calculated it, the men she takes in that room can't go the distance."

More nothing.

"As in, they can't bring it home," I clarified, just in case he was not instantly revolted by these words and setting me aside, never to touch me again, because he didn't get.

Still nothing.

I kept sharing.

"In other words, they can't bring it home for her, obviously, but also for them."

Nothing.

"We think it's you, or, um…the cardboard cutout of you in your Colts gear. We think they find it intimidating. Still, although this is disappointing for Teri and, as I mentioned, an alarmingly frequent occurrence, she hasn't moved it."

That was when I got something.

Sam's body started shaking so violently my body started shaking with it. Then his jaw left my hair because he shoved his face in my neck and roared, yes, *roared* with laughter as his arms went super tight.

It felt nice.

Well, that didn't work.

Onward!

I sifted through my mind, drunkenly attempting to latch on to a new strategy. It found one and I sallied forth.

"I don't have a college degree," I informed him when his laughter died.

His face went out of my neck, his jaw went back to my hair, and he muttered, "You don't?"

"Nope."

His jaw left my hair so his lips could go to my ear where he murmured, "Hmm."

That felt nice too.

Like, *really* nice.

Argh!

Onward!

"You graduated from UCLA," I told him, though he had to know this fact unless he had patches of amnesia and forgot bits of his life, which was highly unlikely, because, since I borderline Internet stalked him, I would know about it if he had.

His mouth went from my ear and he agreed over my head with a "Yep."

"You grew up there," I kept telling him about his life. "In LA, that is."

"Yep," he agreed again, but his voice was vibrating like he was laughing but yet not.

Undeterred, I carried on.

"You grew up in a not very good neighborhood, so within weeks of you signing your contract with the Colts, you bought your mom a house in Malibu."

Sam went back to silence.

I didn't.

"On the beach," I continued.

Sam said nothing.

I kept going.

"Because of the lessons you learned from your mom, you told *Sports Illustrated* you wouldn't accept any endorsement contracts for products you didn't actually use and feel good about endorsing."

"This is true," he muttered, completely unperturbed at the extent of knowledge I held about him.

I sighed.

I sipped more champagne.

Another tactic came to me so I announced, "I have a dog."

"You do?" Sam asked.

"Yep, her name is Memphis."

Sam said nothing, but he moved away from my back, though only so he could pull me gently from the balustrade while turning me. When he did, he took the glass of champagne from my hand and set it on the balustrade before he grabbed my hand and pulled me down the terrace.

I kept talking. "She's a King Charles spaniel."

Sam led me through some doors and I looked up at him, intent on my course so only vaguely noting he tipped his chin up toward someone, and when my eyes went in that direction, I saw Luci grinning madly at us. I gave her a wave so as not to be rude because her gaze had moved to me, but I did this still talking as Sam guided me along the outskirts of the partygoers.

"A King Charles spaniel, just in case you don't know, is a small dog. She's soft all over, brown and white. She has fluffy, floppy ears and big, sweet, dark brown eyes. But she's also yappy. She talks a lot, she has a lot to say, and unless you're her momma, you wouldn't get it. It would just seem like yaps to you. She's also overly friendly. Many people find that annoying."

This last was a lie. Everyone loved Memphis.

Sam guided me to some stairs and up them. What he didn't do was speak.

I decided to get direct to the point.

"How do you feel about small, overly friendly, yappy dogs?"

At my direct question, because he was a gentleman, Sam answered it.

"I prefer big, not overly friendly, not yappy dogs who can sense danger and bark loud."

"I don't think Memphis can sense danger," I told him. "I think Memphis likes everyone, including criminals. Though I can't say that with any certainty since I don't think she's met any. But if I had to guess, my guess would be she'd like them."

"That's too bad," Sam muttered as if it was all the same to him, and he guided me into a room, closing the door behind us.

He moved me through the dark room as I abandoned Memphis and found another topic.

"I live in a small town," I told him as the room lit dimly when Sam turned on the lamp beside a bed.

"Yeah, baby, you told me," he said quietly.

I noted he was shrugging off his suit jacket. I also noted him tossing it to the end of the bed. I then noted his shirt looked even better without his jacket on. He sat on the bed and instantly pulled me in his lap. Just as instantly he fell back, taking me with him and twisting so we were lying side by side, facing each other.

I was drunkenly determined to follow the path I was on, thus I found nothing amiss in our current situation. I simply settled my head into the pillows and found his eyes.

"Outside my wedding gown, which was gorgeous, by the way, though not as gorgeous as this dress, and seriously, Cooter was not worth how gorgeous my wedding gown was, but obviously, now you know that. So outside of my wedding gown, this is the first gown I've worn in my life. I didn't even go to my proms because Cooter thought they were stupid and I was seeing him all the way back then."

I noticed Sam's brows had drawn together slightly but, surprisingly, not at the stunning news I didn't traipse through life in fabulous gowns. Instead, he asked, "Your husband's name was Cooter?"

Excellent!

I should have started with that!

Cooter having the hick name to beat all hick names said it all about me.

"Yep," I answered.

"Was that his real name?"

"No, his real name was Jeff, but no one called him that."

"Ever?"

I nodded, my hair sliding on the pillow. "Ever."

"Not even when he became an adult?"

I shook my head.

"Jesus," he muttered.

"Yep, he was a hick. He was, like, *the definition* of a hick."

Sam just held my eyes.

"He was a fan of yours too, considering you were good at what you did and you played for the Colts, which was his team. That was, he was a fan of yours until you quit and went into the Army. He thought that was crazy. He couldn't believe you gave up the chance of earning that kind of money to join the Army," I shared.

"Kia, honey, I think it's clear the guy was a dick," Sam replied softly.

"This is true," I muttered.

Suddenly, Sam took control of the conversation by asking, "How old are you?"

"Twenty-eight," I answered.

"Jesus," he muttered again.

"What?"

"You look it, but your eyes say you're older."

I latched on to that. "Am I too young for you?"

He grinned but didn't reply.

I felt his grin slide along my skin in a sweet way but powered through it and suggested instead, "Too old?"

He started chuckling and again didn't answer.

I sighed.

Sam's arms, which I belatedly noticed were wrapped around me, gathered me closer.

"So, this is the first time you've worn a dress like that?" he asked quietly.

"Yep," I answered, nodding my head on the pillow again at the same time tilting it back because it was now closer to his.

"You wear it like you were born to it."

Wow. That was nice.

"Wow. That's nice."

Yes. I thought it, then I freaking said it.

Idiot!

He grinned.

Then he asked, "You think you wear it like you were born to it, maybe you *were* born to it?"

I blinked once before I considered this.

Then I answered, "No."

"No?"

I shook my head.

"Why not?" Sam asked.

"Well, because that's crazy. I live in the small town I've lived in my whole life. I married a hick who cheated on me and beat me. He didn't have a college degree and worked for a sheet metal factory and not well, if his performance evaluations and the nasty moods he'd get into after he got them were anything to go by. I also don't have a college degree, and until recently, when I came into some money, I worked as an administrative assistant for five accountants and my job was b-o-r-i-n-g, *boring* in a way it was a wonder I didn't lapse into a coma daily by three o'clock. I mean, they were nice guys, but seriously, accountants and the work they did..." I trailed off and faked a yawn.

Sam grinned again.

I kept babbling.

"I got my first passport delivered two months ago. I had my first manicure, pedicure, facial, and massage two days ago. I think, with all that, it's safe to say I was *definitely* not born to wear a gown like this."

"I was born in the barrio," Sam returned immediately. "My father came and went as he pleased. He was gone more than he was there, but when he was there, he was more of a dick than your dead husband. He took my mother's money, ate her food, drank himself sick, cheated on her openly, beat the shit outta her and slapped my brother and me around. He didn't work, not once that I knew, but she did. She worked hard. She kept us fed. She kept us clothed. But that was all we had and it sucks but you feel that as a kid, no matter how hard she worked so we wouldn't."

I stared, lips parted at his open, honest, deep sharing and he continued.

"But even with all that shit, since we were kids, and maybe before when we couldn't even understand what she was sayin', she told us we were bigger than the shithole that surrounded us. We were better. We were meant to live large. And she believed we'd do it. Find some way outta that fuckin' place. And by the time we got old enough to make decisions, she'd been fillin' our heads with that so long, it sunk in. We believed her and we both worked our asses off to get out."

He paused and I nodded because it seemed he needed indication that had sunk in. Then he went on.

"I had added luck. God saw fit to grant me a talent that would lead my way. But Ma told me over and over, the talent He gave me was fleeting and fragile and I should not rely on it, so I didn't. I studied. I didn't drift through college, I earned my degree. My brother wasn't born with something like that, so he found his way out and joined the Army about two days after he graduated high school. He stayed in it. They gave him the means and he got himself his degree and got on the officer track. He was going to be career Army. That was his goal, even his dream. But whatever his dream, like Ma said we would both do, we made it. So we got the fuck out right after high school and never looked back."

Touched by this as well as awed, I whispered, "That's very cool."

"Yeah," he said through a smile. "But you don't get me, honey. I'm here beside you, wearin' this fuckin' suit, and I wasn't born to be here either. But I'm here, same as you. And wherever you are, however you got there, if it's good, you're meant to be there either because you earned it or life led you there and you were smart enough to hold on."

Nine glasses of champagne or not, I found this concept profound.

Therefore, I shared that with Sam.

"That's very profound."

His body shook mine and the bed when he chuckled, then replied, "It isn't profound, Kia, it's the God's honest truth. You're tellin' me the woman I met at breakfast, saw last night, and I'm holdin' in my arms right now is a fraud. But I'm tellin' you you're wrong. She isn't. She's you."

That was profound too.

I studied him before I shared, "I think I need to ponder this."

His arms gathered me closer as he chuckled again and muttered, "Yeah, you do that."

"I will," I agreed, tipping my head back further to look at him.

"Good," he murmured, tipping his chin down further to look at me.

Suddenly (and I didn't know why and drunkenly didn't care), I whispered, "I think I love your mom and I don't even know her."

"She's the kind of woman you love, even if you don't know her," Sam replied.

"She sounds like it."

"What's your Ma like?"

I pulled in breath, let it out softly and said, "Like a mom. She cooks comfort food. She goes overboard with Christmas decorations. She knocks herself out for you every birthday because, for her, that was a day that changed her life in a way she liked a whole lot and she wants you to know it. We did the whole stereotype thing. Kyle, my older brother, was Mom's little man and still is, even though now he's big. I was daddy's little girl. So Mom was the one who was tough on me and Kyle got away with everything with her. And Dad was the one who was tough on Kyle and I could get anything I wanted if I ran to Dad. But when I say tough, I mean in the sense that parents are supposed to be tough. They were good parents, then and now. I love them both and they both love me."

"And how'd they feel about your husband?"

"They hated him," I answered instantly.

"Yeah," he whispered.

"They tried," I whispered back quickly, not wanting him to think they didn't. "That was what I was thinking about last night when you saw me. I was thinking how I should have noticed they were trying and let them help me."

Sam's face warmed, his eyes grew understanding, and his arms gathered me closer.

Then he said gently, "We're not goin' there, baby, not now. Now is for us. I shouldn't have asked."

"Okay," I agreed readily because I didn't want to go there. Not now. Not in Sam's arms. Not after drunkenly remembering to warn him about me and then drunkenly forgetting I was supposed to be doing that and, instead, loving living this moment with him. So much, there was no way I was letting it go.

"Okay," he whispered.

And that was when I pressed closer rather than Sam gathering me closer, and I lived that moment with him. Talking about my brother, my mom, my dad, Paula, Teri, and Missy and listening to him talk about his mom, his brother, Luci, and his friend and brother-in-arms, Travis "Gordo" Gordon.

And apparently falling asleep, living that moment with him, because, hours later, still wearing my gown, I woke up in much the same position—in his arms, pressed close, and feeling something I hadn't felt in years. Something precious I lost, and even precious, I didn't notice it was missing, but something I recognized as precious instantly when I got it back.

Safe.

And this brought me to now, awake, in my gown, the sun shining into the bedroom where Sam and I slept together.

I had done everything Celeste had told me not to do (except gorging myself on food). I had drank too much and shared too much.

Shit.

I pulled in a silent, steadying breath, and eyes glued to Sam's gorgeous, sleeping face, carefully I disentangled myself from his body, slid away, rolled, and found my feet at the side of the bed.

Twisting the instant I did because I heard him move, I looked to see he simply settled more onto his front and one of his hands had gone up and disappeared under my pillow.

I let out my breath.

Then I scanned the room that also had a tiled floor and a scattering of plush, attractive, lush, comfortable-looking furniture but, obviously, in the bedroom, it absolutely invited you to take a nap.

Amongst other things.

Hmm.

I tiptoed to an armchair so my thin heels wouldn't sound on the tile and sat on it. Then I bent forward and unstrapped my shoes, not believing I'd slept in them, much less my fabulous gown. I was also trying to remember when I'd drifted off to sleep, hoping that I didn't do it when Sam was talking as that would be rude, at the same time hoping I didn't do it when I was talking because that would be embarrassing, and realizing, either way, I was screwed.

I set the shoes aside and did another scan of the room, seeing it had a huge, polished wardrobe and two doors. One was the one we used to enter the room. The other I hoped was a bathroom.

Careful to be quiet, I made my way to the door, opened it and discovered I was right. I slipped in, closed the door, turned on the light, did my business, and while washing my hands, I froze when I caught sight of myself in the mirror.

Not because I was wearing last night's makeup, which, thankfully, didn't look smudged and scary.

But because my hair was down and falling around my shoulders in messy, curly waves and I remembered something about last night that I'd forgotten.

I remembered getting into telling Sam the story of Kyle and his buddies taking me and Paula (who had been my friend since high school) to our first kegger whereupon me and Paula got totally hammered. When they brought us home, both Paula and I hurled in Mom and Dad's backyard, causing Kyle and his buddies to tell us repeatedly, loudly, and without any hope of success to be quiet. This resulted in Mom and Dad catching us. I was giggling at this, Sam was smiling at it, and throughout telling him the story, his fingers were working in my hair, pulling out the pins.

It felt nice then, and staring at myself in the mirror, it felt nice remembering it.

But it was more.

After I'd finished that story by sharing with Sam that Mom and Dad had forced Kyle and his buddies to apologize in person to Paula's parents and then mow their yard free for the summer as penance, Sam shared a story with me.

It was the story of the first time his brother called him when he was hammered to ask Sam to come pick him up. Sam did, but Ben hadn't shared that it was not only Ben who was hammered—his girlfriend and her three friends were with him and also needed rides home. They were not hammered but completely shitfaced, and Sam unwisely loaded them all into his car whereupon three of the four females *and* Ben hurled *in* his car. He had to sell it because he could never get rid of the smell.

And while he was telling me this and I was giggling, he was running his fingers through my hair.

That felt nicer, and staring at myself in the mirror, it settled in my soul how much nicer it felt. Not only last night but right then, remembering it.

Okay. I was either seriously in trouble or…

I was seriously *not.*

I stared into my eyes in the mirror and as I did, I found my lips whispering, "Fearless."

I pulled in a breath, turned from the mirror, switched off the light and exited the bathroom, moving to the arched, windowed double doors with their gossamer curtains, my eyes on a still sleeping, still beautiful Sam.

I got to the doors and opened them, stepping out on the small, stone balcony. The curtain falling behind me, I drank in the view.

Wherever you are, however you got there, if it's good, you're meant to be there either because you earned it or life led you there and you were smart enough to hold on.

Sam's words came back to me, and no longer drunk on champagne or the beauty of being held in his arms, I realized that Sampson Cooper was a great many things, nearly all of them good, but one of them was wise.

On this thought, two arms closed around me from behind and I was pulled into a long, hard body as a stubbled chin swept my hair from the side of my neck right before lips whispered there, "Mornin', baby."

Those two words slid over my skin, coating it, again giving me a glorious moment of feeling invincible.

Wherever you are, however you got there, if it's good, you're meant to be there either because you earned it or life led you there and you were smart enough to hold on.

I closed my eyes.

Then I whispered back, "Morning."

Sam turned me to face him. I opened my eyes, then his body pressed mine into the balustrade as I tipped my head back to look at him and see his eyes were already moving over me.

They came to mine and he whispered, "Right now, honey, I'm gonna kiss you."

My stomach clutched.

Oh God.

Okay. Oh God. All right.

I was supposed to be fearless, but right then, I…was…*not.*

"Sam—" I started, but his head dropped until his lips were light on mine and I shut up.

"No," he said quietly, his lips moving against mine. My heart stopped beating and his voice dropped super low, super rough, it was rich velvet when he went on, "No, baby, you fell asleep before I could taste this mouth. I'm not gonna miss another chance."

That said, he slanted his head and kissed me.

I instantly freaked out.

This was not because Sampson Cooper, my fantasy man obsession, was kissing me. Sam had become way more than just that. He wasn't even close to that anymore.

This was because, except for a couple of guys in high school and some other guys who didn't count during spin the bottle at parties in junior high, I had kissed no one but Cooter. I grew not to like the way he kissed, then I grew not to want him to kiss me and I learned quickly that if I didn't kiss him back in a way he'd like, he'd give up trying.

So I didn't know if I even knew *how* to kiss. I'd forgotten or never really learned.

And I *needed* at that moment in my life not only to be able to do it, but to be able to do it really, really well.

And needing it and freaking out about it, my head filled with garbage and I blew it.

I knew it by feeling it and I knew it when Sam's mouth broke from mine, his head coming up. I opened my eyes and saw his, for the first time since I met him, were guarded.

Oh *God*!

Sam had just kissed me, it was awful, and it was all my fault.

God!

I was mortified. Total humiliation. So bad, I couldn't bear it.

So I didn't.

I had to escape.

So I did.

I ducked my head, jerked sideways out of his arms and skirted him, heading toward the bedroom, all the while mumbling, "I need to find Luci and ask if I can use—"

I didn't get to the bedroom and I didn't finish mumbling.

I found my hand caught in Sam's firm grip and my arm tugged. Hard enough to change the direction I was going, not hard enough to hurt. I flew backward, and as my body moved, Sam twisted my arm so my body twisted with it and my arm was held behind me. My front slammed into his as his other hand came up, his fingers sifting into my hair, then fisting gently to tilt it to the side at the same time he pulled it back.

This shocked me, but not in bad way. Oh no, not bad at all.

It was *hot.*

Then his mouth slammed down on mine.

Oh man.

That was hot, too.

Then his tongue thrust into my mouth.

Oh *man.*

That wasn't hot.

That was scorching.

And it burned through me from mouth to toes and even up into my hair, blistering. My belly plummeted, my breasts swelled, my body melted into his, my arm wrapped around his shoulders to hold on, and my tongue tangled with his because I liked what he was giving me, but I wanted *more.*

When I did this, he growled into my mouth, his fist in my hair twisting, his fingers laced in mine doing the same. Both I felt, not with pain but with a fierce kind of possession I liked. Oh God, yes, I liked it a lot. So much, I felt wet and heat flood between my legs. My hand glided up his neck to cup the back of his head and hold him to me and I pressed deep, returning the gift by moaning into his mouth.

When I did, he pressed forward, arching me backward over our arms, deepening an already deep kiss, demanding more, and my moan turned to a whimper. Not of fear, pain, or weakness but of open, unadulterated *need.*

Sam tore his mouth from mine, my eyes flew open, and my lips immediately protested on a breathy plea of "Sam."

But not a second later, his fist in my hair was an arm behind my knees and his other hand released mine but held on tight at my back. I was swept up in his arms and he made it to the bed in two strides of his long legs. Then I was down on the bed, the warmth and weight of Sam's body on mine. His mouth was back to mine and this was better—way, *way* better—because it came with his hands on me, all over me, and it came with the opportunity of my hands being all over him.

He felt good. God, so good. I was right. He was hard everywhere.

And I liked it.

He pressed his hips into mine, tight, deep. I felt them. I liked what I felt and more heat rushed through me.

God, yes, *yes.* I was right. He was hard *everywhere.*

I forced a leg out from under him and wrapped it around the back of his thigh, reciprocating the gesture, lifting my hips to fit them to his. His lips left mine to trail down my cheek to my ear where he whispered, "Fuck, baby."

I liked that too.

A lot.

So much, I arched my back, turned my head and ran my tongue up his neck to his ear.

God, he tasted as beautiful as he just was.

"Fuck," he whispered, then his teeth nipped my ear and I trembled instantly, top to toe.

Then, no joke—no *freaking* joke—I heard the creak of a door swinging open and a sultry voice crying, "*Buongiorno!*"

Sam's head shot up and his neck twisted.

Seeing as my head was to the bed, just my neck twisted.

And there was Luci, wearing a fabulous outfit, looking stunning, holding a stack of fluffy folded towels and grinning at us unrepentantly.

This went on awhile—Sam and I tangled in a carnal clench on the bed staring at Luci; Luci standing a step inside the doorway, gazing at us with a huge grin and not moving.

Finally, Sam asked on a growl that was clearly frustrated, clearly impatient, and clearly angry, so it was also clearly very scary, "Are you serious?"

"You're in luck," she announced. "I have exactly two unused toothbrushes."

I blinked.

Sam growled again, but this one was unintelligible.

"Sam, *caro*," Luci said, striding in (yes, striding in!), "Kia can see the lake from that bed, but she'll see more of it from the boat."

Was she serious?

And was this happening?

And, if it was, *why*?

I didn't ask these questions. Instead, I stayed silent as Sam rolled off and sat up, pulling me with him so I was sitting up too, but close, and he settled us with my back to his chest and one of his arms wrapped around my belly.

He did this saying, "Woman, you know I'm trained to kill."

She smiled at him, then ignored him and looked to me.

"And Kia, *cara*." She dropped the towels on the foot of the bed plus two toothbrushes in their plastic wrappers and a tube of toothpaste bounced off the top of the pile and onto the bed. "It's morning and you have something to look up on my computer."

I stared up at her having experienced all of this still snug in the warmth of heated, brilliant foreplay, the like I'd not only never experienced at the hands of a (now I knew) seriously not very talented Cooter, but also the like I didn't even know *existed*, and the mistaken belief that, in short order, I would return to that.

Suddenly, that dispersed, what was happening intruded, and what could I say?

It was admittedly a little weird and it was definitely crazy.

But it was also hilarious.

So I burst out laughing.

Luci's sexy chuckle joined my laughter, and honest to God, it actually sounded like it was accented with Italian, which was way cool.

Sam dragged my laughing body across his lap and both his arms clamped around me as he declared, "Just to be clear, I'm not finding anything funny right now."

This made me sober, but I did this unfortunately with my eyes on Luci. Meaning I caught the sultry, sexy, smack-you-back beautiful Luci as she *snorted.*

That's right! I saw and heard a famous model *snort*!

I burst into giggles this time and Luci was right with me.

"Fuck me," Sam muttered.

I giggled harder.

So did Luci.

Sam allowed this.

For approximately two-point-five seconds.

Then he clipped, "You came, you interrupted, you annoyed. Now, you wanna get out?"

I swallowed my laughter, slapped a hand on his chest and cried, "Sam!"

Sam didn't even look at me. He kept scowling at Luci.

"*Certamente*," she muttered.

"Well?" Sam instantly countered when she didn't immediately vanish in a puff of smoke.

I pressed my lips together.

Luci planted her hands on her hips. "Breakfast is in half an hour, Sam. You need to get back to your hotel and sort yourself out. I'll sort Kia out. Then you can enjoy your day together."

"We were enjoying it before you walked in," Sam shot back.

I smacked his chest again but this time snapped, "Sam!"

He looked at me. "What?"

"What?" I returned.

"Baby, *she walked in on us*. She's got eyes. She didn't miss it."

I looked at Luci and griped by using universal female griping language, "Ohmigod!"

Luci smiled at me.

"You still haven't left," Sam prompted Luci.

"All right, all right," she mumbled, flicking her hand, turning and gliding like the catwalk model she used to be to the door. "See you at breakfast."

"Close the door," Sam ordered.

She closed the door.

I turned my head to look at him in order to say something to him about being rude, but I didn't finish turning my head and got nowhere near saying anything because I found myself on my back, Sam's solid, heavy torso pressed to mine and his face an inch away.

"Sam," I breathed, suddenly not feeling snippy but remembering our kiss. Not the first one that was crap; the second one that was *everything.*

"Today, I'll show you Lake Como, even though I don't know fuck all about Lake Como. I do know how to drive a boat. Tonight, no parties, no friends, no nothing. You, me, dinner. Later tonight, just you and me. You with me?"

"I'm with you," I whispered, and I was with him. *So* with him.

His face got even closer and his voice got that sweeter, deeper, rough-like-velvet I liked so much when he said gently, "Baby, when I say just you and me, I need you to get I mean *just you and me.* Now, do you get me?"

"I get you." This time it was a whisper that sounded a lot like a wheeze because I got him. I *so* got that I was going to *get* him.

His eyes held mine. I watched with a deep fascination that affected me systematically when they heated and he whispered, "You taste even better than you look and you're unbelievably fuckin' beautiful. Christ," his head dipped so close, I felt his breath on my lips as his blazing eyes burned into mine, "I can't fuckin' wait to taste the rest of you."

Oh man.

Oh God.

Oh *man.*

I couldn't either.

While I concentrated on breathing and not doing anything stupid like pushing him off, running to the door, locking it, ripping my expensive dress off and then launching myself across the room at him, he twisted us again so he was seated and I was in his lap.

His hand gliding up my neck into my hair, he turned my head to look at him and he ordered, "Give me your room key and tell me what you need. I'll pick it up."

This threw me and it mostly threw me because what I needed included panties. I might have just gone at it hot and heavy with Sam, not to mention slept in his arms, not to mention spent hours yammering on telling him my deepest secrets and my not-so-deepest secrets, but I wasn't ready for him to see my panties.

Still, I needed them. And if I was correct, to save myself from the nightmare that would end in me vowing never to eat again that I knew would be me if I tried on any of Luciana's clothes, I needed an entire outfit.

"Kia, baby," Sam called into my frenzied thoughts, and I focused on him.

Then I mumbled, "Um..."

To which he grinned. His hand left my hair so both arms could give me a squeeze and he proved yet again that he could totally figure me out.

I knew this when he whispered, "In case you didn't get me when you told me you got me, honey, 'just you and me' means I'm gonna be in your pants tonight before I take them off. So right now, get over what's polluting your head and tell me what you need so I can get to the hotel, get it, get back and get your fine ass on a boat and far away from a now up-in-*both*-our-business Luci."

I stared at him and forced myself to think about this. I made some decisions. Then I told him.

When I was done telling him, he stared at me.

Then he burst out laughing.

I was perplexed as I watched him, and when he stopped, I asked, "What?"

"You need all that to go on a boat?"

I tipped my head to the side not thinking "all that" was all that.

"Well, yes."

He grinned. Then he stood at the same time he slid me off his lap and put me on my feet, but he didn't take his arms from around me, and looking down at me, he muttered, "I'm gonna brush my teeth. You're gonna find Luci to get a paper and pen and write me a list."

"Sam, it isn't that much."

"Baby, I need underwear, jeans, a shirt, shoes, and deodorant. I've got a good memory but lost track when your list became five times that." His arms gave me a squeeze. "Find Luci. Paper. Pen. List."

"I'm not high maintenance," I informed him quickly. "All women would need at least that."

"Not true. You *are* high maintenance, and before you twist that to pollute your head, I don't care about that either. I like it. I get to best the challenge, then enjoy the benefits. But right now, to move us on, what I need is a *list*. Yeah?"

I studied his face, thinking that it appeared Sam Cooper could get grumpy.

So I felt my best course of action was to agree with a "Yeah."

He grinned before he dipped his head and touched his mouth to mine.

Seriously sweet.

He lifted his head, turned me out of his arms and gently pushed me toward the door.

I accepted the prompt and kept moving, but I looked back to see him bent at the waist, his long arm stretched to the toothbrushes, one of his hands in the bed.

God, I was a freak because I thought he looked hot even reaching for a toothbrush.

Then I thought it prudent to look where I was going so I didn't run into the door.

I was leaving the room but eventually coming back to him.

I was coming back to him.

On that thought, I left the room.

And I did it smiling.

6

GOD GRANTED YOU MORE TALENTS

I was sitting at Luci's kickass wrought iron table outside on her terrace, my heels to the seat, my knees to my chest, sipping a cup of coffee while wearing her bright orange silk robe with huge even brighter scarlet-red flowers on it that she let me borrow when she brought me a bunch of stuff so I could shower.

Upon seeing it, I told her it was totally awesome and she told me she bought it not far away and promised we'd go there before I left so we could pick one up for me.

"They have one exactly the same, but this enchanting purple with a splash of vibrant pink flowers, *cara mia*, that would be *perfect* for you."

I agreed instantly, wondering what Luci would consider was an "enchanting purple" that was "*perfect* for me," completely forgetting my vow to quit blowing my admittedly large but shrinking-by-the-day cash stash on stupid stuff and telling myself everyone needed a good robe.

Still, I knew by the feel of it that robe was expensive so I didn't figure everyone needed *that* good of a robe.

But…whatever.

One more splurge.

Nothing wrong with that.

Right?

My hair was wet and combed back. I'd consumed a bowl of fruit and two pieces of toast that was more delicious than any toast I'd ever had except in Paris. My experience was that Europeans didn't mess around with bread, no doubt about it. I didn't know what it was, but their bread *rocked.* What made it better was that the toast was spread with Nutella, which meant I went from really liking Luci to seriously liking her, considering her breakfast included Nutella.

She'd gone to turn on her laptop so I could pull up my webmail and I'd moved to studying a view I knew I'd never find anything less than amazing.

I was thinking that it was weird and cool she had a party last night that included loads of people, food, drink, red-coated valets, and white-coated waiters, but today, her house (or what I'd seen of it on my way to the table) was completely tidy and sparkling clean. Not a glass half full of champagne or a stray cocktail napkin in sight. It was like magic.

I was also thinking that last night, I'd laid it out for Sam, and right then, he was picking up my stuff so we could spend the day then the evening and finally the night together.

Which meant I wasn't just studying the view.

I was studying the view, smiling.

Yes, again.

I heard Luci speaking in Italian and I twisted my head in surprise to see her approaching, a cell to her ear. And I was surprised because she'd walked away not a minute ago.

And she didn't have her laptop with her.

She stopped by my side, said something, then said, "*Ciao.*" She took the phone from her ear and extended it to me. I noticed she had the same phone as me right before she said, "I heard it ringing as I was walking by, *cara.* Your bag is in the other room. I answered it. It's a lady called Celeste."

Suddenly, my cell phone morphed into the head of a ferocious, snapping wolf with rabies, though I didn't know if wolves could get rabies, but my phone wolf had them.

Definitely.

"Kia?" Luci prompted on a shake of my phone.

Oh man. Here we go. Celeste was probably curious about how my date went.

Now it was nine thirty in the morning after I slept in my fabulous gown *and* my fabulous shoes *with* a man I had practically just met. Something Celeste was way too cool, chic, and sophisticated to ever, *ever* do.

I reached out, took the phone, whispered, "Thanks, Luci," then hesitantly put it to my ear and said softly, "Hey, Celeste."

"Well?" was her reply.

I blinked at my knees.

"Sorry?" I asked.

"Well? The woman I just spoke to told me she was Luciana Gordon. The Luciana, I assume, whose party you told me you were going to last night."

Oh *man.*

"Celeste, um...well..." God! "Honey, last night, I had a bit too much to drink."

"Excellent."

I blinked again.

Then I repeated, "Sorry?"

"*Ma chérie*, you were tense. Champagne is excellent at relieving stress. This is good."

"Okay, well..." Shit! "Maybe I should have said I had *way* too much to drink."

Silence, then, "And how is that, Kia?"

I sucked in breath.

I didn't want to tell her this and I *really* didn't want to tell her this with a Luci who had not gone back to get her computer but instead settled herself in the chair by me at the table and was currently pouring herself a cup of coffee and therefore also was going to stay awhile. I couldn't get up and wander away because I figured that would be rude. Maybe not as rude as Luci's obvious eavesdropping, but still rude.

So I had no choice.

And that was why I glued my gaze to my knees and whispered, "I…something happened, and I couldn't help it. See, um…"

I paused, took a breath, and rushed the rest out.

"I didn't tell you this, but I'm a widow and my husband was abusive, and last night, like, ten minutes after we got here, something happened. Sam wanted my attention so he got it and he was kind of physical doing it and I, well…I freaked out, exposed my secrets, because I kind of couldn't, um…*not* react. And he, well, then *he* freaked out in his, uh…Sam way because he freaked *me* out. He was really upset and he promised me he'd never hurt me and shared about his life and when I told him I couldn't trust him not to hurt me, that was when he promised me he'd make me believe he'd never hurt me. Then he spent the rest of the night being really nice and he was all, well…"

I tried to find a word.

I couldn't find a word so I emphasized, "*Sam,* being a gentleman and making sure I wasn't left out of conversations and stuff like that. So, I, well, I kind of haven't told you this, but I'm wealthy. But I'm, you know, *new* to being wealthy. I was just a normal person before and will eventually not be on vacation. I'll go home and be normal again and I got kind of drunk and felt Sam needed to know I was not, you know, like him. So I told him I wasn't and he told me he didn't care, but it was more than him not caring. He told me he was like me and told me I was not the fraud I was trying to convince him I was, I was just me. Then we spent the night talking about family and friends while lying in bed. I fell asleep in his arms and today he's taking me out on a boat and showing me Lake Como."

I finally shut up and sucked in breath, continued to ignore the completely unmoving Luci and I waited.

Celeste didn't speak.

Shit.

"Celeste?" I called softly.

Nothing.

I kept trying. "Are you disappointed in me that I…well, didn't take your advice? Especially when you were so kind, and that I, you know, kept from you I'm normal?"

That was when she spoke.

And this was what she said.

"*Ma chérie*, you are many things and one of them is not normal."

I blinked at my knees again, not sure if this was good or bad.

She kept talking.

And she was doing it quietly.

"Thomas and I, we had a daughter."

She said "had."

Oh God.

Oh no.

Oh *shit.*

"Celeste," I whispered.

"We lost her when she was twelve. She had leukemia. That was four years ago."

Oh *God.*

Oh *no.*

Oh shit!

"Honey." I was still whispering.

"She was blonde with green eyes."

I closed my eyes, which were green, but still felt them fill with tears.

"Her name was Clémence."

OhGodohnoohshit!

Celeste kept speaking quietly.

"I know you are not her. I know this. But that does not mean the last three days I have not enjoyed thinking that if Clémence was still with us, grown up, grown beautiful, and off on some adventure and she found herself where your mother lives, your mother would see her and think that she reminded her of you. She would take to her and share with her like I have with you, giving her something more than she would have found on her own. A gift. A treasure. What I hope I've given you."

The wet spilled out of my eyes.

"You have," I whispered brokenly because my voice was clogged with tears.

"And when you needed me yesterday, *ma chérie*, I must confess, not having my Clémence to share those kinds of moments with, I was more pleased you turned to me than you could ever be grateful I assisted you."

Ohmigod! That was so nice, so beautiful, and so *freaking* sad.

And it was so all of that that I felt my body jolt as my breath hitched with my sob. I also felt Luci's arm wrap around my shoulders and her cheek press into my hair.

"And lastly," Celeste whispered, "I am not disappointed in you. I know of this man, *ma chérie*, most everyone does. Thomas admires him and I must admit I do too. I suspected your secrets were dark, though I am sad to know what they are. But I am not disappointed in the least you are bright enough to see that all men are not like your husband and you are strong enough to take a risk that must certainly frighten you by trying again."

My body jolted again as another sob tore up my throat. Luci held on tighter, and at that moment, I heard a barked, angry, "What the fuck is goin' on?"

I swallowed, Luci moved away and I twisted in my chair to see Sam stalking my way.

Yes, *stalking*.

Oh God.

Oh no.

Oh shit.

His eyes were on my wet face, then they sliced to Luci and he demanded to know, "Who's Kia talkin' to?"

"A woman named Celeste," Luci whispered, and Sam's eyes cut back to me.

"Is she upsetting you?"

"I—" I started.

He'd arrived and he bent, one hand to the arm of my chair, one hand wrapped around the back of my neck, and he got in my face to ask, "Yes or no, baby. Is she upsetting you?"

"Well, obviously yes, Sam," I answered. His face got dark, he made a move that my guess (what I didn't know was accurate) was to pull my phone from my ear, so I hurried on, "But not how you're thinking." I dashed my hand over my cheeks and finished, "We're having a heart-to-heart, a good one. I mean…uh, a bad one but a good one."

Sam's brows were knitted and his eyes were intense. He was clearly not liking me swiping at my wet cheeks and I knew this because his gaze followed those movements and that was when his brows shot together.

But now he was studying me.

I let him do it for a moment before I whispered, "Honey, she's still on the line."

He studied me again. Then his hand slid from my neck to my cheek, taking my hair with it, his thumb extending to glide through the wet still on my skin. The pads of his fingers dug in briefly before he let me go and pushed away.

I let out my breath.

Sam said to Luci, "Girl, I need coffee."

I said to Celeste, "I'm back and I'm really, really sorry."

And Celeste said to me on an excited cry that was so far from her polished sophistication, my body jumped in surprise, "I approve, *ma chérie*! Oh, *I approve*!"

"Uh…sorry?" I asked.

"He has a lovely voice, like velvet," she observed.

I blinked again at my knees. I looked at Sam, who was now sitting, eyes on me.

Then I burst out laughing.

Still laughing, I agreed, "Yeah. Totally."

"He's taking you out on the lake today?"

"Yes."

"Lovely. The views from the lake are spectacular. Now, I know you're busy, but perhaps before you leave, we can meet him, if only for a drink. Thomas would so enjoy that and I would too."

My eyes slid to the lake. "I'll, uh, talk to Sam and we'll see."

"*Bien*," she whispered.

"But regardless, before I go, we'll see each other again."

"Oh yes, *ma chérie*. We will definitely do that."

"And I need to pay you back for yesterday."

I heard her cultured but still rich and beautiful laughter, then she said, "Oh no, *ma chérie*. You must give me that."

"But, uh, it was *you* giving to *me*," I pointed out.

"Yes, and the result was I walked out of your hotel room after seeing a vision of beauty. It was a gift to have a hand in that, even if it was simply nail varnish and a sweep of cosmetics. And you walked out of your hotel room to spend the night with a gentleman who earned your secrets in ten minutes. And it was a gift to have a hand in that too."

Seriously, did I already say I loved Celeste?

I *totally* did.

"Okay, then *my* gift is, whether it's with Sam or not, when I see you and Thomas again, I pay for dinner."

"Oh my, Kia, I don't speak of such things. You'll need to discuss that with Thomas."

Which meant I so totally was not buying dinner.

Great.

Okay, well, whatever.

"I'll call you tomorrow and we'll set something up."

"*Très bien*," she murmured.

"All right, honey. I have to go finish getting ready."

"Have a wonderful time, Kia."

"I will, Celeste. We'll speak soon."

"Of course. *Adieu, ma belle*."

Adieu, ma belle.

Freaking cool.

"'Bye, Celeste."

She rang off. I slipped my phone on the table and looked to Sam just as Luci walked out with another pot of coffee.

"You okay?" Sam asked.

Luci poured.

I answered.

"That's my Lake Como bud, Celeste. She just told me she had a daughter with blonde hair and green eyes named Clémence who died when she was twelve of leukemia. Since we met, she's been super awesome. This is because she's super awesome, but also because, I just learned, I remind her of her daughter. I kind of lost it when she told me that so, uh..." My eyes slid from a solid and staring at me Sam to a frozen and staring at me Luci. "Sorry for the drama."

"Jesus, baby," Sam whispered.

I bit my lip.

"That's very sad," Luci whispered.

I nodded.

Sam kept staring at me.

"I'm okay now," I assured him.

He kept staring at me.

"Sam, I'm okay," I whispered.

His eyes moved from me to Luci, then back to me before they slid to the lake. He appeared to be thinking, but he also appeared not to wish to share what he was thinking. I knew this not because I'd absorbed knowledge of all things Sam by sleeping in his arms, but because he didn't share what he was thinking.

I left it at that and took a sip of my coffee in preparation for going back upstairs and finishing getting ready.

I only got the sip in before Luci put Sam's coffee cup in front of him and announced, "I'll go get my laptop so you can check your e-mail."

Off she went, gliding gracefully through the doors to the kitchen before I could make a peep.

When my eyes moved from where Luciana disappeared, they went through Sam on the way back. A Sam who was putting his coffee cup down and turning to me.

And when he did, he said quietly, "Celeste, your Lake Como bud, can I take from that you met her here?"

I nodded.

"And she just shared about her kid?"

I nodded again.

"Just like that?"

I thought about it. Then I said, "Well, kind of. I mean, we got close very quickly so it hasn't been long, but I don't know. I feel a connection with her, a connection she's now explained so it isn't weird. I mean, we've shared. Nothing that personal, but my guess is, it would get that personal eventually. It was just sooner rather than later."

"Luci likes you," he informed me, and I smiled.

"I can tell."

"No, baby, Luci *likes you*."

That was when I blinked because he was telling me something. I just didn't know what.

Sam carried on.

"I told you she was up in my business. What I didn't tell you was, not only is she all over my ass to hook up and get down to the business of makin' babies, she's all over my ass because she pretty much hates every woman I've been with that she's met. She isn't here often. That party last night is something she does when she comes home so she can see all her friends. She's still got the house she lived in with Gordo, a house that's close to mine, and she spends most of her time there. So when I say she's in my business, I might not have mentioned she's got opportunity."

That didn't sound good.

"Why didn't she like your other, uh…women?" I asked.

"I didn't say she didn't like them, honey. I said she hated them, as in hated their fuckin' guts."

"Okay," I said slowly, drawing it out. "So, why?"

"How would I know? Obviously, I liked 'em."

Well. Obviously.

"Until I stopped liking them," he finished.

Well, obviously about that too.

I made no reply.

"But, gotta admit," he muttered distractedly, his eyes sliding to the lake, his hand going to his coffee cup, "none of them were like you."

I was curious to know what that meant, even though I was kind of freaking out about this conversation. But I didn't get the opportunity to figure out how to shape my question so as not to sound overly nosy, fishing for compliments, or gossiping cattily because that was when Luci returned.

"Here we are!" she called, gliding forward carrying an open laptop, which she rounded Sam with. She shoved my dirty dishes aside with one hand and plonked it on the table in front of me. "All ready. I have Wi-Fi or whatever. Sam set it up for me the other day so you're good out here."

Sam could set up Wi-Fi. This meant he was trained to kill, trained to read people and was good with computers.

Interesting, useful(ish), and scary.

I leaned forward but didn't take my heels from my seat as I slid my finger on the mouse pad, clicked, and plucked out the web address one-handed and called up my webmail, then Paula's e-mail, which had the subject line: Woot! Woot! Perfect!

I clicked the link and stopped breathing.

It was.

Perfect.

It was one of The Dorchester's three-story, two-bedroom units. This meant it had a dining room rather than dining area. This also meant it had a study or family room area that was kind of a balcony that opened up over the first floor. This meant it wasn't awesome, it was *awesome.*

Therefore, looking at it, I whispered, "*Awesome.*"

"Let's see!" Luci cried.

Suddenly the laptop was twisted away from me and toward her and Sam, and instantly, I felt panic.

This was because The Dorchester was cool and that particular unit was *awesome.*

What it was not was a swanky, exclusive hotel. It was also not what an ex-pro-football player who had numerous endorsement contracts could afford. Nor was it an Italian villa with an extended garage that housed five trashy but mind-bogglingly expensive automobiles.

Shit.

"Uh…I, uh…" I stammered then blurted, "It's in Indiana."

Sam's eyes went from the laptop to me, and Luci, who was standing beside him and bent to look, twisted to me.

Neither of them spoke.

They thought it was rinky-dink.

I looked to Luci.

"Uh, we don't have villas in Indiana, er, I don't think, or at least, I've never seen one."

Luci's face softened and her lips smiled before she said quietly, "It's lovely, *cara.*"

"Uh…thanks," I muttered, then slid my heels off the chair and stood, saying quickly, "I'll e-mail Paula after I get ready." My eyes moved to Sam. "Is my stuff upstairs?"

He shook his head, put his coffee cup down and his hands to the arms of his chair as he muttered, "I'll get it."

He didn't push up.

This was because Luci announced, "Kia thinks she's normal."

My breath clogged and I was pretty sure my eyes bugged out.

Sam's gaze cut to her.

"Come again?"

"She told her French friend she was normal," Luci explained. "Not like us."

Sam's gaze cut back to me.

I wondered if there was additional sentencing if you were tried and convicted for clobbering ex-supermodels.

"Kia, *cara mia*," Luci said to me, and I tore my eyes from a perplexed Sam to aim them at her. "The pictures of your future home are lovely. It's much like Travis's and my home in North Carolina."

Oh yeah. I forgot Sam lived in North Carolina. He'd stayed where he'd last been stationed.

Wow. That was a long way away from me.

"Except smaller," Luci finished.

"Uh..." I mumbled.

"Girl, give us a minute," Sam said to Luci, and Luci turned to him.

"How many minutes with Kia are you going to need, Sam?" she asked tartly, clearly wishing to be in on finishing the intervention she'd instigated after outing further pieces of my dramatic conversation with Celeste she'd eavesdropped on.

His eyes cut to her and they stayed locked on her as he stood, his head tipping down to hold her gaze as he straightened and hers tipping back to hold his.

Then he rumbled, "A lot."

"Right," she whispered, turned to me, bugged out her eyes, then she glided away.

I watched her go before I looked to Sam.

"You're not like us?" he asked.

"That was taken out of context," I explained. "Luci only heard my side of the conversation."

"So, baby, tell me, how did she take it out of context?"

"Well—" I started but didn't finish.

This was because Sam cut me off to ask, "I thought we got past this last night."

"Actually, I was telling Celeste about last night. That was how it was out of context."

"Okay, then why did you look like you were holding back the urge to grab Luci's laptop and throw it over the balcony when she turned it so we could see pictures of the place you're thinkin' of buying?"

Okay, now, *seriously*.

Did the man miss *nothing*?

I glared.

Sam waited.

I kept glaring.

"Baby," he growled.

I threw up my hands and cried, "What do you want me to say, Sam? Look at her."

I threw an arm out in the direction where Luci disappeared, then swung it out again and went on.

"And this place. And *her cars*." I flicked a hand out to him. "And you. You're hot, you're famous, you're rich, and if that wasn't enough, you kiss really *freaking* well. I mean, God granted you more talents than just playing football and being an excellent commando, Sam, trust me. Clearly, He does not have an even hand. And I'm, well..." I threw up my hands again and said kind of loudly, "*Me*. So, okay, I got a little weirded out by you guys looking at my possible new pad because it isn't Malibu or Lake Como or whatever. Put yourself in my shoes. How would *you* feel if you were me?"

I barely finished with the word "me" before I found myself not standing three feet from Sam but instead plastered against his body, one of his arms tight around me, the other hand in my hair, cupping the back of my head, and his face an inch from mine.

I had not recovered from this maneuver, like, *at all*, before Sam asked, using his sexy, rough-like-velvet voice, "God granted me more talents than playin' football and bein' an excellent commando?"

Oh man. I totally needed to learn when to *shut up*.

"Sam—" I whispered and he grinned, and he did that in a sexy way too so I (way too late) shut up, my mind taking that opportunity to remind me what his mouth tasted like, and his skin, and I shivered.

His grin got bigger *and* sexier.

Then his eyes heated, his eyelids lowered a sexy centimeter, and he muttered, "Fuck."

"What?" I pushed out on a breath.

"You wearin' anything under this?"

Uh-oh.

"Uh..." I mumbled but that, too, was breathy.

Sam was clearly feeling impatient with the flow of information so his hand went on a voyage of discovery and trailed light as a whisper over my behind.

Even light, that felt so good I sucked in breath, shivered again and my knees got weak.

"Fuck," he repeated on a mutter when his voyage of discovery gave him confirmation on the intel he'd assumed. And now his voice was heated, which meant I heated, like, *all over.*

Oh man.

"How bad you wanna take this boat trip, honey?" he asked, his voice now low as well as sexy and rough.

"What boat trip?" I asked back, my voice still breathy.

Sam grinned again.

I blinked. Then it came back to me.

"Uh, Sam, I'm only here three more days and I've got to fit Celeste and Thomas in there and Luci is going to take me to buy a robe like this and, uh..." *You!* "Anyway, I might never get back here so I should pack everything in that I can. In other words, I kind of want to take this boat trip, like, *bad.*"

Something changed in his eyes, flickering then fading away, taking the heat with them but not the warmth before he whispered, "Right." Then his hand still resting light on my ass glided back up, his arm wrapped tight around my waist and he continued, "Then go get dressed. The sooner I give you your boat trip, the sooner I can bring you back, feed you and then have you all for me."

Oh *man.*

I was rethinking how bad I wanted the boat trip.

But I whispered, "Okay."

He gave me a squeeze as his head dropped and he also gave me a mouth touch.

Then he let me go.

I concentrated on walking away without him cottoning on my legs were still trembling and not holding out much hope at succeeding.

But when I turned to go into one of the many double doors that opened onto the terrace, I looked back at Sam and stopped, most of my body inside the house, but my head leaned back and turned his way.

He was standing, but he'd shoved back the screen of the laptop, his chin was dipped and he was studying it. His hand came up, grabbed the top and shut it with a firm snap. His eyes went to the lake, and his profile, I noted, looked preoccupied.

With what, I didn't know.

How important it was, I also didn't know him enough to know for sure.

But it looked pretty important.

I didn't know what to make of that, since before he got that look, he was looking at my possible future home.

And that freaked me out.

But if I was ever going to get my boat trip, I couldn't waste time on freaking out.

I had to get ready.

So I left Sam to his thoughts and did just that.

The problem was, once I got upstairs, I had to come right back down because my stuff wasn't there, so I had to ask Sam where it was.

And Sam being Sam meant he didn't tell me.

No, he got up from his chair, went to the overnight case of mine he'd commandeered to bring my stuff to me, and carried it up for me himself.

After he left, when I tested it by lifting it, it weighed approximately five pounds. Still, he didn't let me carry it up a single flight of steps.

Okay, yes, damn.

Seriously, I liked Sam Cooper.

I knew Sampson Cooper was awesome.

But Sam Cooper was turning out to be a whole lot better.

7

THAT'S ALL YOU'LL GET FROM ME

I was sitting back, sipping my wine and thinking I'd never had a better day, not in my life.

Not in my life.

No Christmas. No birthday. No vacation with my family. And certainly not any times I'd spent with Cooter.

This was saying something. Cooter was an asshole and tore me down, but my family was awesome and even when I was married to him, holidays and birthdays were great. But before Cooter, they were the best.

But no day came close to that day with Sam.

None.

My eyes slid to the side and there he was. Right there.

He was wearing faded jeans that fit him better than any jeans I'd ever seen on any man. He also had on a lightweight, white, button-up-the-front, long-sleeved shirt that was made of soft linen. He had the sleeves rolled up nearly to his elbows. It was kind of wrinkly, but Sam could make even wrinkly hot and I knew this because the evidence was sitting right beside me. Further, that shirt looked amazing against his perfect, brown skin. He wore all this like his tuxedo, with a casual, masculine grace that was immensely appealing and even more immensely cool.

What had I been missing all these years not paying attention to his clothes?

It didn't bear thinking about.

For my part, I decided to introduce Sam to the real me, albeit the new, improved real me since everything I was wearing I bought in Paris. I had on a pair of black, cuffed, tailored shorts, which were *short*. As in serious leg. As in Sam didn't tear his eyes away from them for a whole minute when I walked downstairs at Luci's ready to take my boat tour, which I felt indicated I'd made another excellent fashion decision. This I wore with a slim, metallic gray, snakeskin belt and my charcoal-gray suede, T-strap, flat sandals. I'd also paired it with a tight-fitting, ribbed, heathered, dark gray tank that had a panel of kickass lace at the top back.

This last, as with my legs, I caught Sam staring at too, numerous times that day.

Numerous.

I was thinking he liked me in shorts and tanks just as much as pretty sundresses, gowns, and high heels.

This was a relief.

This was also awesome.

We'd just eaten dinner at a restaurant Luci had suggested and it was a good suggestion. The location was in the hub of it all and the food and wine were fabulous. We were seated outside, and when we got there, it was early for dinner in Italy and it wasn't very populated except by American tourists. But now that we were done, it was filling up and the sidewalks and streets were getting busier.

The atmosphere seemed alive. You could hear the hum of conversation, smell the garlic from the kitchen, the cars and scooters going by. Being out in it, I felt great, jazzed, as alive as our surrounding.

And the best part of this was being with Sam.

And the best part of that best part was partially that, even before we ordered, Sam had moved his chair right next to mine so we were close, but he found ways to make us closer. He did this by resting his arm across my thighs, his fingers curled in or sometimes stroking my skin, his head twisted to look at me when he spoke or facing forward when he scanned his surroundings (which was weirdly often, like he was expecting something). Sometimes, even when he was eating, and definitely when he was sipping his wine, he kept his arm across my lap. But if his food took his arm away, he kept his thigh tight to mine, not losing some form of connection.

I liked this. I liked the closeness, intimacy, his touch, his warmth, and all of what this said about how he felt about me.

I also liked that it was proprietary.

To me, it said I was touch-worthy. He liked the feel of me. He wanted closeness. He was being clear he found me attractive.

But to those outside our little bubble of intimacy, it was claiming. Don't look. Don't even think about it. I was taken. I was his.

Some women might find this overbearing.

I thought it was beautiful.

And I was glad we didn't miss our boat tour and even Sam agreed. Being out on the lake in the sun, the wind in my hair, the views breathtaking, eating Luci's delicious packed lunch on the cream leather-covered bench seat at the back of the glossy boat with Sam while we chatted more about family and friends, sharing ourselves, it was great. Beautiful. The perfect day.

I couldn't quite decide which views were better, from the water or from the shore. What I knew was, I was glad I had both. And better, sharing it with Sam, who, after our night together, I had no issues talking with, being myself, exclaiming openly when I saw something cool, pointing it out, sharing it with him. It helped that he was no less courteous and attentive than he'd been before, helping me in and out of the boat, pulling me in his lap when he was seated behind the wheel to keep me close, folding his arms around me and stuffing his face in my neck when I made him laugh.

It was sublime.

Freaking *sublime.*

The whole day.

Every second.

"*Il conto, per favore,*" I heard Sam murmur, and my eyes went from a mint-green Vespa shooting by, wondering how much one of those cost and also wondering if I could get one in Indiana, to Sam, who was also leaning back, wineglass in his hand, his torso slanted slightly to the side toward me, arm over my legs, but his eyes were on the waiter, who was nodding at him, smiling, and moving away.

"I thought you didn't know any Italian," I remarked, and Sam turned his head to look at me.

"Asked for the bill, baby, didn't recite a poem."

This was true.

I grinned at him.

He grinned back.

Then his face got serious. He took a sip of wine and set his glass on the table.

Then he did something even more beautiful.

He moved his arm from my lap but twisted his torso to me and replaced it with his other arm, wrapping it around my crossed thighs and pulling them even closer, tighter to his, so I was forced to uncross my top leg and hook it around his knee. My bottom calf slid under my chair, my torso twisting toward his. Doing this, he successfully created a private cocoon, a bubble of intimacy seated at a crowded sidewalk eatery.

"Need to talk to you about something," he said softly, his eyes holding mine, and immediately, I leaned to the side even as I bent closer to him. I put my elbow on the table, my head in my hand, and my eyes stayed locked to his, giving him my undivided attention and making sure he knew he had it.

I rested my other hand on his hard thigh and whispered, "What, honey?"

He didn't speak for long moments as his eyes held mine, then moved over my face, my hair, down my torso to my elbow on the table, and back to my eyes before he did something else beautiful.

He lifted his hand and trailed his fingers down my hairline, starting at the temple, then back to tuck a heavy fall of hair behind my ear.

After he did that, he said something even *more* beautiful and he did it in his soft, sweet, rough-like-velvet voice.

"Christ, you're beautiful."

Oh God. Oh man.

I liked that and felt those words glide along my skin, coating it, and I knew I could live a week invincible at the feel of them.

"You would know, you see it in the mirror every day," I replied quietly, watched his eyes warm and also watched his mouth twitch as he shook his head.

He settled his hand at my waist and got to it.

"I know you don't have a lot of time left here, but you said you were goin' shoppin' with Luci."

I nodded.

"I need you to feel her out."

"About what?"

"You knew your girl Celeste for three days and she shared about her daughter. I need you to find out where Luci is at about Gordo."

"I know where she's at," I told him, and his brows drew together.

"She talked to you about it?"

"With words?" I shook my head slightly, then compounded it by saying, "No. With her eyes, definitely."

"Come again?"

I leaned closer to him and whispered, "She's lost, Sam. Lost and grieving. She's in pain. You think *I'm* full of shit? Everything you see of Luci is completely full of shit. She's trying to hide it so people won't approach her about it, but she's doing a really bad job. Obviously, I've known her a day so I can have no idea if it's improved. What I can tell you is, it's still bad. As in," I leaned closer to him, "*really* bad."

"Fuck," he whispered back, his face betraying his concern, the fingers on both hands giving me a squeeze.

"Um…sorry," we both heard, and we both turned our heads to see a man standing beside our table, looking nervous, his eyes darting between Sam and me, and finally coming to rest in a way that it looked like he wished they didn't on Sam. "I, uh…" he went on, "don't mean to disturb you, and I know you hear this all the time, but I'm a really big fan."

Holy cow!

A Sampson Cooper fan interrupting our dinner.

Wow.

I stared up at him, fascinated.

That was to say, I stared at him fascinated until I felt the fingers on both of Sam's hands give me another squeeze, this one deeper, communicating something I wasn't certain I got until my eyes went to him. I saw his jaw was hard and I tensed and stayed that way, even when I watched his jaw relax. And I stayed tense because it seemed this took effort, like he was forcing back his reaction.

I looked back to the man as he continued talking.

"I just, I see that you're busy and…well, I didn't want to come over, but my wife said this opportunity would never present itself again. And, you know, she said it was crazy since we live in Wisconsin, but we're here and you're here so it's like…fate. And I should, you know, not anger fate or, uh…whatever. "

He drew in a deep, embarrassed breath and kept going.

"So I just want to say that I was a real big fan of yours when you played ball, but I admire the decision you made so I also, uh…want to thank you for what you did for our country. You, I…well, my son knows all about you and you're kind of his idol. He's seventeen and he plays ball, but he's, you know, he's okay at it. Not great, but he's pretty good. Still, he's going into the Army like your brother did, like you did. He says that's what he really wants to do and we're real proud of him. But both of us, me and my wife, we think he made that decision because of you." He paused, then finished, "Um… that's it, uh…I guess."

I felt for him. He was really nervous and obviously wanted to be there just as obviously as he didn't.

I looked back at Sam to see his eyes weren't on the man but looking across our table to something else. I followed the direction of his gaze to see a heavyset woman with a peculiar hairstyle, her upper face behind a camera, which was aimed our way, her lower face taken up with a mammoth smile.

"That your wife?" Sam's voice asked, and I looked back at him then the man.

"Uh...yeah," the man answered.

"Right," Sam replied. "Let me pay my bill, finish talkin' to my woman and I'll come over. Kia can take a photo of you and your wife with me. Your boy'll probably like that shot better than whatever's gonna come out of the ones your wife is takin' with her finger over the lens."

The man's head snapped toward his wife, as did my gaze, and I stifled a giggle when I saw Sam was right. She was still shooting away, but her finger was totally right over the lens.

"Oh...I..." the man started, and I looked back at him. Then he finished, "You'd do that?"

"Sure," Sam replied. The man smiled huge and my belly got warm.

"That would be...well, wonderful," the man whispered. "I'll, uh, let you finish up, then."

"Great," Sam said.

"Ma'am," he said to me and dipped his head.

I smiled at him.

He rushed back to his wife.

I looked at Sam, who was watching him go with an expression I couldn't read and this was because his face was carefully blank.

"That was nice of you," I noted cautiously, and his eyes came to me.

Uh-oh.

His eyes were easily read. He was pissed.

"You know," he said quietly, his voice rough with quelled anger, "I'd really like to know who wrote that fuckin' book so I could hunt their ass down and rip their goddamned head off."

Oh man.

"Sam," I whispered, squeezing his thigh.

"No joke, Kia. Honest to God, seriously? I'm at a restaurant, wrapped around my woman, clearly havin' an important, private conversation and they think it's okay, it's fuckin' *fate*, for fuck's sake, that they can interrupt us?"

"He was really nervous, honey."

"Yeah, I'm not feelin' this about him. He didn't wanna be there. I'm feelin' it for her, who's right now takin' photos of us, baby, still. But her finger is no longer over the lens."

I felt my eyes get big and I breathed, "Really?"

"Uh...yeah."

Oh man.

"Do you get that a lot?" I asked.

"Uh...*yeah*," he answered.

Wow. I mean, I figured it happened and maybe even a lot. I'd just not experienced it before, and although not unpleasant, this was because it was a novelty to me. If it happened all the time, it would get very old. Especially when Sam was, as he said, wrapped around me and we were having an important conversation, something our position and body language said and it was something no one could misread.

"Even if you were still playing ball—" I started, trying to find some way to soothe him, but he shook his head.

"Tripled since I got outta the Army and that book came out. It happened when I was playin' ball, definitely. But nowhere near as bad. By now, I'd be retired or lookin' at it and also lookin' at a future where eventually that shit would fade and become rare. I was good, people know me, they'd recognize the name, but it wouldn't be commonplace. Now, who knows? I just know it's been over a year since that book was published and it hasn't died down, not even a little bit."

I was confused.

"So why did you say you'd have your photo with them?"

"'Cause he wasn't lyin'. His kid likes me and his kid is goin' in the Army. His kid could see and do some serious shit because he admires me and wants to follow in my footsteps. That's a responsibility, honey, and his kid's facin' that. And if he gets a kick outta havin' a photo of his parents with me, it takes five minutes of my time and I give it."

Without my brain telling it to do so, my hand lifted to cup his jaw. I leaned into him and I found myself touching my mouth to his before I started to pull back.

I didn't get far. Sam's hand at my waist shot up, wrapped around the back of my neck and held me there.

I bit my lip and stared into his eyes, which were now a lot less angry.

And after our day, after how he'd been kind to that man and why, I decided to share another secret.

"I like you, Sam Cooper, like, a lot," I whispered. "You're not a good man. You're a *really* good one."

"Remember that, baby," he returned instantly. "That feelin' you got about me right now, remember that 'cause that's what you get from me too. And honest to God, whatever this is and wherever this goes, I promise, that's all you'll get from me."

He held my eyes and I let him.

He was making a point, a point he'd made with everything he'd said and everything he'd done since the very second I met him.

A point, right then, I finally got.

Then I nodded.

He bent toward me and touched his mouth to mine.

He let me go, turned his head, mine followed the direction of his gaze and I saw the waiter there. But Sam didn't disentangle our legs or move away when he leaned forward to pull his wallet out of his jeans and pay. He paid in cash, the waiter smiled, bowed and moved swiftly away.

Sam's hand went to my thigh, curled around and his fingers gave me a squeeze as he muttered without any enthusiasm whatsoever, "Let's do this."

"Wait," I said quickly. His eyes came to mine and my hand went to the side of his neck. "Just to finish what we were talking about, when I go shopping with Luci, I'll feel her out and let you know. If it would be uncool for me to say anything, ask anything, I promise, I won't push it because she'll know that's coming from you. But if I think I can get her to open up to me without any blowback on you, I'll do it. Are you okay with that?"

He grinned and answered, "Yeah, honey, that works."

"Good," I whispered, then pulled in a breath and muttered, "Let's get this done."

Sam, being Sam, curled a hand around the back of my knee, lifted my leg from his, set it gently down, got up, pulled out my chair and helped me out of it. I nabbed my purse and settled the strap on my shoulder. He grabbed my hand and led me to the American couple.

As we approached, I saw the woman was nearly bouncing in her chair. The man looked like he wished he had a syringe filled with a fast-acting sedative he could stick her with. And yes, I didn't know the guy, but that was exactly what he looked like.

"*Ohmigod!* You're with your girlfriend!" the woman cried when we were within five feet of her table. She shot out of her chair (her husband coming up much more slowly) and her eyes shot to me. "Are you a model?"

"Uh…no," I answered.

Her brows shot together. "An actress?"

"Uh—" I started, but she cut me off.

"I haven't seen you in any movies. What movies have you been in?"

"I'm not an actress. I'm an administrative assistant," I told her, and her jaw dropped.

Then she jabbed her husband with her elbow three times and exclaimed, "How *neat* is that?" Her eyes moved to Sam. "I love that! I just *knew* when you settled down it wouldn't be with some fancy actress or something but a girl-next-door type. I *knew* it." She turned to her husband. "Didn't I know it?"

"How 'bout we take this shot so you can get on with your dinner," Sam suggested, tipping his head to the nearly full plates of food on their table.

"Oh, we're good. We're fine," she assured Sam. "I know! Would you like to join us? I know you're done eating, but you could have a drink or a glass of wine or something."

"Actually, I need to get my woman home," Sam declined.

"Why? The night is young," the woman noted truthfully but rudely.

"Tilda," her husband muttered, taking her arm.

"Well it is," she told him, then looked at Sam. "We'd love it. It'd be an honor to have a drink with a hero."

"Yeah, pumpkin," her husband said with strained patience. "But maybe this hero would like some private time in a romantic place with his lovely lady."

"Nonsense," she shot back, indicating that the flame had died between Tilda and her hubby because if Lake Como couldn't wake up the romance, nothing could. And clearly the romance was dead between them—so dead, she couldn't see that the romance might not be dead for everybody. She looked to Sam and me and declared, "Nothing better when you're in a foreign place and you meet folks from home. Feels like you *are* home."

This was an odd thing to say, considering you were in a foreign place to experience that place and *not* be home.

Then again, Tilda was an odd woman.

But I couldn't think of Tilda, because, as this wore on, I felt Sam's hand get tighter and tighter in mine so I felt it was time to step in before he broke bones.

"Actually," I started my lie, "Sam needs to get me back to our hotel because I'm expecting an important call from home and I need privacy when I take it. Truthfully, we don't have a great deal of time so I hate to be the one to rush this, but do you mind if I take the shot? Then we really need to go."

"Oh," Tilda mumbled, her face falling. "I hope everything is okay."

"Me too," I replied, taking matters into my own hands and reaching out to the camera that was sitting on their table. "But I'd hate for my call to come while we're on the sidewalk or something so…" I trailed off, grabbed the camera and lifted it toward me. "Is there something special I need to do?"

"Point and click," the man said quickly as he shuffled around the table toward Sam, dragging his wife with him.

To my shock, and apparently, seeing the visible tightening of his entire body, also to Sam's, Tilda wrapped both her arms around Sam's middle, plastered her front to his side, turned her head and smiled scarily at the camera. Her husband stood awkwardly off to Sam's other side and smiled just as awkwardly.

Sam, being Sam, wrapped an arm around Tilda's shoulders, placed a hand on one of the man's shoulders, and looked at me.

"Right, say cheese," I called.

"*Cheese!*" Tilda screeched.

Her husband and Sam just smiled. I took the shot.

"One more, just in case," I said swiftly, then, "Ready, set, go."

"*Cheese!*" Tilda repeated her shriek.

Sam and her husband just kept smiling. I took the shot.

I handed the camera to Tilda who nearly snatched it out of my hands, turning it around to look at the display even as she brought it toward her.

"Thank you, really," the man muttered to Sam. "Kenny'll like those."

"They're *great*!" Tilda cried, then looked up at Sam and me. "Now one with Coop's girlfriend in it."

"We have to go," Sam's rough voice rumbled.

"Just a quickie," Tilda stated.

"We have to go," Sam's rough voice repeated on another rumble, this one firm and unyielding. So much so, Tilda's body twitched and her eyes snapped to him in shock, though how she could be shocked, I did not know, but I was not a rabid celebrity hound who couldn't take a hint, either.

"They have to go, pumpkin," the man murmured.

"Enjoy your meal and your vacation," Sam said, curling an arm around my shoulders and guiding me away. "My best to your boy, yeah?" Sam finished, his eyes on the man.

"Yeah. Thank you, Mr. Cooper," the man returned.

Sam tipped up his chin to him then to the woman, but he did this while continuing to lead me away.

The restaurant was a ten-minute walk from our hotel. We'd been walking two when the noise came from my throat because I couldn't continue choking back my laughter.

"I know, fuck," Sam muttered, totally with me.

"She hugged you," I forced out, all three words sounding strangled.

"I know," Sam repeated, then, "*Fuck*."

I couldn't hold it back anymore. I giggled.

Sam's arm around my shoulders gave me a squeeze. I tipped my head to look at his profile and saw him smiling.

I faced forward again, controlled my hilarity, and asked, "Now does *that* happen all the time?"

"People gettin' *that* in my space?" Sam asked back.

"Yeah."

"Fuck no," he answered, and finished on a mutter, "Thank Christ."

I giggled again.

Then I sobered as something hit me. It was unpleasant, scary even…and weird.

"Uh…Sam?"

"Yeah."

"Can I ask you something?"

That got me another arm squeeze and an "Anything, baby."

I pulled in a breath.

Then I reminded him, "I borderline Internet stalked you."

His voice was filled with humor when he replied, "Kia, honey, the shit you spouted last night? Nothin' 'borderline' about it."

Uh-oh.

"Well then—" I started but stopped when Sam stopped our progress, turned me to face him, and pulled me loosely in both arms.

"Different," he whispered when my eyes caught his.

"How?"

"You remember how we met?"

Uh...*yeah*. I'd never forget. Never, ever, ever.

"Yeah."

"I didn't talk to you, would you have talked to me?"

Ah. I saw his point.

"No," I said quietly.

"Right, no. You wouldn't have talked to me. Definitely not asked me for a picture. And absolutely you wouldn't have pressed up against me."

This was true.

"Though," he grinned down at me, "even if you had, I wouldn't have minded *you* doin' it."

"Sam," I whispered.

"Seriously," he said as he kept grinning.

I rolled my eyes.

Sam kept speaking after his grin faded and his face got serious.

"So. Different," he whispered. "You were respecting my privacy."

"Actually, I was terrified of you."

He grinned again.

"Either way works for me."

I rolled my eyes again.

I rolled them back and asked, "So it doesn't creep you out that one of my best friends has a cardboard cutout of you?"

"Fuck no," he answered immediately. "I get a cut of that shit. She probably paid for a six-pack of beer."

At his words, I burst out laughing.

When I quit laughing, Sam was smiling down at me.

"You got a room at home wallpapered with my pictures?" he asked.

"Uh…no," I answered.

"You ever send me sick-ass letters describing the house we'd live in, the pets we'd have, the names of all our children, goin' into detail about how we'd make those kids?"

Ick!

"Definitely no," I told him.

"A shrine?"

I started giggling but shook my head and repeated, "No."

He let me go with one arm and turned us on our way again, muttering, "Then we're good."

I walked beside him, my arm around his waist, and asked, "Have you received letters like that?"

"Yeah."

Ohmigod.

My head jerked to look up at him. "Really?"

"Yeah, pre-Army had a woman. She sent me at least a hundred of them."

Okay, *that* was creepy. I was now seeing there were degrees.

"I don't know what to do with that," I told him.

"I didn't either. I just didn't reply. It died when I quit playin' ball and never came back. She probably found some other guy who plays ball to fixate on."

"Doesn't that creep you out?"

"Absolutely."

"How do you deal with it?"

"I don't. Not anymore. Got an agency who reads that shit, sends me what I need to see, files the rest."

Hmm. Interesting.

I got another arm squeeze before Sam said softly, "You should know, Tilda gets a wild hair, pictures of you and me at a restaurant in Lake Como, wrapped up together, sittin' close..." he trailed off, and I stopped dead.

This was because I knew what he meant.

She could sell them to someone or even just put them on a social network site and they'd spread like wildfire.

Oh.

My.

God.

He turned me into his arms again as I tilted my head back to look at him.

"Ohmigod," I whispered when my eyes found his.

"That shit happens to me all the time, baby."

I knew that. I'd seen him with a variety of babes. But none of them were me, even though I'd wished they were me.

And now they could be!

Oh.

My.

God!

He studied me as I freaked out.

"Doesn't that freak you out?" I asked him.

"No."

"But...we barely know each other!" I cried.

Yes, *cried* and *loud.*

He pulled me closer, his arms getting tight and his face dipping close to mine.

Then he asked, "This feel good?"

"What?"

"Us."

I sucked in breath at his question.

Sam kept speaking, and when he did, he yet again rocked my world.

"It does to me. That shit, it's my life. I can't care. I did, I'd lose it. So I see it or live it, then I let it go. Now, I'm worried about you 'cause this feels good. If it feels this good now, that means it could get better. What happens tonight is close to what happened this morning, it's *definitely* gonna get better. But right now, it feels good enough I give a shit about it stayin' this good, enough to work at it, enough to *make* it better. And I don't need to find a woman I finally feel good with and have her not able to handle the shit that comes with me."

I was still holding my breath and staring at him.

"Kia."

I kept holding my breath and staring at him.

His face got even closer and his arms gave me a squeeze.

"Kia, baby, breathe."

I let out my breath.

What I didn't do was speak. Sam waited, but my brain was too full with the idea of "us," I couldn't get it together to answer.

"Baby, I need to know if you can handle the shit that comes with me," he prompted gently.

That was when I blurted, "I liked Sampson Cooper not because he was hot and rich and cool. I liked Sampson Cooper because my husband was a dick who treated me like shit and I knew Sampson Cooper was a good man, a decent man, a loyal man and I preferred to spend my time with that man, not with my husband."

It was Sam's turn not to speak.

I kept talking.

"But I like Sam Cooper better."

Sam closed his eyes.

And it was my turn to give him a squeeze, and when I did, he opened his eyes and I whispered, "So, yeah. Definitely yeah. I can handle the shit that comes with you just as long as it comes with you."

I watched his eyes heat right before his hand slid up my back, into my hair, cupping the back of my head, tilting it and his mouth slammed down on mine.

Then he kissed me, not like he'd been doing all day, sweet lip touches that settled in my soul.

No.

Like he did that morning.

A hot, wet, deep kiss with lots of brilliant tongue action that made my knees get weak.

I held on and kissed him back.

It…was…*brilliant.*

He tore his mouth from mine, growled, "Hotel," and he started us walking again.

This time faster.

A lot faster.

Oh.

Man.

8

BURY HIM

Sam led us directly to my room, no discussion over "yours" or "mine."

Decisive.

He was not wasting any time.

But by the time we got there, I was not so sure about "us" anymore.

In fact, I'd convinced myself this was all a huge mistake.

And I'd convinced myself of this because I'd had one lover.

Cooter.

And I found out that morning, just with the little I did with Sam, that Cooter hadn't been very good at what he did. Even with experience with me and whoever else he'd slept with along the way, he hadn't gotten any better. And this was true even before he'd started hitting me, which had made me want nothing to do with my husband touching me.

The sorry fact was, I had never really enjoyed sex with Cooter. I tried but never got there. We'd had our moments, sure. But they were few and they'd caused no fireworks. Sparklers, maybe, but those sputtered out and died.

There was a pocket of time I'd tried to be all I could be for Cooter in bed in hopes that it would make him happy enough so he would be less inclined to get pissed and take it out on me.

This did not work and I quit trying.

But it stood to reason that Cooter went to Vanessa and any of the other women he might or might not have cheated on me with those times he was late home because it was actually me who wasn't good at it. I was not his first, but he had been my first and only and he hadn't exactly taken his time to teach me nor had he made our bed a safe place to learn.

And it was clear with the first kiss Sam and I had shared that I didn't know what I was doing. Just with kissing. So the rest of it might be even worse.

And that couldn't happen.

It couldn't.

After the last twenty-four hours with Sam, it couldn't end like that.

The horrible kiss was humiliating enough. If I couldn't satisfy Sam in bed, that would be mortifying.

And by the time we got to my door, I'd convinced myself that was what was going to happen. That hot kiss with Sam this morning and the one five minutes ago were flukes.

I couldn't tell him this. I couldn't explain any of this.

"Baby, your key?" Sam prompted as I stood staring at the door, trying to figure out how to get out of having sex with Sam and how to talk him into being my hot guy friend who I made out with twice instead.

My head jerked up to look at him, then it jerked down and I pulled my purse off my shoulder, dug inside and came out with my key.

Whether it was because Sam saw my hands shaking (and they were) or he was just being Sam, he slid it gently from my fingers, unlocked the door, pushed it open and held it for me to precede him.

I didn't want to, but I did.

Sam followed me and the door closed behind him.

I stopped breathing and my stomach clutched.

Sam hit the light switch and several lights came on around the room.

That jolted me to action.

"Sam—" I started, but he was right there, his hand wrapped around the side of my neck, pulling me in and tilting my head back with his thumb at my jaw.

His face was so close, it was all I could see when he whispered, "Breathe, baby, just breathe. Stay with me. Two minutes. Stay with me. Then I promise to make it okay."

Two minutes?

He promised to make it okay?

"Promise me you're gonna stay with me," he ordered.

I bit my lip.

Two minutes.

I could do that. Right?

I nodded.

He let me go instantly and moved around the room, turning off all the lights but one by the bed.

Then he came to me and guided me *to* the bed.

Oh no.

"Sam—" I began again.

"Baby, you promised."

I did.

I shut up.

He turned me and gently pressed me to seat me at the side of the bed. Then he bent, hooked a hand behind my knee, lifted my leg and slipped off my sandal. Repeat with the other one. Then he sat down beside me.

I sucked in breath.

"One more minute, Kia," he said gently.

I turned my head to him and nodded again.

He pulled off his boots and socks.

That done, he turned to me, and in a smooth, swift movement, he wrapped an arm around my waist and hauled me up the bed so we were lying perpendicular across the middle of it, both down to our sides, facing each other.

Okay, no.

No.

I didn't know how much time was left on Sam's two minutes, but I had to break my promise.

And that was why I whispered, "I don't think I can—"

His hand cupped my cheek, his thumb out to press lightly on my lips and he whispered back, "You don't have to Kia. I can."

I shook my head, and even with his thumb still at my lips, I told him, "I'm not…I don't think I'm good at this."

"Trust me."

Oh God.

No way!

I could *not* fuck this up. It would ruin everything and the everything we already had was *everything*.

I could live without having more. At that point, I was sure of it.

"Sam—"

His hand went from my jaw to trail down my shoulder, my arm, my wrist, and then my hand. He pulled it to him, dipping it under his shirt, then sliding it up and my fingers hit his hot, sleek skin.

The grip my panicked thoughts had on my mind instantly released as it registered the feel of his skin. The muscle under it was hard, solid, but the skin was so warm it was hot and so soft it was silky.

It felt nice. Very nice.

Sam's mouth touched mine gently as his hand moved mine up the skin of his side, taking his shirt with it and the added lip touch was sweet.

"I'm gonna take care of you," Sam whispered against my lips.

"Okay," I whispered back.

My hand moved of its own accord to experience more, explore the definition of the muscles of his back, take in more of his hot silk. Sam's hand came to my jaw, gliding back and up into my hair as his head moved, his lips sliding across my cheek to my ear.

"I'm gonna taste your mouth again," he whispered, and I shivered.

He slid his hand down my neck, down my spine, light, sweet.

God.

So freaking sweet.

"I'm gonna taste your skin," Sam kept whispering and then he did, touching his tongue to the sensitive area under my ear and I shivered again, pressing slightly closer, my hand continuing its exploration at his back. "There," he whispered at the skin below my ear. "Here," he went on, his hand now whisper-soft and moving up my side. "Here," he kept whispering, his hand moving in over my ribs. "And here," he continued, his thumb drifting at the underside of the swell of my breast.

I drew in breath as my belly plummeted and heat gathered between my legs.

His mouth slid back to mine, and his eyes holding mine, his lips moving on mine, he whispered, "And also here."

Then his thumb moved up, dragging across my nipple. I gasped and he kissed me, his tongue driving inside my mouth.

Oh yes.

Yes.

I kissed him back, pressing close, lifting my leg and hooking it over his hip, my arm going tight around him. He dragged his thumb back, this time deeper, tighter, harder against my nipple, and I whimpered into his mouth.

"Yeah, Kia, baby, give me that," he growled into mine, and he kissed me again, longer, wetter, taking more.

I pressed my hips into his and gave it.

Then he did what he told me he'd do. Suddenly, his hands were in my tank, going up, and it was gone. Before I could think, his mouth was on me, on my neck, down, on my chest, down, his body bending, his lips and tongue gliding down the skin of my side, then up over my ribcage. All the while his hand moved on my back, down over my bottom, soothing at the same time heating, light but enticing.

My head was tipped down and I watched and trembled as he glided his lips along the underside of my breast, then I watched him move up and he tugged my nipple in his mouth over the black lace of my bra.

My back arched as the beauty of his mouth drawing my nipple deep soared through me and I moaned.

Then I was on my back. My bra was gone and Sam was bent to me, his mouth at one nipple, sucking deep, his hand at the other, fingers cupping, thumb circling, and I lost track of everything but how good that felt, what it was doing to me, what was building inside of me.

Need.

There was no other way to describe it and there was nothing else that penetrated my world but that intense, driving *need.*

"Sam—" I gasped, both my hands cupping his head, and my hips bucked.

He surged up and was over me.

"You ready?" he whispered.

"Yeah," I answered and I was. I didn't know exactly what he was referring to, but I also didn't care.

Whatever it was, I wasn't ready. I was *ready.*

Without delay, Sam moved me in bed, righting us so my head was on the pillows. Then my shorts were gone. After those, my black lace panties. Then my legs were spread, and honest to God—honest to *God*—Sam's big hands running along the insides of my thighs, pressing my legs apart, almost brought me to orgasm.

It was good they didn't because then his mouth was on me.

My hips surged up.

Oh man.

Oh *God.*

That was *good.*

Sam threw my legs over his shoulders and cupped my ass in his hands, pulling me to him even as I dug my heels in and helped.

He worked me with his mouth and it started *good,* but it became *awesome* and my hips rocked in his hands and my hands moved to his head to hold him to me.

I felt it.

And I'd never felt it, not once, unless it was me giving it to me.

It was going to happen.

Oh God. I couldn't believe it. *It was going to happen.*

Then it happened.

One of my hands flew to the headboard, my other one stayed at Sam's head as I gasped and cried out, heels digging in as it washed over me, consuming, beautiful.

Oh God.

Perfect.

Heaven.

Nothing—*nothing*—ever had come close.

My eyes drifted open and there was Sam, eyes on me, one hand in the bed at my side, arm straight, his other hand between my legs, fingers trailing, light, sweet.

Dazedly, I noticed he was still fully clothed.

Oh God.

Shit!

He'd given me that and I'd done nothing for him.

His eyes left my face and his chin dipped so he could look at his hand between my legs.

"Jesus," he whispered, "can't fucking believe it. Your pussy's as beautiful as you are."

My freak out stalled and my breath caught.

"Tastes as good," he kept whispering.

Oh wow.

His finger slid inside and that felt so awesome, my eyelids lowered.

"Feels as good," he murmured.

"Sam," I breathed.

"I gotta have this, baby," he said gently, his finger moving out then in.

I started breathing harder.

"Now," he added, his eyes coming back to mine.

I started breathing even harder.

"You ready to take me?" he asked.

I started panting.

I also nodded.

Sam bent low and kissed my belly. Then he pushed up, knelt between my legs and pulled his shirt over his head, tossing it aside.

Seeing his chest, his broad shoulders, his defined stomach, his cut arms, I panted harder.

I also sat up because I knew what the skin of his back felt like.

I had to experience his chest.

So, legs wide, knees bent, soles of my feet in the bed, I sat on my ass in front of Sam, moving my hands on his chest, fingers trailing, exploring, discovering, memorizing.

He felt great.

I leaned in and put my mouth to him, then the tip of my tongue.

Oh God.

He tasted even better.

He was doing something, what, I didn't know until my mouth shifted down and I saw him rolling a condom on.

But I didn't see the condom, really. I saw Sam and Sam's hand at his cock.

He was hard all over, I already knew that.

What I didn't know until that moment was that he was beautiful all over too.

My head tipped back and I whispered, "Is that for me?"

He grinned down at me.

Then his hand cupped the back of my head, pulling me up as he bent low, and against my mouth, he answered, "All for you, baby."

He touched his mouth to mine before he lowered me back, but took my hand and guided it to his cock while he settled again into his other hand in the bed, arm straight, looming over me.

"Guide me," he rumbled, and I didn't delay. I moved him, pulled him, watched his jaw clench, a muscle jump in his cheek. I got the tip inside and just that felt perfect.

My hand flew away as he surged all the way in.

No, no. I was wrong.

This was perfect.

He started moving, slow, deep, his eyes on mine, his free hand roaming my skin.

I was wrong again.

This was perfect.

"Fuck," he muttered, his hand at the base of my throat, his cock driving deeper, going faster, harder. "Fuck," he repeated, his hand moving down my chest between my breasts. I lifted my legs at the knees, pressed the insides of my thighs to his hips and he drove in deeper, then faster and harder. "Beautiful," he kept muttering, his hand down at my belly, then down. "Every inch." He planted himself inside and stayed deep, grinding. "Inside and out," he finished and his thumb hit me.

Okay, no.

This was perfect.

Sam kept thrusting and watching and that was hot. His thumb pressing and rolling was hotter. Both my hands went to the headboard and I pushed into it, driving myself down as he drove himself up, and that, *that* was *amazing*.

"Sam," I gasped.

"Ride me, baby."

"Sam!" I cried.

"Fuck yes," he growled, and I came again. My back arching off the bed, my hands pressing deep into the headboard, grinding myself down on him, as this one tore through me, hot, searing, devastating.

Still coming, I felt Sam's heat and weight hit me. One hand plunging into my hair, fisting, he pressed my face into his neck. The other arm wrapped low on my hips, clamped tight and took over driving me down on his cock. I wrapped my arms and legs around him and alternately breathed, whimpered, moaned, gasped and tasted his skin.

Then his hand in my hair pulled my head back, his face went into my throat, his cock thrust deep and he growled his orgasm against my skin.

And call me crazy but hearing it, feeling it, Sam's big, warm body heavy and covering me, listening to his orgasm was almost better than actually having the ones he'd given me.

And the ones he'd given me were freaking *spectacular.*

His fist relaxed in my hair, but his hand didn't leave it. His fingers sifted then twisted gently, tangling in the strands and staying there as Sam kept his cock rooted, connected to me. As I tilted my chin down, his head slid up so I felt his breath under the skin of my ear.

Finished, I was languishing in the feel of all that was him—his heat, his power, his weight all held tight in my circling limbs—the aftermath, the connection of Sam still deep inside, his breath at my ear.

Then it hit me he wasn't speaking.

And then it hit me that Sam communicated. It couldn't be said I had a lot of experience with guys, but my friends did and they talked about them all the time, talked as in bitched. And one of the things they bitched about the most was that the men in their lives never communicated.

Sam did.

All the time.

He was open. He was honest. He shared.

But now he wasn't saying a word.

Oh God.

Shit!

"Uh..." I forged into the silence and asked quickly, "Was that okay?"

Sam didn't answer immediately.

Then he didn't answer at all but instead asked, "What?"

I kept my eyes glued to the ceiling and repeated, "Was that, uh...okay?"

Sam's head came up and he looked down at me.

God. *God.*

He was beautiful.

Even more beautiful covering me and connected to me.

"Was that okay?" he repeated my question.

"Uh...yeah."

He stared at me.

Then he burst out laughing, throwing his head back to do it and everything.

In the middle of it, his body suddenly collapsed on mine. I wheezed when I took his massive weight, but I took it for a nanosecond before he rolled, performing a miracle as he did because he kept us connected, even when he was on his back, I was on top, and somehow I ended up straddling him.

I lifted my head up and looked down at him to see he was still laughing.

"I wasn't being funny," I whispered.

Both his hands came up to either side of my head and I watched him struggle to control his continuing laughter as he took in my face.

"Was it okay for you?" he asked.

Okay was not the word for it. Okay was not just not in the ballpark. Okay was not even in the same galaxy.

I did not share this with Sam.

Instead, I answered, "Yeah."

He kept chuckling, but he moved his hands from my head and wrapped his arms around me and repeated my "Yeah."

It was safe to say I didn't know what to do with that.

So I sought clarification.

"So is that a 'yeah,' it was okay for you, or a 'yeah,' you heard and comprehended *my* 'yeah' through your amusement?"

"Both," he said through a grin.

"Oh," I whispered, my eyes moving to the pillowcase. "Okay," I finished.

"Kia, eyes on me," Sam ordered gently.

My eyes slid back to him to see he wasn't smiling anymore and there was no trace of hilarity. He was focused, intent, and serious, but all of that in a tender way that made something important shift inside of me.

"Makin' you melt for me, then makin' you light up for me, listening to you get excited, feeling it, tasting it, *eating it.*" His words made me shiver and it helped that his hand was gliding up my back, my neck, and into my hair. He pulled my head down so my face was an inch from his and he continued on a whisper, "Feelin' you come against my mouth, watchin' you drive yourself down on my dick, listening to you moan as your pussy clenched around my cock when you came, baby, yeah. That was all okay. That was better than okay. It was fuckin' *beautiful.*"

Such was my relief, I closed my eyes and dropped my head so my forehead was resting against his.

I opened my eyes and lifted my head when he asked, "Okay?"

I nodded.

He smiled a small but sweet smile as his arm around me gave me a squeeze.

Then he ordered, "Kiss me, then get off me. Yeah?"

I nodded again. I pressed my lips to his and would have pulled back, but his hand in my hair kept me there and his arm around my back held me tight as his mouth opened, his tongue touched my lips, my lips opened, then his tongue touched mine.

When Sam let me lift my head, I pulled myself off, sliding Sam out of me (which kind of sucked because he was still hard and he felt good there). He then rolled me to his side.

He yanked the covers from under me, pulled them up over me, exited the bed and headed to the bathroom.

I closed my eyes and drew in breath.

Okay.

Sam thought that was beautiful.

So did I.

I let out my breath, opened my eyes and smiled.

Sam came back and I watched with no small amount of fascination as he pulled off his jeans, tugged back the covers and got in bed beside me.

He slid close, then pushed an arm under my body, pulling me so into his side I was plastered partially to it and partially on top of him.

I lifted my head just as the fingers of his other hand tangled in the hair at my shoulder, gave it a gentle tug and my eyes hit his to see his were on me and they weren't serious. They were deadly serious.

"Okay, baby, now that my cock is no longer inside you…and when it is, that is a place he'll never be…I'll say this straight. You don't get it straight, we work on it. But I'll say it straight and maybe it'll penetrate and you can focus on the Kia you are, not the Kia he dragged down and made you be."

Uh-oh.

I wasn't sure I was big on where this was heading.

"Sam—"

"Just let me finish, yeah?"

I didn't want to say yeah so I didn't.

But I nodded.

Sam didn't delay.

"I am not him, Kia. Your dead husband is dead. Before he was dead he was a dick. He was a moron. He was an asshole. And now he's gone. You're in bed with me. *Me.* Whatever you had with him in your life and your bed, that's as dead as him. I'm here because I wanna be here. And in about ten minutes, when we're done talkin' about that asshole and he's gone again, I'm gonna get you wet and hot for me and I'm gonna be in you because I wanna be in you. And trust me, I'm a man so I can say with a fair amount of authority there are not many men who would not kill for the chance of bein' naked in a bed with you naked and pressed up against him after he got the gift you just gave me. It's just that that man is now me and he's gonna *be* me for a good long while. Do you get me?"

"I…I think so," I stammered, staring into his serious eyes.

"Where was I unclear?" Sam asked, and I blinked.

"Uh…you were pretty clear," I told him.

"So you don't think you get me. You actually get me."

I kept staring.

And I got him, which meant I had him.

I *had* him.

My heart leapt as that settled into my soul.

"Yeah, Sam. I get you," I whispered.

"You need to talk about him, dig him out so you can release the shit he planted in you, we'll talk, baby. I'll give that to you. Anytime. Except one. When we're in bed, it's you and me. Don't bring him here. Leave behind the shit he planted, because, Kia, honey, you're beautiful. You have a fantastic fuckin' body. And when you let go, swear to Christ, you could make me come just with the noises you make when you get excited."

"Wow," I whispered.

Sam grinned.

Then he whispered back, "So let that shit go, baby. The way you kissed me this morning and the way you were before I broke through tonight, let that shit go. That isn't you. That's what he planted in you and that motherfucker is dead. Bury him."

Bury him.

Bury Cooter.

I already did.

And yet, I didn't.

And Cooter Clementine was very, very dead.

It was time to bury *all* of him.

"Okay, Sam," I agreed quietly.

His hand in my hair moved, taking my hair with it, and it glided along my jaw as his eyes roamed over my face.

Then his fingers slid out of my hair, he wrapped both arms around me and rolled. I went over him, to my back, and Sam was on top of me.

"Right," he said softly. "Now, you were in the middle of usin' your mouth on me when I interrupted to fuck you. Let's go back to that."

Oh yeah. That sounded good because he felt good and he tasted good.

I wanted to go back to that.

"Okay," I breathed.

Sam grinned.

Then he kissed me, hard, wet, and deep.

He rolled us so he was on his back, I was on top and we got back to what I was doing before he interrupted to fuck me.

After a while of further exploration and discovery on my part, which I enjoyed a whole heckuva lot, and, considering I significantly widened my search area and was relatively thorough, Sam enjoyed more, Sam broke out another condom.

By the time Sam finally let me pass out, the sun had started kissing the sky and he'd broken out two more.

So I already had proof, when God was handing out talent, He was generous with Sam in a lot of areas.

One of them was stamina.

Good to know.

9

UNCLEAN

My eyes drifted open when I felt the covers drifting down. Then I felt Sam's lips at the small of my back, his hand light on my bottom and his lips drifted up while his hand drifted down.

I was on my belly. I turned my head just when his lips drifted over my shoulder and his hand pressed between my legs.

I sucked in breath.

Sam's eyes caught mine.

"Mouth," he growled.

Without delay, half asleep but fully turned on, I lifted up and gave him my mouth.

Twenty minutes later I was grinding down on his cock, Sam's head was tipped back, mine tipped forward, and our lips were brushing, our heavy breaths mingling.

I moved to glide up, but his arm around my waist tightened, holding me down.

"Baby," I breathed.

"You're stayin' an extra day in Italy. I'm takin' you to Parma to see the da Vinci," Sam declared on a rumble that I heard as well as felt…straight through me.

"Okay," I agreed instantly and tried again to push up, but he kept me down.

"Then I'm goin' to Crete with you."

I froze. My half-mast eyes opened to full and looked into his.

"Really?" I whispered, uncertain whether to laugh or cry with glee.

"Really," he whispered back.

I held his eyes and didn't laugh or cry. I just experienced the glorious feeling of my heart leaping with joy.

Then I agreed, "Okay."

He smiled.

I smiled back.

Then I tilted my head and kissed him, hard.

His arm loosened and I moved.

I was standing in front of the full-length, oval mirror, swiping mascara on my lashes, when I heard a key in the lock.

My eyes went to the reflection of the door in the mirror and I watched Sam walk in wearing another pair of faded jeans that fit really well and another shirt, this one light blue, and I knew it was made of linen because it was already wrinkly.

We'd showered in my room and he'd gone to his room to change, leaving me to do my gig in my room.

And I had, including blowing out my hair, doing the Celeste perfume business and donning a sundress I bought with Celeste. This one was shorter than the one Sam had seen, and clingier. A lot like a tank top but in dress form, lotus-pink, and clearly it had Sam's approval, considering his eyes moved to it the minute he cleared the door and didn't leave it (or, I should say, the ass vicinity of my back in it) as he walked across the room to me.

I also had most of my makeup done.

This meant one of two things: one, Sam primped like a girl, though when he made it to me, I registered he smelled good so I figured he put on some cologne or aftershave, but other than that, it didn't appear his toilette was extensive except to shave; or two, something had held him up.

I watched him in the mirror as, eyes still on my ass, he slid a hand along my ribcage. He fit the front of his body to the back of mine and his eyes moved to my reflection in the mirror (specifically the breast vicinity).

Before I could figure out whether or not to ask what took him so long, Sam, just like Sam, told me.

"Luci called," he said, his gaze moving from my breasts to my eyes.

"She okay?"

"I don't know. I'm not a woman. She wants to shop, and bein' a man, that would indicate she's not."

I grinned, then leaned forward a bit and went back to swiping mascara while explaining, "She's perfectly fine."

"Right," he muttered, and my eyes went from my wand to him watching me. Suddenly, I felt funny so I stopped.

"Are you saying she wants to shop with you or with me?" I asked.

"She wants to shop with both of us."

I blinked into the mirror because not only was this voiced with dread, Sam was wearing a borderline look of dread on his face.

Yes, the mighty, huge, hot guy, ex-commando Sampson Cooper appeared to fear shopping.

"Are you..." I hesitated, studying him closely, "*scared* of shopping?"

His eyes had drifted down to my breast area again, but at my question, they shot up to my face. Both his arms closed around me, he shoved his face in my neck and burst out laughing.

Hmm. Maybe I read him wrong.

"Scared of shopping," he muttered into my neck, then burst out laughing again, his arms going so tight, they squeezed the breath out of me.

Yes, it would seem I read him wrong.

It appeared he didn't fear it. He loathed it.

So noted.

"Sam, I need to finish with my mascara," I told him.

His head came up and he kept chuckling as his eyes caught mine.

"So finish," he invited, his voice still vibrating with residual laughter.

"I can't, you're putting me off."

His brows drew together. "How?"

"I don't know. Holding me, watching me, being hot. That puts a girl off."

His brows relaxed, but his body started shaking again, his mouth spreading in a huge grin through which he asked, "Me being hot puts you off?"

"Not, say, when I'm sitting, drinking wine next to you, or, uh… other times. But when I have to concentrate on something important and get it right and you're watching, then, uh…yeah."

His big grin became a bigger smile. "Mascara is important?"

"Sam," I snapped.

His eyes left mine in the mirror because his head dipped and his mouth went to my ear, and I watched as I listened to him whisper, "I was watchin' you go down on me and I was a lot hotter then, baby. Now *that* was important and you didn't seem to have any problem concentrating."

Heat rushed between my legs, hot and wet.

Oh God.

"Sam," I breathed.

"Fuck." His nose brushed the skin below my ear as his hand at the side of my ribs slid up to the side of my breast. "You smell good."

Apparently, Celeste's perfume discovery tactic worked.

Also noted.

"You feel good," he went on, his thumb extending and gliding under the swell of my breast.

I bit my lip and locked my shaking knees.

Sam's arm around my belly dipped low, his fingers curled into the hem of my dress and his eyes came back to me in the mirror.

"And you look good," he murmured, his hand ducking under my dress.

Oh God.

"Sam," I repeated on a breath.

His hand slid into my panties.

"Can't keep my fuckin' hands off you."

Oh *God.*

"Sam—"

I stopped talking as I sucked in breath and my head dropped back to his shoulder when his finger hit the spot.

Oh man. That felt *nice.*

His finger worked me. I moaned, turned my head and pressed my forehead into his neck. His other hand pulled down the top of the dress, taking with it the cup of my bra and his fingers started working my nipple there.

God.

That felt nicer than nice.

"Jesus, fuck, look at you."

I pressed my forehead in his neck.

"Fuckin' look at you." His finger at the spot slid down and filled me. "Beautiful."

Both of my hands went to both of his. He kept playing with my nipple and finger fucked me before going back to my clit, pressing and rolling. I felt it with my hands and I felt what he was doing and both felt freaking *great.*

I whimpered.

His finger moved to slide back inside.

"Gotta have that again, baby," he growled in my ear.

I twisted my neck and did my best to focus on his eyes.

"Take it," I whispered.

His hands moved away instantly, both going to yank up my skirt. Mine went to yank down my panties. He lifted me up, they fell from my ankles, and I found myself on my hands and knees in the unmade bed. Sam was on his feet behind me, his hand brushing my ass as he worked the fly of his jeans. Then he was inside me.

He drove forward.

I reared back.

He did it again. So did I.

We'd had a lot of sex so this lasted awhile.

A good long while.

A freaking fantastic one.

I came on a moan, my hands going out from under me, sliding forward as my back arched into the bed, my ass to the ceiling. I heard his growl then his grunts as he powered in harder, faster. Then I listened to his groan when he came.

After, I remained in position, getting my wits sorted, feeling him glide in and out while the fingertips of one hand drifted over my behind and hip and the other hand stayed curled around my waist. I liked that. He did it often, showing me tenderness after he took me hard.

He pulled out, hauled me to my feet, back to him, and yanked my dress down. He held me close to his frame with an arm around my ribs as he righted his fly.

He turned me, lifted me, stepped in, put a knee to the bed, then we were down, me on my back, Sam on top of me.

And it was then he kissed me, long, deep, and sweet.

I liked that too. A lot.

He lifted his head and I looked into his satisfied, beautiful, dark brown eyes, liking that they were satisfied but liking it more that I could give him that

"I think I dropped my mascara wand," I informed him.

He blinked.

Then he grinned.

Then he muttered, "Tragedy."

I grinned back and went on, "And my mascara tube."

"I'll notify the media."

My grin turned to a smile, but I said through it, "Shut up."

He shut up, but he did this by kissing me again, longer, deeper, sweeter.

Yeah, I liked that a lot.

He released my mouth but kissed my nose.

Oh. Wow.

He'd never done that before.

That was sweet too.

Very sweet.

Something occurred to me and I whispered, "I have to go clean up."

"Yeah," he murmured, touched his mouth to mine and rolled off.

I rolled the other way, got up, tagged my panties from the floor, went to the bathroom and did my thing.

I was washing my hands and looking in the mirror when it hit me Sam always put on a condom. Always, no matter how heated it got, and so far, each time it got seriously heated.

And he clearly didn't just now.

This was not a big deal. I was on the Pill.

But Sam was so careful, he was probably concerned I wasn't and was too much of a gentleman to ask.

I needed to set his mind at ease.

I wandered into the room to the mascara wand and tube I'd dropped. I retrieved them and inspected the wand. All seemed well so I slid the wand into the tube, turned to the mirror and went back to swiping.

I did this while, hopefully casually, noting, "You should know, honey, I'm on the Pill."

My eyes flicked to Sam reflected in the mirror, reclining on his side, elbow in the bed, head in his hand, eyes on me, and I saw and heard him mutter, "Good."

Right.

That was done.

Not hard at all.

I could do this—be in a healthy relationship, communicate, move on.

Easy.

I swiped the brush against the edges of my lashes. Three times one side. Three times the other.

Except for gloss, makeup done.

I was screwing the wand into the tube and had moved to my cosmetics case to drop it in when Sam said, "Unless you've had one, we'll find a clinic, here or in Crete, get you a test."

I dropped the mascara in my bag and dug for my pink lip gloss that would go great with my dress while asking, "A test?"

"AIDS, other STDs."

I froze. Then I blinked at my bag. Woodenly, I straightened and turned to him.

"What?"

"AIDS and other STDs," he repeated. "You already had one?"

Numbly, I shook my head.

Sam kept talking. "We'll get you one. Make sure you're clean. Then, since you're on the Pill, we can lose the condoms. Shouldn't have done that just now. You in that dress, outta my hands. Won't do it again until we're sure you're clean."

I was…*clean*?

I didn't know what to say.

But I knew what to feel.

Unclean.

I turned back to my cosmetics bag and blindly dug for my lip gloss. It was blindly because my eyes had filled with tears so I couldn't see a freaking thing.

"Kia?" Sam called.

"Mm-hmm," I answered, but even my mumble sounded thick.

"Baby?"

I swallowed, then answered, "Yeah?"

That sounded thick too.

I blinked to clear my eyes, and my fingers had just found the lip gloss when Sam's hand closed around my other one and he wrapped both our arms around my belly.

Softly, in my ear, he said, "Your dead husband stepped out on you. It's fucked, but it doesn't negate the fact that I'm fuckin' you, which means I'm also fuckin' whoever *he* fucked. I gotta be careful and *you* gotta make sure you're safe."

"Right," I whispered, cleared my throat because my voice sounded croaky and I requested, "Could you, uh…let me go? I need to finish getting ready."

"Kia—"

"Just lip gloss, jewelry, then my shoes, and then I really need to get something to eat."

"Kia—"

My hand holding the gloss pushed at his arm as my hand held in his tried to twist free, even as I leaned away from him and assured, "I'll be ready in two minutes, tops."

He pulled the gloss out of my hand, tossed it back in the bag, then captured mine and wrapped both arms around me.

I went solid.

His mouth went back to my ear and he deduced, "You hadn't thought about that."

I hadn't.

No.

I already felt unclean enough at the hands of Cooter.

The thought of that, the thought that that was what was in Sam's mind every time he made love to me, enough to remember to protect himself from me, made me feel filthy.

Of course, he was only being smart.

That didn't make me feel any less contaminated.

I didn't reply.

I listened and felt as Sam drew in a deep breath, his chest expanding against my back, and I listened to his long sigh.

Then he said, "I fucked up."

Yes. He did.

He could have handled that subject with a lot more care.

He didn't.

Whatever.

Onward.

"Really, let me just—"

He let my hands go, turned me to face him and his arms closed around me tight.

I lifted my hands to his biceps, put on pressure and tipped my head back to look at him.

"Sam, really, it's lunchtime. We slept through breakfast. I'm hungry."

"I should have felt you out, been more aware."

Yes. He should have.

He didn't.

Onward!

"It's okay. Now—"

"It isn't."

I snapped my mouth shut and glared up at him.

His eyes moved over my face and he whispered, "I'm sorry, baby."

I nodded. "Like I said, it's okay. Now, really, I've had some coffee in the room, but I have to have some food."

He stared at me a moment before he noted, "You're pissed."

I wasn't.

I was *unclean.*

"No, I'm not."

"You've got a right to be pissed, honey."

"Do I have to be hungry while I'm pissed?" I asked. His eyes studied my face again and he slowly shook his head. "Good, then can I put on lip gloss and shoes so I can go get something to eat?"

"Yeah," he answered but didn't let me go.

"Uh…are you gonna let me go so I can do those things?"

His eyes studied my face yet again.

I sought patience.

Then he said quietly, "Yeah." And he let me go.

I retrieved the gloss, walked to the mirror and put it on. Considering that our abbreviated conversation about Luci intimated that I would imminently be shopping with her, and my few times spent with Luci indicated she was a fashionista (as she would be, of the tallest order), I added dangly, spiky earrings, a couple of thick, jingly bracelets, and a long, thin-chained necklace with a jingly, spiky pendant at the end. I unearthed my bronze sandals, sat on the bed and strapped them on.

Sam had seen them before but…whatever.

He was a man. He didn't care about shopping. He probably didn't care about shoes.

Once they were on, I got up, went to my purse, hooked the strap on my shoulder and looked to him.

He was standing where I'd left him, except now his arms were crossed on his chest, his legs were planted slightly apart and he looked like a gladiator who was in the ring, they just let in the lion, it was weak, sickly thus easily defeated, and he was disappointed with the challenge.

"Aren't you hungry?" I asked.

He held my eyes a moment, then answered, "Yeah."

"Then let's go."

He held my eyes another moment.

Finally, he jerked up his chin, uncrossed his arms and swung one hand to the door.

We went.

I disconnected, slid my phone in my purse and picked up my piece of bread, muttering, "Celeste and Thomas are good to have dinner with us tonight. Thanks for that."

I took a big bite of bread, trained my eyes on the view of the lake and chewed.

Sam had no reply.

I put the bread down, picked up my fork and stabbed at my salad, saying, "Maybe when Luci gets here, we'll ask her and she'll want to join us. Would that be okay with you?"

Sam again made no reply.

Since I'd asked him a direct question, I turned my head to him and stopped dead at what I saw.

He wasn't eating. He was sitting back in his chair, forearms on the arms of the chair, hands dangling, eyes on me, face hard.

I'd never seen him look like that, ever. I'd seen him pissed. I'd even seen him angry.

But I'd never seen him like that.

"Sam?" I whispered.

"Yeah, Kia, remember me?"

I blinked, set my fork down and straightened away from my food. "Sorry?"

"Just to remind you, sweetheart, I'm the man who fucked you four times last night, twice today."

Oh my God.

Did he just say that?

My eyes darted side to side at the busy tables around us before I leaned into him and hissed, "What on earth?"

"Good question," he returned.

"What?"

"Not likin' the wall, Kia."

I felt my brows snap together and I repeated, "What?"

He leaned into me and it took everything I had not to rear back at the look on his face, and he clipped, "Think I explained last night. And I did it, incidentally, after I fucked you during which you came twice. Somethin' by your reaction at the time and after, he never gave you, Kia...my guess, not once. Further evidence of what I explained last night, and that is, I am *not* that asshole."

"I know that," I snapped.

"You fuckin' do not," he shot back. "I fucked up earlier, pissed you off, maybe hurt you. I don't know if it's one, the other or both and I don't know because you slammed up the wall to hold me back so I have no clue. What I do know is, you aren't talkin' about it to me, workin' it out with me. I also know you're sittin' next to me but you're so far away, I can't reach you."

"Sam, I said it was okay," I reminded him.

"You lied."

I sucked in breath and sat back.

Sam's hand darted out, caught me behind the neck, pulled me back to him and I sucked in another breath, this one a whole lot different and I watched his eyes flare dangerously.

"Oh no, fuck no," he whispered angrily. "First, do not pull away from me when we're talkin', especially when it's about something important. And second, again, do not fuckin' mistake me for him. I'm not gonna hurt you. I want *to talk to you.*"

"Maybe you can do it without getting physical," I suggested acidly and went on just as acidly, "Or without being a jerk."

"Yeah? I asked earlier and you shut me down. Walked here with you, ordered, got served, started eatin' and you shut me out. So I'm tryin' other options to see if I can break through."

My heart was beating wildly but right then my throat clogged with fear and this was not fear of Sam, but a sudden, overpowering fear I was fucking up.

"I'm new to this, Sam," I whispered. "To something being..." I paused to find a word then finished, "healthy."

"Yeah? Well, let me clue you in, sweetheart. Shit happens, we talk it out. You do not *shut* me out."

I stared into his glittering, no less angry eyes.

And there it was. I was fucking up.

"*Buongiorno!*" we heard called and I tore my eyes from Sam who dropped his hand from my neck. I watched Luci approach. She was fiddling with her purse, head down and talking. "I know I'm early but I'm also hungry and I like this restaurant. I'll get some pasta, eat quickly and then," she looked up, "shopping!"

She stopped dead and stared at us, her lips parting and her eyes darting between us.

Clearly, neither Sam nor I were doing a good job hiding the fact that she'd interrupted an intense conversation.

Then she murmured, "But, I think I must go and…" she looked around her, "do something first. I'll be back in—"

"No, that's okay," I said quickly, suddenly finding my body pushing back my chair. "Sit. Eat. I, um…we'll…" I stopped talking. Eyes glued to Luci, I surged up, panic controlling my movements. I grabbed my purse and whispered, "I suddenly don't feel so well. I need to go back to the hotel and lie down. Enjoy shopping."

Then I took off, dashing through the tables like the fraught heroine in a romantic comedy.

Enjoy shopping?

Ohmigod!

I was a nut. I was an idiot. I was a loser.

And I totally could not do this with Sam.

I wasn't going to bore him away.

I was going to annoy him away.

God, he was so *pissed.*

And he couldn't have sex with me without wearing a condom in case he *caught something from me.*

Something *Cooter* might have given me.

Before last night, I'd had one lover, and still, he'd tainted me.

And if the tests didn't come back clean…

I closed my eyes and nearly ran up the sidewalk, going as fast as my sandals would take me, my breath coming heavy and not from rushing—from holding back emotion. I didn't know whether to cry, scream, or find something to throw because I was so *fucking* angry.

At myself.

But especially at Cooter.

I slid through the doors to the hotel and raced up the stairs, pulling my key out of my bag as I went.

I was standing at my door, making my second attempt to slide the key in the lock, when an iron arm clamped around me.

I choked back my surprised cry, twisted my neck and looked up to see Sam's hard jaw, a muscle ticking in his cheek. The key was pulled from my hand, Sam inserted it and we were in my room.

I tried to escape, pulling free from his arm, but he caught me, twisting me on the way back so the front of my body hit his. His arm went back around me tight, but his other hand slid into my hair, holding my head steady, so I was right there when his face got in mine.

I expected him to blow. My body braced and I winced, preparing for it.

But when his voice came, it was soft, gentle, but still velvet rough.

"Talk to me, baby."

I stopped wincing and looked into his eyes.

Then I told him the truth.

"You don't need this drama."

"Kia—"

I cut him off. "Luci doesn't either."

And she didn't. Neither of them did.

God.

God!

I ran away from the table like the *fraught heroine in a romantic comedy.*

How humiliating.

"Don't worry about that shit. Tell me what's in your head."

"Sam—"

"What's in your head?"

"I can't—"

His face got closer. "Tell me. What's in your head? Tell me everything that's goin' through your head."

"I'm unclean," I blurted, and his head jerked.

"What?" he asked.

"Sam." I shook my head. "Just let me go."

"Kia—"

"*Just let me go!*" I shrieked, losing it. Tearing out of his arms, taking four quick steps back, I yanked my bag off my shoulder and threw it on the bed.

He started toward me, but I lifted up a hand as if to fend him off and he stopped.

"He hit me," I whispered. It just came out and I watched Sam's body go rock solid, but I couldn't stop the words flowing so they kept coming. "He backhanded me, and he did it so often, I had a scale. How bad it was. I'd rate it. My head whipped to the side, that was a one. He took me to the floor, that was a ten. And that was the worst because, if I hit the floor, more often than not, he'd kick me."

Sam didn't move, not an inch, not a twitch. His eyes didn't even leave me.

"He wore steel-toed boots to work."

Sam moved then, or at least the muscle in his cheek did.

He knew what I was saying.

"I tried to leave six times, Sam. And never, not once, did I call Mom or Dad, Kyle, Missy, Paula, Teri. Even Ozzie. What was the matter with me?"

"Kia—"

"They would have helped."

"Kia—"

"It was like, like…" I shook my head and threw up my hands. "Like I didn't actually *want* to leave."

"I need to come to you," Sam said gently, but I shook my head again.

"No."

I took another step back, compounding the denial, and kept right on talking.

"I…he…he'd get mad when I left and he…it was bad when he got me back, Sam. I learned. I learned not to leave. And he was mean and not just mean to me. I mean *mean.* I tried to figure it out, what changed in him, why he wasn't who I'd dated in high school. He was always cocky, but he was never mean. But after he got kicked out of college because his grades were so bad, and we got married and life wasn't so easy, he wasn't the glory boy anymore. He had to work at things and he got mean. And I worried he'd do shit like slash my friends' tires or get them in trouble at work or follow them, mess with them, freak them out. My mom had a heart valve replacement, like, seven years ago. She's okay now, but it was scary before we figured out what was wrong. She couldn't take that. Teri and Missy are single. Paula only got married last year and Rudy would never let anything hurt her, not ever, but that wasn't…she hadn't started with him until I…until after I gave up."

"Baby—"

I kept talking, fast, my breath coming faster, speaking right over Sam.

"He had this guy…at work…he hated him. God, he *obsessed* about him. Everyone liked this guy, especially Cooter's boss. It drove Cooter wild. Just wild. He started messing with him. Screwing around with his car. Doing crazy shit. God, he'd come home, tell me what he did. I couldn't believe it. It was so crazy, but he giggled himself sick. He loved it. Every minute of it. Then there was an accident at work and the guy got hurt. It was bad. So bad, he's on disability now. He hasn't worked since. Cooter never said anything to me, but he calmed down after that and I don't think it was just because the guy wasn't around. I think it was because he *made* the guy not *be* around. I couldn't do that to my family. My friends."

"No, honey, that's understandable," Sam said softly, moving a step toward me, but I took a step back and he stopped.

"But all of them, Sam, I could have rallied all of them. I see that now. These past couple of days, it's come to me. They were there to help. Some of them even *told me* they were there if I needed them, and they told me this because they *knew* I needed them. It was hurting them, watching him tearing away parts of me. And now, looking back, I know he couldn't have taken them all on. Especially if I'd talked to Ozzie. Ozzie knew. Ozzie has seen a lot in his life, his job. I knew he knew what was happening to me. I should have talked to Ozzie. He would have helped me."

"You weren't thinkin' then. You were scared and protecting them and yourself."

I shook my head, closed my eyes, then opened them and looked at him.

"He was my only lover and he made me unclean."

"Kia, we don't know—"

"You fuck me, you fuck him, and I can't have that for you. I can't do that to you. So I can't have you."

His face changed, like an understanding. It washed over his features leaving a beautiful warmth in its wake, but it didn't penetrate, even when he whispered, "Baby, that's crazy."

"He contaminated me and he can't contaminate you."

"We don't know that."

"We know."

His head cocked to the side. "You know?"

"I don't know how many women he was with. It could be dozens. But it doesn't matter." I shook my head. "It doesn't matter." He melted as the tears filled my eyes because it hit me, and when it hit me, it crushed me. "He's already contaminated me."

The weight of this knowledge was so heavy, my legs gave out, but I didn't hit the floor. Sam caught me in his arms. I was up, then we were both down on the bed, Sam cradling me, and I burrowed closer, sobbing into his chest.

"That's right, honey, get that shit out," Sam murmured into the top of my hair and my body bucked with another sob.

He cradled me closer and held me for a long time because I cried for a long time. Finally, the tears came slower and I lay in his arms, held close, tight and sniffling.

"Took it too fast, movin' on you, takin' you to bed. Fucked up, mentioning that shit to you," he muttered like he was talking to himself, his hand moving soothingly on my back.

I lifted my hand, dragged my fingers across my cheek, stared at his shirt and mumbled, "You should really go."

His hand stopped moving and both arms closed around me as he asked, "What?"

"You should go."

"Where?"

"Away from me."

"Kia—"

I sucked in breath, lifted my head and looked at him. "I'm…you were right. He broke me and you need—"

"I know what I need, baby. You don't. Don't tell me what I need. Only I know."

"Well *I* know it isn't me."

He held my eyes. Then he grinned.

Then he said gently, "Last night, I was pissed and losin' it. That woman, rude. Takin' our time, up in my space. She kept talkin', I woulda said something that woulda made her kid not like me so fuckin' much. You moved right in, sorted it out, got them what they wanted and us on our way. Been in that position too many times, Kia. Not one woman standing by my side has felt my patience go and stepped in for me. Not one woman…except you."

I stared at him, stunned at this news. I mean, his hand got so tight in mine, how could his other women not know and, well, *do something*?

"Really?" I asked.

"Really," he answered, then went on quietly, "You wore those shoes you're wearin' now the first time I saw you."

I felt my lips part.

He remembered.

Holy cow. He remembered my *shoes.*

Sam's eyes went to my mouth and he muttered, "She gets it."

"Sam—" I started, but he immediately talked over me.

"Silver shoes the second time I saw you, blue dress."

I closed my eyes.

I knew what he was saying.

He remembered everything about me.

"Gold when you went out with me."

I opened my eyes and felt tears filling them again as he kept right on going.

"Your Lake Como bud, Kia, baby, she didn't tell you about her kid because you remind her of her daughter. She told you about her kid because you remind her of her daughter and you are all she hoped her daughter would grow up to be. Beautiful, funny, friendly, classy. I know why Luci liked you at first. You looked good, pure class but effortless, not a wannabe. You looked like what she thinks would fit me. I don't know what you did to take it beyond that, but whatever it was, you did it. By the time I got to you with the champagne, you had Luci. Not one woman I've ever been with that she's met has had her approval at all so definitely not that soon."

"But—"

His arms gave me a tight squeeze and he shook his head.

"You did that, Kia. *You.* You talk about your family and your friends and they're loyal to you. It's obvious they love you and *you* inspire that. That fuckin' asshole didn't contaminate you. *He* was contaminated and I'll bet he wanted to contaminate you, but I *know* he worked hard at doin' it. He looked at you, saw how gorgeous you are, how people care about you, and he knew if you woke up, you'd see he was the piece of shit he was. So he had to drag you down so you'd never see him for what he was, leave him behind and find what you deserve."

"But…you and me, when we're, uh…intimate—"

His arms gave me another squeeze, pulling me up his chest so we were face to face and turning me deeper into him, tangling his long legs with mine.

He asked quietly, "All that you just gave me, you haven't told any of your crew that shit, have you?"

I shook my head.

"Buried it."

I pressed my lips together and nodded.

"Buried everything. Didn't deal. Just thought you could move on."

There it was yet again. He had figured me out.

"Yeah," I whispered.

One of his hands came up, his fingers gliding around my ear, tucking my hair behind it, as he said, "Honey, shit like that you can't bury. You've gotta deal with it." His arm went back around me and both closed tight. "And part of what you gotta deal with is that he stepped out on you, and you gotta be strong enough to face another possible consequence of him bein' a piece of shit. It'll probably be nothing, but you gotta face it, find out, then put that behind you just like you need to face all this shit before you put it behind you. You can't bury it. You gotta look right at it, see it for the shit it is, understand that completely, and *then* put it behind you."

I stared into his beautiful face knowing he was right. Knowing, as all this stuff came up and I couldn't hold it back, that I had to deal with it. I wanted to bury it, but that wasn't working. So I had to face it.

And that sucked.

I stared at his beautiful face and it came to me for the first time since we lay in bed at Luci's house talking that this was Sampson Cooper.

And he could easily find a woman who was not a total mess, crying in his arms, running through sidewalk eateries like the fraught heroine of a romantic comedy, needing to get an AIDS test because her dead husband was a piece of shit.

And that was why I whispered, "You really should go."

I watched his eyes flash before he muttered softly but impatiently, "For fuck's sake, Kia."

"Sam, you're *Sampson Cooper.* You can find a woman who's not a pain in the ass, *easy.*"

"Yeah?" he shot back. "Has it occurred to you that I'm thirty-five and I haven't?"

Actually, no. It hadn't occurred to me.

Sam kept talking.

"I got the bitches who are very, *very* aware I'm Sampson Cooper. Last night, you told me you like Sam Cooper better. Last night, *I* fucked you, *I* ate you and you sucked *my* cock. Not them. They do not see Sam Cooper because they don't want Sam Cooper. They do not suck my cock. They suck Sampson Cooper's cock and tell all their friends about it."

Oh God. That stunk, but I bet it was true.

He kept going.

"Then I got the bitches who look good, dress nice and think their shit don't stink. They are not high maintenance. They are not divas. They *define* both. They get up and go to bed convinced the world revolves around them, even me. They knock themselves out to do one thing, lead me around by my dick like they have every other guy who's taken a dip in their pussy. Then they get pissed and seriously fuckin' bitchy when they can't do that."

That stunk too, but I bet it was also true.

Sam continued his litany of his experience with the not-so-fairer sex.

"Then I got the bitches who play cat and mouse, twistin' themselves in knots to convince me I'm the cat when I'm always the fuckin' mouse. I'm not a mouse, Kia. No fuckin' way. That shit doesn't fly with me."

Hmm. I wasn't sure what to make of that.

I didn't get the chance to decide. He went on.

"And I got the bitches who are so desperate to keep their claws in me, the whole relationship is a sham. They hide everything and show me nothin' but what they think I want to see. Some of 'em are good, even I can't see through them. Luci can, but I can't. Then they fuck up...they always fuck up, no one can keep that shit up without eventually fuckin' up...and I see through them. And every fuckin' second they spent with me is a lie because they haven't given themselves to me."

His hand tangled in my hair and he kept going.

"Not you. Right off the bat you're shy, hesitant, you lay it out about your husband and you're honest that you know who I am. Then you tell me you Internet stalked me, your girl's got a cutout of me and you got a yappy dog. With you, for the first time in a long fuckin' time, maybe even all the way back to high school, I'm the cat. You are not gettin' this so I'll lay it out. I like the challenge and I like it because even when you withhold from me, I like what I see. But when I break through, I see what I'll get when I finally get all of you. Even with this dance we got goin', baby, you are not lying, you are not pretending, you're just you. I've had a number of pains in the asses. I know when I find one who's gonna be worth it."

"Uh...Sam," I started, then pointed out, "when the cat catches the mouse, it usually kills it and eats it."

He grinned at me. It was different than the sweet, understanding grins he'd been giving me. Lots different. So different, I felt my nipples tingle just looking at it and his hand drifted through my hair as he pointed out in return, "Yeah, and you like it when I catch my mouse and eat it."

This was definitely true.

My body melted into his and my eyes dropped to his mouth. His hand in my hair brought my face closer, then my eyes shot back to his, my body tensed, my hand pressed into his chest and he stopped.

"I ran through a restaurant like the fraught heroine in a romantic comedy," I reminded him on a whisper. "That's crazy. That's drama. That's—"

"Real," he cut me off. "Shit was overwhelming you, you had a reaction and you're allowed, Kia. You didn't hide that either."

He moved, rolling me and pulling us down in the bed so my head was to the pillows, his arms were still around me, his torso was resting on mine and his face was super close.

"What you didn't do was, when I fucked up, hurt your feelings, you didn't call me on it. I keep tellin' you I'm not him and I'll keep doin' it until you work him outta you, baby. But in a healthy relationship, people fight. And in a healthy relationship, a fight does *not* end with you on the floor takin' a kick. That shit will *never* happen with me. In a healthy relationship, you're allowed to get pissed and in my face. Fuck, I need you to do that so I know what buttons not to push, where I can't go, and avoid those places. And I'll do the same for you. It's part of learning how to take care of each other. It's fighting, but it's a form of communication and it's also a form of trust. We have words, we come to terms, we learn about each other and we move on stronger."

This made sense, but…

"Sam, I'm getting that there's a lot I need to deal with and—"

"I'm here."

Those two words, said so quickly, firmly, they settled in my soul, deep, and they felt good there. Very good.

But…

"You…I, you…" I hesitated, then finished, "You should know that there's a lot of it *and* I haven't dealt with *any* of it. When Ozzie told me Cooter was dead, he told me it would hit me, but he didn't mean the way it's turning out it's hitting me. This, what just happened now, was the first time I cried since Cooter died, and not because he's dead, but because I need to mourn the time he took from me. With all the stuff that's coming up, I don't think I'm done. I have to talk to my folks, my friends, and *deal*."

"Who's Ozzie?" Sam asked.

"The sheriff. I've known him since I was a little girl."

"Right," Sam mumbled but said no more.

"Sam?" I called, and his arms gave me a squeeze to say he was listening to me. "What I just said, you…maybe you and me…maybe this isn't the right time and—"

He started chuckling.

I was so surprised at this reaction, I stopped talking.

Then he said through his chuckles, "Baby, I'm *here*. Honest to God, even you can't twist in your head the last two nights we've had and the day we shared yesterday and think that it isn't worth goin' through some bad shit with you to get to those kinds of good times."

Oh God. That settled in my soul too and it felt even better.

Sam continued, "We got the rest of Italy and we got Crete. When we're in Crete, we'll talk about what we'll do after Crete."

"After Crete?"

"Kia, you live in Indiana, I live in North Carolina and this is *not* a vacation fling."

"Oh," I whispered.

This was not a vacation fling. I hadn't really thought it out beyond the present, but it was safe to say the fact that Sam had felt good.

No.

Freaking great.

Sam kept speaking.

"But right now, we got that and what you gotta get is you're safe to be real with me. Shit comes up, I'm here to help you sort it. And, baby, I like where I am a fuckuva lot because you *are* real. That's the whole reason I like where I am." He grinned again. "Outside the fact you're fuckin' gorgeous, you got great fuckin' legs, you look good in clothes and a fuckuva lot better out of them."

His grin faded and his eyes changed. They warmed in a way they warmed me and he finished.

"So don't worry about that. If it happens, roll with it. I'm here and I'll roll with it with you."

I stared into his warm eyes. They didn't move. They held mine, firm and steady, and the warmth didn't cool.

He was going to roll with it with me. Like my dad taking my hand in the haunted house while everything around me was scary, Sam was offering to take my hand, make me safe and lead me through.

Wherever you are, however you got there, if it's good, you're meant to be there either because you earned it or life led you there and you were smart enough to hold on.

I needed right then to be smart enough to hold on.

I pulled in a deep breath.

Then I whispered, "Okay."

He held my eyes, looking deep, assessing where I was at.

Then he decided he liked what he saw and he whispered back, "Okay."

"We left our food and Luci—" I started but didn't finish.

Sam bent his head, touched his mouth to mine, then in a fluid motion he rolled us and I found myself on my feet and in his arms by the side of the bed.

I tipped my head back to look at him to see he was already looking down at me.

"You go fix your face," he ordered, and my hand flew to my face, but he shook his head and his lips twitched. "Yeah, you'll think it's a mess when it's not, but I'm gettin' from you you give a shit about the way you look so you'll wanna fix it. I'll call Luci and tell her you had a thing, it's sorted and we'll be back in fifteen. That work for you?"

I nodded.

Sam dropped his head and touched his mouth to mine again.

When he lifted his head an inch, he asked quietly, "Are we sorted?"

I nodded again but added a verbal "I think so…for now."

He bent his neck to touch his forehead to mine a second while murmuring, "Good." He let me go, turned me, and with his hand low at my back, giving me a little push toward the bathroom, he muttered, "Face."

I kept moving toward the bathroom but looked back to see Sam had his hand in his back pocket, pulling out his phone, his long legs taking him to the windows.

My legs took me to the bathroom.

I looked in the mirror and swallowed a scream.

Eyes red and puffy, mascara everywhere. It was such a mess I had to start from scratch.

Sam had seen me like this and told me it wasn't a mess.

He was wrong.

But I had fifteen minutes to sort it and get back to Luci, which meant I really only had ten.

So I didn't have time to think about how Sam could think me post-crying jag was not a mess or even how he could see me that way and not even so much as wince.

I had to fix it and get to the restaurant. Luci was alone and probably worried.

And, post-drama (again), I remembered I was still hungry.

10

SKIPPY'S

"We'll let you young people enjoy the rest of your evening. Kia, *ma chérie*, walk with me?"

That was Celeste and I looked at her as she spoke, seeing that Thomas was catching her hint and he got up and pulled out her chair so she could rise.

We'd had dinner together—Sam, Luciana, Thomas, Celeste, and I—and then moved to a bar for after-dinner drinks. It had been a fabulous time, a natural fit with all of them. Thomas and Sam hit it off instantly, talking sports, and Celeste and Luci hit it off instantly, talking fashion, restaurants, and spas. We laughed at Thomas's stories about people he met and things he did while he traveled. We laughed at Luci's stories about people she met and things she did while she modeled (and traveled).

Now it was late, and even though Sam had just bought Luci another drink, it was also apparently time for Celeste and Thomas to call it a night.

And it was probably the last time I'd see them. We'd exchanged contact information during before-dinner drinks, but that afternoon I'd called a very curious Teri (but I didn't share, not the time or place, nor did I have the two hours to explain it all to her) to deal with the changes to my schedule and she got me on a flight to Crete a day later. The same one Sam booked when we popped by Luci's to use her computer in order for him to do just that. Sam and I would be driving to Parma the next day, spending the night and coming back the day after, leaving early the day after that. That meant no more time with Thomas and, worse, no more time with Celeste.

Looking up at her, feeling suddenly bereft, I felt my chair move slightly and my neck twisted to see Sam had risen and was helping me up.

Farewells were exchanged. Luci and Celeste promised to meet for lunch. Sam gave Thomas a handshake and bent to let Celeste touch her cheek to his. She moved into me, wrapping her hand around my elbow, turned her head and tipped it to Sam, saying, "We won't keep her."

Apparently, I was going alone.

I looked to Sam. He tipped up his chin, a small smile on his face saying he got the message, then Celeste moved us away, Thomas following.

Thomas had found our table, a table on the back terrace around a corner and mostly secluded from the rest of the bar but still having a fabulous view of the lake. After we were out of sight of the table, Celeste leaned deeper into me, her hand giving my elbow a squeeze.

"Official approval, *ma belle.* He's lovely."

I turned my head to her and whispered, "I know."

"He has a lovely friend too. You can tell much from the company a man keeps. This says good things about him."

I grinned and repeated, "I know."

Her face inched closer and she asked, "If you know, why do I sense hesitation?"

I shook my head. We were still walking and I looked to my feet as I spoke.

"I don't know. Probably silly, but he is who he is and I am who I am and right now I come with a lot of baggage on top of that and… I don't know. I guess I wonder when he'll figure it out. I mean, he's explained what he sees in me, but I've got a lot to process. What we have is very new, and as I process, for Sam, it could get very *old.* And I can't stop thinking that, as I deal, eventually he'll remember that he can have anybody so he'll wonder why he's putting up with me."

At my words, Celeste stopped us firmly, turned toward me and opened her mouth to speak.

But it was Thomas who spoke.

"So can you."

Both Celeste and I turned our heads to him and it was only then I saw how close he was.

"Sorry?" I asked quietly.

Thomas got closer, his head tipped to the side and his eyes moved over my face.

Then he smiled a strange, small, sad smile and he said softly, "Kia, I just walked through a bar and every man we passed turned to watch you. If you think you've been at a party with Sam, to dinner with Sam, and he has not noticed this too, you would be wrong. That man is not stupid. That man knows that if he doesn't take care of what he's found, someone else will do it. He's Sampson Cooper and he is no fool. He knows a good thing when he sees it, my love. And you're right, he's very likely a man who could have anybody. That is, anybody who is his to have. So being no fool, he made certain not to delay in laying claim to you."

I stared up at Thomas, surprised, before I reminded him, "He hasn't laid claim to me. We've only just met. This is very new. Anything could happen."

Thomas leaned in close and whispered, "Too true. So I shall look forward to when we meet again. A time when I'm certain he will have chased away those ghosts that haunt your eyes and I'll remind you of this moment. A moment when the beautiful Kia doubted her power over a powerful man and she's content in the knowledge that not only did she do very well, but he did too."

That was *so* nice, my eyes filled with tears and Celeste's fingers squeezed tight.

"There *is* a reason I love him, you know," she whispered in my ear. My head turned to her and she was smiling.

I fought back the tears and smiled back.

Then I looked at Thomas and whispered, "Thank you."

His eyes moved over my face before they moved to his wife. His hand came up, his fingers curled around my arm and he gave me a squeeze before dropping his hand and whispering back, "No, my love, thank *you*."

I pressed my lips together.

Celeste moved back to my side and guided me forward, murmuring, "We must forge on. It wouldn't do to burst in gales of tears *in a bar*."

She sounded so horrified by this possibility, I couldn't help but giggle.

I walked them to their car and gave Thomas a hug and a kiss on the cheek. I moved to Celeste and she immediately folded me in her arms and she didn't do the cheek to cheek to cheek. She pressed her cheek to mine and kept it there.

My eyes started to sting again and I whispered in her ear, "Please, come visit me. I promise to share my treasures with you like you did with me."

"We will plan, *ma chérie*."

"I don't have a spa, uh…yet, but you can meet my mom. She's a really good cook."

"Better than any spa."

She was right about that.

Neither of us moved. Neither of us spoke.

Until Celeste whispered, "Why can I not let you go?"

I knew why and I held her closer, whispering back, "Honey."

Her head turned slightly, her lips almost on my ear, and she whispered in a way that sounded urgent, "Please take to heart what Thomas said. I know it must be difficult, but this is a good man, *ma chérie*. Trust him to take care of you."

My heart skipped a beat and I nodded.

"But more, trust that you're worth taking care of." She pulled slightly away and wrapped her fingers around my upper arms. "*Oui?*" she asked softly.

I smiled. "*Oui.*"

"*Très bein.*" She smiled back, gave my arms a squeeze, tipped her head to the side and whispered, "*Au revoir, ma belle.* We will see each other again soon."

"Soon, Celeste."

She closed her eyes, pulled in breath and let me go. She opened her eyes and grinned at me before she walked to her husband, who was standing at her opened door.

She folded in.

Thomas gave me another smile as he rounded the hood and called, "Get back to your friends, love."

I nodded but stood there, and when Thomas started up and pulled away, I did it waving and I kept waving until they were no longer in sight.

I walked through the bar toward the back terrace, and as I did it, Thomas's words came to me and I stopped looking at my feet and started to look around.

Then I looked back down to my feet because, at a quick scan, I saw Thomas was right.

Four men were looking at me and I caught the last one's eye before looking past him and he smiled.

Holy cow.

I didn't know what to do with that. I didn't know how to process it. Ten years ago, I'd caught Cooter's eye and back then *I* felt lucky. So lucky, I didn't even look at another guy.

And by the time I might have looked, I wouldn't. It was too late. I was too scared. I was in too deep.

So it had never occurred to me *they* might be looking.

These thoughts so consumed my head, I was on the terrace and had just begun to turn the corner when I saw Luci cozied up to

Sam, sitting very close, her head on his shoulder, and I heard her say, "You mustn't tell her. She's too vulnerable."

I stopped and took a step back, rounding the corner, my breath flying out of me.

"Luci—" I heard Sam begin, but Luci cut him off fervently.

"*No*," she hissed on a whisper. "You cannot tell her of these things, Sam. *Never*. And I think you see that you must stop doing them."

"I've told you more than once, girl, this was the last job."

"Yes, you have, Sam, and you also told me that before *this* job," she returned.

"This was for a buddy," Sam replied.

"There will always be another *buddy*," she shot back, her voice on the last word pure acid.

"Luci, girl—" Sam started on a growl, but I turned, tiptoeing away not knowing where I was going. I couldn't go back, interrupting an intense and private conversation I clearly was not meant to be hearing. But I didn't know where to go.

So, even though I had half an amaretto at the table, I went to the bar inside and ordered another one.

Fortunately, I could do this, considering amaretto was an Italian word.

Unfortunately, after I did it, I realized that I didn't have my purse with me.

Damn.

I tried to figure out how to smile and sign language my way through telling the bartender I needed to run and get my purse when the bartender put the snifter on the bar, started pouring, and I saw a bill slide across the bar to him.

I turned to see the man who had smiled at me standing beside me.

Uh-oh.

"You're American," he stated, and I stared up at him, vaguely noting he was Italian. Also vaguely noting he was very good-looking and not-so-vaguely noting I somehow had to get out of this but not knowing how.

"Uh, yes,—"

"The hair," he explained, his head tipping toward mine. "I can tell by your hair."

"Oh, right. Well then—"

"And you are quite tall. American women are often quite tall."

"Oh, okay. Listen, I should—"

"And shapely," he went on.

Oh man.

"Right. Thanks, I think, but—"

"I am Angelo."

"Uh, hi, um—"

He leaned into me as the bartender swept his bill away and left my snifter where it sat.

Shit!

"And you are?"

"Well, I'm Kia, but—"

He leaned in further. I leaned a little back, hopefully making a point and failing when his eyes dropped to my chest and he murmured, "Kia. That is very pretty."

"Uh—"

His eyes lifted back to mine, then they went over my shoulder and higher. He paled and leaned back right before an arm closed around my chest and a pair of lips brushed my shoulder before coming to my ear and I heard Sam whisper, "There you are."

Oh man!

His lips went away from my ear and I heard him ask, "Somethin' you need?" and my neck twisted and my head moved back to see his eyes locked on Angelo and not in a friendly, *I'm an American on vacation and thus will at all times act like a diplomat for my country* kind of way.

Oh *man*!

"Uh, Sam, honey, this is Angelo and he bought my drink because I forgot my purse," I lied as I threw a hand out to Angelo. Then I looked to him and said, "Um, Angelo, this is Sam, my, uh… special friend."

Ohmigod!

Did I just call Sam my "special friend?"

Before I could spontaneously combust with mortification, Angelo, eyes on Sam, spoke. "I see." His eyes came to me. "The lovely Kia, I will leave you to your friend. Enjoy your drink."

He inclined his head at me, turned away and melted into the people around the bar.

Well, that was well done.

Sam turned me so we were front to front, then his arms locked around me.

Uh-oh.

I was beginning to learn the feel of the different ways he could hold me and this felt like *danger*!

I took my time looking up at him.

My eyes made it to his face.

I was right.

Oh man.

"Sam—"

"He bought you a drink?"

"Sam, listen—"

"And you gave him your name?"

Shit.

"Sam—"

"You've got a drink at the table," Sam pointed out, again talking over me.

"Sam!" I snapped.

"What?" he asked.

"I, well…I forgot my drink at the table." This was a lie. "And the farewell with Celeste was kind of emotional." This was not a lie. "So

I needed one, like, STAT." This was also not a lie, but what he didn't know was that he was talking to Luci about stuff I couldn't hear but I heard, so I couldn't get to the one I already had. "And I was thinking about stuff so I wasn't thinking I didn't have my purse when I ordered it. Before I could figure out how to sign language that to the bartender, Angelo stepped in, and he let me say less than *you* normally let me say when you've got something to say and you keep interrupting me."

"So you let him buy you a drink," Sam stated.

"I'm not sure it was a 'let' situation since it all happened so quickly, but strictly speaking, yes."

"The word for 'no' in Italian, baby, is *no*." Sam leaned into me on the last word and I glared at him.

"I know that."

"So next time, use that. We'll look up the Greek word for 'no' so you'll be sure to know how to stop from letting that happen when we're on Crete."

"It's hardly going to happen on Crete."

"You been to Crete?"

I shook my head.

"Greece?"

I shook my head again.

"Right, well, heads up, Greek men are known worldwide as accomplished players and they like blondes. And my guess is they really like blondes with legs that go on forever, asses that, just from lookin' at 'em, they know they want in their hands and—"

"All right, all right," I interrupted him. "Your point is made."

That was when his face got super close and his arms held me in a *warning!* way.

I was not wrong and I knew this when he said, "Good. Then I'll take this time to be certain you totally get my point. Italy, Crete, Bangladesh, or Skippy's, *I* buy your drinks. No other man does. You don't give them your name to be friendly or at all unless I'm standin' right beside you and they get where I'm at. Now, do *you* get where I'm at?"

I didn't answer him. I was stuck at something he'd said in the middle of acting like a Neanderthal.

"Skippy's?" I asked.

"What?"

"You said Skippy's," I told him.

"Yeah."

"What's that?"

"It's a crab shack close to my house that Gordo and I hung at and now where Luci and I hang at."

I stared at him.

He was an ex-football player. He was an ex-commando. Ex-football-player commandos hung at bars called "Thor's" or "Jethro's Fire Rocket Barbeque" or "Hellhound Roadhouse."

Not "Skippy's Crab Shack."

"You hang at a place called 'Skippy's'?" I asked.

"Yeah," he answered.

"Skippy's?" I repeated my question with fewer words.

"Uh...yeah," he repeated his answer with another syllable and a lot less patience.

"Is its full name 'Skippy's You Can Eat 'Em but You Gotta Wrestle 'Em First Crab Shack?'"

Sam had no answer for that. He just stared down at me.

Then he didn't answer but instead asked, "Right, how the fuck am I pissed that I go to find my woman and see some guy in her space, find out not only did she let him buy her a drink but she gave him her name. I make myself clear about how I feel about that, and instead of her confirming she gets me, she's talkin' about Skippy's, and for some fuckin' reason, instead of me pushin' she gets me, I wanna laugh my ass off?"

He sounded disgruntled.

Since I didn't have an answer, and I also didn't want to make him more disgruntled, I decided to shrug.

Sam tipped his eyes heavenward and sighed.

I bit my lip.

Sam tipped his eyes back to me and stated quietly, "No, Skippy's is just Skippy's. The best fried crab sandwich you'll find on the eastern seaboard, and I say that with authority seein' as Gordo and me put some research into that. And no, Skip does not make you wrestle the crabs before eatin' them. Now, honey, takin' us back, do you…*get me*?"

"I get you," I whispered.

He stared down at me.

Then he muttered like he was talking to himself, "I don't know if I want her to figure out she's fuckin' gorgeous so she isn't so fuckin' clueless when a player marks her or if I'm glad I finally got one who looks as good as her and has no fuckin' clue."

"Are you wanting me to participate in this discussion, or are you having a conversation with yourself?"

"Your participation isn't required," Sam replied.

"I didn't think so," I mumbled, my eyes sliding away.

That was when I felt Sam's body shaking and I looked up to see him grinning. One of his hands went to my jaw, he tipped my head further back, and to my shock (but it couldn't be said, displeasure), he laid a hot, wet, deep, heavy, and *long* one on me.

I was holding on tight and breathing erratically when he lifted his head and muttered, "Now *they* get me." Then he turned me, tagged my drink and walked me back to the table.

I drank my half amaretto while I chatted with Luciana. And while we chatted, Sam had one of his arms draped around the back of my chair, his torso toward me (and in the direction of Luci), his other arm draped across my lap.

When I was into my second amaretto, Luci needed another drink so Sam got up to get her one.

But before he did, his hand gave my thigh a squeeze that caught my attention. My head turned to him and he caught my eye, the eye catch meaningful, I just didn't know what it meant. I felt my brows draw together and tipped my head slightly, his gaze cut swiftly to

Luci and back. Light dawned, I gave a slight nod, then he gave my thigh another squeeze and took off.

I turned to Luci to see she was watching Sam leave.

She turned to me and announced, “I very much like you two together.”

I smiled at her.

Then I whispered, “I very much like us together too.”

She smiled back before she scooted her chair close, turned into me and confided quietly, “Sam very much likes you two together too.”

I pulled in a soft breath and shared, “I’m beginning to get that.”

She studied my face a moment and deduced, “He is breaking through.”

“It would be hard not to, considering he’s using a sledgehammer.”

She threw her head back and laughed and I did it with her (without the throwing my head back part).

With a smile on her face, she righted her head, but her eyes went to the lake and she murmured, “Our boys, they are not subtle.”

My heart skipped.

Our boys.

Before I could say word one, she did.

“I was at a party when I met Travis. I was very confident, which was what I liked to think. My father said I was vain. Back then, I think I was. Young, I had so much attention, I liked it. I saw Travis across the room and I chose him. In that day back then, that was all I had to do. I chose them and they came to me and I made them dance. I caught his eye and he came to me. I tried to make him dance.” Her eyes slid to me and her smile was small and melancholy when she whispered, “Travis Gordon was not a man who danced.”

I didn’t know what to do, whether to touch her, take her hand, but before I could do anything, she looked back toward the darkened lake and kept talking.

"He walked away. Five minutes he spoke with me, then he tipped his chin up at me, said, 'Enjoy your evening,' and walked away. I thought it was a game. It wasn't. Three hours we were at the same party and he didn't look at me again. I thought he was trying to make me come to him while I was trying to make him come to me. Finally, I saw him leaving and he didn't even glance my way. I knew then he was not going to come to me, and worse, he was not playing any games. And it occurred to me that if he left, I would never see him again. And, I don't know, I found I simply could not let him go." Her voice dropped to a whisper. "So I followed him."

She fell silent.

I waited.

She spoke again.

"I caught him outside, walking down the sidewalk. I had on very high heels and I was nearly running. If I had…if we didn't have…" She pulled in an unsteady breath. "It would have been quite humiliating if things did not turn out the way they did. But he heard my heels, he stopped and I made it to him. Immediately, he asked, 'Done with that shit?'" I watched her profile smile another small, wistful smile. "What could I say?" She turned her head to me. "I said, 'Yes.'"

I smiled at her and mine was small too, and probably melancholy.

She looked back to the sea.

"Right then, he said, 'Tomorrow night, I'm taking you to dinner. If you make an excuse, I'll know it's a game and offer rescinded. With that bullshit in there, you bought that. Now, are we going to dinner?'" She paused, then whispered, "'Offer rescinded.' So Travis."

"I take it you said yes," I prompted softly when she didn't go on for a while.

She nodded and looked at me. "Oh yes, *cara mia.* I said yes and that was the most important word I said in my life until a year later when I said the words, 'I do.'"

I felt tears sting my nose and was about to reach for her hand when she suddenly twisted to me and reached for mine, grasping it tight, moving into my space and her other hand came up to cup my cheek.

"Three hours I played my game. *Three hours*," she said quietly, quickly, vehemently. "You must know what I would do to get back those three hours with my Travis."

My hand grew tight in hers and I whispered, "Luci—"

Her face got closer. "Do not be as foolish as me, Kia. Do not waste even *three minutes* with a good man. Do not."

"Honey, maybe we should talk about you," I suggested carefully, and this was not a fishing expedition for Sam. This was Luci and me and Lake Como and Travis Gordon having a lock on her heart from the grave, so tight it was never letting go.

"No, you are off to Parma tomorrow, then Crete, and I am not going home to North Carolina for two months. I have little time with you and I need you to learn from my mistake, Kia. I *need* it."

"Luci, that's what I think we should talk about."

She shook her head, determined to stay on her subject. "Sam is a good man."

"I know."

"And anything can happen tomorrow."

"Luci, please." I lifted my other hand and took hers from my face. Holding both of hers in mine between us, I shook them. "Nothing is going to happen tomorrow and—"

"The future is always very bright, Kia, until suddenly, one day, it becomes nothing but black."

Oh God.

"Luci—"

"Do not be angry at him, but he has shared with me about you. Not much and not much more than what I have assumed from hearing you talk to Celeste on the phone. And I care for Sam, very deeply. He was Travis's friend and he is mine, and after I lost Travis, I…I don't…Well, I don't know what I would have done without him.

We have grown even closer since and I want him to be happy. But I would not steer you or any woman wrong to make that happen. He is a good man through and through, Kia. He will take care of you. I know this to be true. Let him take care of you, *cara*. Let him make you happy. And while he's doing it, you make him happy too."

"Luci, honey, we just met a few days ago."

She looked me straight in the eye and declared, "You know."

I pulled in breath.

She went on, "And he does too."

"I—"

"And I did too. And Travis told me many weeks later, he looked across that room and saw me and he knew. And when he approached me and I was not what that looked promised him I'd be, he was very disappointed. But three hours later, he was filled with joy, because when I ran after him, he knew he was not wrong." She shook my hands. "And he was not. Nor is Sam. Nor are you."

I held her eyes. They were fretful and I did the only thing I could do.

I gave her my promise.

"I won't waste a minute, Luci. I promise."

Instantly, she smiled gleefully and released my hands but put hers on both sides of my head, pulling me forward. She kissed one of my cheeks then the other, pushed me back and demanded, "You must inform me the minute Sam proposes and I will immediately speak with Massimo."

I blinked through a heart spasm and a belly plummet. The latter was at the thought of Sam proposing. The former was at the mention of the fabulous designer known only as "Massimo."

"Massimo?" I whispered.

"Why, yes," she replied, letting me go, whisking up the dregs of her drink and sucking them back. She replaced the glass on the table and informed me, "He designed my wedding gown. He adores me. We're the closest of friends, outside Sam, of course. At my request, he would be delighted to design yours too."

I was pretty certain I wheezed audibly at this announcement, but Luciana didn't hear it because at this point Sam returned with her drink. He sat next to me and wrapped himself around me again.

Luci started chattering again while I controlled my hyperventilating and did this by sipping my amaretto. Eventually, I got myself together enough to join the conversation. I finished my drink, Luci hers, Sam his sparkling water, and Sam said it was time to call it a night. He escorted us both to the pavement, got Luci a taxi, deposited her in it and she was whisked away while waving.

Sam waited until he had me in the Lamborghini and we were on the road for the twenty-minute drive back to the hotel before he asked, "Well?"

I took in a breath.

Then I said softly, "As we suspected, it's bad, Sam."

"How bad?"

"Bad as in, if there is any possible way that you think she'd agree to professional grief counseling, she should start immediately."

Sam was silent.

Carefully, into the void I asked, "How did Travis die?"

"Assignment" was Sam's short, uninformative answer, and my mind harkened back to them talking earlier, something I'd completely forgotten about. Since I was not supposed to have heard it and he didn't know I did, I couldn't ask if Travis's assignment was official or if, perchance, it was unofficial. And further, if perchance Sam was also taking unofficial assignments, which, frankly, scared the bejeezus out of me.

So I said nothing.

This time, Sam broke the silence. "How do you know this?"

"She's lamenting the three hours she played a game with him the first night she met him, wishing she had that time back. Regretting her decision to try and make him dance. She remembers every word they spoke to each other that first meeting and can recite it. And she told me the most important words she's said in her life are, 'I do.' Last, she said that the future is always bright until one day, suddenly, it turns black."

"That's bad," Sam muttered.

"Yeah," I agreed.

Sam sighed.

I remained silent for a while.

Then I asked, "Should we ask her to come to Parma with us tomorrow?"

"I'll think about it, baby," Sam answered quietly. "But I think I need to call her father tomorrow. Vitale is worried, we've talked. She listens to him. I'll tell him this and see what he says."

"Okay," I said softly.

Sam reached out, took my hand and pulled it to him.

I thought he was going to hold it and he did. But first, he lifted it to his mouth and brushed my knuckles against his lips before he dropped it to his thigh and muttered, "Grateful for that, honey."

For a second, I didn't speak. For a second, the whisper-soft touch of his lips on my knuckles, the sweet way he did it, why he did it, grateful to me for talking to a friend he was worried about, took that moment to burn in my brain.

Then I whispered, "Not a problem," and squeezed his hand.

He squeezed back.

I kept my gaze steady out the windshield and thought of Travis Gordon being impatient with the lushly attractive Luciana's game, walking away from her, and when she ran after him, asking, "*Done with that shit?*"

That was so Sam. In fact, he almost said the same thing to me when he thought I was playing a game.

And Sam was so big, so strong, so powerful, so vital, I couldn't imagine him suddenly being none of those things and instead being nothing but gone.

So I sucked in breath through my nose and remembered my promise to Luci not to waste a second.

Fifteen minutes later, my promise was put to the test when we were standing outside my door. Sam slid my key out of my hand, opened it and held it open for me to go in. He followed me, threw the key on the table by the door and stood there.

I was walking in, pulling my purse off my shoulder when I noticed and looked back at him.

"Come here, Kia," he ordered gently.

I threw my bag on a chair and walked to him, head tilted in confusion.

When I made it to him, his arms slid loosely around me, he tipped his chin down and he said quietly, "I've been pushin', and today, I see I pushed too hard. I'm gonna give you some space tonight. You get up, call me, and I'll meet you for breakfast before we go."

I stared up at him.

He bent his neck and kissed my nose.

My nose.

"Sleep well and have good dreams," he whispered, gave me a light squeeze, let me go, turned, opened and walked through the door.

I stood there while he did all that, except, when the door started closing, I caught it.

I moved into it, leaned into the hall and asked Sam's departing back, "You're leaving?"

He stopped, turned and looked at me.

"You need space," he informed me.

"Don't tell me what I need, Sam. Only I know what I need."

He held my eyes.

I leaned further forward, stretched out an arm and grabbed his hand.

That was all I had to do.

In half of one of his long strides, he was at me, crowding me and I was back through the door. Then he bent, and with a small, surprised cry, I was over his shoulder. The door clicked shut, and in five strides, Sam tossed me on the bed.

Then he followed me down.

Eight hours and forty-five minutes later…

Sam and I walked into the dining room together holding hands.

When his eyes caught sight of us, dropped to our hands then back to my face, I didn't have to speak Italian to translate the maître d's look of pure, unadulterated glee.

11

THAT MEANS SOMETHIN' TO ME

Five days later...

It was mid-morning and I was at the pool waiting for Sam to finish working out so I could make the big move from the pool to the beach.

This was the way our days were rolling out. Up (make love), breakfast. I would go to the pool. Sam would go to the hotel gym to work out or take to the streets for a run. Then Sam would shower, come and get me (this was an added or alternate making love time slot) and go with me to the beach. In the afternoon, we'd find food, and since Sam would be d-o-n-e, done with lying around at the beach, I'd shower. We would jump in the Jeep he rented and explore.

On our first day there, I learned Sam was not a lying around on the beach man. He was an action man. Although I was a lying around on the beach gal, it was cool he was an action man because exploring was fun. It was also cool that even though he was an action man, he gave me my time by the pool and beach and he did it without complaint.

It was a nice compromise, something I'd never experienced before in my life. With Cooter, I did the compromising. I didn't know what it was like to have a fair dose of what I wanted before I gave in to what someone else wanted.

It felt good.

And with Sam, giving in wasn't giving in, as such. Giving in led to some great times.

For instance, we found a tiny, awesome fishing village set in a spectacular bay while we were exploring. We got there late afternoon and stayed there well into the evening because the open taverna where we had dinner had a band that was killer. Greek music, lots of clapping and, in the end, dancing. Though, Sam didn't dance, but an old guy pulled me up and I had a blast.

We also found the cave where Zeus was born after driving up a hair-raising mountain road that was totally worth it once we climbed further up the mountain on foot and then climbed down to Zeus's birthplace.

We also found another beach, which was the best seeing as it had absolutely nothing built around it at all. You had to trek to it and it was pure and beautiful and so relaxing, regardless of the fact that we were not the only ones there. Even Sam was happy to hang.

And the best part of Sam winding down and hanging was that a lot of the time he did it, he did it lying on his side next to me in the sand, elbow in the towel, head in his hand, chest on display, talking to me quietly. Or he'd roll to his back, pull me up on his chest and run his fingers through my hair while we talked quietly. Or he'd get to his feet, pull me to mine, guide me to the sea and we'd drift around, my legs around Sam's hips, my arms around his shoulders, his hands at my ass, him treading water or floating, and we'd again talk quietly.

After our explorations, except when we stayed at the fishing village, we went back, found dinner, then wandered to an open-air tavern and had drinks. We wandered back to the hotel and had a different kind of fun that wasn't relaxing until after its culmination.

In other words, Lake Como wasn't heaven.

Crete was.

It was perfect.

No dramas. No rushing out of restaurants like the fraught heroine in a romantic comedy. Just sun, beautiful vistas, relaxing beaches, exploration, being together and discovering each other.

The only thing that marred this was, without a variety of things to pull our attention away from each other, such as grieving friends, new acquaintances, and the aforementioned crises, it was beginning to unsettle me that Sam couldn't relax.

It was definitely part Sam being an action man and not content to wile away the hours doing pretty much nothing.

But it was more.

He seemed aware and alert all the time, like he was when we had our first dinner together. He was into me, giving me his attention, listening to me, talking to me, but even as he did this, he scanned, he observed, both our surroundings and mostly the people in them.

I tried to tell myself this was a leftover from being a commando, trained to be aware of every nuance of your environment so you were not taken off guard.

But he'd gotten out of the Army ages ago and we were in Crete, not Afghanistan. Sure, there were always a variety of dangers anywhere you were, but unless we were behind locked doors to our rooms, this was Sam's constant state.

And I'd overheard what I overheard Sam and Luci talking about, and try as I might, I couldn't un-hear it. Sam didn't mention it. In fact, he continued to be open, honest, and communicative but… not. I freely mentioned him being an ex-commando, usually in a teasing way. He'd grin, smile, even laugh. But he wouldn't share.

Maybe he thought I knew. Considering I'd Internet stalked him, it would stand to reason that I'd read the book about him (which I had).

But as our time together wore on, as I learned more about Gordo and how deep their connection was, but only through fun stories of what men got up to when they were carousing, not war stories. As I learned about his brother, Ben, but only amusing stories of brothers getting up to mischief and not how he was lost or how Sam felt about that. And absolutely nothing about his time or activities in the Army, why he got out, anything. It became less about him thinking I already knew (when I couldn't possibly) and more about him keeping things from me.

And considering a great deal of the time we shared included intimate moments and quiet conversations where he guided me through stories of Cooter. What Cooter had done. How I'd felt. Why I'd made the decisions I'd made (and Sam had gone to great lengths to assure me my behavior was perfectly natural, my decisions were rational based on my circumstances, my actions were understandable considering they were self-preserving and I shouldn't beat myself up about them). With all that, it was clear he was not shying away from deep, meaningful, revealing conversations.

They were just all about me.

On this thought, with my sunglassed eyes trained on the waters of the pool, my cell beside me rang. I picked it up and looked at the display, seeing it said Paula Calling.

I was surprised. It was way early at home. I was also freaked because it was way early at home.

I took the call and greeted, "Hey, honey."

"Problem," she announced, sounding frustrated.

Oh man.

"What?"

"Well, the other person bidding on that unit at The Dorchester upped their offer by $10K. Ten *freaking* K! Again! The text just came in. *Just now.* You made your last bid two days ago and they're texting me at five o'clock in the freakin' morning!"

I closed my eyes.

I had been on the phone quite a bit since our last full day in Lake Como. These conversations included chatting with Celeste, who was making it clear our relationship was not going to die after I left Lake Como (for which I was thankful). They also included chatting and texting with Luci, who was making it clear she was intent on building her relationship with me right along with Sam, even if she and I were in different countries (again with the thankful part). And they also included talking to and texting Paula about The Dorchester unit.

I'd made five thousand dollars more than asking price on my house, which was awesome. I had my deposit. Paula was sorting all the mumbo jumbo. I was ready to roll.

But even though the housing market had been stagnant (or worse) for over a year, not only did I do well on the sale of my house, now I was in the bidding war to end all bidding wars to get that unit.

A unit I hadn't even seen.

I'd finally offered asking price, thinking that would end it. They'd countered with $10K more. At Paula's suggestion, I'd countered with $5K more. Now they were countering with $10K more.

That meant The Dorchester unit would go, currently, for twenty-five thousand more than the list price.

That was insane.

But I wanted it. My house was sold, and once Paula sorted the mumbo jumbo, we would close and I'd have no home, not to mention I had the money.

I had no clue what to do.

I opened my eyes and informed Paula of this fact in those exact same words.

"It's all about how much you want it," Paula replied. "There's nothing like The Dorchester anywhere around. The only other condo unit is totally not as cool or well-kept as The Dorchester and it's all the way out on Six, which is, like, at least a fifteen-minute drive from Kroger and that's not during rush hour. But it's way cheaper and I know they have several units on the market. You could go for a house, but you said you don't want to deal with a yard. You could move out of Heartmeadow, but then I'd have to kill you. So really, how much do you want it?"

It wasn't just that.

Sure, I had bunches of money, but if I kept throwing it around, I wouldn't have any at all. And I'd quit my job before going on vacation. Not because I didn't like who I worked with, just that I never liked what I was doing, as in *at all*. It bored me stiff and I had a new chance at life, so I decided I'd go for it, whole hog.

I had thoughts of going home from my vacation and going to school, getting a degree or learning a vocation. I just had no idea what degree I'd get or what vocation I'd learn. I'd quit dreaming years ago. I never imagined I'd have this opportunity, and not only that, the sky being the limit. Heck, I could even go for a master's degree, become a lawyer (not that I wanted to do that), pretty much anything.

The plethora of choices I suddenly found myself confronted with as to which life path I wanted to explore was too much.

I was supposed to be sorting all this out on vacation, but instead, I was spending all my time cavorting with a hot guy and using all my headspace thinking about said hot guy.

Shit.

"I need to think about this," I told Paula, but I didn't need to think about it.

I'd never bought a house. Cooter and his parents dealt with everything when we'd bought our house.

But of the things I'd learned about Sam, I knew he had bought several.

I didn't need to think about it. I needed to ask someone with experience what I should do.

Paula cut into my thoughts.

"Right, think. You need to process, call. You want to counter or back out, text. But whatever you do, don't do any of it for three hours. I gotta crash. This Heartmeadow real estate heat up is draining me dry. I haven't had a commission in three months, now I got so much going on, I can't keep it all straight. I need sleep and I need to give my man a break from this shit. When that text came in, swear, babe, I thought he was going to throw my cell out the window. You know how Rudy likes his beauty rest."

Rudy didn't like his beauty rest. Rudy totally crashed after giving Paula the business, something Paula referred to as Rudy needing his "beauty rest." She'd shared this with us (repeatedly). She thought it was adorable. Then again, Rudy, Paula also shared (repeatedly), was energetic so after a session he'd have to crash, and the way she described it, anyone would.

Apparently, but not unusually, Paula had gotten herself some that night.

Though, this reminder highlighted that Sam was even more energetic than the most energetic encounters Paula had described, he was five years older than Rudy and he was always up before me or he fell asleep after me.

Interesting.

"Yo, babe? Are you in a Crete coma or are you with me?" Paula called, and my head twitched as I came back to the conversation.

"Sorry, honey. I'm here and can do. Three hours, no sooner, you'll hear from me," I told her.

"Okay, and while you think, remember you'll be home soon. The Dorchester isn't the only place. Who knows what'll open up? We can go to viewings. You can stay with Rudy and me or your mom and dad if you don't find a place before you close on your house."

Hmm.

No.

Or, more accurately, *hell no.*

That was not going to happen.

I loved Paula and Rudy and they had a kickass guest room, but they were semi-newlyweds who acted like newly-newlyweds. It was cute in small doses. Being a bedroom over, probably not so much.

And I loved my mom and dad, but if I was under my mother's roof, she would insist on feeding me. I'd been a married woman with my own house for seven years and I had not once provided Thanksgiving or Christmas dinners for my family. This was Mom's domain. She taught me how to cook, but she was not only a taskmaster and drill sergeant, she usually ended up shoving you out of the way and taking over, especially if you did something she thought was crazy, like, say, drain the grease from browned hamburger before dumping in the spaghetti sauce. She went ballistic when I did that, shouting, "That's where all the flavor is!" I had a hot guy who was *way* into my body the way it was. I didn't need to gain seventy-five pounds and lose him.

Obviously, I didn't tell Paula this.

Instead, I said, "Thanks, sweetie. Sleep well and we'll talk later."

"Gotcha," Paula replied. "Can't wait for you to be home, babe. Hear all your stories. Look at your pictures. And just have you home."

I totally loved my girl Paula.

And she was totally going to *freak* when she heard my stories and saw my pictures, because the last few days on Crete, more than once I'd asked a passerby to take one of Sam and me. I had at least a dozen.

And all of them were *awesome.*

We said our good-byes and rung off. I looked at the time on the display of my cell and calculated it.

Sam was either taking a shower or going to arrive back at the room imminently to do so. Therefore, instead of talking to him about something as important as my future home while kids were squealing doing cannonballs in the pool or bunches of people were squealing while doing water sports in the Mediterranean, the cool, quiet confines of our room was a better place to have the conversation.

I got up, tied my sarong around my bikini bottoms, gathered my stuff, and hoofed it up to our room.

The hotel was built into the side of a steep hill. It was also exclusive. This was partly because it wasn't so much rooms as pretty, white-walled, terra-cotta tile-roofed, little bungalows dotting the hill with meandering paths between. There were some that had two rooms in the unit. But Sam and mine didn't. When we checked in, he upgraded my reservation so our room wasn't a room with bathroom and balcony attached to someone else's room with bathroom and balcony. It was a room with a lounge, bedroom, bathroom, and veranda that was all ours.

It was also awesome.

But it was close to the top, private, and a heck of a climb.

Sam ran it on the days he ran.

I did not. Ever.

I made it to the top, pleased with myself that I was only breathing kind of heavy rather than wheezing (like the first time I took the trek). In the cool, shadowed, covered entryway, I shoved my sunglasses back on my head and was putting my key in the lock when the door was flung open.

My body jolted in surprise, then it went solid when, before I could get my wits about me, Sam's long fingers curled on my upper arm and he yanked me into our room.

Not gently.

Not rough in an *I'm gonna pick you up, throw you on the bed and ravish you* way.

No.

He just *yanked* me into the room.

He slammed the door, pulled my kickass, wood-handled, straw beach bag out of my hand and tossed it on the couch.

I blinked at the couch then automatically started backing up when Sam's big body was suddenly in my space and advancing.

My head jerked to him and I saw he had his phone to his ear. He was sweaty, in workout clothes, and he had a face like thunder.

I stopped breathing.

With his furious eyes locked to mine, Sam stopped advancing, but I didn't stop retreating. I went back five more steps until I ran into a chair.

That was when I stopped.

But even moving, I didn't…no, *couldn't* tear my eyes from the fury in his.

And vaguely I realized that he'd not only yanked me roughly into the room, he'd also made it so he was between me and the door. A big, powerfully built obstacle I had no prayer of breaching.

My heart stopped beating.

What was happening?

"Yeah," he bit off into his phone. "No comment. I don't comment on that shit. You know I don't ever comment on that shit." Pause, then his eyes went from sweltering to scorching. "I'll talk to her."

Oh God.

What was happening?

"Right. Later," he clipped, and took the phone from his ear.

My body involuntarily jumped when he disconnected, but Sam didn't speak, move, or take his burning eyes from me.

With difficulty, I pulled in breath and forced out, "Sam—"

He cut me off with a harsh "You forget to share somethin' with me?"

I stared at him, my mind reeling, trying to catch a thought.

The answer was, yes. We'd known each other a week and a half. There were probably a lot of things I had not yet shared with him. I just didn't know which one he was referring to or how—or for that matter *why*—some mysterious person on the phone was sharing unknown things about me.

"I—" I began hesitantly.

Sam interrupted me again, and when he did, his voice wasn't harsh. It was abrasive.

"Like, say, that piece of shit you married and the piece of shit he was bangin' callin' a hit on you?"

Oh God!

How did he find out about that?

And further, how did I forget to tell him that?

"They didn't get that far," I whispered, then jumped and moved back, taking the chair with me as I watched his body move with uncontrolled rage. His arm cut through the air on a vicious sidearm slice and his phone went flying into the cushions of the couch with such strength, it rebounded right out and clattered to the tiled floor.

He turned back to me.

"You got five million dollars outta that gig for whatever reason that motherfucker took out a policy on himself while he was plannin' on whackin' you. That's why you're here. That's why you were in Como. That's why you're dressin' like a fuckin' socialite and spendin' five hundred dollars on a fuckin' robe, for fuck's sake."

My breath was now coming quickly just as my heart was beating fast. Too fast. Dangerous fast. And, stupidly, my mind took that moment to remind me that I really, *really* shouldn't have bought that robe with Luci.

"How do you know all this?" I asked quietly, my voice trembling.

"Tilda?" he shot back, and my heart started beating faster.

I didn't answer, but the answer must have been on my face because he continued.

"Yeah," he ground out. "She posted that shit somewhere, who the fuck knows where, but it spread like that shit *always* fuckin' spreads and it went where it *always* fuckin' goes. My agent got a call from a reporter who said they were breakin' the story that I was on vacation with an ex-administrative assistant, current millionaire who came into her new fortune because her husband, who took a shotgun blast to the head, was plotting to make *her* dead. His alternate piece of ass was currently out on bond, awaiting trial for conspiracy to commit murder. And they wanted to know if you or me wanted to make a comment."

Oh.

My.

God!

Ohmigod!

I couldn't…this wasn't…I couldn't wrap my head around this. *Any* of it.

I never thought I'd ever be asked for a comment on *anything.*

And…

Ohmigod!

If this stuff was spreading and someone was going to write an article about us, my friends and family would find out!

"None of my friends or family knows about us," I blurted.

"*Who the fuck cares?*" Sam roared, and I pushed back.

Feeling chair, I scurried around it and kept retreating until I hit the wall of windows that faced the sea and only then did I realize I was shaking from head to toe.

Sam's eyes never left me, but they were working as was the muscle jumping in his cheek. His jaw hard. His fury filling the room.

Then he said in a carefully restrained voice that even *sounded* like it took effort to achieve, "Pissed at you, Kia. Seriously fuckin' pissed, but I'm not gonna hurt you."

I didn't reply.

"How could you keep this from me?" he changed the subject to ask.

I kept quiet and kept shaking and kept my eyes glued to him.

Sam went back to the other subject and reminded me, "I'm not him."

I nodded but kept quiet, shaking and my eyes didn't move.

Sam held my gaze.

Then he started talking again.

"You know me. You knew me before you met me. You gotta know that nearly everyone I fuck is laid out for the world to see. Most of the time, they aren't interesting except, say, when one of them has a murdered husband who was plotting with his side bitch to whack her and she comes out a millionaire. Now that shit's gonna be all over the fuckin' place and you fuckin' *Internet stalked me,* sweetheart. You knew it would and you did not give me the heads up."

"I—" I began, but he cut me off again.

"Regardless of this media shit, it's kinda important to know the woman I'm bangin' has a hit out on her."

I was beginning not to like the way he was talking to me, especially how he was referring to me.

Like.

At all.

Including the fact he called me "sweetheart" only when he was pissed at me.

"It didn't get that far," I repeated.

"You're wrong," he fired back, and my heart and breath stopped again just as I felt my lips part. "Your friend Ozzie?" he asked. I nodded and he went on, "Keepin' you protected. And when I say that, he was doin' it in more ways than givin' you peace of mind by not sharin' that the hit was called, it was paid for, and once done, there is no way to get in touch with whoever the fuck they hired in order to call it off."

My hands clenched into fists as pure fear saturated my system.

Sam kept sharing.

"He's had a man on you for months, all the while tryin' to track down whoever got the call. His hope was they heard your ex was dead and his woman was facing conspiracy charges and he'd figure he got an easy payday, know you were protected and back off. His worry was he wouldn't hear or wouldn't care and would carry out the job regardless. Until they track that motherfucker down, they can have no clue. He's been in fits since you've been gone, thinkin' that guy's after you here, which he could be."

This couldn't be true.

"That's crazy," I whispered.

"It sure the fuck is. It's also the fuckin' truth," Sam returned.

"How do you know this?"

"My agent set one of his assistants on it. They called Boothe County Sheriff Department. To say Barney Oswald was relieved to hear you'd hooked up with me is a serious fuckin' understatement. Peace of mind for him. For me, I got a woman with a hit on her, I had no clue and now I have significantly limited intel and no fuckin' weapon."

I couldn't believe this.

This was *unbelievable.*

"Why didn't you tell me?" Sam asked again.

"I—" I started again.

"I can't fuckin' *believe* you didn't *fuckin'* tell me," Sam growled, and I snapped.

Just like that.

I snapped.

I didn't remember the last time I'd snapped. It had been years since it was safe for me to snap.

But that didn't mean right then, with Sam, I didn't snap.

I sure the heck did.

"If you'd shut up a minute and let me *talk*, maybe you'd get an answer to one of your questions!" I shouted, and when I did, Sam's face turned to stone and his eyes turned to granite.

Okay, he was pissed. Maybe he had a right to be.

But I had a hit out on me!

And he wouldn't let me fucking talk!

"I didn't know this," I told him.

"Sweetheart, five million dollars says differently. Oswald's deputy shared that you called the fuckin' thing in," Sam retorted.

"I wasn't done," I hissed.

Sam's jaw flexed and I kept going.

"Pardon me, Sam, but I think you're forgetting that things have been a little crazy for me, and not just the last two weeks, but the last," I leaned in, "*seven years of my life.* Then my husband gets half his head blown off by a guy *I liked.* Milo is *cool.* And now Milo is *incarcerated* because Cooter and Vanessa are assholes. At the same time, I found out Cooter cheated on me and now I can guess it was probably repeatedly. I'm twenty-eight and I have no clue who I am. I just sold my house and I'm in a bidding war that's out of hand for that condo unit, so soon I'll have nowhere to live. I quit my job, so I have nothing to do. I came on vacation to sort my head and decide what to do with my life then I met *you.* And that wasn't exactly your everyday, run of the mill girl meets boy situation but girl meets famous, rich hot guy who she's had a faraway crush on for years and suddenly finds herself sleeping with."

I took a deep breath because I needed one, though it did nothing to calm me, and I kept ranting.

"I didn't exactly forget, but I also didn't exactly remember. I wasn't keeping it from you. I don't know why I didn't tell you. I just didn't. That doesn't mean I wouldn't get around to it. But, you know, it's been a lot nicer since leaving Italy to focus on the pool and beach and Greek music and dancing and good food and hot sex and not on the fact my dead husband and his girlfriend wanted me dead. So forgive me for not coming clean and telling you the minute I met you like I told you about Cooter being killed. I've been freaked out, unsure, and pretty stinking scared because I like this a lot, you and me."

I gestured between us with a hand and kept right on blabbing.

"This is something I *never* thought I'd have, and my apologies to the Sam Cooper who means a great deal to me, but it's partly about the fact that I'm suddenly sleeping with Sampson Cooper when that's an unheard of reality after years of fantasy. It's also about the fact that I was in a shitty, rotten marriage that was hell from the minute I woke to the minute I went to sleep. And now I have something the *exact opposite* and I don't know how to cope!"

My voice was rising so I took another breath, but I still didn't stop.

"So, if I didn't share that my husband wanted me dead while all that was going on, I'm sorry. A thousand apologies. Now, too late...but by the way, Sam, my husband was more of a piece of shit than you can comprehend because he wanted me dead and fully intended to do something about it. But the good news is, he left me his pension, he inexplicably took a five million dollar life insurance policy out on himself and left me that and he left me his dog, who might be yappy but I love her. Now you can consider yourself fully briefed."

I ended this diatribe with deep sarcasm and chest rising and falling rapidly. And I ended it glaring at him.

Sam held my eyes and kept his jaw clenched. He did this a long time.

Too long.

Long enough for me to think of a couple of other things I wanted to say.

So I said them.

"And just an FYI, *sweetheart*, you mentioned when we fight it's about learning what buttons you shouldn't push and which places to avoid. So, like you say, straight up, I don't like it that you call me 'sweetheart' only when you're pissed at me and I do not like to be referred to as 'the woman you're banging.' If those are deal breakers for you, then I'll move to a different room and maybe I'll luck out and run into another commando who'll take me to bed and keep me safe while Ozzie searches for the man who's out there maybe or maybe not planning to off me."

The minute I stopped speaking, Sam growled, "You lost it."

"I have not lost it," I snapped.

"No, baby. I mean, you had the high ground but you lost it by not shuttin' your trap and instead throwin' out there that you'd find another commando to fuck. That was low and it was *not* cool."

"Ah." I threw my hands up. "I see. So you can mouth off and say things I don't like, but I can't?"

"No, not shit like that."

"Right." I crossed my arms on my chest. "I get it, Sam. Stuff you say bothers me, it isn't as important as stuff I say that might bother you. Do I have that right?"

"You've had two lovers, him and me. He gave you nothin' for as long as you had him in your bed. You do *not* get nothin' from me. *I* get to show you that. *I* get to give you that, and not even my first when I was sixteen was my first to give that to. It means somethin' to me that when my mouth or my cock or my fingers are between your legs and I know what your face looks like, I know what you're feelin', I know I'm the only man who ever gave that to you, and that's all for me. That means somethin' to me, Kia. And you throwin' out you'd spread your legs for someone else and take that from me, that isn't just 'stuff that bothers me.' It's a fuckuva lot more."

It was my turn for my jaw to clench and it did this because I was grinding my teeth together. And I was doing that because I realized, belatedly, I'd stepped over the line.

"We fight, we fight, but we do not fight dirty," Sam tossed at me.

I held his eyes and kept my mouth shut, now because I was clenching my teeth, trying hard not to cry.

Sam crossed his arms on his chest but said quietly, "Come here."

"No."

Yep. That's what I said.

No.

His brows went up.

I explained.

"I need space. I need some time alone to come to the terms with the fact that my life is in danger. I need to figure out what my next move is. And I need some time to deal with this scene."

"What you need is to let go of that emotion you're holdin' back and what *I* need is for you to give it to me."

God! I *hated* it when he figured me out.

I shook my head and said, "No, Sam."

He studied me.

Then I watched the tension flow from his body, and his voice back to velvet, he ordered gently, "Honey, come here."

I held his eyes a moment before I twisted my neck to look out the window to our veranda and beyond, to the startling blue of the Mediterranean Sea. My body followed my neck, I turned my back to Sam, and I rested my forehead against the cool glass, staring at one of many extraordinary visions Cooter and Vanessa's evil plans gave to me. But I couldn't think, *whatever.* Not anymore.

It wasn't over.

They actually *hired* a hit man to murder me.

And Ozzie knew.

And he thought I was too fragile so he didn't tell me.

God.

On the things-in-life-that-sucked scale, this was seriously at the top of the list and would be for anybody.

Not surprisingly, on that thought, Sam was done with giving me space and I felt him fit the front of his body to the back of mine as his arms closed around me.

"They actually put a hit on me," I whispered when he did.

"No beach, no pool, and we're not hittin' that island today," Sam said quietly. "I gotta shower and make some calls, then we'll talk about what's next."

I stared at the view and sighed.

Then I said, "Whatever."

"Room service. You don't open the door, and in about two seconds, I want you away from this window."

I sighed again.

Vacation over. Fun on the Mediterranean abruptly terminated.

Cooter, dead and still a major pain in my ass, was finding new ways to haunt me.

Shit.

Sam moved me away from the window to the couch and I sat on it, knees to chest, soles to seat, arms around my calves, as he moved to the windows and drew all the curtains.

He came back and crouched in front of me.

"I have friends," he said softly.

I bet he did.

So much for Luci not wanting him to take another job. Another job sat down to breakfast with him eleven days ago.

Of course, that "job" was paternally manhandled to his table by an overly romantic, matchmaking Italian maître d', but still.

"Mm-hmm," I mumbled.

"Barney Oswald just got himself a shitload of help."

I sighed again.

He straightened, bent into me and wrapped a hand around the back of my neck as his face got in mine.

"I won't let anything harm you," he whispered, and I knew by the timbre in his voice he was very, *very* serious. But even if the timbre in his voice didn't say it, the hard, glittering look in his eyes did.

"Can you do me a favor?" I asked quietly.

"Anything."

"I know it's you and I know you're allowed to have a genuine reaction to whatever happens, including getting pissed off, but until I'm used to it, can you at least *try* not to scare the shit out of me when you get angry?"

I watched remorse score across his features. I hated to see it and I uncurled an arm from my legs.

I wrapped my fingers around his forearm and squeezed as I whispered, "Seven years, Sam. I'll do my best to get over it, but I had it for seven years. And you're bigger, you're stronger, and when you get pissed, that's all I can see. If he could hurt me, you could break me. I know you've promised me you won't and you've given me no indication you ever will. I know this is all about me and I have to work on it. I'm just asking you to help."

"I'll check it," he whispered back instantly, and I gave his arm another squeeze.

"I know you won't be able to do that…it's impossible…but I'm asking you to try."

"Baby." His face got closer. "I'll…*check*…it."

I stared into his eyes and somehow I knew he'd check it.

And there it went. That settled in my soul too.

"Well, in your defense, it isn't often you find out the woman you're banging has had a hit put out on her."

Sam stared at me. Then I watched his face warm and my heart warmed with it.

He leaned in, touched his mouth to mine, pulled back an inch and said softly, "Shower. Calls. Then we'll figure out what's next."

I nodded.

He moved in again to kiss my nose before he let me go and strode into the bedroom.

I watched him until he disappeared.

Then I watched the space where he disappeared.

I shoved my face in my knees and made a mental note to call Paula in three hours to tell her I was the woman Sampson Cooper was currently banging before she pulled up any of her gossip sites at the office (which I knew she did first thing while listening to phone messages), found out before I could tell her and lost her marbles.

Then suddenly, I whispered, "I fucking hate you Cooter Clementine" to my knees.

Cooter, being dead and buried in Indiana, had no reply.

12

MY GIRL DESERVES GENTLE

After Sam had a shower and got on the phone, I hopped into the shower and did what I did since I started things with Sam. Which meant the whole shebang of shaved legs, shaved pits, all over lotion, half squirts of perfume in strategic areas and a cute outfit of white short-shorts and a tight-fitting, coral-pink, eyelet camisole that kicked ass with my tan.

Seeing as we were on the Med and I was confined to quarters due to the possibility that my life would imminently be snuffed out, I forewent makeup and the big blow out of my hair as such effort was clearly unnecessary. But I did blow out the long fall of bangs that fell past my eyes, because really, if I didn't, it could get scary. The rest of my hair I was going to let dry curly, wavy and untamed, and if Sam thought it made me look like a wild woman raised by apes, so be it.

I had bigger things to worry about.

Seriously.

And anyway, he'd seen me at the beach and he hadn't escaped in the middle of the night so I figured I was good.

I went to the bed, lay on my back, cocked my knees, stared at the ceiling, tried and failed to eavesdrop on Sam's various conversations in the lounge, gave up on that and was far more successful in plotting Cooter's grisly death and imagining it to its culmination.

Unfortunately, Cooter was already dead.

Still, a girl could dream.

I also counted down the minutes to when I could start calling my family and friends. I wasn't sure I was going to get into the fact that my life was in danger. That might be too much after the "Sampson Cooper is doing me" news.

I had an hour left to wait and Cooter had died in twelve bloody, painful, macabre ways in my murderous fantasies that were even more bloody and macabre than having half his head blown off when I felt Sam's presence enter the room.

I kept my eyes to the ceiling even as I felt Sam's presence enter the bed.

He stretched out beside me and I felt his hand come to rest on my belly.

"What are you thinking?" he asked quietly.

"I'm plotting Cooter's murder," I answered.

This brought silence and then, "Baby, he's dead."

"Good, I can't go to prison for plotting the murder of a dead man."

"Kia—"

I turned my head and caught his eyes. "Sam, he *put a hit on me*."

Sam pressed his lips together, his eyes went hard and scary, and I made a mental note not to remind him my dead husband hired a hit man to murder me.

It was clearly time to change the subject.

"In an hour, I'm starting the round of calls to my friends and Mom and Dad, telling them about us."

"All right."

"I'm not informing them of the, uh…other stuff."

"Probably a good idea."

I drew in breath.

Sam spoke.

"Do you want some good news?"

"Yeah, Sam, that would work," I replied, and he grinned.

"Clinic in Heraklion called. Your tests came back clean."

Well, thank God for that.

Sam had located a private, clean, exclusive (by the looks of it, though I wouldn't know since he'd insisted on paying, something he insisted on doing all the time; I hadn't so much as bought a drink) clinic in Heraklion and I'd gone for my tests the afternoon of the day we arrived on Crete.

So there you go. Cooter didn't give me herpes. He just put a hit on me.

At least that was one way Cooter didn't screw me from the grave.

"Excellent," I muttered and my head turned back, my eyes going to the ceiling.

Sam's hand pressed into my belly and he asked, "What're you tellin' your folks about us?"

I stopped breathing.

Oh God.

What *was* I going to tell my mom, dad and friends about us?

I forced air into my lungs and my eyes slid to Sam.

"Uh..." I mumbled, and he grinned again.

Then his hand slid around me and he pulled me to my side, facing him. My legs fell into his, his immediately shifted to tangle with mine, and he pulled me into his solid heat.

"How's this?" he whispered. I stared into his warm, intense eyes and stopped breathing again and he kept talking. "We met. We clicked. This is somethin' we both wanna explore so that's what we're gonna do. Right now, things are up in the air so when we go home, you might be comin' with me to my place in North Carolina or I might be goin' with you to Indiana. You'll let them know when we know."

I consciously made myself breathe again and asked, "North Carolina?"

"If I think you're safer there, that's where you're goin'."

This made sense.

But I totally could not do this.

"Sam, I can't go to North Carolina with you."

His brows drew together and he asked, "Why not?"

"Well, Memphis, one. My house just sold and I have tons of stuff to do, two. I haven't seen my family or friends in five weeks, three. I've never been gone this long before in my life and they miss me, four. And I'm going to be homeless if I don't get my shit sorted and find a house, five."

To this, Sam countered with, "You got a man who knows you live in Heartmeadow who's got you in his crosshairs."

If we were writing lists, this would go in big block letters at the top of the con list for returning to Indiana.

Shit.

I closed my eyes and tipped my chin down.

Sam kissed the top of my head.

God, he was sweet.

"Tell me about the unit," he murmured.

"They upped their offer another $10K."

"Back out."

I opened my eyes and tipped my head back, shocked by this instantaneous and decisive reply.

"Really?"

"Baby, it's a condo in Heartmeadow, Indiana, not a co-op on Central Park. You're lookin' at least at putting thirty large over asking price into it in a market that is far from stable. The market could nose-dive and you'll be sittin' on a condo that's worth less than you paid for it, and in this market, that could conceivably happen in a day. No shit. This is a bad investment. Back out."

Right.

Well, that was easy.

Except…

"But I want it," I told him.

"I see that, but that doesn't change the fact that it's a bad investment, and when I say that, I mean a *really* fuckin' *bad* investment."

Hmm.

"My buyers have gone fast-track and Paula says I could close on my house in three to five weeks. One of those is already gone. If I don't find something, where do I live?"

"This shit gets sorted, move in with your folks for a while."

"Do you like my ass?"

His head jerked slightly on the pillow, then he answered, "Uh… yeah."

"Would you like it if it was five times the size?"

He grinned and his arms gathered me closer.

Then he muttered, "I'm not gonna answer that."

This was a good choice.

"Mom doesn't drain the grease off hamburger meat when making chili, spaghetti, anything. And she might *say* you can help in the kitchen, but what she means is, you can stand there, drink a beer and chat with her while she concocts meals that are at least five thousand calories a plate. Even the vegetables are fried. So, no. I am not moving in with my parents."

"Honey, you're twenty-eight. Buy and eat your own food."

At his statement, I even *felt* my eyes get big.

If I tried to bring carrot sticks and yogurt into my mother's house and inform her she could not find some way to fry the former or use the latter in a cake, she'd lose her mind.

"Are you *nuts*?" I cried, the last word rising three octaves.

Sam burst out laughing.

I watched because I liked it, but I didn't participate partly because there was a good possibility he thought I was overreacting when I…was…*not.*

When he stopped laughing, he smiled down at me and muttered, "Strike that. Your mom obviously is serious about her command of the fridge, and we're with your parents and I fuck you, you can't moan the way I like to make you moan."

That was when I felt my mouth drop open as well as my eyes get wide again.

"We're not having sex in my parents' house."

He started chuckling and through his chuckles he said, "Baby, again, you're twenty-eight."

"And honey, you grew up in LA where things are fast and loose. This is *Indiana.* This is in *the Bible belt.* LA and all the rest of the world may have hit the new millennium a good while ago, but Indiana is firmly stuck in the '50s and they...are...never...coming... *out.* And my parents are happy as clams right there until...they...*die.* You do not sleep with your boyfriend in the same bed in your parents' house, and even if we were married for twenty years, we would not stay at my parents' house and have sex. If we did, the house would explode and then everyone in Heartmeadow would know we tried to have sex at my parents' house!"

Sam burst out laughing again, but this time, he rolled into me while he did it.

When he was done, his torso on mine, smiling down at me, he murmured, "Right, so, I find a way to make you safe and get you home to your mom, your dog and your friend who has a cutout of me in her bedroom, you close on your house, we're staying in a hotel."

"We can't stay in a hotel. The only hotel in town is a motel and that was where Cooter was murdered so that's out. I like the people who own it. They go to my church. Still, it's the principle of the thing. It wouldn't do for me to stay at the motel my husband used to cheat on me then got half his head blown off in. I'd have to ask Celeste about how appropriate amongst the jet-set that is, but I'm thinking her answer will be a big, fat no."

Sam was grinning when he replied, "Probably."

"Definitely."

"Then it's North Carolina."

My body tensed and I whispered, "Sam—"

I stopped talking when his face got to within an inch of mine and all humor fled from it.

"Right, I like you, baby. I'm hopin' you're gettin' that I like you a lot. A big part of being able to keep doin' that is you need to be breathing," he stated.

I bit my lip at the scary veracity of his words and he kept talking.

"And I like fuckin' you and I'm hopin' you're gettin' that I like that a lot too, so I wanna keep doin' it. And if you're in the bedroom you grew up in and I'm on the couch and your dad feels like wrestlin' me out the door if he hears a floorboard creak, that is not gonna make me happy. The motel that piece of shit bought it in is out. So what we gotta do is, we gotta get you home, connect you with your people for a few days, get your fuckin' dog and get your ass to my place in North Carolina. My place is big, it's got a security system, I have guns and I feel more positive about the fact I can keep you safe there. Is this a plan?"

"You'd take Memphis?" I whispered.

"Does the dog come with you?" he asked.

"Yeah," I answered.

"Then yeah."

My body relaxed and I said softly, "Then yeah, we have a plan."

He closed his eyes and I saw relief in his face for the briefest moment, but I saw it. I definitely did. And it rocked me because I knew he liked me, but it wasn't until I saw that that I had an indication of just how much.

And it was then I understood his earlier anger.

It wasn't so much he was mad at me.

He was angry because he had feelings for me, he'd found out I was in danger and he was hot guy, ex-commando worried.

"Sam," I whispered, his eyes opened and his mouth came to mine.

"We got an hour before you call home and at least that until I get some callbacks. Your tests came back clean. I don't have to wear a condom so all I get to feel is you, so I know what we're gonna do with that hour."

"Sa—" I started his name but didn't finish.

His head slanted and he kissed me, hard, wet and long.

And then we did what Sam knew we were going to do.

So it was over an hour before I was again clothed, sitting cross-legged on the bed, certain my hair was beyond wild and raised by apes. Sam was murmuring on the phone in the lounge and I had my cell in my hand.

Mom first.

I hadn't spoken to her since Florence, and obviously, a lot had happened. Further, Mom was not big on not being in the know with what was up with her kids. She'd had seven years of me keeping secrets, living in denial, and thus shutting her out. From that, I'd bought nearly five months of Mom being more up in my business than Luci was in Sam's.

This could go in a variety of ways, not all of them good.

Shit.

I sucked it up, scrolled to her contact and hit go.

It rang twice, then, "Sweetie! You're home in three days!"

I smiled. "Hey, Mom."

"Oh, Kia, honey, are you having a good time?"

"Yeah, Mom, it's been great."

"Good, I'm so happy. And you've lit a fire. I've been talking to your dad for *ages* about taking me to Europe, and just the other day I saw him on the Internet looking at tourist sites for London. I think I'm going to have a good Christmas present this year!" she declared gleefully.

I kept smiling. "That's cool, Mom. Listen—"

She cut me off. "I'm calling Paula, Missy, Teri. We'll have a get-together. Margaritas, your dad's brats on the grill, and you can show us all your pictures. I cannot *wait* to see your pictures."

"Mom, I've met somebody," I blurted.

Silence.

No.

Loaded silence.

And it was listening to her loaded silence that I knew more than I already knew: that my mom had been through hell. The first and only boy I dated, I married. It was a supremely bad decision and the weight of her silence meant she wasn't feeling confident in my ability to choose another one. Especially on vacation in Europe where I could get played by a whole new field of losers. Probably also especially due to the fact that Cooter had been dead for just shy of five months and she might suspect this was a rebound.

"You know him," I told her.

"I…know him?" she asked hesitantly.

"Or, I mean, you know *of* him."

"Kia—"

"It's Sampson Cooper," I said quickly, then finished, "Sam."

More silence, then a shrieked, "*What?*"

I pulled the phone away from my ear on a wince, then put it back and told her, "I, uh…met him at breakfast about a week and a half ago. In Lake Como. We, um…hit it off. He came to Crete with me."

"You met Sampson Cooper, hit it off, and he's in Crete with you?" Mom stated.

"Yeah."

"You met Sampson Cooper, hit it off, and he's in Crete with you," Mom repeated, and I grinned.

"Uh…yeah."

"I don't…I can't…this is…" Mom stammered, and through her stammer I heard Sam call from the other room, "Baby?" and I knew Mom heard it too because she instantly stopped stammering.

Sam didn't stop speaking.

"It's lunchtime. I'm starved. I'll order. Have a…fuck, sorry."

He'd been walking in looking down at an open binder, but then he looked at me and saw I was on the phone.

"Mom," I told him, then bugged my eyes out at him.

He smiled and muttered, "Right."

He threw the binder at the foot of the bed, skirted it, came to me, wrapped his hand around the back of my head, leaned in to touch his lips to mine and said right there so I knew Mom would hear and I also knew that was exactly his intention, "Tell her I look forward to meetin' her."

"Ohmigod," Mom breathed in my ear as Sam grinned again, let me go and straightened.

"I'll let you get back to it. Have a look." He tipped his head to the binder. "Or you want me to order for you?"

"If you're hungry, just order for me," I answered.

"All right, baby," he replied, then strode out of the room.

I watched his ass in his jeans while he did it, somewhat mesmerized.

"He calls you 'baby?'" Mom whispered to me and I jerked my attention back to her.

"Yeah," I answered.

"Coop calls my baby, *baby*?" her voice was rising, both in octave and in volume.

"Mom—"

"*Ford!*" she screeched, and I took the phone from my ear but had no problem hearing her because she was still shrieking, "*Ford, get in here! Get in here right this instant!*"

I put the phone back to my ear. "Mom—" I started, but it was Mom's turn to have a conversation with her man that I was not a part of, except hers was about me.

"Woman, Jesus. What the hell?" I heard Dad ask.

"I'm talking to Kia," I heard Mom answer.

"Oh shit," I heard Dad mutter and my heart flipped.

Damn. He'd lived through hell too.

Mom didn't delay. "She's met someone."

"Oh shit," Dad repeated and my heart flipped again.

"*Sampson Cooper!*" Mom screamed, and I had to take the phone away then put it back when I heard her going on. "I just heard him, *right on the phone*. He calls her *baby*!"

Silence from Dad.

Not from Mom.

"And he said he's looking forward to *meeting me*!"

Suddenly, I heard the phone jostle, then Dad's, "Kia?"

"Hey, Dad," I said softly.

"You doin' okay?" he asked.

"Great, Dad," I answered, deciding to focus on the fact that I was, indeed, doing great outside of being scared silly that there was a hit on me.

"Havin' a good time?" Dad asked.

"Fantastic."

"This shit your mother's sayin'…it true?"

I paused, then quietly, "Yeah, Dad."

Silence, then a quietly returned, "No shit?"

I drew in breath.

Then I whispered, "No shit."

Silence again.

I knew my father liked Sampson Cooper. He said over and over again he was a good ballplayer, even when Sam was playing for the UCLA Bruins. Dad was super pleased the Colts got him in the draft. And I remembered him having a conversation with a bunch of his buddies (and Cooter, who was not a buddy, he just happened to be there) where Cooter was dissing Sam for his choice to leave football for the Army.

Dad had said firmly, "Man's got mettle. One thing to play at warrior, wearin' pads on a field. Another thing all together to *be* one."

Cooter had no reply to that, but his face got hard and his eyes got scary, though, luckily, he got over this before we got home and he could take it out on me.

Dad broke the silence. "How'd this happen?"

"Well, we, uh…were in the same hotel in Lake Como. We were seated at tables next to each other at breakfast. Then the maître d' moved me to his table, we started talking, hit it off, he asked me out. I went and we've kinda spent nearly every minute together since."

And it occurred to me just then, this was true. Except when Sam worked out or ran, when he went to his room to get clothes, and when he left me at Luci's to go back to the hotel, we had not been apart, like, at all.

Whoa.

More silence, then gently, "He know about your recent business?"

Boy did he ever.

"Everything," I whispered. "He's, uh…I've, well…" I pulled in breath. "He's not had a very good time of it, Dad. Being away from home, having time to think, stuff has come up for me and Sam's borne the brunt of that. I've tried to, well, push him away and we've had some dramas. He's helping me work through stuff."

"He's helping you work through stuff," Dad whispered back.

"Yeah," I kept whispering.

More silence.

I broke the silence.

"Dad, all the things you might think he is, he is, but he's more. He's very wise and he's very protective and he can be gentle—"

"Gentle," Dad whispered and I felt my throat close. "My girl deserves gentle."

Oh *man*.

"Dad," I choked out.

But it was Dad who cleared his throat, then he asked, "So, where's this goin'?"

I drew in a calming breath and answered, "He's coming back to Indiana with me and I'm going to deal with some stuff I have to deal with there. Then Memphis and I are going to his house in North Carolina for a while."

"Inseparable," Dad muttered.

"Sorry?"

"Nuthin', honey. I look forward to meetin' him, you tell him that."

I nodded, even though he couldn't see me, but said stupidly, "Uh…he's not Sampson Cooper."

"Say again?"

"He's not Sampson Cooper," I repeated, then explained, "It's just that, well, when you first meet him, that's all you'll see, but he's not Sampson Cooper. He's not Coop. He's Sam."

"He's Sam," Dad repeated after me.

"Yeah," I whispered.

"Right," Dad whispered back, my phone binged and my brows drew together. "What's that?" Dad asked.

"I think I have another call," I told him.

It was probably Celeste. She could leave a message and I'd call her back.

"I'll let you go," Dad said.

"No, that's—"

"You go, take your call and we'll see you in a few days. Can't wait to have you back home, honey."

"Right, Dad."

"Love you, Kiakee."

Man, I loved it when Dad called me "Kiakee." And, lucky for me, he did it all the time.

"Love you too, Dad."

"Love you, sweetie!" Mom shouted in the background.

"Love to Mom too," I told Dad and my phone binged again.

"'Bye, honey," Dad said.

"'Bye, Dad," I replied.

He disconnected. I took the phone from my ear and grabbed the next call, putting it back to my ear before seeing the name come up on the display.

"Hel—"

"*What the fuck?*" I heard Paula screech, and I took the phone from my ear with a wince again then put it back.

"Paula, sweetie, I'm so sorry I didn't text. I've decided I'm backing—"

"*What the fuck, fuck, fuckity, fucking, fuck, fuck, FUCK?*" she shrieked.

Again, I did the phone and ear business, and when she stopped squealing, I hesitantly put it back and started, "I'm not sure that unit is a good invest—"

I didn't finish.

This was because Paula announced, "I am, right now, sitting at my computer, looking at you wearing a *kickass* tank with some serious *kickass* lace at the back. But it is *not* the awesome tank I see but freaking, freakity, freak, freak, *freaking Sampson Cooper* wrapped around you and *you're kissing*!"

Ohmigod!

"Uh…" I mumbled, thinking fast.

"Uh! Uh!" Paula shouted. "What the fuck?"

"Paula, swear, I was *just* going to call and tell you that I, um… well, I met Sam in Lake Como and we kinda hooked up."

"*You kinda hooked up?*" she screamed.

I did the wince, phone, ear thing again, then put it back and whispered, "Paula, honey, you're going to shatter my eardrum if you keep shrieking at me."

"Oh, so sorry, babe. I mean, you hooked up with *Sam*, who would be *Sampson Cooper*, in freaking *Lake Como, Italy*, and there are pictures of you on the Internet *making out with him*. So, you know, considering he's a major freaking hot guy, he's been the love of your life for *years*, and you're in *Lake Como, Italy, making out with him*, I was a little out of sorts. I'll keep a freaking lock on it."

"We weren't making out," I told her and tried to hark back to if we were.

"You're standin' on a sidewalk goin' at it, girl," she returned, and I blinked.

Oh God.

Oh shit!

Tilda had followed us and taken pictures!

What a stalker bitch!

Shit! Sam was going to be pissed!

"Uh…"

"And then there are others. You two sittin' at a table, all cozy, him *way* up in your space." I heard the mouse button clicking in the background. "You got your elbow on the table and you are *way* up in his space right back. Holy crap. Holy shit. I cannot believe my eyes." More clicks. "*Ohmigod!*" she shouted. "He's smiling at you in this one! Ohmigod! I'm going to have an orgasm just looking at it."

"Paula—"

"Holy crap."

"Paula—"

"Holy freaking shit."

"*Paula!*" I shouted.

"*What?*" she shouted back.

"How many pictures are there?" I asked.

"Like, about two dozen."

Oh my God.

She went on, "Most of them are you and him sitting at a table talking or drinking wine, but others are of you at the same table, snuggled close, talking and not drinking wine. Then there are three of you going at it on the sidewalk."

Apparently, Tilda had been taking pictures of us not only after her husband came to chat, but before then, after Sam had given her her picture with him.

What a greedy cow. Sam had taken his time to be cool and she'd followed us.

"That greedy cow," I griped, totally pissed and also totally forgetting Paula was just learning this mind-boggling news. "Sam was so cool with her, taking a photo with her and her husband for their son. And then she followed us, took our picture while we were necking, and posted them for all the world to see."

"Uh…babe," Paula put in, "you wanna tell me how in *the hell* you're necking *at all* with Sampson Cooper?"

"I told you, we met and hooked up. He's here now with me, in Crete. And he's not Sampson Cooper, he's Sam."

Silence (finally).

Then softly, "He's there with you now?"

"Yeah."

Then sounding hurt, "Why didn't you tell me?"

Oh man.

"Paula—"

"I find out on a gossip site. What's *that* about?"

"I…well, honey…" I sucked in breath, then I let it out and explained, "Things in Lake Como, I…I met him and he likes me, sweetie, like, a lot. And just when we met, things started to hit me. Things I couldn't push to the back of my mind anymore. And, well, they started to come out and he was there and he's…" My voice dipped. "He's amazing, Paula. Everything you can imagine Sampson Cooper to be, Sam is better. He's been wonderful to me."

Another moment of silence, then, "Have you slept with him?"

Oh man.

"Yes," I whispered.

"Ohmigod," she breathed.

"Paula—"

"Is he good?" she asked.

"I…you know, I'd rather not talk about that. For Sam. He's… women in his past…well, that's between Sam and me, okay?"

"He's good," she whispered her correct guess.

I changed the subject.

"He's coming home with me. We're going to deal with stuff, get Memphis, then I'm going to North Carolina with him."

"Ohmigod."

I made no response.

Then Paula said, "He's into you."

"Yeah," I confirmed.

"Like, a lot."

My belly started to get warm and I whispered, "Yeah."

"Ohmigod, this is so…*cool*."

I grinned. "Oh yeah."

"Wow. I cannot wait to meet him. This is *so cool*. Rudy is already stinking flipping. I'm still at home, I showed him the pictures. He *loves* Coop. You know that. And Teri is gonna *fah-REEK*!"

"Yeah, I know. And Paula, I'm going to call her and Missy just now. But just to say, I'll be home soon with Sam and you guys all have to be cool about that. He is who he is to the world, but he's something else in real life and this is real life, not TV, not the Internet, and you all have to be cool."

"I can be cool," she assured me.

"No freaking out. No asking for autographs. No asking for photos. This is just Sam."

"I can do just Sam. So can Rudy."

We would see.

"Okay," I said.

A pause, then, "You're happy."

Outside the hit called on me, absolutely.

I didn't say this. I just said a soft, "Yeah."

"Oh, honey, babe, oh God." I heard tears in her voice. "Oh my God, I love this for you. *I love it.* I told you your luck had changed."

She was right and wrong about that, both in big ways.

She let out a sobbing hiccough.

"Paula, sweetie," I whispered.

"I love this for you. I *love this for you,*" she said through her tears.

"And I just love you," I replied.

Another sobbing hiccough.

I let her do her thing for a while, then I called softly, "Paula, honey, I have to go. I need to call Missy and Teri."

I heard her pull in a steadying breath, then she murmured, "Right."

"See you soon."

"Can't wait."

"Me either, sweetie," I said quietly.

"I love you, Kia, and I'm so happy for you it isn't funny."

"I love you too. Oh, and let the unit go. Sam says it's a bad investment in this market. We'll do some viewings. I know you'll find me something else."

"You bet your bippy," she told me. "And Sam's right. This market is volatile. Now that it's not five o'clock in the morning and I'm thinking clearly-*ish* after this whole thing with you and *Sam,* I'm seeing that's crazy. We'll get you sorted. Yeah?"

"Yeah."

"All right. Later, babe."

"Later, sweetie."

We disconnected. I drew in breath, staring at my phone then I jumped when I heard Sam say quietly, "Thank you, baby."

My eyes flew to the door where he was leaned against the jamb, arms crossed on his chest, one foot crossed at the ankle.

Seriously, he was hot and I suspected he was so hot, I'd never get used to how hot he was.

Which was cool.

"Thank me, what?" I asked.

"Your girl asked what I was like in bed, you didn't tell her. Thank you."

I blinked. Then I asked, "You were listening?"

"Fuck yeah."

I felt my brows draw together before I asked, "Why?"

"Mainly because I've had women play me in the past, I got burned. They were good. You could be the master and I gotta say I'm pretty fuckin' pleased to find out you're not. You're what I thought you were. You're just Kia."

Okay, it kind of sucked he'd eavesdropped, but then again, I'd been trying to do that to his conversations all morning.

And he had a point. Once bitten, twice shy. A gazillion times bitten, two gazillion times shy.

"Yes, Sam," I said quietly. "I'm just Kia."

He held my eyes, his entire face warm, his eyes both warm and intense, and I really liked when he looked at me like that.

Then he said, "Lunch is comin'. More good news, got a buddy who's got a buddy who's got a place here. He's also got skills and hardware. He's retired so he's also got time. This means he's okay with bein' another pair of eyes. You and I do our thing here, he'll kit me out and have our back."

I stared at him.

Then I sought clarification.

"Are you saying he's going to be our bodyguard?"

Sam nodded once. "That's what I'm saying."

"And are you saying that he's giving you a weapon?"

Sam nodded again, his eyes never leaving me, and he repeated, "That's what I'm saying."

I went back to staring at him mutely.

Sam, being Sam, felt like being communicative.

"He's good, he knows what he's doin', and between him and me, no one will get at you. We can enjoy the rest of our time here and get you home. In the meantime, I got boys doin' their thing to see about coverage in Indiana. By the time we touch down in Indianapolis, you'll be golden."

Wow. Seriously. He was not wasting any time looking out for me.

I didn't know what to do with that. The only thing I knew was that it felt really freaking good.

"Okay," I whispered.

"I'll be talking to Barney Oswald too, baby, just so you know."

"Okay."

He studied me in a way that it occurred to me maybe I didn't quite understand his simple statement.

Sam confirmed my assumption.

"When I say that, I mean I'll be talkin' to him to find out what's up with his search for this guy, and I'll be talkin' to him to find out why the fuck he didn't give you a heads up."

"He's a really good sheriff, Sam, has been for years because he's a good guy and he's protective of his citizens. But he's known me since I was a little girl. He hunts with my father and I know he figured out what went down with Cooter and me."

"That might be so, but it was a jacked decision."

"Sam—"

"It was jacked, Kia. I know this because you went off to fuckin' Europe unprotected. The least he could have done is informed your dad or your brother so one of them could have talked to you, talked you out of goin' and assessed where your head was at about whether you should know it all or not. Not to mention, you should have had a security system installed in your house, even if you're sellin' it."

"Kyle lives in Tennessee, Sam, I told you that. He's too far away to do anything."

"What you tell me of your brother, Kia, Kyle lives in Tennessee or fuckin' St. Petersburg, Kyle will wanna know his sister is in danger, then he'll wanna see to it that his sister is protected and safe. The men in your life should have been briefed. Barney Oswald screwed the pooch. That is not gonna happen again."

He held my eyes and I thought it prudent to nod, seeing as he was a commando, I was not, so he probably knew what he was talking about.

Not to mention, he was totally right about Kyle. Dad and Ozzie were buddies. Dad could probably be talked into not being pissed. Kyle was going to freak.

So I nodded.

There was a knock on the door at the same time there was a chime on my phone in my hand.

"Lunch," Sam muttered.

I looked at the display and muttered back, "Teri."

Sam looked at my phone, looked at me and grinned.

Then he turned and disappeared on his way to the door.

I took the call, and learning, I didn't put it to my ear when I started, "Hel—"

"*Oh my fucking God!*" Teri shrieked.

I grinned.

"Room service," I heard in a Greek-accented voice.

I wondered briefly what Sam ordered for me.

Then I put the phone to my ear.

13

YOU'RE HAPPY

Three days later...

Sam took the key from my hand, inserted it in the lock in the front door of the soon-to-be-not my home in Indiana, turned it and opened the door for me.

I shoved in.

I had my overnight bag and purse over my shoulder and both my hands were laden with duty-free shopping bags.

Sam had his bag over his shoulder and was rolling both my huge, stuffed near to bursting pieces of luggage.

I was always grateful that Sam was a gentleman. It was one of the plethora of things I liked most about him.

But at that moment, I *loved* it.

With a droop of my shoulders that I wanted to do five seconds after hooking the straps on them, I dumped all my stuff on the floor five feet in.

Yes, even my purse.

"Leave them there, baby," I muttered to Sam as I meandered through the living room to the hall to my bedroom.

I got to the bedroom, flipped off my flip-flops and was crawling on all fours up the bed when I heard Sam call, "Kia, honey."

"Nap, fifteen minutes, then I'll call Mom and go get Memphis," I mumbled.

Then I collapsed.

After that, I promptly passed out.

Indeterminate hours or minutes later…

I woke up but didn't open my eyes.

I hated my house, but I had to admit, it was cute and this was mostly due to Cooter's mom having good taste, since even back then (red flag?), I had no say.

But it was not built of high-quality materials, which meant the walls were very thin.

Therefore, I clearly heard Sam's conversation in my living room with an unknown man.

"…set up?" I heard the end of whatever Sam was saying.

"Full coverage, four guys, three shifts. Couldn't do the alarm but got trips set on doors and windows. You bunk down for the night, last shift'll set 'em. Anyone trips 'em, the whole neighborhood'll wake up."

"Good," Sam replied.

Then I heard indistinct noises that sounded an awful lot like the noises people made on TV and in movies when they were expertly fiddling with a gun.

"Know you favor a nine millimeter. We're on that. Right now, that's gonna have to do," the unknown man told Sam, proving me right. Sam was expertly fiddling with a gun.

"How long before you can get your hands on the nine?" Sam asked.

"Tomorrow," the man answered.

"Good," Sam repeated.

"You gonna keep both?" the man asked.

"Yeah," Sam answered.

"Would too," the man said, then asked, "How you want us to play this?"

"Don't care you get made. He sees she's protected, that's fine with me," Sam replied.

"Copy that. You got hunters?"

"Yeah, but they're workin' mostly blind. Sheriff has shut down. Need a brief with him, then I'll have more intel for you and the boys out workin' this."

"Right."

I heard the front door open and Sam's "'Preciate this."

A moment of silence, which I suspected included a cocky, masculine head nod or jerk of chin, then, "Town talk, he knocked her around."

I sighed.

"Town talk is not wrong," Sam said in what was weirdly a seriously annoyed growl, and when he went on, I would know why. "But even knowin' it, not one fuckin' person did fuck all about it. Seven years."

"Jesus."

"She's done with livin' scared," Sam stated.

"Yeah," the man agreed.

"So like I said, appreciate this," Sam kind of repeated.

"Yeah," the man replied.

The door closed.

I lay there, eyes closed, feeling the bizarre but far from unwelcome sensation of being in my house, a place that was unsafe for me for years, and feeling safe and doing it at a time when I was arguably more unsafe than I'd ever been.

But it was more. It was knowing Sam was not messing around with making me safe and that was far from unwelcome too.

But I was getting used to it.

Even so, it was not becoming any less precious.

Wanting to roll out of bed and go to Sam, exhaustion wouldn't let me and I hoped he'd come to me.

I fell asleep again before he did.

Four hours after arrival home…

My eyes flickered open and all I could see was the wall of Sam's chest covered in a light blue seriously-wrinkled-from-three-hellish-flights shirt.

I blinked, feeling weird, and I knew this was partly because of the three hellish flights but also because of jet-lag.

Then it hit me my cheek was on Sam's shoulder, one of my legs was tossed over one of his and my arm was around his gut.

He wasn't moving. He was breathing steady so I carefully lifted my head so as not to wake him and looked at him.

Stubble. Fabulous eyelashes. Gorgeous.

Sam.

In my bed.

In the bed I had shared unhappily with Cooter.

All the beauty that was Sam, right there, where Cooter had laid his head.

Okay, call me crazy vindictive, but I freaking loved that. One look at Sam lying there beside me could easily wipe out seven years of the memory of Cooter doing it.

And I knew this because it did.

I cautiously pushed up, then bent to brush my lips against his, thinking he'd continue to sleep, I'd get up, call Mom, write a note, go get my dog and maybe pop by the grocery store for some food to make us dinner.

I was pulling back when both of Sam's arms closed around me, he rolled, and I ended up on my back with all of Sam on me.

"Honey," I whispered, my arms moving around him, my eyes catching his.

"Two choices: I eat you then fuck you in bed then we shower, or I eat you in bed then I fuck you in the shower."

I stared up at him, indecisive due to being just awake and jet-lagged not to mention spoiled for choice.

"Uh…" I mumbled.

Sam, always decisive, decided.

"Eat you and fuck you here, then shower," he muttered.

His head dropped and he kissed me.

Then he ate me.

Then he fucked me.

After that, we showered.

I was standing in the bathroom in nothing but my brand-new, beautiful, silk, purple-with-big-pink-flowers robe that cost more than many people's rents, rubbing moisturizer on my face. Sam was in the bedroom having dragged all our luggage in after we took our shower, thus I had my robe and moisturizer. He was wearing nothing but a pair of jeans.

This was our state when it happened.

I was rubbing moisturizer in but mostly looking at Sam out of the corner of my eye because he was bent over, pawing through his bag, probably looking for a clean shirt, but the muscles of his arm and back were flexing and contracting. It was more than a little fascinating, so since I was concentrating, I saw it when his head snapped up.

Then I heard, "There's a car in the drive. Where do you think they are?"

Mom.

"Maybe they went to the grocery store."

Teri.

"Maybe their flight was delayed or something. Kia said she'd text when they landed and she hasn't texted."

Oops.

By the way, Paula.

Then there was a yap.

Memphis!

Sam's head was no longer looking toward the door of the bedroom but turned to me in the bathroom, his brows up, but he was still leaning over his big, leather duffel bag.

"Memphis and the girls," I said on a smile, putting down the moisturizer and starting toward the door, my mouth opening to shout my greeting.

I didn't make it before I heard.

"Ohmigodohmifucking*GOD*!"

Teri.

Sam's head jerked back toward the bedroom door and I started rushing, but while doing so, I heard whispered, "Holy fucking shit."

Paula.

I made it to the bedroom to see Teri, shoved by Paula, who was shoved by my mother, all entering the room.

Memphis did too, bouncing and yapping straight to me.

I totally forgot about the girls.

"Baby!" I cried and crouched. She jumped into my arms and immediately started licking my jaw as I held her at the same time giving her scratches and straightening. "I missed you, girl. I had a *great* time, but I sure missed you."

She yapped then she licked me.

"Kia, baby," Sam muttered, my head moved from grinning down at my dog to him to see he was straightened and his eyes were still at the door.

I looked to the door.

"He calls her baby," Teri breathed, her eyes big and glued to Sam.

"I know," Paula breathed, her eyes big and glued to Sam.

Mom just stared at Sam, eyes big and glued to Sam's chest.

No one moved or said another word.

"Is this what you guys call being cool when you meet Sam?" I asked, cuddling my dog and glaring at them. "You're all drooling. Even you, Mom." And, uh…*yuck*. "For goodness' sakes," I finished.

Three female bodies jerked and their eyes came to me. Then *they* came to me, rushing me and nearly bowling me over. Memphis yapped. Thinking the attention was for her, she started trying to lick them all as a gift for them being generous with their attention as they huddled and hugged me.

Teri and Paula took a half a step back (Mom stayed latched to me and Memphis) and all three grinned at me.

"Girl, that robe is fah-ree-king *fabulous*," Teri noted, her eyes doing an up and down on me. "Where'd you get it? Paris?" she asked when her gaze settled on my face.

"Lake Como," I told her.

"Scorching!" she declared, and I smiled at her.

Mom's hand came out. Her fingers curled around my jaw, she turned my head to her and she studied me.

Then she remarked, "You're tan."

I grinned at her.

Her eyes went funny and she whispered, "And you're happy."

My grin wobbled because I read her eyes were happy too, and I hadn't seen that, not in a long time. Not when she was looking at me.

She let my jaw go and her gaze went to Sam.

So did mine, Teri's, and Paula's.

Memphis yapped into the silence.

Sam now had a shirt on, partially buttoned. It was pale yellow and cotton (not linen), but it was still wrinkled from being in his bag.

Nevertheless, he worked it.

Mom let me go and walked to Sam as he did up another button.

"You're Sam," she declared, extending her hand.

"I am." He took her hand and smiled down at her.

"Ohmigod, *hot*," Paula breathed, and I shot a killing look at her that she missed seeing as she was staring at Sam.

"I'm Essie Rigsby. You can call me Essie. I'm Kia's mom," Mom pointed out the obvious since I looked nearly exactly like her except less round and younger.

"I guessed," he muttered, giving her hand a visible squeeze before letting it go while saying, "Good to meet you."

"And you," Mom whispered.

"Ohmigod, I think I'm gonna cry," Teri muttered.

Memphis yapped.

"Right, okay, how about this? I'll finish the introductions *not* in my bedroom. Is that a plan?" I suggested.

"No freaking way," Paula replied, then moved quickly to Sam. "Hey, Sam. I'm Paula. I've been best friends with Kia since forever, and if you want to know any dirt, any dirt at all, all you have to do is ply me with tequila."

"Paula!" I snapped because this was totally tactless at the same time totally true, which made it tactless *and* scary.

She didn't even look my way and this was probably because Sam was smiling down at her, squeezing her hand and she was visibly transfixed.

Then she pulled herself together to whisper, "Dude, I so totally know we're supposed to be cool with you, but I gotta have this one. You...are...*awesome* and my husband loves you."

"Paula, seriously—" I started.

"My turn!" Teri shouted over me, then rushed to Sam and knocked Paula out of the way (yes, *knocked*). Paula went flying, Teri grabbed Sam's hand and declared, "I'm not going to be cool. I clocked you when you were a Bruin. I'm into football. Kia isn't, so in girl land, normally, that would mean I could lay claim to you and get first dibs. But, obviously, in real life it doesn't work that way, which kind of sucks, but whatever. I still get to meet you and you're in my best friend's bedroom and she's wearing a robe and I think that...is...*awesome*."

She ended this breathy, bright-eyed and leaning into him.

All right, now I kind of wished the hit man was aiming and about to fire through my window.

Unfortunately, the curtains were closed (something Sam was particular about) so he would be shooting blind and he might hit my mom or Sam.

"Teri, seriously?" I asked.

"You the one who has a cutout of me in your bedroom?" Sam asked over me, releasing Teri's hand, and she turned woodenly toward me.

"You told him that?" she breathed, noticeably pale and obviously mortified.

Shit.

I threw a quick glare at Sam before I rearranged my features and looked back at Teri.

"Well, uh…I was in my trying-to-drive-him-away phase and it kind of slipped out," I explained.

"You were in a driving-him-away phase?" Paula asked and my eyes went to her. "Babe, are you loco?"

"Maybe at the time, temporarily," I muttered, my gaze sliding to Sam to see now he was smiling at me.

"I'll say," Teri muttered back.

"Right," Mom cut in, and I looked to her to see she was digging in her bag. "Ford's chomping at the bit, wandering around with the matches, ready to fire up the grill." She pulled her cell out of her purse and looked at me. "You were supposed to text when you got in. If you had, we would have told you to pop by but you didn't. So, sorry, sweetie, but surprise, your dad and I planned a welcome back party for you and it's kinda happening right now."

"What?" I asked as Sam moved to me, slid an arm around my shoulders and pulled me into his side.

The room went still. No one moved. No one spoke. They all just stared at Sam, me and Memphis.

All except Memphis, who yapped and tried to reach Sam's fingers at my shoulder with her tongue.

"Hello?" I called into the void. "What? There's a party happening right now?"

Mom blinked, then focused on me but not my question. "Couldn't see it in my head, but there it is right in front of me. You two look real cute together."

Sam chuckled.

I snapped, "Mom!"

"What?" she asked.

"Party?" I prompted.

She nodded, turning her attention to her phone, muttering, "Margaritas, beer, brats, Essie's world famous homemade onion rings and Nutter Butter, hot fudge, ice cream parfaits for dessert."

There it was. Mom's world famous homemade onion rings were double dipped in beer batter, which meant they not only had twice the batter, that batter absorbed twice the fat and, thus, they were awesome. And Nutter Butter, hot fudge, ice cream parfaits were wicked good. They had crumbled Nutter Butters in them, hot fudge she made that had two sticks of butter and half a bag of sugar in it, and my mother actually wrote to a frozen yogurt manufacturer once to request them to provide her with the knowledge of what was the point. So, suffice it to say, the ice cream would be premium.

I looked at Sam and said, "Told you so."

Sam smiled down at me.

"Freaking, freakity freak, that smile is good," Paula whispered, and my head jerked to her.

"Would you stop perving on my boyfriend right in front of me?" I snapped.

"Babe, your boyfriend is Sampson Cooper. You gotta get used to that shit. I'm doing my best friend duties and helping," Paula fired back.

"Ford," I heard Mom say and looked to see her talking on the phone. "Yeah, they're here. They made it, safe and sound. They needed a little..." She paused, took in my robe, her gaze gliding over Sam's half-buttoned shirt but studiously avoiding Sam's eyes, and she kind of but not totally lied, "Rest. Kia needs to spend half an hour on her hair and twenty minutes on her makeup and they'll be over."

"Yep, that's your mother," Sam muttered.

I shot him a look.

He ignored the look, let me go and took Memphis from me, lifting her up so they were eye to eye.

"You Memphis?" he asked my dog. Memphis yapped her affirmative while I stared at them thinking that no one but no one (but *no one*) but Sam could make talking to a King Charles spaniel eye to eye cool.

Sam curled Memphis into one of his arms and rubbed her head with his other hand. Memphis panted happily and Sam's eyes came to me. "She's cute."

"Told you that too," I said softly.

He grinned at me.

"Right!" Mom stated loudly, shoving her phone in her bag. "Your father says the match has been struck, the grill has been lit. This means I need to get home and man the deep fat fryer. You've got half an hour. Bring your camera." Her eyes went to Sam. "Very nice to meet you, Sam, and see you in half an hour." Her eyes swept through the girls. "Out to the car. Kia has to get ready and iron Sam's shirt, so we need to leave her to it."

"I'll iron your shirt," Teri offered, her eyes on his chest, and I could be wrong, but it looked like they were glazing over.

"I think I got it, Teri," I told her.

I watched her body jerk.

"Spoilsport," she muttered to me on a grin.

"All right! See you guys in half an hour," Paula stated, hooking Teri with an arm and moving to follow Mom, who was already out the door. This was because she knew from experience when Dad was at the grill, the whole world began revolving around his grill efforts and she was part of that world so she had to get her ass in gear. "Rudy's at your mom and dad's. He's *psyched*. This is gonna be *so fun*."

"Later!" Teri called on a wave.

"Later!" Paula pulled her out of sight.

"Later, guys," I called as Sam's arm curved around me again and curled me into him and Memphis.

I tipped my head back to look up at him.

We heard the front door close.

"You don't have to iron my shirt," he informed me, and I felt my eyes widen in shock at his intimation, not capable of wrapping my head around the thought of Sam standing at an ironing board, much less ironing.

"Are you going to do it?"

"Fuck no."

Well, there you go. I couldn't wrap my head around it because it wasn't going to happen.

"Sam, just a reminder, you're in Indiana," I told him. "Mom's hint was not a hint so much as a command. We're considered a couple. I might be flogged if I allow my man to go out with a wrinkled shirt. I'm jet-lagged, feel weird, am about to face a party where everyone is going to *not* act cool with you, so I'm not in the mood to fit being flogged in that schedule."

He chuckled and through it offered, "How's this? You get ready but tell me where the ironing board is. I'll set it up."

"That's a plan. The ironing board is in the mudroom off the kitchen."

"Right," he muttered, dropped his head and kissed my nose. Memphis yapped and then he let me go and strode from the room, again rubbing Memphis's head as she panted happily.

My eyes followed.

Then my brain processed through the last ten minutes, the brilliant hour before that and the fuzziness of being in a different time zone when it hit me that he took Memphis with him while giving her head rubs.

Sam liked Memphis.

Awesome.

I smiled, then rushed into the bathroom in order to accomplish the formidable task of folding fifty minutes (my mother was not wrong) of getting ready into twenty.

I failed and we were ten minutes late.

They were eating Dad's brats and Mom's onion rings, we arrived with Sam carrying bags filled with the gifts, not to mention the fact he was Sam, so no one noticed.

14

I LET YOU DOWN

Well, if I didn't already know that the Internet was prevalent in our society, not to mention people in a small town talked, the evidence of this would be overwhelming at Mom and Dad's barbeque, considering how many folks "popped by" to welcome me home from vacation like I'd come home from a two-year Peace Corps assignment at a location where no communication could be had instead of being in Europe for five weeks.

At first, this upset me. Sam was not a museum display, and although a few of the folks who "popped by" were cool, most of them were clearly there for the sole purpose of seeing him. They were starstruck and, thus, acting like big dorks.

Sure, it could be said that just two weeks ago I, too, acted like a big dork when faced with sharing breathing space with Sampson Cooper. But just then, I was jet-lagged, tired and my mother, father and closest friends were meeting my new boyfriend for the first time and he just happened to be an internationally known and beloved hot guy. Even at the best of times and with a new boyfriend who wasn't an internationally known and beloved hot guy, this would put me on edge.

These weren't the best of times so I didn't have the patience for it.

But as time slid by, it penetrated that Sam was a practiced hand at this. He was friendly, accepting and had an ability to make people quickly feel at ease.

What I didn't know was if this was taxing for him.

This was because, almost the minute we hit my parents' deck after Sam met Dad, Missy, Rudy and our elderly widowed neighbor, Mrs. O'Keefe, Sam deposited me in a chair that was resting against the siding at the back of my parents' house, bent to me and whispered in my ear, "We gotta be outside, you're gonna stay right there."

He lifted his head, looked in my eyes, his were serious so I nodded.

Clearly, if someone was insane enough to shoot at me in my parents' yard during a barbeque, my position as decreed by Sam gave them a not-so-good shot.

Also clearly, Sam was not taking any chances with someone being insane enough to shoot me at my parents' barbeque. That said, to actually *be* a hit man, you had to have some screw loose so obviously caution was a good way to go.

So, holding court in my chair at the back and with Sam called to meet half the town, I hadn't had a second even to speak with him much less take his pulse.

Luckily, this died down, but I still didn't have a chance to make sure Sam was cool. This was because we got down to the business of a welcome home—everyone looking at the display on the back of my digital camera as they clicked through photos, them asking questions, me telling stories and giving out presents and those who meant the most to me in the world getting used to having me home and becoming comfortable with Sam.

This was until Ozzie, in uniform, popped by. I suspected Ozzie was there to see Sam, but I also suspected he was there for other reasons, namely to see if I was still breathing.

What I *knew* was, the minute Sam saw him in uniform, got his name and shook his hand, Ozzie's visit was going to take on a whole other meaning as defined by Sam.

Ozzie, being Ozzie, clocked this immediately, and as he sat enjoying a Coke, his eyes often strayed to Sam.

Sam, being Sam, didn't delay in sorting out what he felt like sorting out.

And this was done at three sips into Ozzie's Coke (I counted) with a "Ford, sheriff, let's have a minute inside with Kia."

Ozzie sighed, unsurprised.

Dad's eyebrows shot together and he looked at Sam then me.

"Is everything all right?" Mom asked.

Since it wasn't, Sam didn't answer. What he did do was get out of his chair next to mine, then gently pull me up.

"All's well, Essie," Ozzie muttered, also straightening out of his chair and Dad followed suit, looking slightly bemused and not-so-slightly concerned.

"I'll come with," Mom decided and popped up.

Ozzie gave Dad a look. Sam gave Dad a look.

Dad took in these looks and looked at Mom.

"Give me a minute with Oz and Sam, hon."

"I don't—" Mom started.

"A minute, Ess," Dad stated firmly.

Mom's mouth got tight, her eyes started shooting daggers and I held my breath because I'd had twenty-eight years of this.

Dad was a man's man, through and through. He poured cement for a living. He had his own business doing this. He did the best job of anyone in three counties. And he didn't employ slackers and that was known throughout town, maybe even statewide, seeing as your ass was fired on the spot if he found you not working to his exacting standards.

Also, I knew of two bar brawls he'd gotten into in town, though I didn't know the reasons he had them, but to me, bar brawls for any reason screamed *man*!

He hunted (even though Mom, and then me, when I was old enough to voice my opinion, hated this).

Further, interrupting him during the Super Bowl, the World Series, or the NBA playoffs was punishable by death. I didn't know this for a fact, mainly because I, like everyone else in my family, never interrupted him.

He drank beer, not wine, not cocktails, but if he felt like branching out, he might drink bourbon but only neat. You didn't even *look* at the grill with the intention of using it because that was his domain. He mowed the lawn. He serviced the cars. And on occasion, what he said went.

Mom, on the other hand, although they met and married relatively young, was independent and strong-willed. She'd been a mom and a housewife and still went to night school when I was a kid so she could get her degree, then moved on to get her master's. It took eleven years, but she did it. Through this she worked part-time, finally getting a full-time job in the field she'd studied, Speech/Language Pathology.

Yes, she cooked. Yes, she cleaned. Yes, in our household, Dad never did any of this. And yes, she did all this without complaint. But she had a say in her children's lives and a definite hand in our upbringing. She might have been busy, but she was not absent.

No, strike that. She had a say and an opinion about everything and didn't mind voicing it.

And on the occasions my dad had something to say that he thought went and Mom disagreed, things could get hairy.

Like they appeared to be doing now.

Until Sam stepped in.

"I appreciate you've cottoned on, Essie," he said with quiet understanding. "But there are things I need to share with the sheriff and Ford that I need to keep confidential for now. It's about what I do. What Ford can share with you, he'll share with you later. But I need to be able to be forthcoming and the fewer people who hear this, the better."

Although this could only make anyone more curious, and from the looks on everyone's faces, they were, Sam's rough-like-velvet voice coupled with the quiet understanding could not be denied. Not even by my mom.

She held his eyes for a scary moment though, but she must have liked what she saw because she sat back down.

Without delay, Sam led me into the house then stepped aside, and when Ozzie and Dad followed, Sam looked at Dad and muttered, "Private."

Dad held his eyes this time, nodded and led the way through the kitchen, into the dining room and through to the living room. He closed the glass-paned doors to the dining room and the wood door to the foyer.

When we arrived, staying standing, Sam wrapped an arm around my chest and pulled the side of my back into the side of his front and his eyes leveled on Ozzie.

Before he could speak, Ozzie did.

"Know what you're gonna say, Cooper, and I get you. The deputy who took the call from your people heard your name associated with Kia's, got excited, shared too much. I can assure you he did *not* do this with the reporters who called and I can also assure you he will *not* do this again."

"That wasn't cool, but that is also not why we're standin' here," Sam replied, and Ozzie's eyes shot to Dad before they went back to Sam. He didn't shake his head "no," but his eyes screamed it.

Sam shook his head "no" and then explained it.

"You know he's gotta know," Sam said softly.

"It's in hand," Ozzie returned.

"It isn't," Sam shot back.

"What's this about?" Dad asked.

"Cooper—" Ozzie started, leaning into Sam, but Sam turned to Dad.

"Sorry, Ford, this is going to come as a shock—" he began, but Ozzie interrupted him.

"Cooper, I don't advise—"

Sam looked to Ozzie. "Due respect and understand, Kia has told me about you. She cares about you. She trusts you and she's explained you're a friend of the family. So when I say due respect, I mean it. But with this, you are not makin' the right decisions."

"I got experience, son," Ozzie retorted. "I know what I'm doin'."

"Yeah? You do, then look me in the eye and tell me since she got on a plane and until you heard Kia hooked up with me that you slept good at night," Sam volleyed.

Ozzie snapped his mouth shut.

"What is...goin'...*on*?" Dad bit out, eyes narrowed, body tight.

"Shit," Ozzie muttered.

Sam looked back at Dad. "Jeff Clementine and Vanessa Cloverfield hired a hit man to take out Kia."

My body was already tight through the preliminaries, but it got tighter at these words.

"Yeah, this isn't news," Dad said, again perplexed.

"No, Ford," Ozzie put in quietly. "They didn't conspire to do it. They *did* it."

Dad took a step back, his face going pale. I made to move away from Sam and go to him, but Sam's arm tensed and I couldn't get away.

Dad was staring at Ozzie and he whispered, "What?"

"Vanessa pawned a bunch of stuff and talked Milo into gettin' a second mortgage on their house, sayin' she wanted a new kitchen or somethin'. They found a broker who hooked them up with a man who could do the job they wanted done. They made contact, they paid and the hit was placed on Kia," Ozzie explained.

"You are shittin' me," Dad was still whispering.

"I wish I was, Ford," Ozzie was now whispering.

Dad shook his head, looked at me, Sam, then Ozzie, and asked, "Okay, well, so? Clearly Vanessa called it off."

"Unfortunately, no," Ozzie replied. Dad blanched and his eyes shot to me while Ozzie kept talking. "The broker took a percentage, gave the contact details to Coot and Vanessa, and it was all done electronically. Three e-mails. One to inform. One to confirm wire transfer of the money. One to confirm they wanted him to go through with the hit. They were warned that once they sent that third e-mail, that account would be made invalid. They would not hear from him again and could not call him off."

Dad's throat was working, his eyes, locked to me, were working, and I tried to pull away from Sam again but his other arm went around me, caging me in.

Ozzie went on.

"We had a man on her, Ford, all the time. We don't really have the resources to do it, but we did it. And we're doin' everything in our power to track this guy down."

"And you went off to Europe," Dad said to me. "Jesus, God, Kia, what was in your head?" he clipped.

"She didn't know," Sam stated, and Dad's eyes sliced to him.

"Say again?" he demanded.

"Kia didn't know," Sam kind of repeated.

Dad's eyes sliced back to me then Ozzie when Ozzie spoke quickly.

"We thought, what Kia'd been through, what you all had been through, what you all were facin', considerin' Coot was gone and the time had come to face it, not to mention what he left behind just knowin' all he was up to with Vanessa, we wouldn't add to that burden."

"You wouldn't add to that burden," Dad whispered.

"Ford—" Ozzie started.

"*Are you out of your ever-lovin' mind?*" Dad thundered at Ozzie, and I watched Ozzie clench his teeth.

He held Dad's eyes, but he didn't answer.

Dad tore his gaze from Ozzie's and shook his head, running his hand through his hair while doing it and muttering, "I don't...I cannot believe this shit. I cannot *believe* this *shit.*"

"Right," Sam put in. Dad's eyes cut to him and Sam announced, "This is where we're at now. The sheriff's talkative deputy gave me the heads up three days ago."

Sam looked at Ozzie.

"So you need to know there are four men in your town who'll be visible watching Kia and her home. I'll get you names and pictures so your men can identify them. They are carrying concealed and three of four of them have a license to do that in this state. I'll ask you to look the other way with the one who doesn't. I can assure you he's trained and he knows what he's doin' or I wouldn't have him on Kia. I'm also carryin' concealed and I don't have a license in Indiana either. I'll have a weapon on me at all times and another one in Kia's house, and since I couldn't get home to North Carolina to get my own hardware, I do not hold permits for either."

Ozzie's eyes were getting bigger and bigger as Sam spoke, but Sam wasn't done.

"I'll ask you to look the other way on that too. There are also two men hunting this guy at my request. They'll need information, which means I'll need a full brief from you and I'll need to talk to Vanessa Cloverfield. So as not to fuck your case against her, you'll not have anything to do with that. But she doesn't talk to me, I'll escalate my tactics to get her to talk to me. You'll need to look the other way on that too."

"Son, you cannot ask me to do that," Ozzie replied, then finished, "*Any* of that."

"I just did and you'll do it," Sam returned, and Ozzie's face started to get red.

"Cooper, I understand—" Ozzie started, but I felt Sam's body get taut at my back and I braced because I knew, for whatever reason, he was done.

"No, sheriff, you *don't* understand. If you did, at the very least Ford would have been aware of this situation before Kia's ass was on a plane. For three weeks, she was wandering Europe alone and unprotected. For a week and a half, she was with me and I had no clue."

He lifted a hand and stabbed an angry finger Ozzie's way.

"You do not know who this motherfucker is, therefore you do not know what resources he has available to him. She should never have been on that plane. In the months after you learned about this situation, she should have had more than the Sheriff Department's protection but also the protection of her family and a security system installed in her house. Or, seein' Ford's reaction, her ass moved to this one and a system installed here. None of this happened. And months have passed and you have not found this guy."

Ozzie started to look uncomfortable as well as pissed, but Sam kept going.

"My experience, you haven't found him yet means you got nothin' on him and your leads have gone stone-cold. So he's not in the wind, he *is* the wind. And when that shit happens, your boys can be brilliant, but unless they're trained to lock down that kind of target, they got no hope. They also got other shit to do. I do not. The hunters I called in on this do not. And the men at Kia's back have one focus, *Kia*."

This made me feel all warm, safe and protected, but I didn't get a chance to fully process that because Sam wasn't quite done.

"I know you are not unaware of the last seven years of her life and what she's been livin' with behind closed doors at the hands of that piece of shit. Now he's still controlling her life and he's fuckin' dead. I got the power and the means to make certain that shit stops and I'm gonna do it. And last, I'll give you the heads up that I do not make threats so take that into consideration when I say, I'm doin' this and you do not wanna stand in my way."

When Sam was done, I was holding my breath. Ozzie was holding Sam's gaze. And Dad was staring at Sam like Santa Claus and the Easter Bunny popped in to give him a brand-new hunting rifle and a year-round permit to shoot all things cute and furry *and* a basket as big as a house filled with chocolate. In other words, like he'd just hit the mother lode.

The silence stretched, so before I passed out, I decided to start breathing again.

Finally, Ozzie spoke.

"I'll admit those leads are cold, Cooper, but they're cold for us, they'll be cold for you."

"First, what's cold for you is not cold for my boys. And second, I'll ask, you sure you got all you could get from that piece of shit's bitch?"

Clearly knowing who Sam was referring to, Ozzie answered, "Vanessa was very forthcoming as advised by her attorney. She's arguing that it was all Cooter's idea and she was along for the ride without collusion but with a fair amount of coercion. So I suspect her attorney wants to show she's been helpful in order for it to assist her case."

"Interesting to see if the woman who pawned a bunch of shit and conned her husband, who she drove to committing murder into getting a second mortgage to pay for a hit can convince a jury of that bullshit, but I don't care about that. I asked if you're sure you got all you could get from her," Sam returned.

"And what I'm sayin' is, yeah. She's up the creek without a paddle. I reckon she thinks that's her paddle," Ozzie stated.

"Then you haven't got all she could give you," Sam declared.

"How you figure that?" Dad asked, and Sam looked at him.

"Because she's covering her ass. If she was bein' smart and doin' the right thing, she'd come completely clean, cop to what she did, confess and use her tell-all as ammunition for a plea bargain. She's hidin' something," Sam replied.

"You can't know that. You haven't even met her," Ozzie told him.

"Have you found the broker?" Sam asked Ozzie.

Ozzie inclined and twisted his neck but didn't answer. In other words, no.

"My guess, she or the piece of shit met with the broker face-to-face," Sam speculated.

"Yeah," Ozzie confirmed. "She said Coot did, but that guy's in the wind too."

"Bullshit," Sam clipped. "His percentage is probably ten, at most twenty. He's local. He does not evaporate after brokering a deal. He doesn't make the kind of cake that lets him relocate like that, especially seein' as he'd need to activate or create a network of scum everywhere he relocates. He needs business. He'll be reachable. We'll reach him."

"Vanessa told us he told Coot that he also doesn't have contact with his men," Ozzie informed Sam.

"Then either that bitch lied or the broker lied to her. If he doesn't, he knows someone who does. He can hardly get them assignments without some form of contact," Sam returned.

"We thought of that, but we got a warrant for her computer and she gave us details and he's unreachable. No one's even heard of him," Ozzie returned.

"Then she met with him personally and that'll hurt her case, so she's hidin' somethin' from you. She'll give it to me. And the way I'll get it means either during or after your department will get a call from her. If she tells you I'm there, your boys take their time showin' up. If she calls after I'm gone, you cover my ass," Sam demanded.

"You have got to know askin' me to do that is not only unlawful, it's insane." Ozzie was getting heated.

"I get that you got a responsibility to all your citizens, including that bitch. I feel for you. That's gotta tear you up. But straight up, I don't give a shit about that either. You'll cover my ass." Sam was still cool as a cucumber.

"You need to stand down and let my boys handle this," Ozzie snapped, at his end.

"And I'm tellin' you, I'm not gonna do that," Sam retorted.

"Then you'll find trouble in this town," Ozzie returned.

Sam was silent.

I waited.

Dad waited.

Ozzie waited.

Sam finally gave it to Ozzie.

"Seven years, you knew," he said quietly.

Ozzie *and* Dad sucked in breath.

I held mine.

Sam wasn't done.

"You, of all people, had a responsibility to her."

"I—" Ozzie started, but Sam cut him off, no longer cool. Totally pissed.

"Don't," he bit off. "Do not. Do not stand in front of her and make excuses. Do not do it. Her friends, her parents, they were caught in his web. She was fragile and they had to be careful not to break her in trying to deal with that shit or tip him into making it worse. You have no excuse."

"She never called it in, never made a report," Ozzie said softly. His eyes came to me. "Darlin', I'm sorry, but—"

Sam cut him off. "That's an excuse."

Ozzie's gaze sliced to Sam and he clipped, "You clearly do not understand the sometimes extremely frustrating limits of law enforcement."

"Yeah, I do. But not for men who hunt with an abused woman's father, who've known that woman since she was a little girl. Men like that make shit happen so that shit *stops*," Sam fired back.

It was time, I felt, for me to intervene.

I did this by lifting both hands and wrapping my fingers around the arm Sam had around my chest, twisting my neck, tipping my head back to look at him and whispering, "Sam, honey, that's not fair."

Sam looked down at me. "Did you tell me you were contaminated?"

Another audible breath from my dad.

I stared in Sam's eyes, silent.

"Did you tell me that, baby?" Sam asked.

"I…yes," I whispered.

"You're terrified of me when I get angry. Not an adrenaline rush, you get the shakes. I see 'em, it's so fuckin' bad."

"Sam." I was still whispering.

"First, a woman like you with a family and friends like yours, beauty like yours and a personality like yours should *never* feel like she's contaminated. I do not know how that feels for you, baby, but I do know what your face looked like when you said it to me and I held you in my arms when you cried after you confessed that shit. So I can guess and that is not right. *That* is not fair. And you jumpin' straight to that kind of fear because you were trained to do so at the hands of your dead husband is also not fair."

Sam looked to Ozzie.

"I know you're a good man. I can see you warred with this for a long time. I can also see you carry a burden for the decision you made. So what you need to do now is stop makin' decisions that cover your ass and start makin' them to take care of Kia."

"You don't understand what you're askin' me to do," Ozzie said quietly.

"I do and I'll do my best to make sure nothin' I do blows back on you. That said, shit happens and I'm focused on makin' Kia safe, so if it does, you need to suck it up and think quick to cover my ass and yours."

Ozzie stared at Sam and Sam held his stare.

Then Ozzie looked very briefly at me, but he avoided Dad's eyes before he looked back at Sam.

"You hurt Vanessa, I won't cover for you."

"I'd like to rip the bitch's head off, but that's not how I work," Sam replied.

Ozzie tipped up his chin, then continued, "Whatever you get you also give to us."

"Done," Sam agreed.

"You track either the broker or his man down, you give them to us."

Sam shook his head. "No fuckin' way."

"Then no deal," Ozzie fired back.

"We get what we need from them, you can have 'em. But not until we know shit is locked down and Kia is safe," Sam returned.

Ozzie clenched his teeth.

Then he nodded and added, "Heartmeadow is not the O.K. Corral. Your badasses do not have carte blanche to make it so. They see a threat, they call it in."

"They see a threat, they neutralize it, then they call it in," Sam countered.

"Jesus, Cooper!" Ozzie exploded. "How exactly do you think I can cover for your crew if a man who is not licensed to carry concealed in the state of Indiana or you, who's in possession of two firearms for which you don't have permits, drills holes into a suspected assailant before he becomes an assailant?"

"That is not my problem, it's yours," Sam stated. "And it's the whole reason for this heads up and why Essie is not in here right now learnin' about what's goin' down with her daughter because she also has the right to know. What she doesn't need is to be an accessory to anything that might turn bad."

Oh man.

That didn't sound good.

"Would I be an accessory?" I asked.

"No," Sam answered, tilting his head to look down at me.

"Dad?" I pushed.

"Don't worry about it," Sam replied, this time giving me the wrong answer.

"But—" I started.

"Don't worry about it, Kia," Dad stated, and I looked at him.

"I—"

"I want to know," Dad said firmly and looked at Ozzie. "I want to know everything from now on." Dad looked at Sam. "Everything."

Sam nodded immediately.

Ozzie looked to his feet.

"Oz?" Dad prompted.

Ozzie looked at Dad. "You know I was only trying—"

"No." Dad shook his head. "We'll deal with that later. After Kia's safe. Right now, no more hiding anything. This is my daughter. I want to know."

Ozzie held Dad's eyes a moment before he nodded his head.

Dad looked at Sam. Then he looked at me.

And when he did, he commenced in breaking my heart.

Tears forming in his eyes, he whispered an agonized, "I didn't look out for you."

I pushed against Sam's arms when I saw his tears, heard the tortured tone of his voice, but Sam's arms locked tight.

Dad wasn't done and I suspected this was because Sam felt this was my due and Dad's responsibility to say it.

But I didn't want him to.

"Dad," I whispered, still pushing against Sam's arms.

"We all let you down," Dad told me. "Me especially."

"Dad, don't," I begged quietly.

"You said things have come up for you. They've come up for me and your mother too. And bottom line, we let you down."

"Stop," I pleaded.

"I can't," he said brokenly.

"I didn't ask for your help. I kept my secrets. I—"

Dad interrupted me. "You ask for Sam's?"

My head jerked. "Wh-what?"

"You told me you made it hard on him and there he stands. And there he stood when he laid it out for Ozzie how it was gonna go down. Did you ask for that?" Dad asked.

"I…" I shook my head. "No."

"He's lookin' out for you. I shoulda looked out for you."

"Dad—"

"I gotta say it, Kiakee. I let you down. Your mother let you down." He held my eyes and the tears trembled in his as he whispered, "You thought you were contaminated. My beautiful girl thought she was contaminated." He stared at me and his voice broke when he finished, "I let you down."

I tore out of Sam's arms and ran across the room into my father's.

He shoved his face in my neck and I felt his body jerk as he swallowed a sob. This made one tear from my throat so I shoved my face in his neck and let loose.

I held him, he held me, and then suddenly Dad's head snapped up and he ordered in a thick voice, "No. You stay."

I pulled my face out of his neck to look over my shoulder to see Ozzie moving through the doors to the dining room, shutting them behind him, but Sam moving to the couch and sitting on its arm.

I looked at Dad and lifted my hands to both his cheeks.

"Please don't let him get his claws into you," I whispered. "I couldn't bear that, Dad. It happened. It's over. We deal with what we have to deal with now. We bury it where it belongs because he's dead and we move on. I love you. I always did, I always will. We all made mistakes, including me. You didn't let me down. I didn't reach out so you could hold me up."

"Hon, I understand you see it that way, but I'm your father and I knew. You didn't say it. We didn't see it. But deep down inside I knew and I didn't do anything. I couldn't—"

"Really," I interrupted him, "we don't have to do this."

His hands came up, fingers wrapping around my wrists, and he pulled them down between us and shook them while he said, "Yes, Kia, we do."

I closed my mouth.

Dad held my eyes.

"Your mother and me, we talked about it all the time. We couldn't figure out if you loved him and put up with it because you did. Or if he'd broken you and you were showin' a brave face. Missy talked to us, told us you were not ready to go there and we just needed to keep an eye on you and be there when you were ready. She said if we pushed, we might drive you closer to him and deeper into that mess. But it went against everything I was not to step in. I talked to Cooter at least half a dozen—"

At his words, I felt my body jerk.

"What?" I whispered, my eyes wide, shocked.

"I talked to Cooter."

"You did?"

"Half a dozen times. First, to feel him out. Then I laid it out."

I took a step back and stared at him.

"Seriously?" I asked.

"Yeah."

"You laid it out for Cooter?"

Dad nodded, studying me.

"What'd you say?"

"I said you were not my girl anymore, I didn't know what was goin' on, but if what I suspected was goin' on was actually goin' on, if it didn't stop, I'd stop it."

I shook my head. "But…when did you do this?"

"Year ago," Dad answered, then finished, "Too late."

"What did he say?"

"Gave me a bunch a' shit about how he loved you. Everything was good. You could get moody and you'd been tryin' to get pregnant and it wasn't happening so you were out of sorts."

I blinked.

Then I asked, "What?"

"Honey, though I hope everything is all right in that department, God works in mysterious ways and maybe—"

"I wasn't trying to get pregnant!" I said kind of loud.

"You weren't?" Dad asked, looking perplexed again.

"Uh…no." I threw out a hand. "I mean, seriously, the man beat me." I powered through Dad's flinch. "What kind of idiot would I be to have a kid with a guy like that?"

"Kiakee—" Dad started.

"He lied to you, point-blank," I informed Dad.

"Kia—"

I whirled then informed Sam of something he couldn't miss, seeing as I was being loud but also he was only three feet away, "Cooter lied bald-faced to my father."

"Baby, seriously, you look pissed and surprised, but this is that piece of shit you're talkin' about. How can you be surprised?" Sam asked.

"I don't know but I am." I threw up my hands. "I mean, he didn't just *lie*. He lied about me trying to get pregnant! I mean, how messed up is *that*?"

My voice was rising.

Sam just rose, physically, and came to me.

With both hands on my neck, he bent his face to mine and whispered, "Calm down. He's a dick. You know this. Baby, he put a hit on you. This was the least of his sins. Let it go."

I glared into Sam's eyes.

He was right.

I sucked in breath.

Then I let it go.

But I was still pissed so I turned to Dad, Sam's hands dropped, and I laid it out for my father.

"Right, you know everything now. And it's bad. And I can't say I'm not scared. And I also can't say that I have my head straight about all that's gone on. What I can say is, I don't need the additional guilt of thinking you and Mom are beating yourselves up about this. I understand how you feel and I'm sorry you feel that way, Dad. But the bottom line of it is, I picked him. I married him. I stayed with him and I put up with his shit without asking for help. I brought this on you. You didn't marry him. So please, I need you to work through it and get past it because it's done, that part at least. We all need to move toward letting it go. Can you do that for me?"

I watched my dad's face get soft, and in an equally soft voice, he promised, "Yeah, Kia, honey, I can do that for you. I can talk to your mom too. What I can't say is that it'll happen tomorrow, but I can say I promise we'll try."

I nodded.

Dad wasn't done.

"But what we'll need from you is to know where you're at." His eyes strayed to Sam before coming back to me and he whispered, "First time in a long time, standing right in front of me, I see even a hint of my Kiakee. I'm glad to have her back, but I know there's work you gotta do. What your mother and I need is for you to let us in and help you do it."

"You're already in," I replied firmly and immediately.

Dad studied me for a long moment, but his eyes darted to Sam and back to me before he whispered, "Thank you."

I sucked in another breath as tears threatened again.

Dad's eyes went to Sam and he stated, "You hold me responsible."

My entire body grew solid, because after what Sam laid out for Ozzie, I had no idea what he'd say to Dad. The only thing I knew was he'd say it straight.

I wasn't wrong.

"I don't," Sam replied, and I relaxed.

"For Kia, you don't have to—" Dad began.

"I'm not," Sam cut him off. "I have not been in your exact position, but I have been in a position to know that same shit is happening, to feel powerless, to try to run through every option available and think there are none. I said what I said to Oswald not only because he had the power to step in, but he was objective and not intimately involved. The consequences you might have faced coming between a husband and wife, that wife bein' your daughter, who was too scared to be open with you so you could have no clue where she was comin' from, were not the same for him. He compounded that by makin' an understandable but incorrect decision on how to handle things after Clementine died. I do not hold you responsible, Ford. But it wouldn't matter if I did because Kia doesn't."

I'm falling in love with you, my mind said as I stared at Sampson Cooper, listening to him speaking to my dad as he had to me for the last week. Removing the emotion. Lifting the weight. Taking action. Giving peace of mind and doing it in a time still burdened with the unknown.

With effort, I tore my eyes away from him as this thought seared into my brain, down my spine, radiating out throughout my body. I looked to Dad who was watching Sam, his eyes working, his face suffused with a mixture of feelings he couldn't hide. Concern, gratitude and relief.

Dad nodded and looked to the floor, muttering, "Best get on out. Essie'll wanna be makin' the parfaits."

"Sam and I'll be out in a second, Dad," I said to him as he turned toward the doors and I felt Sam's gaze come to me as Dad looked at me.

Dad nodded and smiled, opened the door to the dining room and stopped, turning back halfway through and looking at me.

"I love you, my Kiakee. God shined His light on me the day He gave you to me, and no matter what has come since, I've never felt different. Not one day. Not for twenty-eight years."

I pressed my lips together, and only when I knew I could reply without it coming out on a sob, did I whisper, "I'm the luckiest girl in the world."

"Kia—" Dad whispered back.

"Even then, Dad," I interrupted him to say. "I just forgot for seven years."

Dad closed his eyes, opened them, gave me a small smile, then his eyes moved to Sam and his smile died. "None of my business, son, and you never have to tell me, but I'll tell you, whatever it was that made you feel powerless, I'm sorry you felt it. You gotta know what that means, seein' as you know I understand it better'n anyone."

"Appreciate that, Ford," Sam murmured.

Dad nodded at Sam, then he let it go and went out the door, closing it behind him.

I watched through the windows until he was gone and I saw through the windows to the outside that Mom was getting up and heading across the deck to the back door.

She was done waiting to find out what was going on.

Poor Dad.

"Kia," Sam called, and I looked at him.

"Thank you," I whispered. His eyes shifted to warm, he started to move to me, but I took a step back, lifting my hand.

His brows snapped together. He stopped, his eyes went to my hand, then back to my face.

"Please, let me say this," I said softly.

He held my gaze, jerked up his chin, and I continued.

"Thank you for assuring my dad I didn't blame him. Thank you for understanding, not blaming him and sharing why with him. Thank you for taking care of me from practically the moment you met me. And thank you for going all out to protect me. I haven't felt safe in a long time, Sam. A *very* long time. I didn't notice it missing, but I noticed the instant I got it back and that was when I woke up in your arms in Luci's villa."

At that, his entire face warmed, his eyes got intense and he started toward me, but I shook my head and took another step back.

He stopped and his head tipped to the side.

"I need to know you understand how much I mean all that I just said," I told him.

"I understand, baby," he replied gently.

I nodded.

Then I pulled breath into my nose, sucking in courage, definitely unsure, and more than a little scared, and went on, "I'm glad, honey, but now I have to be honest with you and tell you I wanted to go to my dad during that. Several times. I know you felt it, but you wouldn't let me. That was hard on him and it was hard on me and a lot of what was hard on me was having to stand separate from him and watch him go through it without me close."

Sam held my eyes for a moment before he said quietly, "I get that."

"Thank you," I whispered.

"But you were doin' that for you, baby. I didn't hold you back for you. I held you back for him."

I felt my eyebrows draw together and I asked, "What?"

"I don't know your dad at all. But I know what I'd do if I found out that Oswald kept that from me. Your dad had to be free to have whatever reaction he wanted to have and not worry about you."

Okay, I could get that.

However...

"Okay, Sam, but when he was blaming himself, he needed me then."

"No, honey, you needed him then. He needed to say it, he told you flat out. I didn't hold you back for the reasons you're thinkin'. I did it because he had to be free to let that shit go and you weren't gonna let him."

This was true.

"Right," I whispered.

"There it is," Sam whispered back and there was an unreadable expression on his face. I couldn't get a lock on it. I just knew it was good.

"There what is?"

"You're gettin' to the place I want us to be."

This time, my head tipped to the side. "What?"

He closed the distance, his hands went to my neck, thumbs to my jaw, tipping my head back and his face came to within an inch of mine.

"Fearless," he murmured.

"Sam, I'm not following."

"You disagreed with me. You faced your fears. You told me what was on your mind. We disagreed. We talked. We listened. You said you feel safe with me but, Kia, honey, you don't believe in it. Just now, you took another step toward believing and I gotta tell you, baby, it feels unbelievably fuckin' good every time you place a little more trust in me."

Oh my God.

That was so beautiful. So sweet.

So Sam.

My body swayed into his as my hands, which were resting on his waist, slid around to wrap around his back and I whispered, "Sam," but said nothing else because I couldn't find the words to say.

His hands left my neck and his arms folded around me as he promised quietly, "I'll earn it all, baby."

I pressed my lips together and nodded before I dipped my chin and did a face-plant in his chest.

Sam kissed the top of my head.

And just as I suspected I would never get used to him being so hot, I suspected I would never get used to him being so sweet.

And I really hoped I didn't.

"We better join the others. Even though I got a week's allowance of fat sittin' in my gut, I don't think it'd be good to dis your mom on the parfaits at this juncture," Sam noted.

I pulled my face out of his chest and tilted it back to look at him, grinning.

"You would be correct," I confirmed, then asked with curiosity, "You count fat?"

Sam burst out laughing.

I watched and waited patiently for him to finish.

He finally did before he answered, telling me something I already knew, "Baby, this body does not come naturally." Letting me go with one arm but sliding the other one up to my shoulders, he moved to my side before he propelled us to the doors. "But I don't count fat. You don't have to count fat to know you're consuming too much when you eat half a dozen onion rings and go through three napkins doin' it in order to sop up all the grease."

He was not wrong about that.

"Told you Mom was a comfort cook," I muttered as he pushed one of the doors to the dining room open.

I pushed the other one and we walked through.

"You did not lie," he muttered back.

We walked through the dining room and the kitchen, but at the back door, I pulled him to a halt, curled into him and caught his eyes.

"Were you okay with before?" I asked quietly.

"Which before, baby?" he asked back, and I laughed softly.

"Well, not the emotional scene with my dad or the tense scene with Ozzie. The before where half of Heartmeadow came to check you out."

"Am I slidin' in bed beside you tonight?" Sam asked, and I blinked.

"Uh…I think so."

Where else would he sleep?

His face dipped closer. "If the answer to that is yes, then yes, I'm okay with half of Heartmeadow coming to check me out."

There it was again. So damned sweet.

I slid my hand up his chest to curl my fingers around his neck and warned, "You're also sliding into bed with Memphis, and heads up, she seems really small, but in a bed, she expands to five times her size."

Sam smiled at me. "I think I'll cope."

"Good."

"Your bed is queen-size, Kia, my bed is king. Eventually Memphis will have plenty of room."

Sam, me and Memphis in a huge bed where everyone had plenty of room.

That sounded like heaven.

I smiled back.

Mom threw open the door and ordered, "Scooch! It's parfait time." She hustled Sam and me out of her way, continuing to issue orders, "Kia, sweetie, get the ice cream and nuke it. Thirty seconds, then check. You might need another fifteen. And grab ten bowls. Ozzie is still here."

"Right, Mom." I started to move away, but Sam caught my hand and I looked back to see his brows raised.

"Nuke it?" he asked quietly.

"Mom doesn't like hard ice cream so she nukes it soft."

Sam stared at me.

Then he shook his head before he bent it to touch his mouth to mine.

His mouth barely landed before I heard Teri shout, "*Hot!*"

He lifted his head and I was relieved to see his eyes smiling.

He let me go and walked outside.

I walked to the freezer to get the ice cream.

15

DON'T CROSS THIS LINE

It was late morning and Memphis and I were in my kitchen with a roll of masking tape and a marker.

Sam was at Vanessa's.

I was a mess.

My mess was multifaceted.

It was partially because I woke up at two o'clock in the morning, ready to face the day. I tossed. I turned. Memphis yapped. I tossed more, turned more, and finally decided to go and toss and turn on the couch so I didn't toss and turn Sam awake. I'd just thrown the covers aside and lifted up when a steel band-like arm hooked around my belly and I found myself on my back in bed with a hot guy mostly on top of me.

"Jet-lag?" Sam asked.

"Yep," I answered.

Sam's hands started traveling and his mouth went to my neck where he murmured, "Mm."

Then his hands and mouth started traveling more. Mine joined them. I got into it and returned the favor Sam gave me earlier, taking him in my mouth. Then Sam got into it and one-upped my favor by giving it to me in a variety of different but delicious positions. I had an orgasm I was pretty sure the neighbors could hear. Sam's orgasm shortly followed. Fifteen minutes after that, tucked into Sam's side, Memphis returning and stretching out in the expanse of bed I'd left her, I crashed on the thought that jet-lag wasn't so bad, at least not when Sam shared my condition.

But when I woke up, I was no longer feeling so hot about jet-lag. Groggy and out of sorts, I was also in bed alone. And, weirdness of weird, I could hear a succession of yaps—they were measured, not random—and I'd never heard Memphis yap like that.

I threw the covers back, lurched out of bed, grabbed my robe, shrugged it on and lurched down the hall, tying the belt.

I stopped dead when I saw Sam sweating in workout clothes, his legs bent at the knees, ankles crossed, fingers curled around the top of the doorjamb. Memphis was on the floor in front of him, yapping each time Sam did a pull-up like she was counting them down.

"Mornin', baby," Sam said as he lowered his body.

Hair probably a rat's nest, eyes fuzzy, head groggy, dazedly noting that Sam clearly didn't share these symptoms with me (not that his clipped hair could form a rat's nest), I stared at him and asked, "What are you doing?"

Sam pulled up, stayed up and grunted, "Pull-ups," over Memphis's yap, then he lowered himself down.

It was then it belatedly hit me that Sampson Cooper—not Sam, *Sampson Cooper*—was in my little two-bedroom, nondescript house in Heartmeadow, Indiana, and I momentarily freaked out wondering what he saw and what he thought of me from what he could see.

Sam pulled up.

Memphis yapped.

Sam lowered down.

Sam pulled up.

Memphis yapped.

Sam lowered down.

I watched.

"You okay?" Sam asked.

"Memphis is yappy," I answered.

"Noticed, honey," Sam muttered, then pulled up.

Memphis yapped.

Sam lowered down.

Sam pulled up.

Memphis yapped.

On Sam lowering down, I asked, "How many of those do you do?"

"As many as I can," Sam answered, pulled up and Memphis yapped.

Sam lowered down.

I continued staring.

He was concentrating on what he was doing. He didn't give one shit about Memphis being yappy. He grew up in a barrio and two times during football games his senior year there were kids murdered. One a stabbing during a drug sale gone bad. One a shooting during a gang war.

Sure, Cooter had had half his head blown off but not in the house and Cooter's murder was the first Heartmeadow had seen in nearly thirty years.

Sam had lived worse. He didn't care about my house and didn't think it said anything about me.

He pulled up. Memphis yapped. I saw his muscles in his arms bunch, exposed by the skintight, sleeveless shirt he was wearing and I went a different kind of groggy.

He lowered down and asked, "Are you in a standing coma?"

"Your muscles in your arms look really good when you do that."

Yes, that's what I said.

Sam grinned.

Then he pulled up and Memphis yapped.

When he was down, I queried, "You keep doing that, won't you pull the wood off the doorframe?"

"This house sold?" Sam queried back.

"Yeah," I answered.

"You care if I pull it off?" he went on.

"No," I replied.

"You got a hammer?" he kept going.

"Yeah," I told him.

"Then we're good," he muttered, pulled up and Memphis yapped.

I turned around and went back to the bedroom to get to the bathroom.

Fifteen minutes later, teeth brushed, hair tamed (ish), face washed, still feeling weird, I wandered out of the bedroom, down the hall and into the kitchen. Sam was no longer doing pull-ups so I had an unobstructed trek to the coffee. I made it then wandered to stand in the kitchen doorway to see Sam doing one-armed push-ups on the living room floor.

Memphis was bouncing around Sam's body as he did this, alternately getting down on her front legs, thinking he was playing.

"Your back looks really good when you do those," I generously kept the information flowing on how hot he looked when he worked out.

"Good to know," Sam pushed out through a hissed breath as he pushed up.

"I mean, it looks good all the time, but it looks *really* good when you do those," I shared.

Sam lowered down, then pushed up but didn't reply.

Memphis ran under his body.

I thought that was hilarious so I giggled.

Sam lowered down, then pushed up, grunting, "You know what's most important during a workout?"

I had no clue.

"Nope," I replied as Sam lowered down.

"Focus," Sam told me, and Memphis jumped over his ankles.

I burst out laughing.

"Jesus," Sam muttered as he went belly to the floor. His arm shooting out, he tagged Memphis and rolled to his back, Memphis in his arms. She was wiggling, panting and licking Sam's sweaty neck. He did an ab curl to sitting with cocked knees, Memphis still in his arms, now licking his jaw. His eyes locked on mine and he announced, "I need a gym."

I grinned. "I'm seeing that."

"This burg have one?"

"I've heard rumors."

He smiled at me.

Then he declared, "I get showered, go get my brief from Oswald, then talk to that bitch. After, we find food, hit the grocery store and find a gym."

All humor fled at the idea of Sam talking to Vanessa.

"Baby," Sam called softly.

"What?"

"Talk to me. What's on your face?"

"I don't like the idea of her sharing your air."

"I don't either but got no choice."

"I don't like that either."

Sam put Memphis down, pushed himself to his feet and came to me. Memphis, seeing his direction, remembered she had a momma and bounced over. I crouched, picked her up and straightened, giving her distracted cuddles by the time Sam made it to me.

He curled a hand around my neck and dipped his chin to look down at me.

"We got a plan. Information, yard sale, as many viewings as you can fit in and we're gone. A week, at most two, then my place, beach, Skippy's and a king-size bed."

I nodded and asked, "Will your badass bodyguard battalion be joining us in North Carolina?"

"Undecided," Sam answered. "This could be done and at my house we don't need them at night. My security system is tight, impenetrable, put in by the best in the business. Man lives not too far from here actually, name's Callahan. But I want you safe and I want extra eyes on you during the day, so, yeah. A smaller crew, but this business isn't sorted before we go to North Carolina, we'll be bringing a few of them with us."

"It's nice of them to do this," I remarked, and Sam's brows drew slightly together.

"Nice?"

"Yeah, to do you a favor like this."

"Kia, honey, one the boys who's huntin' this guy, he's a buddy. I pulled in a marker with him. The boys who're watchin' you and the other hunter I'm payin'."

I blinked and my lips parted.

"What?" I whispered.

"Private detective, lives in the same town as Callahan. Name's Tanner Layne. Callahan suggested him. He's on payroll. He's workin' with a buddy of mine I met in the Army, Lee Nightingale. Lee's doin' me a favor. Lee and Tanner suggested locals they know to look out for you. They're all on payroll."

"You're *paying* them?"

"Yeah."

"*Paying?*"

"Uh...*yeah*," Sam replied. "This shit is time-consuming, has no end date and could get dangerous. Lee owes me for something big. But with an open-ended situation like this, the skills I needed, the peace of mind I expect them to give, they gotta issue invoices. Why the surprise?"

I didn't know what to say.

"Is it expensive?"

His face went guarded and he answered carefully, "The best is never cheap."

"I'll pay you back," I said instantly, and his fingers flexed in my neck.

"No, sweetheart, you won't."

Uh-oh.

He was calling me sweetheart.

"Sam—" I started.

"This isn't a discussion."

"Sam!"

His fingers dug deeper, his face suddenly dipped close and Memphis yapped, but we both ignored her.

"Right, you need to get this. It's important. So I'll lay it out as best I can, but you don't cross this line, Kia. Ever."

Now I was confused.

"What line?"

"I'm a man."

Well, I knew that.

"That isn't news, Sam."

"And you're my woman."

I sucked in breath.

Oh God.

I was thinking this was big.

No, this was *huge.*

"She gets me," he muttered.

"Sam," I whispered.

"I gotta do this and you gotta let me."

"But it's expensive."

"I got money."

"So do I, Sam."

"Kia," he said warningly, his face getting closer. "Don't cross this line. I protect myself. I protect my home. I protect my family. And I protect my woman. I do it how I need to do it. No discussion. Are you with me?"

"Are you saying you're with me?" I asked cautiously.

"I'm saying I want you breathing for long enough to figure that out."

I wanted that too so that was a good answer…kind of.

"So you're not with me?" I whispered.

"Kia—"

"Sam."

He held my eyes.

Then his other hand came up to my neck and he stated, "I feel somethin' for you. It already runs deep. We may as well get this straight…I don't know where this is goin', but I like where it is. I like how it feels. And while we figure it out, it's exclusive. That means you're mine. I protect what's mine. That's where I am. That's where you are. Now are you with me?"

I wanted to be. Boy, did I want to be.

But I wasn't.

So that was why I said, "If this doesn't work, it ends and we're over, I don't want you to find another woman you like being with and me being on the list of how women have screwed you over. This isn't your problem. It's mine. I have the money and I want to pay."

His fingers gave me a squeeze and his face got even closer when he whispered, "That, baby, that right there says you will *never* be on that list. I can tell you not a single woman I've been with even offered to pay for a drink. You are not them. I knew it before, but I know it even more now."

I lifted one of my hands to rest on his chest and whispered back, "Okay, I appreciate that, but I still want to pay."

"You're crossing that line, Kia," he stated, his voice getting an edge.

"Sam, I have to," I pushed.

"No," he returned, his voice now hard. So hard, I blinked. "Right now, this is what we are. Right now, this is working. Right now, there's no chance this is gonna end and we're gonna be over. So right now and for the foreseeable future, you…are…*mine*."

His hands swayed me (and Memphis) gently with each of the last three words and my eyes were riveted to the intensity in his. He could be intense, but this was something different. Deeper. Starker. Profound.

He kept talking.

"You're under threat. I lived from the minute I could make a memory to the minute I tossed that asshole outta my mother's house not able to eliminate the threat that was livin' in my own goddamned home. My mother in danger, my brother in danger, my family, including me, ruled by an iron fist, a fist that lashed out randomly and brutally. That is *not* happening again, sweetheart. Danger darkens my door and threatens what's mine, I'll handle it. This is me and you gotta know this about me. If you can't see it my way, you gotta beat it back, keep your mouth shut and let me do this because we're not having this conversation again. Not after this shit is over for you and, if we go the distance, not in our future. I protect what's mine how I gotta do it and with no discussion. Now, Kia, whether you're with me or you're not, right now, you say you're with me."

I stared up at him, thinking sometimes what Sam said went too.

Therefore, I did the only thing I could do.

I whispered, "I'm with you."

Sam held my eyes, body unmoving, the intensity didn't shift from his gaze and I knew something had a hold on him and I suspected it didn't all have to do with me.

Then he sucked breath into his nose, muttered, "Right," pulled me up to him as his head tipped to me and he kissed my nose. His hands left my neck and he rubbed Memphis's head as he continued on another mutter, "Shower, then I get this shit done."

He turned and started down the hall.

"I'm not your mother."

Yes. That was me.

I didn't know where it came from, but it came from somewhere and then it came right out.

Sam's body locked for a half a second, before stiffly, he turned and looked at me.

"Come again?" he asked quietly.

I held his eyes and pulled in a breath, bent slightly, dropped Memphis to her feet, straightened and looked at him again.

And when I did, I knew where it came from.

So I told Sam.

"What just happened there," I said carefully, "was not about me. You don't talk about yourself very much, but I think you're reliving what happened to you when you were a kid. I'm not your mother.

I don't know what happened with that, but what happened to me is my responsibility, not my dad's, my mom's, Ozzie's, or anybody's. And now I'm in this mess and that's my responsibility too." He opened his mouth, but I lifted a hand quickly and whispered, "I said I was with you, I'm with you. I promise, honey. I'm not crossing that line. It means something to you so I won't."

He closed his mouth.

I kept going.

"But this is still my responsibility. I was young and stupid, but I made the decision I made and it happened. Now it's clean-up time and this is different. This isn't your mom and your brother. I'm not alone. I never have been. If you're sorting through past demons while going through this with me, you need to face that and I think we both need to know that isn't clouding how you feel about what's happening here."

"Clouding how I feel about what's happening here?" Sam repeated, his brows drawing together a little scarily.

That was when I gave it all to him.

"I'm not your mother, Sam. If you're attracted to me because you had to live under that threat without having any power to do anything about it and you want to relive that and make it come out a different way, then…then…" I faltered before I finished, "then we have more to talk about."

I shut up, and when I did, I realized my heart was beating hard.

Sam stared at me.

Memphis yapped.

We both ignored her.

"I…" I began when he said not a word, then ended simply with a prompt of, "Sam?"

"Remember Luci's party?" he asked.

Like I'd ever forget.

"Yes," I answered.

"Remember when I told you he took something precious from you?"

I nodded.

"I know, Kia, and I've known since the beginning, even before I knew he took his hands to you, that he'd broken something in you that, if I took the shot, I'd have to fix. And, baby, you sittin' across from me, shy and cute and open and funny, I did not give one shit that he'd broken you. I knew the minute I saw you laugh, no..." He shook his head once. "Before that, I wanted in there and I'd do anything to get what I wanted."

I felt my lips part, but just like Sam, he was not done, but this time he was *far* from done.

"That didn't have fuck all to do with my mother, my father and what happened to me as a kid. You might not like hearin' this, but what it had to do with was watchin' you walk across that dining room in those sexy-as-hell shoes and that hot, little dress with your long legs and your great tits and all that fantastic fuckin' hair. But mostly, it was a face I knew I wanted to see starin' up at me when my cock was buried inside you."

At that, my mouth just dropped open.

Sam still wasn't done.

"Straight up, you are one fine piece of tail, but now you're *my* piece of tail. When you sat across from me and ignored me, I saw that shit you carry in your eyes, even when your mind is consumed with something else. Then you sat with me and I watched you laugh. I knew that shit would not deter me, no matter how deep it ran. And I can promise you that has not one thing to do with my mother."

He took a breath and kept going.

"The precious thing he took from you is that you have no fuckin' clue it wasn't only me in that room who watched you walk across it, wishin' he was a man who could be buried inside you. And that precious thing also includes the fact that you think for one second this bullshit is your responsibility. He saddled you with that too, Kia. This mess is *his* making, not yours. I don't know how to get that outta your head. The only thing I know is it's gonna be me who cleans up that mess, and like it or not, it partly has to do with you turning out in reality to be one *seriously* fine piece of ass. But also it has to do with you not likin' Eurotrash cars, not rappin' with your posse about what I do for you in bed, you demonstrating you have my back and you bein' able to make me laugh when I'm mildly pissed at you."

He finally stopped speaking and I stared at him.

He had noticed me walk across that dining room.

He wanted me when I walked across that dining room.

Ohmigod!

Sam interrupted my mental freak out with, "Now, we past this?"

"Yes," I whispered.

He studied me.

Then he stated, "Look of you, honey, you're gonna search for some other fucked-up reason I'm with you and I gotta say now, I don't know how much more straight I can be about that."

I didn't either.

"Uh…yeah. You were pretty straight," I agreed quietly.

"Did what I say penetrate?"

"I might, uh…need coffee and to get over jet-lag and then, um… maybe it'll sink in," I told him honestly.

His lips twitched.

Then he muttered, "I'll be here when it does."

On that, he turned around and disappeared in my bedroom.

Memphis yapped, then bounced down the hall and disappeared after him.

Sam was going to have company in the bathroom while he showered. This was Memphis's way.

I kept still and staring.

I'll be here when it does.

Okay. All right.

Wow.

Wow.

I forced myself to turn and lurch to the coffee, discovering Mom or Paula had made sure we had fresh milk for which I decided to buy them both a yacht, that was how grateful I was.

I was leaning with my hips to the counter when Sam came in wearing another long-sleeves-rolled-up-near-to-his-elbows, button-up-the-front shirt (this one chambray), jeans, and boots. He was followed by Memphis, who I was getting thought Sam was the shit, even more than she thought everyone was the shit. She didn't even follow Cooter around with that kind of devotion. Then again, Cooter didn't do pull-ups and push-ups that she could misconstrue as playing with her.

He came right to me, touched his mouth to mine and I smelled his aftershave. Doing that, I decided that he smelled so good the second Vanessa smelled him she'd spill all of her secrets.

He told me he'd be back as soon as he could and he left.

The moment the door closed behind him, his words repeated in my brain.

I'll be here when it does.

He watched me walk through that dining room and he wanted me.

Thomas had said, *I'll remind you of this moment, when the beautiful Kia doubted her power over a powerful man…*

That intensity Sam had was partly about his history, but it was mostly about me.

Me.

Sam watched me walk through that dining room and he wanted *me.*

Thus began my multifaceted freak out because firstly, I didn't know what to do with that intensity directed at me, my problems and Sam's clear dedication to eradicating them which included Sam throwing serious money at accomplishing this feat.

I also didn't know what to think about the fact that Sam *still* wasn't sharing. He seemed to, talking about his childhood not only to me but mentioning it to my dad. But he didn't share much, just nuances, then he moved on.

It was also dawning on me that I might be a little bit of all right, which was something I hadn't considered until Thomas said what he'd said and now definitely after Sam said what *he* said.

And lastly, I was freaking out because I was falling in love with him. I knew it. And I knew from his words and deeds that he was committed to exploring what we had, so maybe he was getting there with me too. But I also knew from his lack of words that he was holding back and holding back didn't exactly say "exploring what we had" or "falling in love," because to start falling, you had to trust the person you were falling for to catch you.

I mean, I didn't know, I was new to this, but I suspected I was right that everyone needed to trust the person they loved to catch them, even ex-commandos.

So I went about my morning, showering, doing the getting-ready gig, unpacking, starting laundry and dealing with putting an ad in the *Boothe County Gazette* for my yard sale. Then I sat down and made a list of things to do.

After that, I unearthed some of the boxes I'd collected prior to going on vacation from the garage. I commenced in going through my kitchen and stuffing boxes full of all my crap, marking the box with bargain basement prices, as well as tacking a piece of masking tape on furniture and repeat with the marking-it gig.

And all the while I did this, my mind was consumed with all of this as well as Sam being with Vanessa, which, I didn't lie, I really did *not* like. Not because Sam might get creative with (and in trouble for) extracting information from her. Just because Vanessa was a bitch. She was a bitch in high school. She was a bitch after high school. And she was a bitch after she got married to Milo, who was a good guy but who, even after they'd tied the knot, she made no bones about letting it be known to anyone who wasn't Milo that she'd settled for him and was not pleased with the track her life had taken.

And, of course, there was the fact she'd put a hit on me.

It was two seconds after I realized I was seriously hungry in a hunger-pains-gnawing-at-the-lining-of-your-stomach kind of way when the front door opened and Sam walked through.

I was standing at the kitchen table now covered in filled boxes, so when my head turned that way, I had a direct line, and the instant I saw him, I went still.

Sam didn't.

He stalked through my living room and into the kitchen, Memphis, who greeted him noisily at the door, yapping at his heels.

He ignored her, stopped and his enraged eyes scorched right through me.

"That bitch is a fuckin' *bitch*," he growled, and I pressed my lips together.

Well, clearly Sam's yummy aftershave didn't work.

I forced myself out of my freeze and turned fully to him.

"What happened?" I asked carefully.

"She called the cops before I got up to her door."

This wasn't surprising.

"Did you get in?"

"Oh yeah." His tone was scary. "I got in."

Eek!

I pressed my lips together and waited.

Sam continued scowling at me.

Finally, I prompted, "Well?"

"Oswald is right now takin' her to the department. I wasn't wrong. She's got more. She's coverin' her ass. I know this because she was belligerent and not in a wronged woman way, in a hidin' somethin' way. Ten minutes after I got in, the cops came. Five minutes after that, her attorney showed. He's shut her down."

"So you didn't get anything?" I asked.

"Nothin' but the fact that bitch sees, lives and breathes green. She hates you, baby. So jealous, it consumes her, and me showin' at her door only intensified that."

I bet.

It sucked for Sam he had to share her air, but I had to admit, I got more than a little kick that my protective, hot guy, awesome boyfriend showed at her door and rubbed her nose in the fact that I had a protective, hot guy, awesome boyfriend.

I did not share this.

Instead, I walked to him and wrapped my arms loosely around his waist, saying softly, "I'm sorry, Sam."

His arms returned the favor and he replied, "I'm not."

My head cocked to the side. "You're not?"

"Kia, honey, she was the mastermind."

I blinked and whispered, "What?"

"What you said. What Oswald said when he briefed me. Your dead piece of shit husband was not the sharpest tack in the box. So this leads me to believe all this was her gig from start to what she still hopes will be the finish. It was her idea."

Holy cow!

"She told you that?"

"Fuck no, but I read it all over her. Her clothes, the way she wears her hair, her house. She wants more, always has, always will. She wants the dream she concocted in high school—married to the star quarterback, livin' large, lordin' her shit not stinkin' all over town. She thinks you took that away from her by marrying that fuckin' guy and she wanted it back, with your ex and the money from your life insurance policy."

"So you figured her out too," I deduced.

"She's so consumed by it, baby, she's not even close to hiding it. And that ten minutes I had alone with her, she reeked of it so much, took everything I had not to gag."

At his words, I thought about Vanessa. I thought about the fact that Vanessa, who had mouse-brown hair, bleached it blonde about a week after I started seeing Cooter. I remembered that more than once she'd come to school wearing the same outfit I'd worn a few days before. I thought about the fact that Milo played high school ball and looked a lot like Cooter, except he stayed fit and attractive mainly because he ran every morning and only drank beer while watching sports rather than downing a six-pack every night. I thought about this fact and it hit me that she didn't even see Cooter the way he was before he got half his head blown off. She only saw what she wanted to see. And it also hit me for the first time with any clarity that the stupid idiot wanted to be me.

And last, I thought that this all creeped me way the heck out.

"Okay, I was creeped out before, what with her wanting me dead, but now I'm creeped way *the heck* out," I told Sam.

"That's because this shit is creepy," Sam told me.

"Why is Ozzie taking her in?" I asked.

"'Cause she's got more and he wants to give it a go, getting it from her. He won't succeed. She'll keep her mouth shut, and if she doesn't, her attorney will do it for her."

"What does this mean?"

"It means I'm out and Lee and Tanner are up. She's not gonna give me anything. They're gonna have to find ways to make her talk or dig up her dirt."

"Right," I whispered just as there came a knock at the door. It was loud, it was hard and Sam's body went the latter, then twisted quickly when the door flew open.

"What the fuck?" Sam growled, and I peeked around him, my mouth dropping open when I watched another man in my life stalk into my living room, face like thunder.

"Jesus, fuck, *Jesus*!" my brother Kyle shouted, his eyes on me, his girlfriend, Gitte, hurrying behind him.

I was having trouble deciding between shouting with glee that he was there and fleeing because he looked extremely pissed. My brother was a good guy, funny and loving, but he was also tall and strong, he took care of himself and he had a temper. Therefore, with the size of his frame and volatility, when he got pissed, *watch out*.

He stopped in the doorway and his eyes flicked to Sam, whereupon he mumbled, "Dude, cool to meet you. Big fan." Then he looked back at me and exploded, "Seriously, Kiakee, what…the…*fuck*?"

Well, there was one good thing about being under threat of death; it took precedence over Sam's fame.

"Uh…Kyle, Sam. Sam, Kyle. Gitte, Sam. Sam, Gitte, Kyle's girlfriend," I quickly introduced, and as I did, I felt the tension leave Sam's body.

"Time for that shit is later," Kyle announced. "Now, *what the fuck?*"

"Uh…I take it Dad called you," I guessed.

"Uh…" Kyle leaned in, then boomed, "*Yeah!* And I'm here 'cause if I go see Ozzie, I'll wring his fuckin' neck. *What the fuck?*"

I moved to stand beside Sam and asked, "Aren't you supposed to be at work in Tennessee?"

"Yeah, but see, they were pretty cool with me takin' off to drive home, seein' as my *goddamned sister* has a *hit put out on her*!" Kyle answered.

"Kyle, honey, calm down," I whispered.

"That doesn't happen a lot." He didn't calm down. Instead, he kept on target.

"Kyle, sweetheart—" Gitte started, unwisely (I thought) getting close to his side.

Kyle ignored her. "And they had no problem believin' that shit, seein' as my sister is currently flavor of the month on all the gossip sites." He crossed his arms on his chest and added wryly, "So, by the way, congratulations, Kiakee, for makin' last week's top ten best dressed on youwearitwell.com."

"What?" I asked.

"Casual section," Gitte put in with a huge grin. "You were number seven with your cute tank, metallic belt and short-shorts."

Ohmigod!

"Seriously?" I asked Gitte.

"Yeah," she answered. "And I think you're number seven because you're a newbie. When you're more famous, you'll *totally* move up the rankings. That outfit was *hot*."

More famous?

Oh God. I didn't know what to do with this.

"Uh...hel-the-fuck-lo!" Kyle clipped loudly, throwing out his arms. "Can we focus?"

I focused then I moved toward him saying, "Kyle, it's cool. I know it's a shock, but Sam has it under control."

I stopped a foot away from him, but he didn't look at me. His eyes were on Sam.

"Yeah, Dad said. My sister lands a famous dude, lucky she lands one who's trained in a variety of ways to kick ass. That said, I'm thinkin' I need to be more intimately acquainted with Sam's plans *and* Sam's intentions toward my sister so I can feel all this Sam Love everyone's suddenly got and know my baby sister is in good hands."

"She is," Sam's deep voice replied at the same time I said, "I am."

"Yeah?" Kyle asked, "How 'bout Gitte and Kia go do some woman shit and you convince me of that?"

"Kyle," I whispered, and his eyes sliced to me. When they did, the fear I saw stark in them, an emotion I'd never seen my brother experience, nearly brought me to my knees. So I repeated on a whisper, "Kyle."

"It's good that motherfucker is dead," he whispered back.

I moved to him and put my arms around him, whispering again, "Kyle."

"Do my time to kill him he wasn't," Kyle went on.

"Honey," I said softly.

"It wasn't sick as shit, I'd dig his punk-ass carcass up and burn the motherfucker," he told me, his eyes roamed my face, then his arms closed around me.

I did a face-plant in his chest.

His arms got tighter. So did mine.

"Can I ask, at this juncture, what 'woman shit' entails?" Gitte asked.

I unplanted my face out of my brother's chest, turned my head and looked at his girlfriend.

Kyle and Gitte had been together for four years. They were a matching set. He was blond, handsome, tall and built. She was blonde, gorgeous, tall and built. They were both sweet and loving, but they were also both chock-full of attitude. The only difference was, Kyle was American and male and Gitte was Danish and female.

Her name meant "strength" and her personality underlined it.

As evidenced by the annoyed look on her face at being relegated to "woman shit." They said men married their mothers and women married their fathers. This was not true with me, but it was definitely true with Kyle and Gitte. Dad had taught Kyle to be a man's man. My brother might work a desk job, but he kicked ass doing it, he pulled down a huge salary, and often, he thought what he said went.

And also often, Gitte staunchly disagreed.

"Gitte—" Kyle started.

"Do I not get to understand the Sam Love?" she asked, her delicate, arched eyebrows arching further, which, knowing Gitte for four years, boded bad things. "Or perhaps Kia and I should retire to her bedroom and give each other facials?"

Uh-oh.

I pulled out of my brother's arms in order to steer clear. I got two steps back when Sam, clearly using his training and reading the room, tagged the back of my tank and pulled me two steps further and into his body.

"Darlin', I think you get me," Kyle stated, though he was wrong. Gitte did not.

"I called off work too, and not to drive all the way up here to give Kia a facial," she retorted, then looked to me and said, "Though your skin is lovely, always. You don't need one."

Seriously, I loved Gitte and not just because she thought I had good skin. Unlike Luci, my brother didn't make me wait to find a good one who I could love like a sister and get drunk with.

"Thanks, honey," I whispered. "You don't either."

She nodded and smiled.

Sam, surprisingly silent, decided not to be silent any longer.

"Right, I'm hungry. Kia's gotta be hungry. There are no groceries in the house, and even if there were, Kia's boxed up all her kitchen shit so we can't fix anything. We need food. You can come with us, eat if you're hungry, don't if you're not. But either way, while I eat, I'll fill you in. *Both* of you."

There you go. Sam was being decisive.

"Is Kia gonna get a hole blown in her while we visit the Pancake House?" Kyle asked Sam, and instantly I decided on pecan pancakes from the Pancake House for lunch.

"No," Sam answered Kyle but didn't elaborate.

Kyle held Sam's eyes.

I waited.

Gitte waited.

Sam stayed silent.

Memphis yapped.

My stomach growled audibly.

That was when Kyle said, "Let's get pancakes." Then added, "Or do commandos eat pancakes?"

Gitte grinned.

I bit my lip through my own grin.

Memphis yapped.

Sam muttered, "Serious as Christ, I spend another day in this burg, I need to find a gym."

That was when I knew I was going to get my pecan pancakes.

And that was also when I laughed.

16

PROMISE

Sam was on his phone in the kitchen talking to the unknown (to me) Tanner Layne.

I was on my couch with Memphis.

We'd had pancakes. Sam had shared his keep-Kia-breathing plans and both Kyle and Gitte had calmed down. We left the Pancake House and went directly where no one went after the Pancake House—the gym. Sam suffered (without showing he was suffering) through the guy at reception practically drooling at the thought of Sam working out there. Then he kindly declined free passes and paid for a week's worth. After that was achieved, we went to the grocery store where most of our cart was filled with fruit, veggies and lean proteins, courtesy of Sam.

Their presence became a boon because we all went back to my house and they helped me work toward getting ready for my everything-must-go yard sale.

When Mom and Dad were off work, we all headed over there and had a family meal that consisted of breaded and fried pork cutlets, fried potatoes and corn fried in butter, all of these prepared in Mom's three ever-present cast iron skillets. This was served with enormous poppy-seed rolls and followed by strawberry pie.

When Sam's plate was put in front of him, he looked at it a nanosecond then his eyes instantly cut to me.

I tried to stop my laughter, therefore I snorted.

"What?" Mom asked upon hearing the snort.

"Nothing," I answered.

Mom glanced between the two of us then unusually let it go.

Sam tucked in, but I imagined he did it while mentally adding about a hundred more push-ups to his workout the next day.

Dinner was good. Dinner was fun. Dinner was like dinner always was when we all got together—a happy occasion that we cherished because we all weren't together very often.

Dinner was also more insight for Sam into me, my family, how we interacted, the deep love we felt for each other. My family talked, shared stories, laughed over history. And without anyone mentioning it but with everyone feeling it, we enjoyed that we could all be us without Cooter sitting at the table like a big pink elephant in the room.

Sam was involved, though quietly. He chuckled. He laughed out loud. He gave me warm looks and my family warm smiles.

But although Gitte was Gitte, involved, sharing her own tales not only of her times with us, but of her life with Kyle in Tennessee and her own family and friends, Sam did not.

At all.

He wasn't removed. He just wasn't sharing. I didn't understand how he pulled it off, but he definitely did.

I didn't think anyone noticed, but I did and it was beginning to nag at me.

We left Gitte and Kyle with Mom and Dad since they had a nice guest room and I did not, and Sam and I went home. Sam told me he needed to check in with his crew of badasses and he went to the kitchen. I camped out on the couch with my photo albums. My goal: sorting the pictures I wanted to keep and dumping the pictures of Cooter.

I did not want to do this, but everything in my house had to be sifted through. I'd already given away all of Cooter's clothes. I'd also already boxed up his belongings and Dad took them to his parents' house so they could have whatever they wanted.

But now it was on to the hard stuff and I decided to get through the worst of it first, then move on to what wouldn't suck as much.

The tension I felt in my shoulders just looking at Cooter in pictures grew tighter when I sensed Sam walking in. On the floor beside the couch was a pile of Cooter memories as well as my entire wedding album. I didn't want Sam to see any of them. I also didn't want to hide.

He'd mentioned more than once that he liked that I was "transparent," so as difficult as it was, I kept flipping through the album in my lap.

Sam crouched beside the pile on the floor, picked up a photo and studied it.

I pretended to ignore him, pulled another photo out of the album and tossed it to the floor.

Sam dropped the photo he was studying without a word then twisted my wedding album toward him.

I deep breathed.

He flipped it open. I flipped a page.

"Baby, *fuck*," he whispered, and my eyes slid to him to see his head bent to look at the album. "Beautiful," he finished, and his gaze came to mine.

I looked down to see a full-page photo of myself standing alone in my awesome wedding dress, carrying my huge-ass bouquet, and my eyes went back to him.

I liked what he said just as much as I hated him knowing I was stupid enough to give it to Cooter, which was to say *a lot*.

"Thanks," I whispered back.

He looked down at the album and flipped a page. I looked down at mine and did the same.

"What are you doin' with this stuff?" he asked.

"Giving it to Cooter's parents," I answered.

"Come again?"

I knew those words weren't directed at the floor and I found I was right when my head turned to him again and I saw his eyes on me.

"I'm giving all of it to Cooter's parents."

"Why?"

Uh…*why*?

"Why not?"

He stared at me. Then he shifted so his ass was on the couch at my bent legs.

"You tight with them?" he asked.

I shook my head.

"It's a nice thing to do, you givin' them memories of that piece of shit. But you don't have to do it," Sam told me.

"I know," I told him.

"So, you're not tight with them, why you doin' it?"

I looked at him. Then I looked at the floor.

I looked back at Sam and said, "I don't know."

"Fuck 'em," Sam returned immediately, and I blinked.

"What?"

"They know what kind of man they raised?"

"I don't know," I repeated, but that was a semi-lie. Cooter's mom was beaten down and broken, just like me. Cooter's dad was a dick, just like him. They knew, or at least his mom did.

After Cooter died, Cooter's dad was beside himself with grief in the way a man like him could be beside himself with grief. He blustered and boiled over and got drunk and told anyone who would listen that if Milo Cloverfield got anywhere near him, he'd pull Milo's intestines out with his bare hands.

Cooter's mom retreated, got even more quiet than normal, and anytime I saw her, which luckily was only briefly the day after Cooter died and then again at the funeral, she looked at me in a way that made my heart clench and my flesh crawl. Pain and grief mixed with jealousy.

And Sam, being Sam, knew this and I knew he knew it when he stated, "Apple doesn't fall far from the tree."

"You did," I reminded him, and suddenly he stood. Using his toe to flip closed my wedding album, he walked from the room and into the kitchen.

Stunned by his actions, I stared after him and kept doing it so I saw him come back with a big, black garbage bag.

He crouched by the photos and shoved them and the album in the bag while I kept watching. He left it at my side when he was done, straightened and looked down at me.

"The rest go in that bag. You get done with that shit, I burn it or I take it somewhere and dump it. You need help goin' through the rest?" he asked, and tipped his head to the three albums I hadn't yet done, stacked up on the floor.

"I'm not fired up for you to see my life with Cooter in pictures," I answered.

"And I'm not fired up to do it, but that wasn't what I asked. I asked if you need help goin' through the rest."

Okay, now, wait. Weird.

He sounded testy.

I tipped my head to the side and asked quietly, "Is everything okay?"

"Yeah, and it'll be great when you answer my question."

Oh man.

Definitely testy.

"I think I got it." I kept talking quietly.

"Gonna put on the game. You watch baseball?"

"Not unless there's someone wandering by my seat, offering to sell me a beer or cotton candy."

The firmness that had set into his features softened and his lips tipped up. Then he turned, walked to the table beside Cooter's easy chair, nabbed the remote and snapped on the TV. He looked at the chair. Then his eyes came to me.

"This where he sat?"

Oh man!

I nodded.

I felt my lips part when Sam tossed the remote on the couch at my feet. He rounded the chair and shoved it across the living room. Once there, he opened the door and shoved it outside, going with it. Five seconds later (I counted), he came back.

Without a word, he retrieved the remote, sat in the cushion at my feet, stretched an arm along the back of the couch, stretched his legs out in front of him and turned his eyes to the TV.

All right, it was safe to say I had no idea what to do with that, *any* of it, starting with Sam not sharing (again) when I turned the direction of the conversation to him and ending with the rather dramatic act of shoving Cooter's chair in the front yard.

I sifted through all of this in my head, trying to decide which one I had the courage to tackle.

Then I noted, "Uh…I don't have an HOA, but I'm thinking my neighbors are not going to be hip on me having an easy chair in my front yard."

Yes. I wimped out.

"I'll get rid of it tomorrow, first thing, on my way to the gym," Sam replied, not taking his eyes from the TV.

"Okay," I said softly.

Totally wimped out.

I went back to my albums. It took a while, but I got through them all, dumping all the photos in the bag Sam provided for me, all the while not sure how I felt about that. Sam was clearly in no mood for me to disagree with one of his decisions and one could not say Cooter's parents were dear to my heart, but it didn't do anyone any harm taking the high road.

Still, they weren't burned or dumped yet. Maybe the next day Sam would be in a better mood and I could approach him about it, explain where I was coming from, and then talk to Dad about taking them over to Cooter's parents' house.

When I set the last album down, Sam's voice came at me.

"Hopeful."

My head turned and I saw his eyes were on me.

"What?" I asked.

"You looked hopeful."

My brows drew together. "Sam, I'm not following."

"In your wedding picture."

Oh God.

I pulled in breath.

"Now something good happens to you, you look surprised and like you can't believe it and you act like you're preparing for it to go away. That piece of shit took that from you too. And until I saw that picture, I didn't get it. Now I do. And it pisses me off."

Well, I was glad to know what was behind his mood except for the part about me not knowing what to do about it.

"I don't know how to respond to that," I told him the truth.

"That makes two of us, honey, 'cause the asshole's dead and I can't hunt his ass down and cave in his face."

Yikes.

"I survived," I reminded him quietly and added, "and I'll heal."

He didn't speak, but something was working in his eyes. I saw it and I waited, but again, he didn't give it to me.

Instead, he muttered, "Right." Then he looked back at the TV.

I licked my lips, then pressed them together, calling up the courage. When I had it, I called, "Sam?"

His eyes remained glued to the TV. "Yeah?"

He didn't want to talk, it was clear. Sam always wanted to talk, but he didn't now and I debated pushing it but decided against it. If he needed space, I had to give it to him and find a more appropriate time to try to get him to open up to me.

So I asked, "You want a beer?"

"No."

"Okay," I whispered, got up and got myself a beer.

This was a mistake. My body was used to being asleep at that time, and after Mom's meal, during which I'd consumed a beer, and compounding it with another one, I passed out on the couch. And I did this at the opposite end of the couch from Sam, Sam not touching me, Sam not cuddling me, and I didn't like not having either. It was the first time Sam and I watched television together, but he was tactile. If I'd been asked to guess, I would have guessed he'd snuggle, even during baseball games. And I suspected his mood was what held him distant.

The next thing I knew, I was being laid on my bed in the dark.

"Sam, honey," I muttered sleepily.

"You awake?" Sam asked.

"Kind of," I answered.

"Good," he murmured, then he kissed me.

His kiss was a shock—not an unpleasant one, but one nonetheless. This was because it was not gentle. It was not leading up to anything. It was already there, wet, hard and demanding.

Instinctively, I gave.

His mouth took more and I gave more and then his hands got in on the action and they took too. First, my clothes, then everything else. In no time I was heated, dazed by the sensual onslaught, pulling at his clothes to get to his skin. Sam helped, yanking them off, and when we were both naked, I went at him. We rolled, we kissed. We rolled, fingers swept, tongues tasted, teeth bit, limbs tangled. We rolled and more of the same, and Sam—his hands, fingers, lips, tongue, teeth, not to mention him giving me access to his body so I could use all the same—took me beyond the need he always made me feel.

It was desperation.

And my voice dripped with it when I was on my back, his finger rolling at my clit, his tongue rolling my nipple, my hand cupping the back of his head, and I breathed, "I need you inside, honey."

Sam didn't delay, shifting so he could hook the backs of my knees around his arms, holding me wide. He positioned and drove in. Looming over me, powering in fast, hard, deep, oh God…*God.* It…felt…*great.*

I pushed up to an elbow and reached out with my other hand so my fingertips could graze the silk of his skin at his chest and then down.

"You feel beautiful," I whispered, and I meant all of him. All of him driving deep and all of him I could feel with my fingertips.

"You like my cock," he growled, planting himself to the root and grinding.

Oh yeah. *Yeah.*

"I love it," I gasped.

"You like what I do for you," he grunted, thrusting hard and fast again.

Okay, that was better. By a lot.

"Love it, honey."

"Beautiful," he rumbled.

"Beautiful," I breathed, pulled in breath through my teeth, arched my neck and prepared for it to wash through me.

Sam pulled out.

My head righted with a jerk.

"Sam—" I started, but he was gone, then I was moving. He was seated, back to the headboard. He pulled me to straddling him, then with an arm wrapped around my waist, he impaled me on his cock.

Oh yes. That was nice. That was freaking *amazing.*

"Baby," I whispered, my head tipping forward, my lips touching his.

"My Kia deserves beauty."

My body stilled, even my breathing.

Oh God.

Sam wasn't done.

"She deserves hope."

Oh God!

"Take it, baby," he whispered against my mouth.

My hands moved to either side of his head and I looked through the dark into his eyes as I moved up and down. Slowly, then faster, harder, his thumb moved to my clit and started rolling and I sucked in breath.

"That's it, Kia, honey, fuck me. Take what you deserve."

"Sam," I moaned. His thumb put on more pressure, my neck and back arched, it tore through me, leaving a wake of sheer ecstasy, and I cried out.

Before I was done, Sam flipped me to my back and pounded deep, his breathing labored, one arm tight around my middle back, the other hand cupping my face.

"Even in the dark, all I can see is how beautiful you are," he growled.

His words tore through me too and their wake was no less beautiful.

I lifted my head and kissed him. He took over the kiss, his tongue driving into my mouth. One of my legs was wrapped around his waist, holding tight, the other one around the back of his thigh, doing the same. My hands were running along the skin of his back when his mouth disengaged from mine, his head snapped back, he thrust in deep and groaned deeper, the sound rumbling through me spectacularly, its origin not from his throat but between my legs.

And I lay under Sam, listening to his breaths even out, thinking of his words, his actions, and how they coated my skin, seeping in, reminding me that with Sam, I was invincible.

I held him close as his head tipped forward, his face disappearing into my neck, and I felt his mouth move there as his hips moved, stroking tenderly.

God, *God,* I loved it when he did that.

My hand drifted up the sleek muscle of his back, his neck, and I cupped the back of his head.

I turned mine and whispered in his ear, "You make me feel invincible."

I felt his body still for a moment before he muttered against my skin, "Good."

I held on, loving the feel of him, his weight, his warmth, all that he'd just given me, allowing myself a moment to glory in that before I did what I knew I had to do and went on, "But I think we have to talk."

Instantly, Sam pulled away. My limbs tightened to hold him to me, but he was stronger. He rolled off, and suddenly, I felt cold. And for the first time since our first date, I felt strangely alone.

His hand came to rest on my belly and his mouth came to mine. "Later. Now I gotta crash."

"Sam—"

His hand pressed in, his head moved back an inch and he cut me off with a quiet yet firm, "Later, baby."

I stayed silent. This was important, at least to me. And it was growing more important every day.

But Sam Cooper gave a lot and he didn't take very much. He didn't want to do this now, that was clear. So I felt I had to give that to him.

So I let it go but still whispered, "Promise?"

His hand slid up my body to curl around the side of my neck and he whispered back, "Promise."

I studied him in the dark and decided Sampson Cooper would honor his promise.

"Okay, honey," I said softly.

I lifted up, touched my mouth to his, pulled away and rolled off the bed. I went to the bathroom, cleaned up and returned to the bedroom. I tagged my nightie from under the pillow, located my discarded underwear, tugged on both and joined Sam in bed.

Without delay, his arm shoved under me and he curled me into his side.

Yes. Okay. Everything would be okay.

I settled.

Memphis jumped up on the bed and sprawled on the side I wasn't using, considering I was on Sam's side.

Sam crashed.

Then Memphis did.

A little later, so did I.

17

YOU OKAY?

Eleven days later…

"You okay, babe?"

I turned my head from watching Sam standing in my yard, talking to my brother, Kyle, to Paula, who was standing beside me, holding my plastic cup refreshed with lemonade, part of the many refreshments my mother brought to see us through the day.

It was early afternoon of my yard sale, and after we finished up, Dad, Kyle, and Sam were going to haul anything left to the Goodwill. Then we were going to Paula and Rudy's for a barbeque. After that, Sam and I were driving to Indianapolis, staying the night at the Hyatt, and getting on a plane headed to North Carolina late the next morning.

Not that there would be much to go to the Goodwill. Firstly, an everything-must-go sale stated pretty clearly that the person having it wanted everything to go and not many people were averse to a bargain. Secondly, everyone in America knew I was with Sam, which included everyone in Indiana, so practically everyone in Indiana showed up.

We had our first person arrive at five thirty in the morning.

Sam didn't even open the door. But he and Memphis got out of bed and walked to it and I heard him shout, "Come back on time. Eight o'clock. No sooner."

Memphis yapped her concurrence.

Then Sam wrote a note, put it on the door and came back to bed. It didn't stop a few people from knocking, but he didn't get up again. At seven thirty, my posse showed and we started dragging stuff out to the yard. The minute we did, all the doors opened on the cars lining the road in front of my house *and* down the side streets and they descended en masse.

Half the stuff was gone by nine o'clock.

Another quarter of it was gone by ten thirty.

Now it was two in the afternoon and only the dregs were left. I'd been so busy, I'd barely noticed if Sam was inundated by admirers (though I did notice many occasions he was chatting with people, but just like him, he seemed to take this in stride). My house was empty save for Sam and my suitcases. I'd hired professional cleaners to come in on Monday and I'd given Mom power of attorney to close on the house for me, something that was happening on Thursday.

It had happened.

All that was Cooter and me was gone except for the dregs sitting on my lawn. I'd sifted through everything and there was nothing left. I'd even sold nearly all of my clothes except ones I'd bought in the months after he died and when I was on vacation.

I felt relief about this and it ran deep. I also felt a shimmer of elation. It was done. I could move on. Any memories I had were no longer physical, they were only in my head and those would fade.

That said, it was only a shimmer of elation because the answer to Paula's question was no, I was not okay.

And I was not okay because Sam had broken his promise.

At first, I'd been patient and given him time. We were busy sorting through the stuff in the house, renting a small storage unit for anything I intended to keep and going on approximately three billion, four hundred and twenty-seven viewings with Paula (none of them fruitful, alas). Then there was hauling stuff to the storage unit, dinners at Mom and Dad's, Paula and Rudy's, Missy's, Teri's, or meeting them at restaurants. There was also finding and hiring a cleaning firm. And working with Teri to arrange travel to North Carolina. And also Sam's workouts and frequent telephone conversations with his crew of badasses and Ozzie.

But after a while, the hard work was done and it was mostly waiting for the yard sale to happen sprinkled with an occasional (fruitless) viewing.

When we had time on our hands, Sam filled it. He did this by telling me he wanted to visit the places he'd frequented when he'd lived in Indianapolis.

I'd been surprised. I knew he lived in Indy for several years, but I didn't know he held any nostalgia for it.

This was because he hadn't told me.

So we went to Eagle Creek Park where Sam said he would go and run; he liked it and he missed it. Though, luckily, he didn't run when we went there, but we did walk for over an hour. We drove around the Circle. We went to an Italian restaurant called Patrizio's, where, the minute Sam walked in, the owner (the aforementioned Patrizio) greeted him like a long-lost son. Interspersed with his many duties running a popular but kind of hole-in-the-wall restaurant, Patrizio hung at our table and I learned more about Sam from Patrizio than I did from Sam. But again, all of it was fun, reminiscing, nothing meaty, nothing profound.

In other words, in our time in Indiana we did a lot, we were together almost constantly, but what we did not do was talk as Sam promised we would.

He was no less attentive, no less gentlemanly, no less Sam, which meant he was no less guarded.

And that was what it was. I'd figured it out. And I'd figured it out not after the first time I gently attempted to steer our conversation to him, his intensity about me and where that was coming from, his history, his heart, and had been just as gently rebuffed. Nor did I figure it out after the second time I, a little less gently, tried to approach him and was again gently rebuffed.

No, it was the last time, last night, after we'd had sex, were cuddling and murmuring about nothing important, when I'd tried to move it to stuff that was important and was not gently rebuffed.

And I did this by cautiously and gently (I thought) asking about his brother, Ben.

"Don't, Kia. Yeah?" Sam had said, his until-then soft murmur suddenly holding an edge.

"Don't?" I asked carefully.

"Don't," Sam confirmed.

"Don't what?"

"Don't push it."

I pulled in breath, then asked, "Push what?"

Sam didn't answer.

No.

What he did was lift up and twist, coldly dislodging me from where I was lounging on his chest. Then he turned off the light and settled in bed with his back to me.

Yes, that was what he did. He gave me nothing and then he completely shut me out.

After the shock wore off (and this took a while), I rolled to my back, cuddled Memphis, and stared at the ceiling, feeling a pain stabbing close to my heart.

Because I knew at that moment that it wasn't about us being new, getting to know each other, feeling each other out. It wasn't about things being intense, our feelings for each other, and all the stuff swirling around me. And it wasn't that we were jet-lagged, busy and there were a million things on our minds.

It was that Sam did not intend to share and I couldn't figure this out. He was demonstrative, affectionate and communicative. He listened, I knew. He always paid attention. He cared what I said about practically everything, even if I was waxing on about how awesome pasta was at Patrizio's.

He just wasn't letting me in.

The one time I put up what Sam called "a wall," he got seriously ticked and tore it right down. But turnabout was obviously not fair play with Sam Cooper.

He'd broken his promise.

And that hurt.

I looked from Paula back to Sam, and suddenly, I felt my head start to throb dully.

I was in unchartered territory.

Of the things Sam *had* shared, he'd made it clear he didn't want me gabbing to my girlfriends about him, though this was mostly about how he was in bed.

I didn't know if it was okay to do what every girl in the world did and that was pick apart her relationship with her boyfriend. I didn't want to piss off Sam, especially not now, when I felt things were at a fragile juncture.

It didn't seem fair if the rules of dating a famous hot guy included the fact you couldn't seek advice from your girlfriends, especially in the beginning and seriously especially at a fragile juncture.

"Babe?" Paula prompted, and I looked back at her. But before I could speak, she handed me my lemonade and declared, "You know, this is good."

My mind on Sam, I didn't know what she was talking about.

"What's good?"

"This." She swept her arm out to the yard. My eyes followed it, and when they did, I saw Teri and Missy heading our way. "This is good," she went on. "Letting that dickhead go. Exorcising him from your life, all of it, all of him. It's good."

"It is, you know," Missy told me when she and Teri stopped close.

"I know," I replied, looking amongst my friends.

Paula was petite, had dark, thick, curly hair, gray eyes and she was a little plump but she worked it.

Teri was tall like me, way rounder than me, but she also worked it. She had ash-blonde, wispy hair she spent a fortune on having cut so it didn't look so wispy.

Missy was also tall, but she was blue-eyed, dark-haired and reed thin by design. She worked out daily at the gym, getting up at five o'clock in the morning on weekdays to do it. Since Rich died, it was another of her obsessions. She dropped fifteen pounds she didn't need to lose due to grief and kept it off due to an obsession with fitness that took her mind off what she lost.

They were my friends, my posse, my best buds. But I had kept them distant from me for years as I lived in hell. They were friends who would have helped me, friends who stood by me, even though I didn't let them in, and still, even learning that lesson, I was undecided about sharing about Sam.

And I didn't know how to feel about this either.

On the one hand, I was falling in love with Sam, and if he could grow to trust me, I could grow to trust that maybe the same thing was happening for him too. And I didn't want to do anything that might harm that.

On the other hand, with Cooter, I'd chosen the way wrong man for me, blinded by false glory, and I didn't want to do that again. Sam was not Cooter, I knew this. And for years I'd given a certain amount of headspace to what signs I might have missed from Cooter, red flags that, if I'd been older, more mature, I would have caught. There weren't many, but they were there. And what had happened last night with Sam completely shutting me out I thought was a red flag.

And my girls could confirm this. Or not. But at the very least, talking to them would mean letting it out and getting different viewpoints because the one I had wasn't so fun.

I didn't know what to do.

"You should be doing a happy jig," Teri told me, "but you look like someone ran over Memphis."

This took me out of my thoughts and I gasped at the very thought of my baby being run over. So did Paula. So did Missy. My two girls loved Memphis. Teri was partial to bigger dogs and ones Cooter hadn't adored.

"Don't say that!" Paula snapped.

"Jeez, don't be so touchy. I'm just saying what she looks like, not that I want anyone to run over Memphis," Teri returned.

"Ohmigod! You just said it again!" Paula cried.

"Seriously?" Teri fired back.

"Okay, I love your brother, but oh…my…*God*." This came from behind me, it came from Gitte, and the last word was breathy.

I looked over my shoulder to see she'd approached. She and Kyle had left the day after they ascertained Sam had my safety in hand. That said, I knew Kyle called Dad *and* Sam frequently to make sure everything was okay. They'd driven up last night, arriving late, to help me with my yard sale and to party with the gang after all that was my life with Cooter was carted away.

Now her blue eyes were big and they were staring across the yard.

"Holy shit," Teri whispered.

"Freaking, freakity, freak, *freak*," Paula breathed at the same time.

"Wow," Missy murmured reverently.

I followed their eyes and blinked. But after my blink, they didn't disappear like the dreamlike visions their utter perfection proclaimed them to be. They were still there, walking across the yard toward Sam and Kyle.

Two men. Both tall. Both dark. Both seriously freaking fit. And both *gorgeous*. One was maybe five (ten at the outside) years older than the other, but this did not detract from his absolute lusciousness.

"Who are those freaking guys?" Paula asked on a whisper.

"I have no idea," I answered, with my girl posse still gratefully drinking in the talent. In other words, I had not torn my eyes away from the two men.

They made it to Sam. There were smiles, chin jerks, head nods, handshakes and so much hot guy hormone floating in the air around them, it was a wonder every female in a two-block radius didn't instantly become pregnant.

Kyle was introduced. Then Sam's head turned, his eyes flowed through me and to the street where he gave another chin jerk. I followed his gaze and saw a man, short, bulky, negative body fat, seeing as he had so much muscle, his muscle was competing with his other muscle to control his frame. He had sandy blond hair close-cropped to his head and was wearing a jacket, even though it was eight-two degrees with seventy-five-percent humidity. I watched as he got out of his vehicle and leaned to the side.

Bodyguard.

Jeez, I'd been so busy selling my life with Cooter and freaking out about what happened last night with Sam that I hadn't even noticed him.

I looked back Sam's way to see him leading the hot guy crew toward the front door.

"We'll be a minute, honey," he called to me as he approached the door.

My eyes went from him to hot guy number one, then older hot guy number two, both of whom were looking at me with small, polite (but hot) smiles on their (hot) faces, then back to Sam.

They were his hunters. I knew it.

I shifted to start toward him and began, "I'll—"

"No," Sam cut me off. I stopped moving and saw he had too, his eyes on me. "Later."

I stared at him and that was it. Sam said "later," he meant later. And I knew this because he immediately opened my front door and him and his crew (and Kyle) disappeared behind it without another word.

That was when I stared at the closed door, unsure if I should stomp inside and demand to be let in on what was happening in *my life*. Or whether I should burst into tears because I was frustrated, and further, it couldn't be denied, Sam had hurt me last night. He'd actually *hurt* me—something I never thought Sam would do. Or whether I should scream at the top of my lungs to get rid of some of the tension that was bunching my shoulders, up my neck and throbbing in my head.

I was unable to come to a decision before Teri, who clearly was so mesmerized, she didn't hear my earlier answer, asked, "Do you know those guys?"

In the intervening days since my arrival home, I'd let my girls in on what Vanessa and Cooter did as well as what Sam was doing about it, so I answered, "I think they're Sam's friends who are dealing with my hit man issue."

Four sets of female eyes went to my front door.

Teri muttered, "I wouldn't mind my life, or other parts of me, being in their hands. Either one of them."

"I bet neither of those guys would have a problem with Sam's cardboard cutout being in the room while he gave you the business," Paula noted.

"There you go. Finally, a solution to that problem," Missy put in. "You need a badass. That way you can keep your cutout of Sam and still get yourself regular orgasms."

Teri looked at Missy. "The only badass in town was Milo and he's not in town anymore because he's at the penitentiary. And I didn't know he was a badass until he blew half a man's head off."

"I have to admit, Heartmeadow is kind of a badass wasteland," Missy muttered.

"Tell me about it," Teri muttered back.

"Rudy's a badass," Paula threw out, and we all looked at her but said not a word. "He is!" she asserted, correctly reading our looks. "He'd never let anything happen to me."

"Uh, girl, I don't know if you were here just now, but those two dudes are like Sam. That is to say, they could disarm Milo on a rampage and then break him in two, after which they'd successfully lead a mission to dismantle a terrorist sect intent on ending American society as we know it. You're right, Rudy would never let anything happen to you. But we just were introduced to visions of pure badass and, love him to bits, but for the first time in my life seeing the real thing, Rudy is no badass," Teri stated.

"Uh...excuse me?" A female yard sale patron joined our huddle, thankfully before Paula could attempt (unsuccessfully) to defend Rudy's badassness. "This box says five dollars. Does that mean everything in it?"

I nodded. "Sure does."

"Will you accept three?" the patron asked.

I opened my mouth to answer in the affirmative, but Paula got there before me. "Woman, from what I can see, what's in that box is worth fifty dollars. You're getting it for five and you wanna pay three?"

"Paula," I whispered.

"It's a yard sale," the patron retorted. "You're supposed to haggle."

"It's an everything-must-go-because-your-dead-husband-was-a-serious-dickhead sale and that means you pay the price my girl spent her time writing on the box and walk away happy you got yourself one freaking huge-ass bargain," Paula returned.

"You don't have to curse," the patron shot back.

"Honey, you just got here, but it's been pandemonium, seein' as everything that's been carted away was *the definition* of huge-ass bargain. And her dead husband wanted *her* dead. There is no other word for a man like that but dickhead," Paula parried, and the patron looked at me.

"Yeah, I read that. That's just awful. Though, you done real good for yourself, hooking up with Coop. And you're climbing the best-dressed list. I saw you in your bikini on that beach on that island and you looked real good."

I stared. Then I breathed, "What?"

"You were on a beach in a white bikini and you were tan, just like now. They had a special summer edition of beach babes on youwearitwell.com and you landed the number four slot," the woman told me.

"You're moving up," Gitte muttered. "Told you."

Gitte sounded happy.

I was freaked.

The patron kept the information flowing. "Same bikini, different picture, you were wearin' like a short, see-through sarong, holding hands with Coop, walking up the beach on bodiesbygod.com, and you got on last week's edition, number six on the Curvy Girls list."

Oh. My. *God!*

People were taking pictures of me. Of us! And I was in a bikini! And I didn't even know it!

Sure, it happened before, but that was Tilda. Tilda was rude and rabid. Tilda doing it wasn't a surprise.

This was.

I had no idea.

The throb in my head became less dull and I checked myself from glancing around frantically as paranoia set in that right that very moment someone was taking a photo of me that would eventually be posted somewhere I didn't know it would be.

"I need an aspirin," I muttered.

"I got aspirin in my purse in the house. I'll go get you one," Missy offered, and headed toward the house.

"So, will you take three dollars for this box?" the woman brought matters back in hand.

Again, before I could answer, Paula did. "No."

"But—" she started.

"Seriously? Not only is it a bargain, you're buying it from *Coop's girlfriend*. You can tell all your friends that *and* that you spoke to her too. That makes it a serious bargain," Paula returned.

"Hadn't thought of that," the woman muttered.

"Five dollars," Paula stated firmly, holding out her hand, palm up.

The woman glanced at the box, then at me, then at the house where I was certain she'd seen Sam disappear. After she did all that, she went for her purse.

I left Paula to it, wandered away and sat in the grass. I was sipping my lemonade and still controlling the urge to survey my surroundings to make certain no one was aiming a camera (or other more deadly technology) at me when Gitte lithely fell to the grass beside me.

She asked Paula's question.

"You okay?"

I pulled in a breath, turned my head and looked at her.

"I have a headache."

She nodded and looked across the yard at the half a dozen people milling about and pawing through stuff.

"Kyle is…" she started quietly, and trailed off.

When she didn't say more, I leaned into her, bumping her with my shoulder and she looked at me.

"Kyle is what?"

"He cried when Cooter died."

I blinked.

Whoa. Shocker.

"He did?" I asked.

"Yeah," she answered. "A lot."

I didn't know what to make of this.

"I—" I started.

"Relieved," she whispered. I then knew what to make of it and I snapped my mouth shut. "If it had gone on much longer, Kia, he would have been Milo Cloverfield. I know it."

Oh God.

I closed my eyes.

What I had done to my family.

Oh God, what I had done.

"He likes Sam," she said, and I opened my eyes. "He likes him very much. And not because he's wealthy, not because he's famous, but because he cares about you in a healthy way."

There it was, my opening to throw out what was worrying me and pick it apart with Gitte. Gitte wasn't only strong, she was cool, she was smart and she had the ability to say it like it was without hurting your feelings. She, too, had more than once brought up the topic of Cooter, and she, too, had been shut down by me on said topic.

But she could and probably would talk to Kyle about anything I shared with her. And Kyle had Sam on speed dial. Further, Kyle could let something slip. It wouldn't be the first time. Heck, half the times I got in trouble when I was a kid was because Kyle had a big mouth.

No.

Gitte was out.

"I'm glad," I told her.

"He's still relieved," she told me. "We both are." She looked to the yard again and shared, "I think half of why he was so intent on driving up was that he was concerned you were with another man, even one like Sam, who he admired." Her eyes came back to me. "But anyone can be something for the public and something else privately. We were both very happy to know Sam is who Sam really is."

Yep. I had done a number on my family.

"He is," I assured her, even though I wasn't feeling so assured. Still, one thing I did know was that he was far better than Cooter. Far, *far* better.

"You need to believe in this," she told me softly.

"Sorry?"

"In you. In Sam." She smiled at me. "I see good things."

I did too.

Until last night.

She continued, "You don't believe in it, do you?"

"We've known each other a month."

"You go to bed beside him. He goes to bed beside you. How long has that been going on?"

I pressed my lips together and tried to calculate it.

I gave up and admitted, "Well, most of that month."

Gitte smiled again. "I believe this."

"Sam didn't waste a lot of time," I pointed out the obvious.

Her smile got bigger. "I believe this too. You, an American on vacation in Italy, he wouldn't wish to let you slip through his fingers."

I pressed my lips together.

"Or," she kept going, "it's *clear* he didn't wish to let you slip through his fingers because here you both are."

"Yep." I looked away. "Here we both are."

She took my hand and I looked back as she whispered, "*Believe,* Kiakee."

I stared into her eyes. Then I nodded.

Celeste and Thomas. Luci. Now Gitte. They all wanted me to believe.

Maybe they saw something I did not. Maybe Sam just needed more time.

Maybe I should just let my mental bullshit go and believe.

We'd only been together a month. Only a month. And he'd been screwed over repeatedly.

I needed to cut him some slack and believe.

So, to my nod, I added a smile.

She smiled back and let my hand go.

I took a sip of lemonade and in my head whispered, *fearless.*

I said it. I wanted to feel it and I tried. But my headache was not going away.

Whatever.

It was just a headache. Eventually it would fade.

Onward.

I made a decision.

"All right, sweetie, let's call an end to this. Load up the dregs in Dad's truck, get to Paula and Rudy's, and start the party."

"Sounds good to me," Gitte muttered, rolling gracefully to her feet.

I followed and moved toward the remaining boxes.

"You okay?"

Sam and I (and Memphis) were in our room at the Hyatt and he'd just tipped the bellman for bringing up our bags on a trolley.

I'd let Memphis out of her doggie carrier. She was exploring.

I was staring out the window at the amazing view of the Capitol and the lights of Indy and I didn't look at him when I answered, "I can't shake this headache."

This was true. Missy had given me aspirin, and a couple of hours later, Paula had given me ibuprofen. Neither worked.

And I had a feeling I knew why.

Deciding to believe in Sam and in us, being the dork I was, lasted around five minutes and started to melt away when Sam walked out of the house with Lee and Tanner.

I was right. Those men were his hunters, Lee Nightingale and Tanner Layne. He introduced them to me, my family, my friends and then they helped load up the remaining boxes of stuff in Dad's truck. They politely declined invites to Paula's barbeque, doing so with hot guy smiles that left all the females staring (and Teri nearly drooling), and took off.

Since there wasn't a lot of stuff, Sam and Kyle didn't have to haul any in Sam's rental SUV or Kyle's car, only Dad had to make the trip. So Sam loaded up our suitcases, I grabbed Memphis, and we went right to Paula and Rudy's. My car was already stowed in Mom and Dad's back shed so I went with Sam.

In the SUV, I'd asked, "So, what was with the powwow?"

Sam's reply?

"Later, baby."

It was said gentle, sweet, but still, it upset me. As far as I knew, he hadn't had a face-to-face with them since we got there, but I wouldn't really know since he never told me anything. They'd talked on the phone often, but one thing I did know was they had not approached the house. Not to mention, it wasn't one of them, it was both.

This made me think they had something important to say.

And when Dad got to Paula and Rudy's, I knew they did because Sam left it for approximately two-point-five minutes before he negotiated a private huddle with Dad and Kyle, *sans* me.

I'd let it go in the car because my head was hurting even more and I had to keep a lock on my reaction because I didn't want to get emotional, however that emotional might be—either losing it and snapping at him, or losing it and getting teary.

After the huddle, even with my head still throbbing, I'd picked my moment and caught Sam when we could be alone.

"Is something up that I should know?" I asked.

Again, gentle and sweet, he lifted his hand, cupped my jaw, his head dipped close and he whispered, "Now's not the time, honey. Later."

He'd kissed my nose, his hand fell away and he moved away.

The good news was, he didn't seem wired and worried. Neither did my dad or Kyle. In fact, studying my father and brother, they seemed more at ease than they'd been for ages.

So, clearly, nothing dire had happened.

The bad news was, if it was nothing bad, I didn't get why Sam wouldn't tell me.

As I stared out the window, I felt Sam fit his body to the back of mine and his arms went around me. Then I felt his jaw settle at the side of my head.

"Important day for you," he muttered.

"Yeah," I agreed.

"It's done," he stated.

"Yeah," I repeated.

His arms gave me a squeeze and didn't let go. He was quiet. So was I.

I waited for him to say something. We had time. It wasn't early, it wasn't late. It was just us. Until we had to be at the airport to check in our bags and Memphis for our flight, which didn't leave until eleven, we had nothing to do but be.

He didn't say anything.

Neither did I.

But I felt my head start pounding.

Before I could figure out what to say, Sam spoke.

"Get ready for bed, relax. I'm gonna take Memphis down and give her a walk. Yeah?"

"Yeah."

"Where's her leash?"

"In my overnight bag."

His jaw went away and his lips swept my neck. Then he let me go.

I turned and watched him dig through my bag and nab the leash. Memphis went mental at seeing it, Sam clipped it on and gave me a smile and chin lift (Memphis gave me a yap), and they were out the door.

I turned back to the window, but I closed my eyes against the view.

Everything Sam danced across the backs of my eyelids. All of it, except what happened last night, was beautiful.

I opened my eyes and stared at a view I knew cost more than the average room, something else Sam gave to me since he was paying for it, like everything else.

And seeing that view, knowing he knew I had a headache so he was taking care of my dog, surmising that he was giving me quiet time to reflect on my "important day," thinking of all that was him and that very day getting rid of everything that had anything to do with the hell I'd lived in my years of Cooter, I could not believe I wanted more.

But I couldn't help it.

I did.

When it came to Sam, I wanted everything.

And I was beginning to fear he wasn't going to give it to me.

18

RANGERS

My headache was gone.

And without the throbbing, a yard sale, my friends and family, and with it being the next day, nothing but Sam and me, waiting around, standing in line, hanging in departure lounges (the swish ones where the rich and famous hung, which was to say where Sam hung, and now me) and sitting on planes, I was no longer confused and concerned and trying to talk myself into being fearless.

I was pissed.

This was because Sam had plenty of opportunity to bring up any of a variety of topics, first and foremost whatever he spoke with Lee and Tanner about the day before.

But he didn't.

In fact, although still unfailingly courteous and demonstrative with affection—holding hands, sitting in the lounge with his arm slung around the back of my seat, reading his *Sports Illustrated* on the plane with one hand resting on my thigh—he was mostly quiet. He was doing that being-aware-of-his-surroundings thing again. This likely because he could not fly with a firearm, and the bodyguard who was coming with us (the other one was driving) who, unlike us, was flying coach and couldn't get into the rich and famous departure lounge, was also unarmed and not with us the whole time.

Though I guessed this, obviously, since Sam didn't tell me he had any concerns.

I spent this time mostly thinking about everything that crowded my head.

Then I spent it getting pissed about it.

Firstly, it was *my* life in danger and I felt I should be kept apprised of that situation.

Sure, I'd had a tough time with Cooter. And sure, when Sam and I met, I'd had my fair share of dramas.

But since Crete, I'd been me, moving onward, dealing with things, getting on with life, and doing all of this totally drama free. Sam noticed everything. He had to have noticed things had evened out for me, and if I did say so myself, I was handling everything pretty freaking well.

Secondly, in the beginning, I'd been clear several times when I didn't feel like sharing. But Sam didn't accept that. He pushed it and got what he wanted. When I pushed it, he shut me out.

Rudely and hurtfully.

And he didn't even mention that night when he'd turned his back on me, falling asleep at my side for the first time since we'd been together without me tucked close. He didn't apologize. He didn't explain. He just went on like it didn't happen.

And as our plane touched down in Raleigh, I decided…no.

That was not acceptable.

I was not able to share my feelings with Sam as a captive audience in a car, however. This was because Sam's friend Hap was picking us up.

"Hap," Sam had shared with me (a miracle!), was an Army buddy who was still in the Army. Hap had dropped Sam off when he went to Italy. Hap had looked after Sam's house while he was gone. And Hap was picking us up.

And Hap, I suspected (though wasn't told), would be bringing Sam his hardware or carrying himself.

Hap's nickname was short for Hap's *other* nickname, "Happy." Hap's real name was George Cunningham.

And, waiting for us at baggage claim, I found Hap was a good-looking, five foot eleven, brown-crew-cut-haired, smiley-brown-eyed mass of compact but bulky muscle. So much of it, it had grown up his neck so he no longer had one.

"Dude!" he'd shouted so loud, several people jumped and turned to look, or that was to say, those who weren't already staring at Sam started staring at all of us.

Then he treated Sam to a man hug that included back pounding that was so hard, I winced at the thuds. They separated and Hap stepped back a foot and faked a one-two punch combo to Sam's body that Sam didn't pretend to deflect. He just grinned down at his friend.

Then Sam turned and started, "Hap, this is—"

But he got no further.

Hap's dancing brown eyes came to me and he finished for Sam, "Your seriously *fine* piece of ass."

I blinked.

Sam tipped his head back to study the ceiling.

Before I could recover and decide whether to be amused or offended, two iron arms closed around me, I was lifted clean off my feet and shaken about seven times.

"For fuck's sake, Hap, put Kia down," Sam growled.

I landed on my flip-flops with a body-jarring thud but could not get away, even though Hap's arms went from around me. This was because his hands clamped on my jaw and he grinned huge in my face.

"Babe, you…are…seriously…*fine.* Shit!" he declared.

"Uh…thanks?" I couldn't help it. It came out as a question.

He didn't answer. He let me go but didn't step back, only leaned back, doing a head to toe and back again, then he asked curiously, "Now, who would wanna take out a fine piece of ass like this?"

As I suspected, Hap had been briefed.

"Bud, let it go once. That's twice. There won't be a third time." Sam was still growling, but it wasn't a semi-amused, semi-annoyed growl. This one was full-on annoyed.

Hap stepped back and tossed Sam a big smile.

He looked back at me and stated, "Luci says you're not only not hard on the eyes but also you're the freakin' shit."

"That's nice since I think the same way of Luci," I replied.

"Everyone does," he told me. "When Gordo landed her…" he trailed off and whistled, feeling this said it all because he strangely (and crudely, I might add) went on with, "Couldn't even jack off to pictures of her anymore. Gordo could sense that shit and he'd rip your dick off, but he'd use your throat to get to it."

I wasn't sure, but I thought my mouth had dropped open.

Hap finished with, "Sucked."

"I, uh…bet," I agreed.

"All right." Sam got close and claimed me with an arm around my shoulders, curling in and tucking me to his hard side. "Not sure you noticed, but we're in baggage claim, not a locker room. And even if we were in a locker room, not feelin' happy vibes you're not checkin' that shit around my woman. So I'll say it once: be cool."

"Dude, calm down," Hap, apparently and surprisingly unafraid of Sam's tone, replied at the same time pressing his hands down. "Kia and me, we're just gettin' the feel of one another."

"Since I got a choice, and I do, I'll tell you to give Kia a different feel for you. One that doesn't make you look like an asshole," Sam returned.

Hap turned his unwavering grin to me. "He wants me to make a good impression so you don't think he's a dick because I'm a dick."

"Yeah," Sam concurred. "That'd be good."

"He's not a dick," Hap assured me.

"I, um…kinda already noticed that," I replied.

Hap's grin got bigger. Sam's arm got tighter.

"Me, the jury's still out, seein' as I haven't nailed down a fine piece of ass like you or Luci," Hap shared.

"Just a bit of friendly advice. You want one, you might want to stop calling us pieces of ass," I shared in return.

Hap smiled wide.

This guy was so rough around the edges, he was jagged. Still, I couldn't help it, I liked him.

So I smiled back.

Luckily, at this juncture, the baggage claim started rolling.

We got our bags, or I should say, Sam and Hap got our bags. I didn't even carry my carry-on and this was because Hap divested me of it. Then we walked to the counter where we could claim Memphis.

They put her doggie crate on the counter and I leaned down to coo through the gate at her.

Memphis yapped, her body vibrating and her tongue trying to lick me through the metal.

There it was. Just like Memphis, her first plane ride didn't faze her. She was clearly no worse for the wear.

On this relieved thought, I heard Hap exclaim, "Jesus, what the fuck is that?"

I straightened and looked at him. "It's my dog, Memphis."

"That is not a dog," Hap declared, and I stared at him.

"She is. She's a King Charles spaniel," I informed him.

Hap didn't tear his eyes away from the crate when he announced scornfully through a lip curl, "She's a big brown-and-white rat with creepy eyes."

Ohmigod!

Memphis's eyes weren't creepy! They were cute!

"She is not," I returned.

Hap looked at Sam. "Are you sayin' that thing is gonna be in my truck?"

I put my hands to my hips. "She's not *a thing*. She's *a dog*. *My* dog."

Hap's eyes came to me. "Babe, you got bad guys after you. A rat won't do shit to a bad guy unless it's got fleas or is carrying the plague. You need a dog with balls. A German shepherd. A Doberman. A Rottie."

Memphis yapped, though I couldn't read if her yap was agreeing with Hap or if she was offended.

As for me, I decided I was pissed again, this time at Hap.

Before I could give Hap indication of my mood, Sam stepped in.

"First, yeah, Hap, Memphis is gonna be in your truck. Second, we got folks bearin' down on us and I'm not in the mood to sign autographs. I'm in the mood to sit on my deck and drink a beer. And last, we got a dog who's been cooped up for a while so we need to get her some time with some grass."

I glanced around and saw two huddles of people eyeing us. One had decided on an approach and had instigated it. One was still considering it.

I turned from them and gave Hap a glare. Hap gave me a grin. I ignored it, grabbed the handle to Memphis's crate and stomped with Hap and Sam to the parking garage.

We luckily escaped the approach of the autograph seekers and made it to the garage unmolested. Sam and Hap loaded our bags in the back of Hap's SUV. I loaded Memphis and me in the backseat. Sam climbed in front, Hap behind the wheel, and away we went.

It was, unfortunately, over a two-hour drive from Raleigh to Sam's place at Kingston Beach, which was outside Wilmington. After his time being stationed in Georgia, Sam had been (and Hap still was) stationed at Fort Bragg in Fayetteville, where Hap lived. Sam had a place there when he was active duty but also had his place at the beach. Since Sam was discharged, he'd sold his place close to the base and now just had the house in Kingston.

As soon as he could, Hap stopped so we could let Memphis have a wander and take care of business. And since I'd never been to North Carolina, the first half hour of the trip was interesting. This was not only taking in the passing landscape but also listening to Hap gab nonstop to Sam, filling him in on stuff that had happened with mutual friends while Sam had been gone, hearing names I'd heard in passing from Sam.

Then, when Hap ran out of news and both men in the front fell silent, as I was prone to do on car rides, I got bored.

Memphis did not. She stood, back paws to my thigh, front paws to the window ledge on the door, nose to the crack in the window, drinking in North Carolina with her doggie senses. I knew she liked it because she licked her chops often and wagged her tail even more.

Finally, we hit Kingston and I instantly fell in love. It was not a mix of old and new, it was just old. The main street consisted of two sides of two-story, sturdy, red brick buildings decorated with American flags and pots of flowers. There were some graceful white-columned structures with rolling lawns on big lots that were stereotypical of the South. There were also some houses built close together and painted in bright pastels that were really cool. And last, you could smell the sea air and hear the cry of the gulls. It was just busy enough to seem populated and friendly, but not overwhelming.

I could totally see why Sam picked this place. It was awesome.

Hap took us slightly out of the town and turned onto a narrow road that managed somehow to be attractive while at the same time not inviting strangers. This was because of the big sign that said, Private Road. Private Beach. Homeowners Only.

Although it was a private road that led to houses on a private beach, the homes were surprisingly mostly older and small-ish, not the grand manses I would have suspected a rich, famous hot guy to live in. They were also built relatively close together. Every once in a while you could see someone bought a couple of lots, scraped the old houses, and put up modern, starkly designed (but cool) beach houses. But mostly the houses seemed vintage and established.

As we closed on the dead end, Hap lifted a hand and nabbed a remote from his sun visor. He hit the button, then tossed it to Sam, who caught it. He slowed and turned.

It was then I realized that regardless of my mood, I was excited to see where Sam lived. He called it his house. He talked about his deck. But he had not described it. I knew he had a place in Indy when he was playing for the Colts but sold it when he quit. I knew he had a place in LA while he was playing for the Colts where he lived outside football season, and he sold that too. This was now his only property.

And I suspected it would be everything—as the tall, black, attractive but not entirely imposing gate swung open and Hap drove through—I saw that it was not.

It was not a huge, modern, starkly designed (but cool) beach house on a triple lot.

It was a small, established, charming beach house on a single lot with a similarly small, established beach house close to it on one side, nothing but sand dunes and grass on the other.

There was a short, curving, black asphalt drive that grew wide and led to a two-car garage. The drive also swung along and up the side of the house. I could see the dune that the house was built into, jutting out from the house on either side. And all the green space around the drive was set with cool, tall, what I would guess were native grasses in bunches. The house was wide, squat and had two stories. And there was a white-painted, narrow walkway that wrapped around the house.

Hap drove up the side of the drive and we unloaded. As the men got the bags, I stood, carrying Memphis's crate with a Memphis I'd reloaded in it. Then Sam led us toward the front of the house facing the ocean.

I followed. Hap followed me. We trundled up a white-painted plank ramp and there it was.

The beach.

The ocean.

Beautiful.

Sam didn't slow to drink in the view and around he went to a long deck that had two tall flagpoles at each end. One flew an

American flag and under it was a black flag with what looked like a yellow diamond from which two wings jutted out the sides. On the other pole was a black flag with a gray skull wearing a forest-green beret with an insignia on it, neon green fire shooting out the sides and crossed rifles at the skull's jaw.

I stopped and stared at it as Sam went on and Hap came up behind me.

"Rangers," Hap said, and my eyes moved from the flag to him.

"Sorry?"

He extended his head to the flag. "Rangers. Army Rangers," he stated, then his head jerked to the other flagpole. "Airborne." He grinned. "Figure you know the one with the stars and stripes."

I stared at him a second, then I looked at the flags.

Rangers?

I could not say I was hip on all the elite training a man in the Army could do.

What I could say was that I knew what a Ranger was. Everyone did.

They were the baddest of the badasses *in the world.*

And I'd read the book about Sam and it said not one thing about Rangers.

I looked back at Hap, my brows knit. "Was Sam a Ranger?"

His face changed. The grin stayed in place and he was wearing sunglasses so I couldn't see if it still lit his eyes, but I could tell he was no longer committed to it.

"Maybe I should let Sam tell you about that," he muttered over the waves crashing against the sand.

Right. Like that would happen.

Woodenly, I turned toward the house, taking it in. It was shingle-sided, the shingles painted gray with grayish-brown shingles on the roof. The woodwork was white. The deck had a plethora of white Adirondack chairs with curved footstools that, pushed together, made the chairs more like lounges. There were also a couple squat, round tables. It led to a deck-long screened porch that, when I walked through, I saw had a rough wood picnic table with two benches on one side of the porch and a wide wraparound bench on the other side, which was covered in dark gray cushions strewn with huge, fluffy, light gray and bright yellow pillows.

Through the double front doors I was in the house.

I wanted to take it in, but I also needed to let Memphis free. So I got out of Hap's way, shoved my sunglasses back on my head, set down her crate and turned her loose. She burst out, emitted a couple of yaps, then put her nose to the floor and commenced her voyage of discovery.

I straightened and did the same but with my eyes as Hap moved up the stairs that were in the middle of the space.

To my right, a big seating area. Lots of windows. To my left, another big seating area that included a large flat-screen TV. More windows. To the right back, over a bar with stools, a huge, modern, clean kitchen with white cupboards, a big island and lots of gray, dark gray, and black speckled, shining granite countertops.

There was a wall on the other side up which were the stairs with a white wooden railing on their open side and dark wood steps (the same wood as the floors underfoot) leading up to the second floor. On the other side of the stairs was the dining room, which had a long, rectangular dining room table, more windows and a low chest.

I was surprised to see it didn't look expensive, posh, or like it had been crafted by a designer's hand. It looked comfortable, welcoming and very, very masculine. There was a lot of space and there also was a lot of furniture. Then again, there was so much space, there could be a lot of furniture and it still seemed airy and roomy and not cluttered. Blacks and grays abounded. Some hints of yellow, army green and red. The furniture was fluffy, wide-seated and invited you to hang out. Any tables were attractive but utilitarian; they were meant to catch keys, mail, books, beverages, or a consumed plate of nachos. Decorative touches were minimal.

There were some framed photos and two framed flags that were much like the flags outside. One black, with the word Ranger in yellow in a banner partially covering a star, under it a gray skull over wings coming from a sword with blue curved embellishments, all in a gray circle. The other was white with a black badge that had the profile of a white eagle's head in it over a banner that stated Airborne in yellow.

And that was pretty much it. No Colts or Bruins jerseys pinned on mats and framed. No shrines to Sam's life in football—trophies, plaques, team pictures, or shots of fabulous plays to be remembered. And no shrines to Sam's life in the Army—pictures with buds wearing fatigues and casually handling massive, scary automatic weapons, or frames displaying patches or medals.

I thought this was interesting, but I didn't know why.

Memphis wandered into the kitchen.

I wandered to the table by the door.

In a frame sitting on the table was a younger Sam wearing a suit, smiling his blinding, trademark gorgeous smile. He had his arm around a handsome man nearly as tall as Sam, wearing an Army uniform. The man was also smiling a blinding smile much like Sam's. His brother, Ben. On Ben's other side was an attractive, older woman with a proud smile and clear Hispanic ancestry, her arm also around Ben, but her body was turned to him, tucked close to his side with his arm around her. Sam's mother, Marisela.

My body jumped and I turned when I heard Sam's voice saying, "Baby, gonna hit the store." I watched his long legs then the rest of his body coming down the stairs as he continued, "Hap's gonna stick around. I'll get enough to cover us and we'll go back out tomorrow." He made it to me and wrapped his arms loosely around me, his chin tipping down to hold my eyes. "I'll get some beer, coffee, milk and dog food. We'll get takeout tonight. Hap's gotta get back to the base so he'll leave after dinner. You need me to get anything else?"

"Breakfast?" I suggested.

"Got oatmeal. Got granola. I'll get some fruit and yogurt. Anything else?"

I shook my head.

Sam dropped his and kissed my nose.

He pulled back an inch and I saw the warmth in his eyes when he whispered, "Make yourself at home."

Make myself at home.

That was nice, *so* nice.

Boy, I wished I wasn't pissed at him.

I nodded again.

He gave me a grin.

Then he let me go, walked into the kitchen and disappeared behind the stairs. Thirty seconds later, I heard a garage door go up, then the growl of what had to be a truck or SUV (a *big* one). A few seconds later, I heard a garage door going down.

It hit me that I didn't even know what kind of vehicle Sam drove.

Then it hit me that everything that was hitting me about Sam was a surprise.

Then it hit me even more than it had been hitting me that I didn't know anything about my boyfriend.

"Yo!" Hap called. My body jolted again and I saw he, too, was downstairs and grinning at me. "You're in a different time zone, babe, but you didn't fly to China. You okay?"

No.

I wasn't.

My boyfriend was a Ranger and I didn't know.

My life was in danger and I had no clue what was going on with that.

My mother was closing on my house in four days, and after that, I'd be homeless.

I had no job and I had no idea what I was going to do with the rest of my life.

And I'd just flown to North Carolina with my boyfriend, who I knew was a gentleman, he had a great sense of humor, my family and friends liked him, he was loyal to his friends and family, he was phenomenal in bed, he liked me, and he also liked my dog.

But other than that, although I'd spent a month with the man nearly nonstop, I really didn't know a thing about him. Or, I should say, nowhere near what I should know, nowhere near what he knew about me, and not enough of what I knew was important.

So, no.

I wasn't okay.

"Great!" I chirped my lie, then asked, "After I get Memphis a drink, can we take a walk on the beach?"

Hap approached, still grinning, and answered, "Yeah, but only if I go with you. It'll be a hit to my street cred, takin' that rat for a walk on the beach, but I'll get in a bar fight or something this week, make up for it."

I smiled at him.

Yes. Hap was carrying. I didn't know where, considering his dark gray t-shirt was skintight, but he was wearing black cargo pants and they had a bunch of pockets, so maybe he had his weapon skillfully hidden somewhere there.

Whatever.

That was his gig. My gig was getting my dog some *agua*, finding her leash, and clearing my thoughts by walking the beach.

"Cool," I grinned back. "Let's go."

"Drive safe," Sam murmured, shaking Hap's hand. "Owe you," he finished.

"You bought dinner and beer and think you still got markers, dude," Hap returned intriguingly, grinning up at Sam, then he turned to me and engulfed me in a bear hug.

I hugged him back, saying, "Text Sam when you get home."

He pulled slightly away, didn't drop his arms but did give me a big smile. "Babe, I don't check in."

"Practice," I replied. "You ever land a fine piece of ass, she'll expect that."

His smile got bigger. "Killer. I get how-to-take-care-of-a-hot-chick lessons from Sam's new pe…I mean, woman. I like it."

"Maybe you should take notes," I suggested on a head tilt and a grin.

His smile didn't waver and his arms gave me a squeeze. He let me go, turned away and flicked out two fingers as he moved to his SUV.

Sam moved to me, sliding an arm around my shoulders, then curling me so my front was in his side.

Hap swung in, fired up his truck, backed out of the drive, and through this, Sam and I didn't move. Sam also didn't wave, but I did. When Hap was out the gate and on his way, Sam's arm came up, he pressed the button on the remote he was carrying, and the gate started to swing closed.

That was when Sam turned us and headed us to the walkway. He kept his arm around my shoulders and we walked side by side.

We made it to the deck and Sam muttered, "Gonna drop this inside and get another beer. Want one?"

I looked up at Sam and shook my head. Sam tipped up his chin slightly and let me go. He headed inside. I headed to the railing of the deck.

The sun was beginning to set; it was late. Sam had come back from the grocery store before we got back from our walk on the beach. This was because Memphis loved the beach so I let her have a lot of time there. This was also because I needed that time to clear my head. I knew this because, even with that amount of time, I still hadn't cleared my head. Hap had walked with Memphis and me, but he did this mostly silent. I didn't know what to make of this, whether he was sensing my mood or whether he was trying to take a read on me.

We arrived back and beers were opened. Hap partook but sipped since he was going to be getting in a vehicle. We sat on the deck and chatted, or I should say, Hap and I chatted, and at this juncture, it was clear Hap was trying to get a read on me, mostly because our chatting consisted of Hap asking jovial, amusing questions that were jovial and amusing to disguise that they were nosy as all get-out.

I didn't have anything to hide so I answered them.

This was clearly satisfactory to both Hap *and* Sam, and I knew I'd earned Hap's approval when the guard he actually did disguise came crashing down and Hap, who seemingly was as happy as his nickname, became seriously freaking happy.

We ordered takeout. Sam went to go get it. We ate it with more beers and then Hap declared he had to go home.

Which brought me to now.

I heard the screen door bang shut, then I heard Memphis's claws clicking on the wood of the deck and I turned to see Memphis and Sam approaching, Memphis a lot quicker.

I bent and she jumped into my arms.

As I straightened, I told Sam, "I don't want her out off her lead. Not until she gets used to her new space. Your deck is open. She could take off and not know how to get home."

"She's fine," Sam replied, leaning into the railing and giving Memphis's head a rub before dropping his hand, lifting his other and taking a drag off his beer.

Memphis began to struggle to get down, and really, she'd been there all of a few hours. I didn't want her out without a lead until she knew the lay of the land.

I started to the house. "I'm gonna take her back in."

Sam's fingers curled around my arm, halting my progress. "Baby, like I said, she's fine."

"She doesn't know the lay of the land."

"She knows your call. She knows mine. She's fine."

"She's *my* dog, Sam!"

Yes, that was what I said. And yes, it came out with a lot more heat and volume than befitted our current conversation. And I knew it surprised Sam because he let me go and his chin jerked back.

I decided to go with it. Fuck it. I wasn't pissed about my dog, but I was still pissed, and so what? I had a hot guy boyfriend. So he was rich. So he was great in bed. So he was famous. So he was a lot nicer than my husband. That last, frankly, was not hard to do.

That didn't mean I couldn't get pissed and act like a bitch, even when the situation at hand didn't warrant it. I was a woman. Women, as far as I could tell from my girlfriends' conversations, did that all the time.

And, anyway, the situation not at hand definitely warranted it.

Therefore, I turned and marched to the door to the porch, through that and into the house, where I let Memphis down. She yapped, her head tilted to the side. She'd read my tone and was doggie confused.

I didn't think I could explain it to her in a way she'd understand so I didn't.

"You got a problem?" I heard Sam ask, and I turned to see he'd followed me.

He looked displeased—not exactly angry but definitely not ready to break out into a smile.

I was suddenly uncertain of my commitment to my tantrum. This was because Sam being displeased bothered me. Sam was not moody. Sam was pretty laid-back. This wasn't to say he didn't have emotions or hesitate to show them, but mostly he was mellow.

And tonight, he'd been mellower than I'd ever seen him.

Clearly, for Sam, it was good to be home, down his private, homeowners-only drive, behind his gate, in his house with its kick-ass security system, and spending time with his friend. He had been relaxed to the point it could even be completely relaxed, though I couldn't know that, but that was how it seemed.

Now I'd shattered that.

Shit.

"Kia, I asked you a question," Sam prompted when I stared at him and didn't answer.

"She's my dog, Sam," I repeated.

"No argument from me on that, sweetheart," Sam returned.

Great. He was calling me sweetheart.

Yes, displeased.

He went on, "But she's also smart and she's a people dog. She's with you or me constantly when we're in the house. She didn't wander all day yesterday when she was out in your front yard during the sale. And she's smart enough not to wander now, especially not knowin' the lay of the land."

"You're probably right, but I'd rather not take any chances. She was a puppy when we got her. Except for staying at Dad and Mom's house, she's never been anywhere else, so I don't know how she'll behave in a new environment," I replied.

"All right, then why the fuck didn't you say that instead of biting my head off?" Sam asked.

"Because you stated in your 'Sam Way,'" I gave the last two words air quotation marks, "that she was fine. In other words, she was fine, I should shut up and do as you say."

Uh-oh.

His brows drew together over narrowed eyes and he asked, "My Sam Way?"

"You can be bossy," I informed him.

He took in a breath and studied me. Then he crossed his arms on his chest.

After he did that, he invited, "Right, Kia, tell me what's really up your ass."

Uh-oh again.

And not uh-oh that Sam was getting more pissed.

Uh-oh because *I* was.

"What's up my ass?" I asked quietly.

"Yeah," Sam answered immediately.

"Were you a Ranger?" I returned, and his brows snapped together again, this time in confusion.

"Come again?"

"Were you a Ranger?" I repeated.

He looked to his right at the flag on the wall, then back at me and answered, "Uh…yeah."

"I didn't know that," I told him.

"So?"

"You didn't tell me."

He studied me again and said, "Sweetheart, you Internet stalked me. How could you not know that?"

"Is it common knowledge?" I asked.

"Uh…yeah," he said again.

Really? How on earth did I miss that?

"It is?" I queried, surprised.

"Yeah, Kia, Jesus. What's the big fuckin' deal?"

"It's not in that book about you," I stated.

"No, it isn't. There's shit in that book that's true and very few people knew until that book came out. There's shit in that book that's missin'. And there's shit in that book that's conjecture and all that *isn't* true. Whoever wrote that piece of trash missed me bein' a Ranger. Don't know how, it's one of the few things that isn't a secret that they didn't include. I also don't care. It was a hack job. They knew just enough to get a payday and made up just enough to make that payday big."

"What parts were missing and what parts were conjecture?" I asked.

"You don't have the clearance to know the first and I don't have all night to explain the last. Now, what I'd like to know is why you not knowin' I was a Ranger made you turn bitch?"

Oh man.

I didn't like that.

"Don't call me a bitch, Sam," I whispered.

"You got another way to describe how you're actin'?" he shot back.

"I didn't know you were a Ranger."

"And this is my problem because…?" He let that hang.

"And it's also over twenty-four hours since you had your powwow with Lee and Tanner and I don't know about that either," I retorted, finally bringing the matter in hand.

He took in another deep breath and on the exhale murmured an annoyed, "I see."

"Are you going to tell me about that sometime in this century?" I asked sarcastically.

"Yeah, but see, yesterday, sweetheart, you let go of the physical manifestations of your life with that piece of shit, which I suspect was profound for you. It also took effort and you were busy all day. Then you got a headache, likely because it took effort, you were busy all day and what you were doin' was profound for you. Then, since I know how tight you are with your family and your posse, and your stay here and away from them is indefinite, I figured you'd want to enjoy your time with them, so I wanted you to have that and not burden you with outside shit."

Damn. That made sense *and* it was nice.

Still.

"Well, thanks for that Sam, but I *did* ask twice to be told. I can see you not wanting to do it through that and me having a headache, but you've had all day today."

"Yeah? Should we get in a discussion about people wanting to whack you when we can be overheard in a departure lounge or on a plane?"

Now *he* was being sarcastic.

But damn again because he was also right.

He kept talking.

"And you think maybe you can give me a chance to relax and be home, which I haven't been, Kia, a lot longer than you, and spend some time with a buddy of mine without that shit intruding for a while?"

Oh man.

Now I was feeling like I *was* a bitch, and a worse one than I thought, because he had valid reasons for his decisions and I hadn't asked nice. I'd been, well…a bitch.

"Okay, honey, maybe I was out of line—" I started.

His brows went up. "Maybe?"

Now, hang on a second.

As soon as I remembered, I forgot to stop being a bitch.

"Okay, Sam, I can see you had your reasons, but it's not like I asked you to tell me when you planned to take out the trash. This shit *is* kind of important. It affects me and you know, my dad knows, my brother knows, but the person it affects, *me*, does *not* know. I'm sorry to cut into your relaxed vibe, but someone out there might be hunting me in order to kill me. It's kinda weighing on my mind."

Sam's jaw flexed.

I waited.

A muscle in Sam's cheek jumped.

I waited.

When I was done waiting and prompted, "Well?"

"Lee and Tanner found the broker."

I blinked.

Then I breathed, "What?"

"They tracked down the broker. They also…" he hesitated, clearly searching for a word and then found a scary one that said it all without saying anything, "*persuaded* him to get a message to the man to call the hit off. Easy payday. He backs off, confirms via e-mail he got the message and is a memory. He keeps his pay, the broker keeps his commission and you breathe easy. Ozzie gets fucked in this scenario, seein' as he can't dismantle that bit of trade, but I don't give a fuck. You're safe and that's all I care about."

"I'm safe?" I whispered.

He shook his head. "We haven't received e-mail confirmation. What we do know is that the broker has been contacted by that bitch since your dead husband died and he's been contacted to tell him the job was still on."

Oh my *God.*

"She did that?"

Sam nodded.

"Oh my God," I whispered.

"Something else Tanner found out was that, in case Clementine was unable to collect your life insurance, that bitch did. Clementine named her as second beneficiary."

God, Cooter was such *slime.*

"I cancelled the policy," I told him.

"I know, but wouldn't matter if you did. Her bein' behind your death would mean she wouldn't collect. In fact, in one of my briefs with Oswald, he told me your insurance company came sniffing around Clementine's death to ascertain if there was foul play that would invalidate his policy."

My breath went out of me.

Therefore, I had to force out my "What?"

Sam shook his head. "You're good. Murder is covered in that policy and Cloverfield was not involved in their dealings. But I don't think she cares her actions invalidate your policy or that it's cancelled. I think the bitch just wants you dead."

"But..." I paused, then went on, "wouldn't it be important for Ozzie to at least have a chat with this broker so he could tell him Vanessa is still plotting to kill me?"

"Don't need it. She purchased an extra cell to communicate with the broker. Seein' as she's just a bitch and not a criminal mastermind, she didn't get a burner. But she did get it under an alias and gave her mom's address to send the statements. Tanner and Lee found it, tapped into it, taped conversations, transcribed them, and also got copies of the statements and printouts of the texts. Oswald has all that shit, and all of it is admissible mainly because Oswald is not gonna share how he procured it and is gonna say he and his boys got it. He's gotta call in some markers to get warrants dated appropriately, but luckily, he's got those markers to call. Yesterday, they arrested her again, seein' as continuing to conspire to commit murder when you're out on bond after being arrested for conspiracy to commit murder is a violation of bond. She'll now most likely be held without bail until her trial, where it is also very likely she'll go down, and hard."

I was stuck on an early word so I asked, "A burner?"

"A disposable phone."

Right.

Then the rest of it penetrated.

"So this is good news," I pointed out, my heart beating faster but the muscles in my neck getting looser.

"Yeah, it is, except the part where she didn't call off the hit. We now know a man is waiting for his moment to take you out, and until we get the confirmation e-mail, we have to assume he still is."

Yeah, except that part.

It was my turn to take a deep breath and I did.

Then I said softly, "This is mostly good news, Sam. I don't understand why you waited to tell me."

"Because the part of it that's not good is *really* not good. You're comin' back to you. Every day you smile more, laugh more; more of the real you comes out or you put back in place more of her. And your friends and family are visibly relieved to have you back, *you*, their girl. You're not there, but you're getting there, and I suspected every step you took to release the life you led with that asshole was leading you there. I wanted you to have that. Not a reminder of just how much of an asshole that asshole was."

This made sense too. And it was also nice.

However.

"Isn't it up to me to make that decision?" I asked.

"No," Sam answered instantly, and my head jerked in surprise.

"No?"

He shook his head.

"Sam—" I started, but he interrupted me.

"We had this conversation. You agreed. And we're not havin' this conversation again."

Now I was confused.

"We've had this conversation?"

"Are you my woman?"

I was still confused. How were we back to that?

"I don't get it," I told him.

"Kia, sweetheart, are you my woman?"

"Mostly," I replied without thinking, encroaching into territory we needed to explore but I didn't think it sensible to breach at this juncture.

I watched his brows snap together again and I also watched his entire body get tight.

"Mostly?" he asked quietly and very, very scarily.

Oh man.

"Yes," I changed my answer hurriedly. "I'm your woman."

"That's a better answer," he whispered, again very, very scarily.

"Sam—"

He cut me off again.

"I protect my woman as I see fit. You agreed to that."

"Well, yes, I did," I concurred. "But how does this fit into that?"

"I protect my woman however she needs to be protected *and* whatever she needs protection from."

Oh.

Now I got it.

"So, essentially, what you're saying is, you decide how I need to be protected, what I need to be protected from, and therefore there are times when you'll decide what I need to know and when."

"No."

"No?"

"No in the sense that there's nothing 'essentially' about your statement."

He couldn't be serious.

"Sam!" I cried.

"What?" he asked.

"I'm not a little girl and that's just…it's just…I don't know what it is, but it isn't right."

"How isn't it right?" he shot back.

I threw out an arm, saying, "I don't know, it just isn't."

Sam uncrossed his arms and planted his hands on his hips, leaning in and exploding.

"Jesus, *fuck*, Kia! When this shit is over we will *never* be back here, so when it's done, we won't have this problem unless, hope to God not, some other shit comes up. But this shit isn't over. There is a woman out there who wants you dead. She's incarcerated now, but the man she hired isn't. This is serious shit and we agreed *I'll* deal with it, so *I'll* fuckin' deal with it."

I opened my mouth to say something but got nothing out as he kept going.

Angrily.

"And, sweetheart, I wake up and live and breathe worry that I'll miss somethin' or someone will fuck up and the consequences of that is you bein' dead and now we know that threat is real. *You* wake up and go on viewings with your girl and giggle yourselves sick. You sit with your mom after eating a chicken breast stuffed with cheese and surrounded by three slices of bacon, which explains why she needed a heart valve replaced, though she clearly didn't get the message, and you two gossip and cackle about everyone in town."

That was true and vaguely amusing. It also reminded me I should have another conversation with my mother about draining the fat off hamburger meat.

But Sam wasn't done.

"You didn't ask to meet Lee and Tanner. You haven't asked to meet the men who are lookin' out for you. I assumed that meant you were puttin' this shit in my hands, where it belongs. And I was glad of it. The only thing I have to hang on to is, I got control of this situation and my woman can giggle with her friend and gossip with her mother. I might worry she keeps eatin' her mother's food, she'll need a heart valve replacement in ten years, but I see you emerging from the shit he left you. I'm good with that and can focus on the *other* shit he left you. What I'm *not* good with is havin' this conversation that you promised me we would not have."

He stopped speaking and scowled at me.

I pressed my lips together a moment before I defended myself. "Okay, I get that, but I have to tell you I wasn't aware of all the nuances of that agreement and I still might not be."

"Then let's clear this shit up," he offered. "You trust that I got matters in hand. You trust I'm lookin' out for you. I pay for makin' you safe. And you trust that the decisions I make are done for rational reasons I've thought through with you in mind. Does that work for you?"

"Um...yes," I muttered.

"Fuck," Sam muttered back.

Since we seemed to be concluding things, I thought it important to add, "I still don't want Memphis going outside off the lead until she's more accustomed to your house."

Sam again scowled at me.

Then he asked, "Fuck me, how the fuck can you piss me off to an extreme, and then right after, be cute and make me want to laugh?"

I was being cute?

I thought it prudent not to ask that question and, instead, remain silent. So I did.

Sam didn't.

He ordered, "Come here."

It was then I thought it prudent to do as he ordered. So I did.

When I did, Sam's arms folded around me and I returned the gesture.

He tipped his head down and caught my eyes. "We good?"

"I don't like it that you live and breathe worry about me."

"Soon, I won't have to."

I pressed my lips together, nodded and then did a face-plant in his chest.

"I didn't ask to meet the guys because, well…with everything else, it kinda slipped my mind," I told his chest.

"You wanna meet 'em?"

"Yeah."

"I'll arrange that."

I sighed and whispered, "Okay."

One of his hands slid up my back, my neck and into my hair where his fingers cupped my head. His other arm held tight.

Okay, well, there it was. We had that out.

It wasn't everything, but it was something.

I still wanted more.

But standing in Sam's arms, in Sam's house, which underlined the fact he was definitely *not* a Eurotrash Lamborghini man, and doing it after he made logical explanations that all were embedded in looking out for me, one way or another, not to mention he admitted to living and breathing worry about me, I'd take this for now.

Definitely.

I was close. Oh *God*, I was close.

I was on my hands and knees in front of Sam. No, strike that. I was on one hand and my knees in front of Sam, my other hand was between my legs, my finger adding to the magic Sam's thrusting cock was making.

It was going to happen, I knew it.

And, as ever, it was going to be *fabulous.*

Before it did, Sam pulled out. I whimpered in surprise and was about to protest when his fingers wrapped around my forearms, he yanked me up so my back was pinned to his front, and my arms were pinned in front of me with his hands at my wrists.

Then his mouth came to my ear and he growled, "Are you my woman?"

I opened my mouth to speak, but he kept growling.

"Or are you *mostly* my woman?"

Oh God.

I should have known he wasn't going to let that slide.

"Sam," I whispered, and his hands gave my arms a gentle shake when I said no more.

"Answer me, Kia. Who am I fucking right now?"

No one since he pulled out.

I didn't point that out.

Instead, I turned my head and pressed my temple into his neck. "Baby—"

"Answer me."

"Are you my man?"

Yes. That's what came out. Naked, on my knees, held captive by Sam, who was the same, that was what I blurted.

He transferred my wrists into one of his hands. His other hand went away. I felt him move, adjust, then I felt his cock drive up and fill me, taking my knees off the bed.

My head shot back.

God, I loved being connected to him.

"What does that feel like?" he growled.

It felt unbelievably good.

"Honey," I whispered.

He ground up as his lips went to the skin under my ear and he whispered back, "You have me, Kia."

My body went perfectly still.

His fingers tightened on my wrists and he repeated, "You have me."

I didn't know what he meant.

But I hoped I did.

He kept whispering, "You just have to take me how I can give it, baby."

I closed my eyes.

"You with me?" he asked.

No. I was not.

But I was thinking maybe I was closer.

"Baby." He ground deeper and his lips moved up, his teeth nipping my earlobe, and I trembled. "Are you with me?"

"Yes, honey," I lied.

He pulled out again then I was on my back. His hands were on my hips and he was sitting back on his heels. He slid me up his thighs and I pressed mine to his sides. He then held me steady, staring down at me in his king-size bed, his eyes intense, his face intense, as he fucked me hard until I came hard and so did he.

It was later. After I'd cleaned up. After I'd pulled on a nightgown. After Sam had turned out the lights, tucked me into his side and Memphis had joined us to sprawl in the vast expanse left to her in Sam's big bed.

His breaths were coming even. My eyelids were drooping.

His hand drifted up my back, into my hair, it fisted and twisted.

It didn't hurt, but it made my eyelids stop drooping.

"None of that 'mostly' shit again, Kia," he rumbled into the dark, his voice deeper, rougher, and not like velvet.

He wasn't angry, I knew that tone. And he wasn't annoyed, I knew that one too. He also didn't sound tired because I knew the sound of that too.

This was something else.

Something new.

I stared at his shadowed chest, knowing somewhere in my soul I'd hurt him when I said that.

I'd hurt him.

Oh God.

What was happening?

I didn't get it, but what I did get was that I was thinking Sam had told me earlier that I couldn't ask. Instead, I had to take it as I got it.

I closed my eyes.

Then I did the only thing I could do in that moment, for him and for me.

I whispered on a squeeze of my arm around his gut, "Okay, baby."

His hand relaxed, sifted through my hair, then drifted down to become an arm wrapped around my waist.

Sam fell asleep about thirty seconds after Memphis.

It took me a lot longer.

19

A MISSION

My eyes flitted open and I saw the wall of Sam's chest as well as the wall of Sam's bedroom. It was grooved wood painted light gray.

His room also had white woodwork and dark wood floors with a big, dark gray area rug under the huge bed. His bed had dark gray sheets and a dark red comforter cover. Black furniture, mission style. Tall, wide dresser, nightstands, attractive lamps over the nightstands built into the wall that swung around so you could position them where you wanted them.

The only thing on the wall was a framed black-and-white photo of a headshot of Walter Payton wearing a white headband and looking over his Bears jersey covered, shoulder padded shoulder, his handsome face reflective.

It was an awesome picture.

Sam was asleep. I knew this from his breathing but also from the feel of him. You could sense his power, always, even if he was only in the vicinity. Now his power was shut down.

Memphis was also asleep. I knew this because she was pressed to the small of my back and immobile.

So I had time. Time to decide what to do about Sam.

But I didn't need time. It came to me immediately.

And what came to me was that *I had time.*

Time to convince him he could trust me. Time to prove to him he could give me his secrets, open his heart, show me his soul and I'd take care of it just like he was taking care of mine. Time in his capable hands to put myself back together and give him the real me.

We were new, I reminded myself. I needed to give him time. I needed to give him me without expecting more than he was already giving me. And I needed to work toward gaining his trust.

No more tantrums. No more dramas. No more pushing.

It would come.

In the meantime, I needed to keep my promise and take him how he could give himself to me.

Because, seriously, what did I have to complain about?

On this thought I pressed into him, putting my lips to his chest, gliding them up to his shoulder, his neck, then to his jaw.

His arm around my waist tightened and he pulled me mostly on his body.

He was awake.

Time to get to work.

I lifted my head and looked down into his beautiful eyes with their spiky, thick lashes. Eyes that were now languid and thus hotter than their usual *hot.* And I grinned.

"I like your picture of Sweetness."

His arm got tighter and his lips turned up slightly at the ends. "You know Payton?"

"Who doesn't know Payton?"

"Thought you weren't into football, honey."

"You don't have to be into football to know Walter Payton was the best running back the game has ever seen."

His lip turn got bigger. "You know what a running back is?"

"No, but my guess is they run and I definitely know Sweetness could run."

His body shook with his chuckle as he rolled, taking me to my back, making Memphis scoot away, and ending with him mostly on me.

My fingers started exploring his back as his hand ran up my neck, his fingers sliding into my hair from the bottom, his thumb extended to stroke my jaw as I kept talking.

"I like your bedroom too."

"Good," Sam murmured, dipping his head and running the side of his nose along the side of mine.

He'd never done that. I liked it. It was sweet.

"And your whole house," I whispered.

His lips swept my lips, then he whispered back, "Good."

"And your view," I kept going.

"Good," he repeated on a mutter as his whole hand slid up into my hair, cupping then tilting my head. His slanted the other way and he kissed me.

I planted a foot in the bed, heaved up, Sam let me roll him so I was on top and I did this all while kissing him back.

I lifted my head and informed him, "But if you have a Ferrari in your garage, that's a deal breaker."

Sam burst out laughing. I watched for a couple of seconds, smiling down at him, before I dropped my head and kissed him again. He laughed into my mouth for a second. I liked the feel of it. He quit laughing, took over and it got heated.

When his mouth broke from mine, I was breathing harder and focusing on his lips gliding to my ear, where he murmured, "Got a Ford F-150 SuperCrew Cab. That work for you?"

My lips had landed on his neck, my mind vaguely processing I had no freaking clue what a SuperCrew Cab was, though I did know what a Ford F-150 was, so I mumbled, "Mm-hmm."

"Good," he mumbled back.

My lips decided they wanted to move down, so they did. Then they decided they wanted to explore, so they did. They decided to further their exploration, so they did. Finally, I slid between Sam's legs, he opened them and cocked his knees, giving me unfettered access. I took him in my hand and didn't delay sliding him in my mouth.

"*Fuck*," Sam groaned, both his hands sifting in my hair on the sides, pulling it back and fisting in it.

My eyes tipped up to him to see his eyes on me. He always watched me working him. He liked how I worked him. He liked to watch. And it must be said, so did I.

I slid him out, held him to my lips, rolled the tip with my tongue and he pushed off on his heels, taking himself (and me) up the bed until his shoulders were to the headboard so he could more easily watch.

Since he was in position, I gave him a show.

He was liking it in a big way, which was about as much as I was liking it, and I knew from experience he was close to ending the show and taking over. This was another way I considered Sam a gentleman. He always finished in me and he only finished after he made me do the same. He might allow me to give, and in so doing take, but he never took it all unless he'd given it all to me.

I loved that about him.

And just when his growls were going so deep, I could feel them in my mouth through his cock, the corresponding wet gathering between my legs, his phone on his bedside table rang.

I slid him out of my mouth and looked at it.

"Ignore it," he ordered, his voice super rough velvet, gliding over me, coating me in invincibility.

Yes, invincibility. I forgot. With Sam, I was invincible.

I could do this. I could be me. I could make him trust me, share with me and fall in love with me. With Sam, I could do anything. Nothing would beat me.

My eyes slid to him as the phone rang again.

"Baby—" Sam started, but I grinned.

He could pull out and make me wait for it.

I could do the same.

I quickly crawled up his body, watching his face turn dark with frustration. My grin became a smile and I reached out and grabbed the phone from its cradle.

"Do not answer that, Kia," he rumbled.

I straddled his gut, looked to the phone, found the on button, hit it and put it to my ear.

"Please, at this hour, do not be a telemarketer," I greeted, my gaze tipping down to Sam, who now had his fingers curled into my hips and an expression in his eyes that said I'd pay for this but in a way I could look forward to.

Several seconds had gone by before I realized no one had answered my flippant greeting.

My eyes went unfocused and I called, "Hello?"

Sam's upper body knifed up, I slid down to straddling his lap, and one of his arms curled around me.

Then a woman's velvety but hesitant voice came at me through the phone.

"Uh...hello. Is Sam there? This is his mother."

I froze solid.

Shit!

His mother!

I'd answered the phone flippantly and it was his mother!

I was *in bed* in *the morning* with Sam and I interrupted *the blowjob* I was giving Sam in order to answer the phone flippantly and it was *his mother*!

"Baby, who is it?"

I unfroze, gave Sam big eyes and waved my hand at him to shut up.

Then I forced myself to stammer, "Uh, yes. He's here, uh..."

Sam pulled the phone out of my hand and put it to his ear.

Oh God! Now she was going to know he was in bed with me!

"Cooper," he said into it, listened for a nanosecond, then his eyes cut to me and he smiled huge. "Hey, Ma."

I tensed to launch myself off him, but his arm around me clamped tight.

Then Sam spoke again.

"Yeah, that was Kia. The one I told you about."

He told her about me? When? Why? What did he say? And, again, *when*?

Sam kept talking.

"We got here yesterday." Pause. "Right." Pause, then his arm spasmed around me, his eyes slid away, his amusement faded and his brows drew together. "No, don't do that."

Uh-oh.

He kept going.

"No, Ma, seriously, we just got here and now's not the time for company."

Uh-oh!

"Ma—" he began, was obviously cut off, then, "Not a good idea." Pause, then, "Ma—" Another cut off, this one lasted longer and ended with a clipped, "Shit. Fine."

No!

My hands lifted, fingers curling tight on his shoulders where they met his neck and his eyes came to me.

"Right, we'll pick you up in Raleigh on Thursday," he said.

No. No. *No!*

My fingers tightened on his shoulders, his eyes moved over my face then they started twinkling.

Twinkling!

Was he *crazy*?

I couldn't meet his mother!

It was way too soon, for one. Sure, he'd met my whole family, but someone was trying to kill me and Sam was my self-appointed protector. There was no way to avoid that.

For another, I couldn't sleep in the same bed with Sam if his mother was in the house. I was from Indiana. I was the daughter of Essie and Ford Rigsby. My mother and father could look the other way and pretend Sam and I didn't have a sexual relationship outside of marriage if we were staying at my house and it wasn't in their face. And they did so contentedly, considering Sam was my self-appointed protector who'd wrangled up a crew of badasses to make sure I kept breathing. This bought you a lot of leeway, even with churchgoing folk in the Bible belt.

But I could not sleep with Sam or *sleep with Sam* when his mother was in the house. And Sam wouldn't allow it to be any other way. I knew it.

Furthermore, his bedroom, walk-in closet and master bath took one whole side of the upstairs. The other side was another bathroom, a guest room and his office. His mother would be in the guest room and there was nowhere else for me to sleep except one of the couches downstairs.

Eek!

Sam again spoke, taking me out of my fevered thoughts.

"All right, Ma, call me or text the details and we'll meet you outside the terminal." Pause. "Yeah." Pause. "Lookin' forward to it." Pause. "No, that'll be fine, considering I've been forced to eat Kia's mom's cooking, I'm sure she'll be good with eating yours."

Forced? What would Mrs. Cooper think, Sam saying he was "forced" to eat Mom's cooking?

Eek again!

Sam went on, grinning into the phone and muttering, "I'll explain it later, Ma. Need to see to Memphis." Pause. "Kia's dog." Another pause. "Yeah, she's cute. You'll love her."

Oh God. I hoped so. It would suck if Sam's mom turned out to be the only human on the planet (outside Hap and, kind of, Teri) who hated Memphis.

It would suck more if Sam's mom turned out to be the only human I knew on the planet (outside Vanessa) who hated me.

Sam kept speaking. "Right. See you soon." Pause. "Love you too, Ma. Later."

He beeped off the phone, twisted, taking me with him, and put it on the cradle. He twisted back and his eyes locked on mine.

"What chance I got that you'll use your mouth to get me hard again so I can fuck you?" he asked through a shit-eating grin.

"Zero," I answered while trying not to hyperventilate.

"Figured," he muttered, still grinning.

"This isn't good," I told him, and Sam's other arm curved around me, both of them giving me a warm squeeze.

"She'll love you, baby," he whispered.

"Okay, well, maybe so, but *you* won't love me sleeping on the couch."

The grin disappeared and his brows drew together. "Come again?"

"Hello? Sam? Again, I'm from Indiana."

"Yeah, well, I'm not and neither is Ma."

I shook my head. "I can't do it. It's impossible. I'll break into hives or something."

"Baby, you're overreacting. Your parents know I'm fucking you."

Ohmigod!

I forced his words out of my head, even as I responded to them. "Yes, okay, but they only didn't give me a lecture or hit us both with their heavy censure because they think it's your reward for keeping me alive. In normal circumstances—"

He interrupted me with another arm squeeze and stated, "In normal circumstances, Kia, baby, you are twenty-eight and you can do whatever the fuck you wanna do. And in our current circumstances, my Ma knows me pretty well. She does not have hang-ups about that shit, but if she did, she knows better than to share them with me or make you uncomfortable. You are not sleepin' on the couch. You're sleepin' with me."

"Fine," I returned, because I already knew that was a battle I'd never win. "But we won't be having sex."

Sam's face got a little scary.

"Kia—"

"Sam."

He stared into my eyes.

Then he burst out laughing, falling to his back, taking me with him. He rolled so he was on top, lifted his head and looked down at me, still, I might add, laughing.

When he got control of his hilarity, he muttered, "Fuck, you're cute."

"I wasn't being cute."

"Yeah, that's why you're cute."

I glared at him.

His face got soft and it also got closer when he whispered, "You're nervous."

Uh...*yeah*!

I didn't answer.

"She'll love you, honey."

I swallowed.

Sam dipped his head, touched his lips to mine, lifted it and, still whispering, said, "Luci loves you, Celeste loves you, Hap loves you, and Ma will love you. Trust me, baby."

I pressed my lips together.

Sam smiled at me.

My stomach, which was in knots, unknotted.

"Okay," I said softly.

"Okay," he repeated softly, then he touched his mouth to mine again, lifted his head and told me, "Gonna take Memphis for a walk. You comin' with?"

"Before coffee?" I asked.

"Yeah," he answered.

"Then no," I replied, and he smiled again. "Make it short and we'll take her out again later."

"Works for me," he muttered, dipped his head yet again and kissed my nose.

He rolled away.

I lay in bed and watched him pull on a pair of loose-fitting, athletic shorts, a tee with the sleeves cut off and a pair of old, ratty running shoes with no socks. Then I watched him move to the door, whistling. Last, I watched him disappear through the door, Memphis bouncing behind him and disappearing too.

I rolled to my back and looked at the ceiling.

I was going to meet Sam's mom in two days.

Yikes.

Fearless, the word sounded in my head.

I took in a deep breath and reminded myself I had a mission.

So I didn't delay.

I threw off the covers, did my bathroom gig and headed downstairs to make coffee.

I was in the kitchen writing a grocery list when I heard the garage door opening and Sam's Ford F-150 SuperCrew Cab truck growling in.

It was late morning. I was showered, clothed and made up. I was also juiced up on caffeine, which was sharing space in my stomach with oatmeal.

Sam had taken Memphis for her walk, came back, changed into workout clothes, which meant he put on socks and a better pair of gym shoes. Then he took off to the gym.

Now he was back.

In his absence, I also had time to inspect Sam's kitchen, finding he had all the accoutrements to the point I was a little surprised. He even had a garlic press.

What single man had a garlic press?

I found this a little disturbing because no single man had a garlic press unless that single man had a woman who at one time lived with him and forgot to take her garlic press with her when their relationship crashed and burned in a fiery ball of flame. Or she was around enough to cook for him repeatedly, thus he outfitted his kitchen with items she'd deemed necessary.

I turned my mind from these thoughts to other thoughts that were only slightly less disturbing. These included the fact that I'd never cooked for Sam. I didn't cook like my mother, this was true.

And I thought my cooking was good. In fact, although Cooter was controlling about *what* I cooked, he never got pissed off about how it turned out.

But I'd noticed that Sam wasn't freakish about his nutrition consumption inasmuch as he didn't demand his vegetables steamed, his chicken grilled and allowed nothing unhealthy to pass his lips. He also would enjoy a beer or three. Still, his selections were all relatively healthy and he leaned toward fish and skinless poultry and away from beef, fats and copious carbs.

I was the queen of beef, fats and copious carbs. Well, maybe not fats, so much, but definitely the other two. If a meal didn't have some sort of bread, even if that meal was pasta, my thought was, what was the point?

Therefore, since I planned on making dinner for him that night, I was kind of at a loss.

I realized as I was staring down at the grocery list that didn't have a lot on it that Sam's truck was no longer growling, the garage door had already come down, but he hadn't come up the stairs from the garage.

My head turned in that direction just as I heard the door to the stairs open. I saw a still-sweaty (thus luscious) Sam round the wall and come into the kitchen.

I smiled and greeted, "Hey, honey."

My smile faltered when the man who I saw standing outside his car at my yard sale followed Sam into the kitchen.

"Hey, baby," Sam replied on his approach.

The man did not approach. He stopped on the opposite side of the island. Memphis bounced in, yapping her greeting to Sam, got a look at the newcomer, dissed Sam and bounced, yapping to him.

The man tipped just his eyes down to my dog and didn't try to hide his revulsion.

Clearly, there were some badasses who didn't think little dogs were cute.

Sam made it to me, slid his arm along my shoulders and stated, "You said you wanted to meet the boys. Two of them came with. Aziz is off duty. This is Deaver."

"Hi, Deaver," I greeted.

"Yo," he grunted, his eyes moving from their disgusted study of a still-bouncing and yapping Memphis to me.

"Um…sorry I didn't ask to meet you earlier. I was, uh…kinda busy," I told him.

He stared at me and made no response.

Weird.

"Do you want coffee?" I asked.

He shook his head but did not verbalize his refusal.

I tried again. "So, are you from Indiana?"

He stared at me a beat, then nodded his head but said not a word.

Totally weird.

"Uh, sorry that you, uh…couldn't join us in the lounge at the airport or that we uh…didn't get you in first class." I tipped my head back to look at Sam and asked, "Why didn't we do that?"

Sam started to speak but Deaver beat him to it and I looked back to him when he did.

"Can't assess a threat drinkin' champagne in first class. Cooper had that covered, not a two-man job. I covered coach."

"Oh," I murmured.

He went on, "And can't scan the area sittin' on my ass in the first-class departure lounge."

"Right," I muttered.

That was when Deaver became talkative…*ish.*

He jerked his head toward the floor where Memphis was sitting on her doggie bottom, sweeping Sam's tiled floor with her tail, waiting for Deaver to lavish affection on her, and he declared, "Need a Rottie."

Here we go again.

"That's been noted," I told him.

"Or a shepherd," he continued.

"That's been mentioned too," I replied.

"Or a mastiff," he went on.

That was a new one.

"Uh..." I mumbled.

"Or a Dogo Argentino."

I blinked. "Sorry, a what?"

"The badass mofo of the canine world," he explained.

"Oh," I whispered, thinking this guy was a little scarier than the average scary.

"Not that," he jerked his head down at Memphis again.

Memphis yapped.

"She's friendly," I defended Memphis, then added, "And cuddly."

Deaver's eyes sliced to Sam, clearly unimpressed with friendly, cuddly dogs and wanting to know why Sam didn't eject my baby immediately.

"And anyway, I have badass mofos of the human variety looking out for me so I think I'm good," I finished.

That was when Deaver decided to share his badass mofo wisdom. "You got a threat, you use every available means to neutralize it."

"Uh, that makes sense, of course. But Memphis would probably yap pretty loudly to greet an intruder so at least we'd have a heads up," I told him.

He again looked at Sam, and since I just met him, I didn't know if it was with respect that Sam had the patience to put up with me and Memphis or if it was with disdain that Sam was putting up with me and Memphis.

I decided I was done meeting my bodyguard so I said brightly, "Nice to meet you. If you should want to, say, use the bathroom or get a bottle of water, you obviously know where we are."

He took the hint and I didn't have to know him very well to see his relief at being dismissed from this particular duty. He jerked his chin up and replied, not brightly, "Right. Thanks. Hope you don't get dead. You gettin' dead means I fucked up and won't get paid."

Yikes!

"Well, I'm glad Sam had the foresight to put that clause in your contract," I muttered and felt Sam's body start shaking against mine.

"Standard," Deaver grunted, jerked up his chin again, frowned down at Memphis again, turned on his boot and disappeared.

Sam's silent laughter became an audible chuckle when I turned into him and looked up.

"I'm not sure I want to meet Aziz," I shared, and Sam's chuckle became a roar of laughter as both his arms closed around me.

When he quit laughing but he was still grinning huge, he replied, "Aziz wasn't raised by Argentine Dogos. He's a little more sociable."

"A little?" I asked, and Sam's huge grin turned into a blinding smile.

"Yeah," he confirmed. "A little. A guy checks the box marked 'friendly' on a job application for bodyguard, he's not gonna get much work."

This made sense.

"Right," I muttered.

Sam kept smiling at me, then he looked to the counter at my list and back at me. "You ready to hit the grocery store?"

"I will be when I ascertain if there's anything in my cooking arsenal you won't feel *forced* to eat."

"I don't have a cast iron skillet, baby, and shortening is not an acceptable addition to my pantry. That help?"

"Yes, but barely."

"We'll figure it out," he murmured.

Yes, we damn well would and I knew this because I was on a mission to make it so.

"Um…if Deaver comes with, he's not going to attack any grocery store patrons for looking at us funny, seeing as you're famous and all, and leave bite marks, is he?" I asked.

He pulled me closer and told me, "Good part of bein' home, in Kingston, people are used to me. Unless it's new folk or tourists, they leave me be."

This *was* good.

"Excellent," I replied.

Sam smiled again. Then he bent his head, touched his mouth to mine, let me go and muttered, "Shower, then store."

"Gotcha," I muttered back.

He moved to the stairs. I turned to my list.

I was scratching out the word "shortening" when I heard, "Kia?"

I turned and looked over my shoulder to see Sam at the wall by the base of the stairs.

"Yeah, honey?"

His head cocked slightly to the side and his eyes moved over me. I held my breath because they'd gone super intense and I suspected he was seeing something, *feeling* something, something I didn't understand, while looking at me in his kitchen.

But he didn't share.

Instead, he said, "Won't be long."

"Okay," I replied softly.

He tipped up his chin and disappeared.

I took in a breath and went back to my list.

It was night, the moon lit the ocean, the sound of waves crashing on the beach shifted lazily toward the deck. All of those, plus a nice dinner and a good day spent with Sam, were lulling me into a relaxation I hadn't felt in years.

Years.

It felt good.

The grocery store mission was successful. I got what I wanted and Sam got what he wanted. I paid close attention to what Sam got, which gave me ideas for dinner. After we left the grocery, we hit the liquor store, then we went home.

And Deaver, who I noted trailing us twice, didn't attack anyone.

A plus.

I put chicken breasts in to marinate and Sam and I took Memphis for a long walk on the beach. We came back and he took me upstairs for a long, energetic session in his bed.

We emerged from Sam's bed late afternoon and I met Aziz.

Sam was right, he was friendlier if not less scary. He was Arabic, had less bulk than Deaver but not less muscle, though his was lean. He had more height, and when he departed, he did not share his wish I didn't get dead. He gave me a look that promised I wouldn't (thus him being not less scary).

The only thing that semi-marred our day was that twice Sam got calls where he looked at the display on his phone, then took them elsewhere. This was not exactly unusual. He had a lot of calls at home where he did that and I suspected they were discussions with Ozzie or his crew of badasses. So I didn't think anything of it, in Indiana or in North Carolina.

That was until, during the second call, I headed upstairs on bare feet to see to unpacking, and I did this while he was in his office on the phone.

The door was open and I heard him say, "Like I said before, tell them I'm considering it, but I haven't made a decision." He paused. I debated the merits of eavesdropping and before I made a decision, he went on, "They're impatient for an answer, then the answer is no. They can keep their shit, then they can wait for me to fuckin' consider it."

It was then, considering his tone sounded frustrated and the conversation was clearly not about my safety, not to mention, I had some anxiety about what it *was* about, harking way back to the conversation I overheard Sam have with Luci, I moved swiftly to the bedroom. For the first five minutes of unpacking, I made way more noise than I needed to. Firstly, I did this to drown out hearing anything Sam was saying. Secondly, I did this because I wanted Sam to know my whereabouts.

When he came into his bedroom, he was no longer on the phone and he was also in his usual not-in-a-sharing mood.

I knew this when he came up behind me as I was bent over my suitcase by the bed.

He hooked me around the waist, leaned into me and said quietly in my ear, "Meant it yesterday, honey, make yourself at home. You need to move shit, move it. I'll stow your bags when you're done."

Then he kissed my neck and moved away.

That was nice, very nice, and I definitely liked it. But it still wasn't Sam sharing.

And it should be noted, Sam didn't grab his bag and unpack his own stuff.

Whatever.

I did it for him.

A bit later, Sam grilled the chicken at his grill on the deck. I made a salad of raw spinach, arugula, cucumber, carrot, mandarin orange slices and pistachio nuts and prepared some wild rice. I ate mine with a buttered dinner roll we got from the bakery at the grocery store. Sam ate his with an extra breast, double the amount of rice, salad and zero roll.

Sam had also made certain that I had amaretto and he did this during the detour to the liquor store on the way home from the grocery.

So now I had a snifter (yes, Sam even had snifters) of amaretto and Sam on a deck at a house on the beach in North Carolina after a good day.

Life was good.

And Sam needed to know that.

So I whispered to the ocean, "Life is good."

Sam made no verbal response. What he did was a whole lot better.

He trailed the tips of his fingers along the outside of my thigh.

I sighed and took a sip of amaretto.

I dropped my hand to rest the base of the glass to the arm of my chair and told the ocean, still whispering, "It was hell, honey."

Sam again made no response, but this time his nonresponse included physically.

I kept whispering. "Everywhere I've been since he's been gone, I thought was heaven."

Sam responded to that, both verbally and physically. His fingers glided from the outside to the inside of my thigh and he pulled it toward his until it was resting there and he muttered, "Baby."

I turned my head to look at him to see he was looking at me. "I was wrong."

His fingers gave my inner thigh a squeeze.

"This is heaven," I said softly.

I saw Sam smile.

Then I heard him murmur, "Glad you like my place, honey."

I shook my head, turned my torso and leaned into my armrest. I dropped both my legs into his, imprisoning his warm hand between them and placed my hand on his chest.

"That's not what I mean," I whispered.

Sam twisted toward me, lifted his free hand and wrapped his fingers around the side of my neck.

"What'd you mean, Kia?"

"Anywhere is heaven as long as it's an anywhere with you."

The fingers on both Sam's hands clenched deep, hard, fast, and I knew it was reflexively because he didn't check it and they caused a hint of pain.

Then he was up and my snifter of amaretto was on the deck railing. My footrest was shoved out from under my heels and I was up, my hand was firm in Sam's, and we were in the house.

He stopped long enough to lock the screened porch door, the front door and quickly punch buttons on the alarm panel.

Then we were in his bed.

There Sam demonstrated to me how I was figuring out Sam demonstrated how much he felt about me.

And two hours later, climbing back into bed after cleaning up and tugging on panties and a nightie, I fell exhausted into Sam's body and fell directly asleep.

So directly, I didn't feel him pull the covers over me.

I also didn't feel him turn to his side or his arms get tight around me.

And, unfortunately, I didn't hear his rough-like-velvet voice softly rumble, "Heaven is you too, baby."

I didn't feel him kiss my forehead.

I didn't feel him tangle his legs with mine.

And last, I didn't feel him gather me super close and hold me that way, even long after he, too, fell asleep.

20

KHAKIS

I woke suddenly when I felt Sam's arms clamp around me. He rolled us, squeezing the breath out of me when he was on top. He rolled us again and we were in free fall.

I cried out my surprise into the dark.

In the split second it took us to fall, Sam twisted so somehow we landed with a bone-jarring thud, me on him, Sam on his back. We stayed that way a millisecond before he rolled us toward the bed.

He was knifing up as he growled, "Stay down."

I did as I was told, heard a drawer open, scraping, then Memphis yapped and kept doing it.

What was happening?

Memphis yapped again, quick successions, in a way I'd never heard her yap before.

A warning.

Fear slithered over every inch of my skin.

Suddenly I heard Memphis growl under Sam's rumbled order of "Drop it on the bed."

"Now—" a man's voice started to say, and hearing a stranger *in the bedroom in the middle of the night,* I quit breathing.

A gunshot blasted the air, loud and terrifying. My body jumped but Sam stayed still, and I noted in shock, he was the one who fired. Memphis yapped, then I heard her claws on the wood floors, and with my baby on the move, without thinking, I jerked into action.

Sam clipped, "Kia, stay the fuck down."

I sucked in air, stopped moving and stayed down as I heard what sounded like Memphis attacking one of her chew toys, but she wasn't playing. She meant business.

"Drop it on the fucking *bed*," Sam bit out.

"Get the dog off me," the man said.

"Drop your *fucking* weapon on the *fucking* bed."

Ohmigod. Ohmigod. *Ohmigod*!

What was happening?

I heard the soft *fumf* of something heavy falling on the bed.

"Now get this fuckin' thing off me!" the man snapped.

"Memphis!" Sam called sharply. The noises Memphis was making stopped, I heard her claws clicking, then I heard another soft *fumf* on the bed and I knew Memphis was moving toward Sam. "On your knees, hands up, palms to me, fingertips at your ears," Sam ground out, then came a barked, "Do it. *Now*!"

Oh God, oh God, oh *God*!

"Kia, up," Sam rumbled.

Immediately, I got up. Sam was reaching across the bed toward something at the same time he had his head back and his eyes and gun trained on the dark shadow of a man on his knees across the room.

"Get me some shorts," Sam ordered.

I didn't delay. Sam was standing there naked, holding a man at gunpoint. I could see this would be uncomfortable.

I hurried across the room, opened a drawer, grabbed a pair of his shorts, left the drawer open and ran back to him. He handed me his gun and I took it without dropping it, even though holding a recently-fired-therefore-clearly-loaded-and-deadly weapon freaked me way the fuck out.

"He moves, you even *think* he's gonna move, shoot," Sam instructed.

"Right," I whispered, and now it was me who was aiming my eyes and a gun at the man on his knees.

Sam took the shorts from me and in about two seconds he took the gun back from me.

I just stopped myself from heaving a sigh of relief.

"Turn on the light," Sam demanded.

I turned on the light and saw Memphis within reaching distance, so I snagged her off the bed and cuddled her to my chest.

"Behind me, stay there." Sam kept the commands coming and I kept doing as I was told.

Then I peered around him at a man with a nice haircut, khaki pants and a golf shirt. He was slim, fit and very alert.

And, lastly, I guessed he was my hit man.

"My next directive to my woman is dialin' nine-one-one. You got two minutes to talk me outta that," Sam told the man.

"We need a chat," the man told Sam.

"I'm guessin' that, since you breached my security system and approached with your gun not at the ready, the fuckin' safety on. Now you got a minute and a half for your chat. Don't waste more," Sam returned.

"I need assurances," the man stated.

"Think your broker gave you those," Sam retorted.

"Need them direct from you. I do not need Tanner Layne on my ass. Man's bad enough, but he comes with fuckin' Ryker and he's a pain in the ass. Now both a' them come with a man named Devin Glover, who's a *serious* fuckin' pain in the ass. I want it direct from your lips, I stand down, you give the order for those assholes to stand down."

"You already got that *through your broker*," Sam told him, clearly losing patience.

"Yeah, well, Layne, Ryker and Glover are pains in the ass, but I've had the opportunity to look into Nightingale and I need to know him and his fuckin' whackjobs in Denver won't get a wild hair and go on a mission just for shits and giggles," the man shot back.

"Don't control Lee or his boys," Sam stated. "My advice to you, now you're on their radar: don't do anything to piss them off. Further advice, you already done somethin' that would piss them off, you disappear and do it really well."

"Fuck!" the man exploded, and I jumped and pressed Memphis and myself closer to Sam's back.

Sam didn't move.

The man started bitching.

"That cunt didn't pay me to put up with this kind of fuckin' headache."

"You made a bad career choice. These are your consequences. Now, do not stand there wastin' my time. I'm givin' you a good deal and you fuckin' know it. As much as it shits me to allow it, a deal's a deal and the deal is, you stand down, you walk outta here and breathe free. You got ten seconds to decide. At eleven, I'm incapacitating you and you're goin' down another way."

"I'll stand down," the man said immediately.

Sam sucked in an audible breath and he was silent for three seconds (I counted).

Then he said with very scary, very quiet menace, a tone that, even knowing him and how he really was, sent chills up my spine, "Anything ever happens to her, *ever*, I will find you, I will hurt you and in the end you will beg me to kill you."

I pressed closer to Sam.

The man held Sam's eyes, but cold-blooded killer for hire in a golf shirt or not, his face had paled.

He nodded.

"Get out," Sam ordered.

He nodded again as he asked, "Can I have my gun?"

Sam didn't speak and I wasn't in a position to see his face, but whatever look he gave the man, it worked. Instantly, the man got to his feet, turned and moved quickly out the door.

Sam turned and looked down at me.

"Grab the phone. Foot of the bed, on your ass on the floor. Dial nine-one-one but do not hit go. You hear anything, feel anything you don't like, you hit go. Yeah?"

I nodded, moved to the phone and grabbed it. Then I moved to the foot of the bed and dropped to my ass on the floor. I hit the buttons and cuddled Memphis to me.

Sam took me in then took off.

I sat there listening hard and breathing harder.

Memphis stayed still, close and silent.

It took seven years before Sam came back.

He came direct to me, dropped both guns to the bed, bent down and pulled me up by my wrist. He stalked to his nightstand, tagged his cell, hit some buttons and put it to his ear. I turned his landline off.

Seconds later, he growled into the phone, "Yeah, I fuckin' know what time it is, but what *you* don't know is I got a fuckin' bullet hole in the floor of my bedroom because Kia and I just got paid a visit by her hit man and he didn't take me seriously, tried to turn the safety off on his gun and I had to make a point. Now, Cal, what I wanna know is, how the fuck did he breach your security?"

Okay, I'd seen Sam annoyed, pissed and downright angry. Even *really* downright angry.

But it was safe to say he was right now enraged.

I cuddled Memphis closer.

"Yeah, that'd be good, you come in person to check it out," Sam kept growling, then continued growling when he stated, "Yeah, he said he'd stand down. And I feel good about it because he knows I missed on purpose but still tore a hole through his fuckin' *khaki* fuckin' *pants* in the dark with my warning shot. I still wanna know how he breached your goddamned system. I have two men on dayshift, no nightshift 'cause it's supposed to be impenetrable. If I thought we were unsafe, Aziz or Deaver would have neutralized him and my woman would not be shakin' like a fuckin' leaf right about now."

He'd torn a hole through that man's khaki's with his warning shot?

Uh.

Wow.

Obviously they didn't mess around in Ranger school.

"Yeah," Sam's voice was now quieter and a whole lot less ticked off, "I know you got three girls under your roof and you get me. I also want my question answered, Cal." He listened, sucked in breath through his nose then, "Right." Clearly the unknown Cal broke through because his lips twitched and he muttered, "Yeah, khakis." A pause before he went on muttering with a, "Fuck me."

Then he chuckled.

I wasn't finding one, single thing amusing.

He must have caught my vibe because his eyes cut to me before he said into his phone, "Kia's about to have a shit fit or a breakdown. I gotta be available for either one. Let me know your plans." A pause then, "Right, later."

He took his phone from his ear.

The instant he did, I remarked, "I find it immensely disturbing that a hit man wears a golf shirt."

Sam's lips twitched then he ordered gently, "Baby, come here."

"But I think it's good to know that Memphis won't be friendly to unwelcome intruders."

"Kia, honey, come here."

"And we must make a mental note to patch that bullet hole in your floor before your mom gets here," I informed him.

Sam gave up on his order and told me quietly, "He wasn't here to hurt you. I hired the best. He was running scared. He wanted assurances."

"I got that."

"Now he's got his assurances and you're good."

"What does he mean by Lee and his whackjobs?" I asked.

Sam hesitated, studying me, and carefully, he answered, "Lee owns a private investigations agency but he dips his toe in a lotta shit. His crew has a variety of skills. They are known to be very good at what they do and not to fuck around. You're smart, you don't get on their bad side. He wasn't smart. He took a job to kill an innocent woman. That was strike one. And that job he took was to kill a woman who'd been abused. That was strike two. For Lee and his crew, you don't get a strike two."

Great.

In normal circumstances, I would find that admirable.

Now, not so much.

"Will they step in, piss him off and make him forget about his promise to stand down?"

Understanding hit Sam's face and he kept talking quietly when he replied, "They step in, he won't get the chance to forget his promise."

"You're sure of that?" I pushed.

"Sure as I'm standin' here."

"You were sure that Cal guy's security system was impenetrable too."

It was a mean thing to say, but in my defense, I was *freaking out.* A hit man in a golf shirt *made it to Sam's bedroom.*

Sam was clearly done with distance and I knew this because he moved to me. When he got close enough to lunge, he did so, grabbing my hand, pulling me around the bed and into his arms.

He tipped his chin down and told me, "That bitch didn't hock a bunch of shit. She hocked a bunch of heirlooms. She also didn't take out a small second mortgage, she took out one on all the equity they had in their place, which was a lot."

His arms gave me a reassuring squeeze and he kept going.

"What I'm sayin' is, I paid for the best to cover you. She found the best she could find to do his job. I was aware this man was a man to take seriously. That guy was a ghost so we had no idea of his skills. We only knew he had them considering his price tag. Now we know one of his skills. He came up here, safety on, knowin' who I was and that I also have skills. He was wavin' the white flag. I felt like bein' safe, and in any uncertain situation, you gain the upper hand. That's why I took him to his knees. He gets me. He understands what I can do. He didn't come here to harm you. He came here to make sure his headaches were done. He's cautious and he's thorough. Neither are a surprise but both are a pain in the ass. But it no longer matters. He's history. That said, I got some calls to make for peace of mind and I need to make them now. You okay for ten minutes while I do that? Then we'll keep talkin'."

I looked up at him.

He had things to do for peace of mind which meant my safety. He also knew I was freaking out and needed him. So he was going to give me that if I needed it and his peace of mind be damned.

Yep. Definitely. I was falling in love with him.

I didn't share that. I said, "I'm okay for ten minutes while you do that."

He gave me another squeeze, let me go with one arm and reached out to the bed. He snagged both guns then he moved us up the bed. He put the guns on his nightstand, took the phone from me and put it in its cradle. He then maneuvered me and Memphis into the bed and got in it with us. He sat back to the headboard, knees bent and held Memphis and me tucked close to his side.

With us positioned, he called Deaver, briefed him quickly and told him he wanted twenty-four hour coverage on the house starting now. After that, he called Lee, briefed him and explained the situation. I didn't get much about Lee's replies due to Sam's side of the conversation being guarded. I decided to bury that in a part of my brain I never intended to access again so I did that. Finally, Sam called what apparently was Tanner's voicemail at work and left a message.

Done with his calls, he tossed his phone on the nightstand, turned to me, both his arms came around me and Memphis and he slid us up his chest.

"Right," he whispered, "how you doin'?"

"I'm good," I whispered back.

"Deaver and Aziz are stayin' in a hotel in town. He's gonna make contact when he gets here. I gotta go down. You wanna come with me or try to get back to sleep?"

There was no way in hell I was going to go back to sleep.

Still, I also didn't want to see a woken-up-and-called-to-duty-in-the-middle-of-the-night Deaver. He wasn't overly friendly by the light of day. I didn't want to experience a Deaver who'd had his beauty rest interrupted.

So I said, "I think Memphis proved she's got my back."

Sam grinned. Then he shifted an arm from around me, pulled Memphis out of my clutch, and held her up, her face close to his.

"Good girl," he muttered.

Memphis aimed and missed a lick at Sam's nose.

Sam handed her back to me.

"I'll be back soon," he whispered.

"Okay," I whispered back.

"You sure you're okay?"

No.

But I was sure I'd eventually get that way.

So I answered for the future, "Yeah, I'm sure I'm okay."

He leaned in and kissed my nose. He gave Memphis a head scratch, disentangled from us, nabbed his gun and moved to the door.

He stopped in it and looked back at me.

"I'll be back soon," he repeated.

God, Sam Cooper was a good man.

"I know," I whispered.

He studied me a second, his face got soft, and he disappeared into the dark hall.

I moved Memphis and myself under the downy cover and into Sam's soft sheets. Then I looked at Sam's alarm clock and saw it was twelve minutes after three o'clock in the morning.

At twenty past, Sam came back and Memphis and I watched as he put his gun on the nightstand. He slid in bed in his shorts and gathered me and my dog in his arms before he twisted and turned the lamp off.

"Deaver on duty?" I asked.

"He did a perimeter check and, yeah, he's on duty."

I nodded, my cheek sliding against his chest.

Sam's arms got tight.

"It's over," I whispered.

Sam's arms got tighter.

I felt tears sting my nose and my voice was husky when I said, "Thank you, Sam Cooper."

Sam rolled to facing me. Memphis jumped out from between us and went to sprawl on her side as Sam pulled me close. I shoved my face in his throat and wept, luckily silently but with extreme relief.

As I did this, lips against the hair at the top of my head, Sam whispered back, "My pleasure, baby."

My breath hitched and I pressed closer.

Sam's arms got even tighter.

And it was then I knew I was wrong.

I wasn't falling in love with Sam.

I was already there.

21

I DID NOT RAISE A STUPID MAN

Two days later...

"I should have brought flowers," I mumbled, staring down the wide terminal hall Sam and I were standing at the end of and doing it like a stampede of bulls was heading my way.

"Baby, relax," Sam whispered, his arm wound around my waist giving me an affectionate squeeze.

Right. Relax. Easy for him to say. He'd known his mother since inception and it was her duty to like him.

"Flowers say welcome," I informed him. "And they make a good impression."

Sam curled his body into mine and wrapped his other arm around me, saying softly, "Kia, honey, you got flowers on the kitchen bar. You got flowers on the kitchen island. You got flowers on the dining room table. And you got flowers *and* chocolates in her bedroom. I think you've got the welcome and good impression down, baby."

This was true. However, I had two plus hours of airport, baggage claim and ride home to navigate before she even saw the flowers and chocolates. And I had to navigate this without doing something that made me seem like a freak, a dork, a slut, or a loser. I wasn't certain I could do that. I was too young when things started up with Cooter even to know I should care that his mother liked me. By the time I learned, I didn't even care if Cooter liked me. I had no experience with this kind of thing.

What Sam said hit me and my panic escalated. So much, I had to share it.

Therefore my hands fisted in his shirt, I got up on my toes and whispered anxiously, "Oh my God, Sam, is that too much?"

"Kia—" he tried (and failed) to break in.

"Four bouquets of flowers *and* a box of chocolates?"

Sam tried (and failed) again. "Kia, baby—"

"I know!" I cried. "You detain her in the garage. I'll run upstairs, grab a couple of the bouquets and the chocolate and throw them over your deck."

His arms squeezed tight, his face dipped close, his smile got so big it had to hurt and he clipped out a trembling with amusement "Kia, baby, fuckin' *relax*. She's gonna love you."

I stared at him, then totally ignored him and noted, "I shouldn't have worn high heels."

He tipped his head back and looked at the ceiling. However, he did this with his body shaking with silent laughter.

I didn't have the time or energy to deal with Sam (again) thinking an un-amusing situation was amusing.

I had to psych myself up.

Unfortunately, this took me through a mental perusal of my outfit.

I was thinking I should have gone shorts and tank or maybe a cute little shirt with flip-flops.

But no. I decided to wear a dress I bought with Celeste. Navy blue, the bodice going straight across the tops of my breasts with a spaghetti strap that started at my armpits and went around the back of my neck. It fit close down to my waist, then flared out in a cute little short skirt. I was wearing my strappy, silver, high-heeled sandals with it. I certainly looked like I belonged on Sampson Cooper's arm and I knew this by the (many) approving looks we were getting.

But Sam wasn't Sampson Cooper to his mother and I was afraid I'd gone overboard.

Taking my mind off that, it decided to move through yesterday, which was good. This was because yesterday was good. In my mission to break through with Sam, yesterday I felt I didn't do too badly.

The day started with the good news that Sam felt pretty confident the hit man was on his way to Bora Bora, never to return to darken our door again. Tanner Layne's morning call sharing he received a confirmation e-mail from the hit man that he was standing down helped.

I thought this was overkill and might be his way of putting us off the scent. Sam (and Tanner and, after Sam phoned him, Lee) disagreed. They all felt that Sam's point had been made *very* clearly as getting a pair of khakis ruined by a bullet was wont to do. They felt the hit man just wanted to make sure that all the players were aware of his intention not to kill me.

I saw the wisdom of believing them, seeing as I had enough on my plate trying to make Sam open up to me at the same time fall in love with me and making a good impression with his mother. Not to mention, they were experts in this crazy shit and I was not.

After Sam took his run, I talked him into hitting town to buy flowers, chocolates and vases (Sam's kitchen was kitted out, but he was not a man who owned vases, which I discovered during my search while he was running). We picked up what we needed then Sam drove us out of town straight to a Jeep dealership. He did not share that a visit to a Jeep dealership was on our day's agenda so I was a little surprised.

I became very surprised when we were met by a salesman, who was clearly beside himself with glee that he scored Sampson Cooper but was still trying to act cool.

After his effusive (but trying to be cool) greeting, Sam told him, "Need to lease my woman a Jeep Cherokee. Thinkin'..." he trailed off, glanced through the lot, then looked at the man and finished, "Green."

I stopped breathing.

The man chirped excitedly, "Absolutely! Let's get you a test drive. I'll go get some keys. Be right back!" Then he sprinted (yes, *sprinted*) into the building.

"Uh…what's going on?" I asked, and Sam looked down at me.

"Gettin' you a ride," Sam answered.

"Um, shouldn't we go to a car rental place or…" I looked around, then back at him. "Do they do day and week rentals here?"

Sam's head cocked slightly to the side and he repeated, "Day and week rentals?"

"The threat is over, honey. I mean, I want to meet your mom so I'll stay for that, but then I have to go home and sort out my life."

"Right," Sam agreed. "But what are you gonna drive while you're here?"

"A rental car and I don't need anything fancy. Just a compact from Avis or something."

That was when Sam's brows drew together and he asked, "No, baby, I mean when you're *here*."

The emphasis on the final word didn't mean as much to me as it obviously meant to Sam, so I wisely decided to tread cautiously.

"Let's back up," I said quietly. "What's going on? And this time, maybe you should add some details to your answer."

Sam studied me a moment before he did as I requested. "You live in Indiana."

I nodded.

"I live here."

I nodded again.

"You need to go back there, family, friends, whatever. When you're there, you've already got a ride."

I nodded yet again.

"When you're here, you need a ride. So I'm seein' to you havin' a ride."

Okay, although there were more words to this explanation, I was still not following.

"Yes, and I can rent one from Avis or something, like you did when you were in Indiana."

Sam's head cocked to the side again *and* his brows drew together again, at the same time, which I thought might be a scary combination.

"Baby, I live here."

I was getting kind of impatient. "I know, Sam."

"And you're my woman."

Uh-oh. Not this again.

I had a feeling there was an additional nuance to me being his woman that he thought I should get that I did not.

"Sam—" I began to tell him this, but he turned fully to me, lifting his hands and curling his fingers around either side of my neck, his face dipping to my face, his serious, so I shut up.

And I would find he was serious when he said, "This isn't a vacation for you. You're not here a few days to relax and enjoy the beach and then goin' home, never to come back. I didn't just buy four vases because my woman wanted to fill the house with flowers. I bought four vases because my woman's livin' at my house and she's the kinda woman who fills the house with flowers."

Oh boy. I had a feeling that explained the garlic press.

Sam went on, "I dig that you gotta sort out what you gotta sort out at home. When I'm there with you, we'll sort out what I gotta sort out when I'm in Indiana once you got what you gotta sort out sorted."

Right, I followed that...kind of.

He kept going. "But we don't have shit to sort for you when you're here except this—gettin' you a ride. So I'm sorting it."

Light was dawning.

"Are you saying I'm going to be here often enough to need a car?"

This got the head cock, eyebrow draw *and* narrowed eyes, which was definitely scary.

"Uh…yeah."

"Oh," I whispered.

"You with me?" he asked.

"Um…yes," I answered, then foolishly queried, "Am I, uh… paying—?"

I didn't finish.

Sam cut me off with a firm, unyielding, deeply growled, "Kia."

I pressed my lips together.

I unpressed them to venture, "Okay, then, uh…can I point out you already have a gas-guzzling utility vehicle and perhaps we should spare the environment another gas-guzzling utility vehicle?"

Luckily, that made Sam grin. His hands went from my neck to become arms wrapped loosely around me and he kept grinning down at me when he replied, "You can point it out, but you're still gettin' a Cherokee."

This was when *my* brows drew together.

"Sam! *I* have to drive it."

"Yeah, and it's safe, if you don't drive reckless and roll it. Someone hits you and you're in a Cherokee, they may not come out breathin', but you will."

This point held merit so I didn't debate it.

Sam finished with, "But you can pick the color if you want."

Well, that was something.

I glanced through the lot, and I had to admit, the green was really cool. It was so dark, it was nearly black. And since Sam's truck was black, they'd kind of match.

I looked back and told him, "I like the green."

"Right," he muttered, grinning again.

At this point, I didn't know what came over me, but I blurted, "You have a garlic press."

This only got me a head cock for which I was relieved.

"Come again?"

I said it. I had to go with it.

"You have a garlic press."

"Yeah," Sam agreed.

"I find that surprising," I shared.

"Why?"

Hmm. How to traverse this?

Luckily, as my mind whizzed from thought to thought, Sam spoke.

"I like to cook, but while doin' it, I don't like to fuck around with shit that takes ten minutes when I can spend twenty-five dollars on something that'll make it take ten seconds."

Whoa. There was a lot there.

I started with the easy part.

"You spent twenty-five dollars on a garlic press?"

He grinned again and asked, "Are you not gettin' that I like the best?"

This was true.

So I kept going, "You cook?"

His grin got bigger and he replied, "I'm thirty-five. I'm a bachelor. I've always been a bachelor and I was an athlete then a soldier. No one's gonna take care of my body but me, so I do, but I like food. You wanna take care of your body and you like food, you learn to be creative. I learned. Before that, I was a kid with a mom who worked full-time. Sometimes she had a part-time job on top of that and I had a little brother. She put me in charge and part of bein' in charge was gettin' both of us fed. Canned soup and TV dinners get old real quick. You want better, you learn to make better. So, again, I learned."

I thought this was cool and sweet.

Before I could share that with Sam, he kept talking as his loose arms got tighter, "You don't race back to Indiana, I'll show you what I can do in the kitchen."

"Will it include carbs?" I asked.

That got me a full-fledged smile and a soft, "I can do carbs."

I melted into him and replied softly back, "Then I won't race back to Indiana."

Yes, that was what I said. I might not have a hit out on me anymore, but my entire life was still up in the air. Even so, I promised to increase my indeterminate stay in North Carolina an indeterminate amount just so Sam would have the opportunity to cook for me.

This was my dedication to my mission. I'd do anything.

"Good," he muttered, and it was then I realized I'd scored.

It wasn't huge. But he talked about his brother, his mother and himself. He'd shared. And he'd made it clear I was going to be around awhile and back often, enough to lease a vehicle.

And that was what he did. He leased me a forest-green Cherokee. I drove it back to his place, and even though I wasn't used to that big of a car, I still thought it was the shit.

That evening, Sam did not thrill me with his culinary brilliance and spoil me with carbs.

He took me to Skippy's Crab Shack.

And it was just that. A shack out in the middle of nowhere, surrounded by nothing but dense trees, accessed by a single-lane, dirt road. It was so dilapidated, how it stayed standing was anyone's guess. The only part of it that had walls was the kitchen. The rest of it was a long, cement porch covered by a rickety roof that drunkenly slanted.

I also met Skippy, who was the antithesis of Patrizio. And not just because Patrizio was an older man who clearly enjoyed his food, but neither of these things hid that he was once very good-looking and still had it. It also wasn't because Skippy looked like his mother birthed him in the blazing hot sun, and although that blessed day was apparently one hundred and fifty years ago, he'd never been indoors since, such was the weathered look of his skin, the complete absence of his hair and the brawny, bulldogedness of his frame.

No, it was also because Patrizio was warm and funny and Skippy was so hard and surly, he was crusty.

I learned this immediately.

As we made it to the edge of the patio under his censorious glower, he took one look at Sam, then he looked at me and declared, "You call me Skippy even once, I'll piss in your beer."

I decided not to reply and spent my energy focusing on not looking freaked out or offended by this greeting.

"His mother named him that, as in, put it on his birth certificate," Sam explained to me while grinning at Skippy. "But everyone calls him Skip."

I could see a brown-skinned, leathery-faced, burly old guy with a serious attitude wishing to lose the "py" on his name. It was clear he'd never been a boy even when he was a boy, so he'd not want a boy's name when he was most definitely all man.

"I've never tried urine, but I'm also relatively certain I don't want to, so you have my word you're only Skip to me," I assured him.

He didn't give any indication he heard me speak when he continued laying down the law.

"I also don't do substitutions, and if you got a lactose intolerance, a nut allergy, you need gluten-free, you're on some stupid-ass diet that means you can't have ketchup or whatever, I don't give a shit. The menu is the menu. You order, you get what it says you'll get and you're happy with it since I also don't do complaints."

"So noted," I replied.

"And I got beer, Coke, Sprite and Diet Coke. You're on an asinine diet, you order Diet Coke. I do not do light beer. I do not serve water. You want light beer or you wanna do something moronic like drink water with fried food, you can find another crab shack," he announced.

"Message received," I assured him.

Skip wasn't done.

"You're with Sam and you feel like tyin' one on, I'll pull out the bourbon. You're with Luci, I'll bring out the vodka. You become a regular and don't get up my nose, I'll keep a bottle a' whatever you like in the Shack. You *ever* bring Hap back here, you're eighty-sixed for life, just like him. Got me?"

Hmm. Wonder what Hap did. I couldn't see him ordering a light beer so I suspected it was something else.

I stared at Skip's craggy face and decided to ask Sam later.

"Got you," I told him.

He examined me head to toe and took his time.

So much of it, Sam asked, "Skip, Ma's comin' to town tomorrow. Need your approval of Kia before we have to hit the road for Raleigh. We got any prayer that's gonna happen?"

Skip glared at Sam while he spoke, and when he was done, his eyes sliced to me.

"So, Maris is comin' to check you out?"

I bit my lip and shrugged.

"Sam was my boy, you'd get approval just because you got a great rack," he informed me.

Jeez. Seriously. What was up with the men Sam hung out with?

"Uh…cool," I muttered.

Skip looked at Sam and continued, "And a mouth made to be kissed."

That was better…*ish.*

"Noticed that, Skip. Now, can we sit and eat?" Sam asked, sounding amused.

Skip looked back at me. "Two fried crab sandwiches, two beers, comin' up."

With that he turned and disappeared into the Shack.

Sam led me to a picnic table, one of the kinds where the seats were attached with angled boards. We mounted the seat on the same side and Sam claimed me by pulling one of my legs over one of his thighs, twisting his torso to me and resting his arm over my lap.

"Skip's a character," he told me.

"Got that, honey," I muttered, and Sam grinned.

His grin faded and he shared softly, "Fifty cents of every dollar he makes he gives to ALS research 'cause his sister died of Lou Gehrig's disease."

My heart squeezed.

"Oh God," I whispered.

"He's a nut, but he's a nut who really fuckin' loved his sister."

I felt my face get soft and I looked toward the Shack.

"And when Gordo died," Sam went on, and I quickly looked back at him, "and Luci lost it, he slept on her couch for two weeks because he didn't like her bein' alone. He made her breakfast every morning and stood over her, makin' her eat when she wouldn't. He left the Shack and made her lunch. And he left it again to make her dinner. He can be an ass. He's hard to take and that's why he never got married, never had kids. That doesn't mean he hasn't adopted a number of them along the way. He adopts you, as you can tell, he's still an ass and hard to take, but he's good people."

"Never judge a book by their cover or talking books that tell you two minutes after you've met them that you've got a great rack," I said quietly, and Sam grinned again.

Then he agreed, "Yeah."

"What did Hap do?"

Sam's grin got bigger before he stated, "Hap's in the Army."

"Right..." I drew it out on a prompt.

"And before Skippy started his crab shack, he was in the Navy."

"Ah," I murmured, nodding my head.

"One night, Skip broke out the bourbon and Hap had too much, didn't shut up. There was a discussion. It got heated. It veered to the Army-Navy game the previous season, which Army just happened to win. Hap rubbed it in and Skip blew a gasket. Eighty-sixed Hap for life and meant it. Hap's tried twice to come back. Skip got out his shotgun and fired buckshot at him twice. Hap's not a big fan of bein' fired on in the line of duty and *really* not a big fan of bein' fired on when he's just lookin' for dinner. So Hap hasn't attempted a third time."

"This is probably wise," I stated.

"Definitely wise," Sam agreed.

I held his eyes and told him, "Celeste said that you can tell a lot by the company a man keeps."

Sam burst out laughing. I smiled and watched.

When he controlled his laughter, he remarked, "Great. Not sure that's good, baby."

My smile died and I whispered, "I am."

Sam's eyes got intense, his face got intense and I held my breath.

He leaned into me, opening his mouth to speak, just when two bottles of beer thudded loudly on the wood beside us.

I choked back growling my frustration when I turned to the bottles to see Skip had deposited them so forcefully, both of them were foaming over. My eyes tipped up to look at him.

"Beer," he grunted the obvious and stalked off.

Sam chuckled and grabbed a beer. He reached out to a napkin dispenser, yanked some out and wiped one down before he handed it to me.

The moment was lost.

I decided to let it go and find my time to make another one.

Not long after, our meals were served.

I was an experimental eater. I would try practically everything. That said, the operative word in that was "practically." And it had to be said that I was willing to try a fried crab sandwich but was still apprehensive about it. After meeting Skip, learning about him and seeing the many picnic tables filled with people and the steady coming and going of cars picking up takeaway orders, I felt better about this. After actually eating it and the mound of homemade, spiced by hand, thin fries that were fried to crispy perfection and covered in ketchup, I knew why Sam was a regular.

After Skippy's, we headed home and finished the evening on the couch, snuggled together, Sam watching a game. I knew he'd cuddle even while watching a game and I was happy to have this verified.

Then bed, great sex, sleep and now I found myself waiting for Sam's mother to show and check me out.

He'd shared, and he'd even done it deeply, about Marisela Cooper. He loved his mother. I knew this.

So I also knew if I stood a chance of making the man I loved love me, I had to make Marisela Cooper do the same.

Of anyone, she knew his many nuances. She'd created both Sampson Cooper and Sam. She knew Sampson Cooper could have anyone and should settle for nothing but the best. And she knew Sam Cooper deserved the best of the best.

And I had to convince her that was me.

And I was scared to death.

"Kia, look at me," I heard Sam call gently, and my eyes, which were staring unfocused at his shoulder, lifted to his. When they did, his face got close. "I know you're worried, and it sucks that you're worried, but I gotta say, I love that you care enough to be worried."

My body softened into his and I whispered, "Baby."

His eyes moved over my face before they locked to mine.

He kept speaking gently, this time soft and sweet, when he said, "You're beautiful always, but you make a little dress and high heels look fuckin' spectacular and when your face looks just…like…that, honey, you take my breath away."

God, God, *God*, I loved this man.

And I had to let him know without letting him know.

So I went up on my toes, my hands slid up his chest to his neck and I pressed my lips to his for a hard, closed-mouth kiss.

Even though it was a certainty people were looking and a possibility someone had at least a camera phone at the ready, Sam didn't hesitate with slanting his head, his arms going tight around me, and he took my hard, closed-mouth kiss straight to a hard, deep, wet, open-mouthed kiss.

Suffice it to say, my body softened even more into his and both my hands slid up to cup the back of his head.

The kiss was awesome, it was hot, it was sweet and it was very ill-timed.

"Sam, honey?" a velvety female voice called from close, and Sam ended the kiss and lifted his head an inch as he turned it.

I turned mine too. Slowly.

And there stood Marisela Cooper.

Damn.

There was a reason Sam and his brother were handsome. I didn't know what his father looked like, but his mother's beautiful skin, beautiful eyes, and now seeing her beautiful, blinding white smile, she'd given him the best of her and her best was *the best.*

She had long, thick, shining black hair pulled back at the tops and sides. At her age, which I was guessing to be in the mid-fifties, it was likely dyed, but either she was very fortunate or she went to an awesome stylist because there was not a gray hair to be found and it didn't look fake.

She was wearing a pair of stylish, loose-fitting, white linen trousers, a pair of stylish, strappy, black high heels and a loose-fitting, man-style, black linen shirt over a white camisole. She'd added a tangle of some interesting silver necklaces, which sat perfectly on her still-smooth, beautiful brown-skinned chest like they'd been arranged by a production assistant during a photo shoot.

Thank God. I was not overdressed.

I knew from Sam that she (very cool at her age back then, I thought) went to college when her son hit the big time and got herself a business degree. While doing this, she'd opened her own high-class, beach boutique in Malibu, which she still ran, that Sam told me was very popular and turned a good profit.

And it was clear she was sporting her wares and they were evidence of why her boutique was popular. She looked fantastic.

Celeste would love her and so would my mom.

She was perfect.

I was screwed.

"Ma," Sam muttered. My eyes slid to him as his arms slid from around me and I saw him smiling his mother's smile right back at her.

I watched him fold her in his arms and I watched her eyes close. My breath stuck when I saw her face get warm, soft and intense, just like her son's, as her arms stole around Sam.

"Sammy," she whispered, her eyes still closed.

Sammy.

Oh man.

She loved her boy. Really loved him.

That was beautiful.

I was totally screwed.

Sam moved away but not far. His hands went to her waist as hers shifted to his biceps and he asked, "Flight good?"

"It was long and it's over. Why you don't move back to California so I don't have to fly five hours to see you, I will never know," she answered.

"Yeah, you say that, then you hit the deck with a rum and Coke and stop bitchin'," Sam returned on a grin.

Her eyes slid to me, I held my breath, then they went back to Sam and she admonished, "Language, Sammy, there are ladies in your midst."

Sam stepped away from his mom, still grinning, and muttered, "Right, Ma this is—"

"Kia," she breathed.

Yes.

Breathed.

What did I do with *that*?

She moved into me and gave me a tight hug.

At first, I was a little shocked. Then I was a little relieved. Finally, I pulled myself together and hugged her back.

"Hey, Mrs. Cooper," I said into her ear. "I'm so pleased to meet you."

She gave me a squeeze but didn't take her arms from around me as she leaned back and smiled warmly in my face. "Maris, honey. Mrs. Cooper is my ex's mother and she wasn't all that nice."

"Okay," I whispered.

She kept smiling at me before her head turned to Sam and she noted, "No Burberry, thank God."

I pressed my lips together.

Sam sighed.

Maris looked back at me. "Sam told me about you after he met you in Italy."

Uh…wait.

Really? *Italy?*

Whoa.

Maris cut into my freak out by continuing to speak. "Then *Luci* told me about you and keeps telling me about you every time she calls. You've won Luci's heart, Kia, an impossible feat."

Thank God. Luci laid the road for me. I just had to travel it.

"Everyone keeps saying that, but knowing Luci, I find it hard to believe."

She gave me a squeezy-hug shake and another smile, then released me.

"Right!" she said sharply, and I jumped. "I will *die* if I do not have a chai, which needs to be seen to prior to getting my bags. Let's go."

It was then she hooked her arm through mine, leaned into me and commenced us walking with Sam trailing and her talking.

"Sam said he met a beautiful girl in Italy, but until I saw the pictures, honey, I didn't believe him. He has good taste, but he finally found a true winner. You're even better in the flesh. I *love* your shoes."

She said the word "love" on another squeezy-hug shake, this one of my arm. I had to admit, I was feeling all-over happy that Sam told his mother about me after he met me and that he included the word "beautiful."

"Thanks," I replied softly, and I looked over at my shoulder to see Sam grinning at me.

His voice rumbled at me, "Told you."

Maris looked over her shoulder too and demanded to know, "Told her what?"

"That you'd love her," Sam answered.

I gave him big eyes, then quickly rearranged my face when Maris looked at me.

"Were you nervous?" she asked.

"Uh…yeah," I answered.

She gave my arm another squeezy-hug shake at the same time waving her other hand in front of her, looking forward, and declaring, "I'm harmless."

"I see that now," I murmured.

"Unless you break his heart," she went on. "Then I'll find you, rip yours out and feed it to my dog."

Yikes!

"I think if that happens, Sam will likely be the heartbreaker," I whispered, and I felt her eyes on me so my eyes moved to her.

And there it was again. Just like her son, her eyes were intense, burning into me, saying something I did not get.

"I did not raise a stupid man," she whispered back, and this time she just gave my arm a squeezy-hug without the shake.

I smiled tentatively at her.

Her smile wasn't tentative at all.

She looked forward again and cried, "Thank God! Chai!"

Then she steered us quickly to the line in the coffee place at the airport.

Right. That went well.

And I owed Luci. Big time.

I ordered an iced latte.

And when the girl handed me my plastic cup, I finally relaxed.

22

NEVER USE IT JUST TO BREATHE

"Look at all these beautiful flowers!" Maris called out.

Since Sam was bringing up her bags, he was trailing me. I was trailing Maris, therefore she'd hit the first floor before both of us.

I was learning that Maris making note of something I'd done with her in mind was pure Maris. She was just like her son—talkative, friendly, warm, demonstrative, decisive and totally bossy. It was super cute how she ordered her tall, powerfully built, definitely adult son around. It was even cuter how Sam put up with it with affectionate patience and indulgent grins.

We took the Cherokee up to Raleigh because it was more comfortable for passengers and meant her bags wouldn't be exposed to the elements. During the ride home, twisted in my seat most of the time to gab with Maris, I had learned that Sam told his mother about me after he had breakfast with me.

Yes, that's what I said. *After he had breakfast with me.*

She'd called him that very day and he'd shared he'd met, as Maris recounted, "a beautiful woman who also manages to be cute."

At his mother imparting this information on me, with affectionate patience and an indulgent grin, Sam had muttered, "Jesus."

"Is that not what you said?" Maris retorted.

Patiently and indulgently, Sam muttered, "Yeah, Ma. That's what I said."

She grinned at me. I grinned back, but I suspected, learning Sam shared this with his mother *after we had breakfast,* my grin was a whole lot brighter.

Luci and the news reported widely that Cooter and Vanessa planned to off me filled in the rest. Therefore, she wasted no time in finding the opportunity to meet me.

"I hope you don't find it offensive that we talk, Kia," she said quietly, studying my face. "We're family; that's what families do."

I liked it that she corralled Luci in her family. I liked that a lot. It said everything about her.

"I have a family, Maris, so I get that," I replied quietly in return.

She grinned at me again. And again, I grinned back.

Sam was right. I had nothing to be nervous about. Then again, it was good that I was nervous because, clearly, Maris was just as pleased as Sam that I cared.

Now we were home, she liked the flowers, and it was all good.

I made sure I was out of his way at the top of the stairs, then turned and smiled at Sam to communicate my relief. He caught my smile, stopped, his hand shot out, hooked the back of my neck, and he pulled me to him, leaning down to kiss me even as he smiled back.

"Luci!" Maris cried.

Sam's mouth still on mine, I opened my eyes to see he had too and my surprise was reflected in his.

His head moved away just as Maris exclaimed, "Oh my God! What a lovely surprise!"

Sam released my neck, left the bag where it was and we both moved into the kitchen to see Maris already out the front door and hurrying through the screened porch.

My eyes went beyond her to see Luci on the deck.

She wasn't alone.

Celeste was rising gracefully from one of Sam's Adirondack chairs.

"Celeste!" I cried happily, running on my high heels through Sam's house and out to the deck (Memphis yapping and following at my heels), where I made a beeline to my friend and threw my arms around her.

"*Ma chérie*," she whispered in my ear, holding tight.

"I can't believe you're here," I whispered back.

"Surprise," she replied softly.

I felt tears sting my eyes as I straightened but didn't drop my arms.

"Best one I think I've ever had."

She smiled at me, took one arm from around me and laid her hand lightly on the side of my face. Her eyes moved over my features. They got soft and I knew from her look that she liked what she saw. Then they moved over my shoulder.

"Sam," she said in her rich, cultured voice and moved out of my arms to Sam.

"Kia!" Luci cried, and I turned to her just in time to catch her in my arms. We gave each other deep hugs, then she pulled back. "Maris told me she was coming to meet you. I told Celeste and we both decided it would be fun to make it a surprise party." She let me go and threw out her arms. "So we're here. Surprise!"

"Awesome," I whispered.

She grinned at me, her head turned and she cried out, "Sam!" like he wasn't two feet away from her but down on the beach during a hurricane and she threw herself in his arms so hard, I saw his body lock so they both didn't go down.

Celeste and Maris were smiling at them and I let Sam and Luci have their moment by introducing the two women.

"Maris, this is my friend Celeste Masterson. We met in Lake Como. Celeste, sweetie, this is Sam's mom, Marisela Cooper."

"Maris," Maris stated, lifting her hand that Celeste took. She leaned in and they did the cheek to cheek to cheek business and pulled apart.

"We brought champagne!" Luci announced, moving to a table, lifting a sweating bottle of Cristal and I noted it was one of three.

Yep, Luci and Celeste had decided it was time to party.

So it was time to party.

"I'll get glasses," I offered and began to move.

"No, baby, I got it," Sam murmured and moved faster than me so I settled.

"I love this!" Luci cried, clapping her hands together. "Everyone together! We need to call Hap!"

I grinned at her even as I studied her.

It was still there, the sorrow, not even a little faded. My grin faltered and my eyes moved to Celeste. She tipped her head slightly to the side and shook it once, almost imperceptibly. I nodded mine once, hopefully the same. I knew from conversations with both of them that Celeste and Luci spent a lot of time together in Lake Como and Celeste and I had several conversations about Luci. Celeste saw the same thing I did. And Celeste was at the same loss as Sam and I were as to what to do about it.

My gaze slid to Maris, who I saw was looking between me and Celeste knowingly. She saw it too. She knew what Celeste and I were communicating and this was confirmed when she reached out her fingers and lightly touched the back of mine.

I quickly filled the loaded silence with, "I love it too, Luci, sweetie. So pleased you both are here." My eyes moved to Maris and I added, "All of you. So pleased *all* of you are here."

Luci shot me a half-fake, half-genuinely-bright smile.

Then she hurried to her purse, declaring, "I'm calling Hap right now."

She dug in her purse.

Maris cried, "What an adorable dog!" and bent down to pick up a bouncing, delighted-beyond-reason-to-have-company Memphis.

Sam arrived with five champagne glasses turned down, their stems tucked between his fingers.

Luci called Hap.

And the surprise party began.

In my nightie, ready for bed, I exited Sam's bathroom to find Sam standing by the bed, emptying his jeans pockets, dropping stuff on the nightstand.

I also heard, distant but definitely there, Hap's snores coming from where he was passed out on the couch. Another indication of why he had not nailed down his own "fine piece of ass." Those snores would drive the most devoted woman either to kill him in his sleep or avoid a jail sentence and leave him.

Hap showed about four hours after Luci called him. He didn't have to go back until Sunday and he didn't drink champagne. Hap drank beer intermingled with shots of bourbon, a lot of both, and Hap was even more happy as well as hilarious when he was loaded.

Once he'd passed out, Maris announced she was calling it a night and Sam had loaded a very tipsy (but still cultured) Celeste and Luci into the Cherokee and taken them to Luci's house.

Now, obviously, he was back.

Sam had finished with his pockets and was pulling his shirt over his head when I asked, "Everyone settled?"

He tossed his shirt on the floor as I watched, tearing my eyes from the vision of his chest to his shirt lying on the floor.

Sam always tossed his clothes on the floor, but in the morning he picked them up and took them to a plastic hamper in his walk-in closet. I knew Kyle didn't do this because I heard Gitte bitch about it. I also knew Dad didn't do it because I had a lifetime of Mom bitching about it (as well as bitching about Kyle not doing it when he lived at home). And I also knew Rudy didn't do it because Paula bitched about it to me on more than one occasion. Cooter *definitely* didn't do it.

Sam did.

It was another thing I loved about him.

I suspected I had Maris to thank for that and, luckily, now I had the opportunity.

"Yep," he answered my question.

I mounted the bed on a knee, and when I got both of them in, I sat back on my calves and softly noted something I'd observed as the afternoon wore into the evening and then into the night, "I think she's worse."

Even as his hands worked the buttons on his fly, his eyes came to me, locked on mine and I knew he knew I meant Luci when he repeated a weighty, "Yep."

"Sam—" I started, but he interrupted me.

"I'll call Vitale tomorrow. He told me he was going to sit down with her, but he hasn't reported in. I'll see how that went."

"Obviously not well," I remarked.

Sam's jaw clenched. Then he removed his jeans and all thoughts of Luci swept from my mind.

He pulled the covers back, climbed in, flicked them over his body and did an ab curl, his long arm reaching out toward me. He tagged me around the waist and yanked so I fell chest to chest into him as he settled on his back.

His arm stayed around my waist and his other hand sifted into the hair at the side of my head, pulling it back, his fingers curling around my skull. I left one hand pressed between us on the warm, silk skin of his chest and curled the fingers of my other one around his neck.

"Your mom sees it and she's worried too," I told him.

"I know," he told me.

"I'm at a loss, Sam."

"Me too."

I thought about it and shared, "Missy never snapped out of it. She breathes, but she doesn't *live*. Do you know what I mean?"

He nodded. "You tellin' me her story, I watched her. Switched off. Existing. Wrapping herself in other people's problems so she won't have to face her own."

There it was. He'd also figured out Missy.

"Seeing Luci, now I think something should be done about the both of them," I said quietly.

"Yep," Sam agreed.

I sighed.

Sam was done talking about sad, worrisome things and I knew this when he started to pull my face to his.

I resisted, whispering, "Sam, your mom's on California time. When I came up, the light was on under her door."

"We'll be quiet," he muttered, his eyes dropping to my mouth at the same time they heated, them doing both making my nipples tingle and he put more pressure on my head.

"Sam—"

Suddenly, he rolled me, and when he was on top and I got a good look at his face, I knew instantly something profound had changed.

"Learn from them, baby," he whispered. "You got one life, never use it just to breathe."

I stared at his face, his intensity seared into me and it hit me that he was *so* right.

I had one life and I lived it for seven years doing nothing but focusing on each day, each breath, not living my dreams, not seeking excitement, not pursuing happiness, not searching for my slice of heaven.

I was done just breathing.

"We'll be quiet," I whispered back.

Sam grinned his approval, then he kissed me.

I woke up in a bed that didn't include Sam or Memphis.

I looked at the alarm clock and saw I'd slept in. Sam was either out walking Memphis or he was already at the gym.

I rolled out of bed, did my bathroom thing, grabbed my fabulous robe and shrugged it on.

I was tying the belt, my bare feet silent on Sam's wood floors, just about to round the railing to hit the stairs, when I heard it.

"I did not raise an idle son."

I stopped dead.

That was Maris and she sounded *pissed.*

I was more than mildly shocked. I knew from what Sam told me and what I'd seen of her that she was not a weak woman. I had no idea how she was before Sam and Ben ousted their father. I just knew from Sam's stories that she blossomed after that and everything about her was proof. She was happy. She dressed well. She lived well. She had a great sense of humor and an easy smile. She worked and enjoyed what she did. She was her own boss. And she raised two boys who turned into fine men.

But she was like Sam, albeit with a bit of feminine drama. She was mostly laid-back, good-humored and easygoing.

At her tone, I learned she *was* just like her son. In other words, she could get *pissed.*

"Ma, Kia's up," Sam returned on a low growl I still heard from my position on the stairs.

"So?" Maris replied, and I started backing up.

"I'd say we'd talk about this later, but we're not fuckin' talkin' about this later. We're not talkin' about this at all," Sam declared.

"Do not use that tone and language with me, Sampson August Cooper," she snapped.

"You're standin' in my kitchen, in my home, talkin' about my life with my woman awake upstairs. Do not fuckin' tell me how to behave in my own goddamned home," Sam shot back on a continued, infuriated growl.

Now I was even more shocked. Shocked stone-still. Sam loved his mother. I couldn't believe he was speaking to her like that.

"Of the many things I'd like to know, *now* I'd like to know why you're so concerned Kia is going to hear us," Maris stated.

"That's none of your business either," Sam returned.

Ohmigod.

"I don't like that, Sam. Kia is—" she started.

He cut her off. "My woman and my business. Not yours."

Yikes.

"I cannot believe you just said that to me," Maris whispered, sounding hurt.

"I did." Sam didn't hesitate to confirm.

Ohmigod!

Maris was silent.

I decided to tiptoe back to Sam's room.

I didn't even get started. This was because Maris broke her silence.

"You cannot go on like you are."

What did that mean?

"I can do whatever the fuck I wanna do. It's my life, Ma. You gave it to me, but that doesn't mean you get to lead it."

Um...*ouch.*

"You have no focus, Sam, no purpose, no drive. You're drifting through life. That is not my son," she returned instantly.

"Honest to God?" Sam fired back, and I knew by his tone she'd pushed him close to the edge. "You do not know what I got or what I don't got, Ma. And I'm tellin' you, whatever that is, it's none of your damn business."

God, I needed to get out of there.

So I did. Carefully rushing back to Sam's room so as not to make any noise, I stopped in it and frantically tried to figure out what to do. Then I noticed the floor was empty except for the rug. As usual, Sam had picked up his clothes and taken them to the walk-in. So I went to the closet and rooted around in the pile of Sam's and my tangled, dirty clothes. I got a bunch of darks, enough to make a load, and headed out.

On the landing, I called, "Maris, see you're up. I know you just got here, but I'm doing a load of darks. Do you have anything that needs to be cleaned?"

Memphis yapped and ran up the stairs to meet me halfway.

Hap grunted, "Fuckin' A. Am I at a bus depot? What's up with all the noise?"

I made it to the bottom of the stairs and saw him hanging over the back of the couch, scowling. I smiled brightly at him and hoped he was hungover enough not to notice it was forced.

"Morning, Hap," I greeted cheerily.

"Fuck," he muttered, flopped back and thus disappeared.

I kept the grin pinned to my face as the clothes I was carrying, my dog and I turned into the kitchen.

"Morning," I said to both occupants, neither of whom were hiding that they were still pissed. So I thought it safe to let my fake grin fade and venture, "Is everything okay?"

Maris looked to the floor.

Sam came to me, wrapped his fingers around the back of my head and pulled me in and up to my toes. He then commenced in laying a hard, short, closed-mouthed kiss on my lips.

He let me go but didn't move out of my space when he muttered, "Hittin' the gym. Be back in a couple of hours."

A couple of hours?

Sam didn't mess around working out. I knew this because he was never back before an hour was up and usually didn't return for an hour and a half. The same with when he ran.

But a couple of hours? Never.

"Okay," I whispered, then kept trying, asking softly, "You okay?"

"Great," he lied, moved away, jerked his chin up at his mother and disappeared behind the stairs.

I looked to Maris. "Did I interrupt something?"

She was watching the back of the stairs, the residual anger on her face now mixed liberally with concern.

She wiped it clean, looked at me, gave me a small smile and didn't lie so much as evade when she answered, "We're family. We talk a lot. We share a lot. And sometimes we fight, though luckily not a lot. It happens, we get over it. My Sammy's like his mama. We sometimes rub each other the wrong way, but it doesn't last long. Promise. Now do you want coffee?"

She was trying to change the subject.

And I was still reeling from what I'd heard, the tone, the words, and most especially that it now seemed very clear Sam was intentionally keeping something from me.

So, cautiously, I replied, "Love some, Maris." I moved toward the utility room but stopped when I came abreast of where she was across the kitchen from me and I said quietly, "But if you ever need to talk…" Her eyes came to mine, mine locked on hers, my heart clenched and my mind made a terrifying, split-second decision. Therefore, I continued on a whisper, "I love your son. But I know he can be annoying. You want to talk, I'll listen, and while I do, know nothing you say will change the way I feel about Sam."

Her lips had parted, her eyes went bright with tears and I decided I was done. I'd been fearless, taken a risk and threw it out there.

Now it was time to get the fuck out of there.

So I dipped my head to the clothes in my arms and asked, "Any darks?"

Maris shook her head.

I nodded and muttered, "Okey dokey."

Then I got the fuck out of there.

I had pushed the footstool aside and pulled the Adirondack chair up to the railing of Sam's deck so I could rest my feet on it.

Memphis was nosing around on the deck for the first time out without a lot of company to keep her occupied. It was a test. But as Sam said she'd do, she was enjoying the space but staying close. I was keeping an eye on her in case she got a wild hair and wandered.

It was late afternoon and Maris was in the kitchen starting dinner. Luci was helping her. Celeste was at the bar, keeping them company. And Sam and Hap had gone to the store to pick up some things Maris needed and more booze.

That morning, after Maris and I chatted for a while over coffee, breakfast and Hap's resumed loud snoring, Luci and Celeste showed. They did it with Luci's flashy, red Corvette stuffed to the gills with beach paraphernalia, as in, stuffed so full her trunk wasn't shut—coolers filled with drinks, sandwiches and snacks; bags filled with beach towels and a variety of suntan lotion, chairs and umbrellas.

Maris and I got changed and we carted all of Luci's stuff down the wooded walkway that led to the beach that Sam and his neighbor shared. Hap, wearing a pair of cutoff jeans as trunks and proving he was indeed made entirely of muscle from jaw to toes, joined us a half an hour later. That was to say, he joined us by arriving, then collapsed facedown on a beach towel Luci laid out for him. He then again passed out.

Sam joined us an hour after that wearing a loose-fitting tank that, to my delight, he immediately took off and loose-fitting trunks he left on.

Hap resurfaced, ate four of the sandwiches Luci and Celeste brought and somewhat revived. This included him jogging to Sam's house and bringing back a football. Sam and Hap played catch while I watched with no small amount of fascination. This was mainly because Sam wasn't so much playing catch as existing with movement. I found it stunning. Throwing, catching, running, reaching—it was all so fluid and graceful, it seemed natural. Not practiced. It wasn't like a dance, it was like breathing.

Except breathing beautifully.

Watching him, I wished my dad was there. Dad would love to play catch with Sam. Sam was definitely Sam to Dad, heck, to my entire family. But there were times he was Sampson Cooper and this was one of those times and Dad would get something huge from that.

Luci joined them and essentially played run after the ball you dropped, which only Luci could make cute and seem like fun. Which she did.

Not long after, Sam came to me, yanked me to my feet and we played two-on-two beach football, a game I didn't know existed. I was teamed with Hap, which I found a surprise until I realized it was because, if I was on an opposing team, Sam could tackle me. Which he did.

A lot.

Hap and I, by the way, lost. This Hap did good-naturedly, but then again, he probably knew we had no shot.

It was a blast and it was then I wished Kyle and Gitte were with us because three-on-three would be an even bigger blast.

Maris and Celeste chatted in between cheering us and indifferently reading their e-books.

We gave up on the game and Luci and I frolicked in the ocean for a while, Sam and Hap joining us, therefore the frolicking became horsing around. Then, exhausted (or at least Luci and I were), we dragged ourselves out of the surf, collapsed on our towels, laid out and soaked up some rays.

Early afternoon we packed it in, which was to say the women hoofed it to the house while Hap and Sam carted up all our stuff. Luci and Celeste went back to Luci's place for showers while Maris and I did the same at Sam's, Sam hitting the shower after me.

The women returned looking prepared to sweep into a slightly casual Cordon Bleu restaurant and Maris emerged from her room much the same. So it was lucky for me I chose a pair of dark green, tailored, cuffed short-shorts and a kickass melon-colored tee that was sleeveless and had awesome drapey bits crossed tight at the neckline, as well as light makeup, light perfume and a touch of cool-as-hell jewelry I'd picked up at a boutique in Paris.

The day was fun and, clearly, neither Sam nor Maris were going to spoil it for anyone by holding ill will about that morning. It was like it didn't happen. Sam was Sam, Maris was who I was getting to know was Maris and that was it.

But now, sitting on Sam's deck with a moment of solitude and a glass of chilled white wine, try as I might, it was creeping back on me.

What Maris said was true. Sam was a professional football player. Then Sam joined the Army and became a freaking Ranger.

But now what did Sam do?

I had no idea except he said he was in Italy on business, business he never explained. And thinking back on it, he'd had a lot of phone calls not only when we were in Indiana, but also when we were on Crete and even when we were on our trip to view *La Scapigliata.*

And most of these he walked away from me to take.

When someone was out there maybe then definitely out to kill me, I didn't think about it. Sam had a mission. Sam had a focus.

Now there was nothing.

And Maris was right. Sam was not that kind of man.

So what did he do?

I could not imagine Sam was a guy who worked out, frolicked at the beach, hung at Skippy's and followed his girlfriend around.

What I didn't know was what was next, not only for me but for him.

What I knew from his conversation with his mother that morning was that whatever was next or, indeed, currently happening with Sam, he wasn't going to share it with me. I had not been spending much time trying, but I hadn't really broken through. Now I knew my small victories were not small.

They were puny.

"Do you wish to have some time alone, *ma belle*?" I heard.

I turned my head and tipped it back to see Celeste, wearing fabulous sunglasses and holding her own glass of wine, standing beside me.

"Absolutely not. Not while you're here to spend my time with," I told her. She smiled, then she moved to drag a chair beside me. When she settled, I said, "I love it that you're here."

"I do as well, my Kia, and not only because I get to spend time with you and Sam, but also because Thomas received his next assignment and he's in *Lago di Como* dealing with packers and movers and I am not. I fear, as much as I have done it, I have never grown to like it. But I am fortunate that my husband loves me so he doesn't mind me flying over an ocean to avoid it."

I turned my head to look at her. "Where are you moving?"

She looked at me and answered, "London."

Drat. That wasn't Chicago or even New York.

As much as I wished she was moving closer, I still smiled and remarked, "Well, I've never been there, so a new place to visit."

"*Oui*," she murmured on a small returned smile, but it died as she turned her head to look over her shoulder, then back at me. "We must talk quickly in case Luci joins us."

Oh man.

"Why?" I whispered.

She tipped her head to the side and I knew she was thinking.

"It is odd…" she trailed off then quickly went on, "You and I, we have discussed it. I sense your anxiety. And Maris's, Hap's, Sam's… but, *ma chérie*, since our return yesterday, something has changed."

I twisted my torso toward her and leaned in. "What?"

She twisted to me and also leaned in. "You and Sam."

I blinked. Then I repeated, "What?"

"She watches you both when you're focused on each other. At first, I thought this was wistful, as it would be. Then the pain started to be more visible. I think watching your relationship blossom with Sam reminds her even more acutely of what she has lost."

"That's not good," I muttered, not wanting to be the cause of even deeper pain for Luci.

"No it isn't," Celeste agreed. "But it's more."

Oh man!

"What?" I prompted, leaning deeper into her.

"Our flight, our travel from the airport, getting settled in her home she shared with her husband and also I noticed a time this morning…she retreats. But this morning, it was different. Kia, *ma belle*, it alarmed me."

Shit!

"Why?"

She shook her head but answered, "Such despair. Not hidden. I do not think her being in the house she shared with Travis is a good thing. She was much livelier in Italy. She was, of course, hiding grief, but now…" she trailed off again.

"Do you know if her father spoke to her?" I asked.

"She mentioned several times since you and Sam departed Italy that she's had lunch or dinner with her mother and father. But she did not share much about it."

Hmm.

I looked through my sunglasses directly into Celeste's and asked quietly, "Do you have any ideas?"

Celeste nodded. "I think the time has come that the ones she loves stop dancing around this and confront her directly. You and I spoke briefly about your friend Missy, and yes, I do agree with your assessment, it is much the same. However, it is also very different. Missy found something to turn her attention to—her fitness and her career. Luciana does not even have these types of anchors. Our Luci is drifting."

Drifting.

Drifting.

That was what Maris said Sam was doing.

Travis Gordon was gone and the two people closest to him that he left behind were drifting.

Oh God.

"Kia?" Celeste called, and I looked at her. "What are you thinking?"

I had a decision to make and I had very little time.

So I made it.

Celeste wasn't going to blab what I said to anyone but Thomas, who I instinctively knew would share it no further. Celeste was safe to share with and Celeste was worldly wise.

Celeste could help.

"I'm in love with Sam," I blurted and watched her lips curve up.

"This is not news, *ma chérie*," she told me.

It wasn't?

Oh God.

Was I that obvious?

I felt my brows go up. "It isn't?"

"If you're trying to hide it, then I must admit I am very surprised, and therefore, I hate to tell you this, my darling Kia, you are failing at your endeavor."

Great.

She smiled big at me and finished, "Spectacularly."

Fabulous.

"Well, um…I don't know if I'm actually trying to hide it so much as…" I hesitated, not knowing how to explain it. Then I decided to tell her just that. "I don't know what to say, how to explain it. I'm in love with him and I know he cares a lot about me. He's great. *It's* great, what we have, but something is missing."

"And what do you think is missing?"

"He's keeping something from me."

Even with her sunglasses on, she didn't hide her surprise.

"You're surprised," I noted.

"Indeed," she murmured. "That is not to say that I do not think Sampson Cooper is a man who has secrets. This is obvious, *ma chérie*. It is to say that I'm surprised that, like you have with him, he has not shared his with you."

"I am too," I muttered.

"This is causing problems," she deduced.

"Not exactly," I replied. "Like I said, things are great. *He's* great and I'm in love with him. I told you what was happening with me and he sorted that. It's all done. It's all good. Except it's, well…*not.*"

She reached out a hand and curled her fingers around my forearm, whispering, "Patience, my Kia."

"But—" I started.

She shook her head, so I stopped.

"Always," she whispered, then leaned in even further, "*always,* when you earn the secrets of someone worth knowing that deeply, you will feel rewarded when he eventually offers you these treasures. So, my darling, *patience.* You will earn them, I have no fear. He will give them to you, and when he does, they will feel like the gift they are."

Right. That was good advice.

I was on the right track.

I just needed to be patient.

I nodded.

Celeste squeezed my arm, let me go and leaned back, continuing with her advice, "Just keep doing what you're doing. I will say that it is obvious that you are in love with him, and my Kia, it is equally obvious that he is the same with you."

I felt my heart clutch and breathed, "Really?"

She smiled at me. "Kia, that man adores you."

Oh God. I hoped so.

"Patience," I whispered, hoping with everything I had—hell, everything I *was*—that Celeste was right.

"Indeed, *ma chérie,*" she whispered back.

We both heard the door open. We both twisted our necks to look between the seats. And we both saw Sam sauntering our way. After his shower, he put on a pair of exceptionally, and no other way to describe them, *deliciously* faded jeans and another long-sleeves-rolled-up, button-up-the-front, lightweight shirt. This one a green so light, it was nearly white.

He looked beautiful.

I smiled at him.

He smiled back.

Yep. Beautiful.

He made it to us, bent deep at the waist, and touched his mouth to my upturned lips.

When he pulled back, he asked, "Am I interrupting girl time?"

"Absolutely not," Celeste answered, then rose, murmuring, "but I need to powder my nose."

Powder my nose. Totally, Celeste was so cool.

She slid a small smile between the both of us and moved to the house.

Sam moved to the railing.

I left my wineglass on the arm of the chair and moved to Sam. He delayed a nanosecond before his arm slid around me and he pulled me into his body.

"Walkin' out, you two seemed intense. Is everything all right with Celeste?" he asked.

"She's extremely concerned about Luci," I semi-told the truth.

Sam sucked in breath through his nose, turned to face the ocean and let it out on a quiet "Fuck."

"Before you got to the beach today, Luci shared that she's cut her trip to Italy short. She's not going back. She's staying here." Sam's eyes came back to me. "At Celeste's advice, I'm going to find my time soon and have a direct chat with her."

"That'd be good, seein' as I talked to Vitale today after I got back from the gym but before goin' out to the beach and he said he tried a couple of times to broach it, but in the end, pulled back. Spoiled her when she was a kid. Spoiling her now. Neither time is right to do that shit, but this time, he should have more balls."

"You're right," I agreed.

Sam, not wearing sunglasses, looked closely at me. "You think it should be me who talks to her?"

"I think that maybe she needs you as a safe haven, so if I talk to her and it goes south and colors the way she feels about me, she still has you. So, no, I think it should be me who talks to her."

He took in another deep breath, and as he did it, his arm around me got tighter, pulling me closer, and he noted gently, "Not gonna be pleasant for you, baby."

"What she said to me in Italy, what Celeste said…I don't think we should ignore the signs, Sam. So, unpleasant or not, it's time for someone to step in and that someone is going to be me."

He nodded and his arm got tighter even as his body shifted closer and he asked, "You know what you're gonna say?"

"I'm going to tell her to sit herself down a year ago with a Gordo who knew in a year he would be gone and ask *her* to tell *me* how Gordo would feel about how she is right now."

At that, his arm got so tight, for a second, it cut off my air, but for a lot longer, it made my heart race at what might have caused that reaction.

I didn't get the chance to ask because Sam remarked, "Baby, you didn't know him. You can't guide that conversation."

"You're wrong," I replied softly. "I know, standing here right now with you, feeling the things I feel for you, this being so good, if I found out that I wouldn't be here a year from now, I'd tell you, and I'd mean it, that I'd be hugely disappointed in you if you didn't feel what you had to feel, then pull your shit together and find someone else who it was good with. And from what I know of him, Travis Gordon would say the same."

He'd been leaning us both into the railing, but at my words, he straightened, taking me with him, and what we were talking about evaporated and something else bloomed. And when it bloomed, it bloomed like a mushroom cloud.

I knew it looking into his face. It was intense, but it wasn't warm. It was hard and his eyes were glittering with something—anger, definitely, but something more. Something deeper. Something distressing. I also knew it because his other hand suddenly came up and plunged into my hair, immediately fisting.

And lastly, I knew it when he rumbled low and menacing, "Do not ever say that shit again."

Oh God.

I'd crossed a line.

"Sam—"

His neck bent suddenly so his face was all I could see.

"Do not *ever* say that fuckin' shit again."

Oh *God*!

"I'm so sorry," I whispered quickly. "You're right. I don't know Gordo. I don't know what he would—"

"No," he growled. "You're right. Gordo would say that. Gordo would be pissed as all hell Luci wasn't pulling her shit together. What *I'm* sayin' is, don't *you* talk about dying. Don't you ever, Kia, fuckin' talk to me again about dying."

What on earth was going on?

"Sam—"

"Don't do it."

"Sam, honey—"

His face got even closer and he snarled, "*Ever.*"

He abruptly let me go and strode away. Not to the house, to the walkway at the side. He took it with long, angry strides, a Memphis I feared he didn't notice bouncing at his heels, and both of them quickly disappeared.

"What on earth?" I whispered, my heart still racing, my breath coming fast and that hard look on Sam's face burned into my brain.

I was in the bathroom, staring at myself in the mirror.

Earlier that evening, Sam had come back, and like I was becoming accustomed to when he had an episode (with me or others), he had sorted it out himself and put it behind him.

And he expected you to do the same.

The Sam who came back with Memphis after a ten-minute walk was not the emotion-unleashed Sam who had walked away from me on the deck. He was a laid-back, mellow, clearly-enjoying-his-beach-house-filled-with-people-he-cared-about Sam.

Dinner was delicious. I was surprised that Maris served a fabulously succulent pork roast, buttered and herbed new potatoes and a delicious salad and not something Mexican.

But I learned during dinner conversation at Sam's big dining room table that Maris's mother was white, her father Hispanic, and Maris had unfortunately perpetuated the family misfortune when she hooked up with Sam's dad. Her father was not a good father; he skipped out on her family when she was a little girl and she hadn't seen him since. Therefore, although he left her mother, her brother and Maris in the barrio, her mother was so bitter about her husband's desertion, she'd blocked her children from learning any of the customs that surrounded them, so Maris knew very little of that side of her heritage.

She also shared that Sam, too, had lost the African American side of his heritage as, not only did he not want anything to do with his father, his grandparents from a very young age did not play any part in his life. Most assuredly not Sam's paternal grandfather, who was black and also who died when Sam was ten after choosing his sparring partner in a bar fight very badly—his opponent had a knife and was not afraid to use it, so he did.

I thought that was sad.

I did not share this because this was the only downer of the evening. The rest of it, we had a great time. Not everyone got tipsy, or in Hap's case, roaring drunk, at the dinner table, so when we moved to the couches, conversation was fast and fun.

It included all of us sharing amusing stories about our lives. Even Celeste got into it, talking about growing up in France, and with her sophisticated manner and beautiful accent, the woman could seriously weave a tale. We were all entranced.

Hap surprisingly, but with keen attention to Luci, which was hidden behind his fun-loving grins, shared about Gordo. I didn't know why he did this, but I suspected he did it because Gordo lived and Gordo was loved and Gordo shouldn't be swept under the rug. He was making a gentle point that everyone needed to move on to happy memories.

Luci braved it and Sam allowed it, also smiling (though not sharing) to hide his acute attention to Luci.

Celeste and Luci left late. Maris handed out cheek kisses and went up. And Hap, Sam and I shared one last drink before I went up, leaving Sam downstairs.

I was hoping he would follow me.

I got my wish. While brushing my teeth, I heard him in the bedroom.

And now I had to decide how to play it: try to talk to him and risk being rebuffed, or wimp out, risk nothing but also give nothing and gain nothing.

"Fearless," I whispered to myself, turned from the mirror, moved to the door, opened it and exited, hitting the light on the way out.

Sam was only in jeans when I got into the room. His eyes came to me. They warmed and he moved to me, sliding his hand along my belly as he passed me and went into the bathroom, closing the door.

Memphis was lying at the foot of the bed, panting at me.

I bent over her, giving her a cuddle before I got in bed and sat cross-legged with the covers pulled up to my waist, waiting.

Sam came out, rounded the bed, and when he was at his side, undoing his fly, I started.

"Can I ask you a favor?"

His eyes came to me, and like last night, he kept working his fly even as they locked on mine.

But this time they were guarded.

Not good.

"Yeah," he answered.

"I know you don't have a lot of room—I mean, you do, just not a lot of *rooms*, but maybe we can get an air mattress for your office or something—but I'd really like to ask Mom and Dad and Kyle and Gitte out here. They'd love it."

The guard came down and his face got soft when he whispered, "Whenever you want, baby."

He tugged off his jeans, then slid in bed beside me.

I uncrossed my legs and slid in beside him. The minute my body touched his, his arms closed around me and he pulled me on top.

I looked down at him, letting my eyes move over his handsome face. I then lifted a hand, placed it against the side of his head and I let my thumb move over his handsome face.

"Kia?" he called.

I stopped watching my thumb glide over his cheekbone and I looked into his eyes.

"Yeah?"

"You okay?"

"Can I tell you something?"

His arms gave me a squeeze and he whispered, "Anything."

I shifted my thumb to his lips and whispered back, "You might freak out that it's too soon, but I know what I know. And when I say that, *I know what I know.* And you don't have to feel anything but what you feel. But life is short and someone really smart, who I admire, told me to be fearless, so here goes." I sucked in breath, closed my eyes, opened them and kept whispering when I told him, "I've fallen in love with you, Sam Cooper."

His body went solid under mine.

Oh no.

Oh shit.

Shit!

I didn't know what I expected, but that was not the response I was hoping for.

"You don't have to say it back. You don't have to pretend to feel it," I said quickly, moving my hand from his face to his shoulder. "I just wanted you to know—"

"Shut up," he growled, and I blinked.

"Sorry?"

He rolled so I was on my back, he was on top and he repeated, "Shut up."

"Sam, I—"

His mouth hit mine. "Shut...*up*."

He kissed me, hard, wet and demanding. Then I didn't have my nightie or panties, all I had was Sam, his lips, his tongue, his hands all over me.

When I was whimpering into his mouth, my legs wrapped around his waist, arms clutching his back, his arm wrapped around the top of my hips, his finger building heaven between my legs and my whimpers got desperate with need, Sam felt it, heard it, knew it, and being Sam, he gave it to me.

His arm around me tightened as he lifted up to his knees, taking me with him. He fell back to his calves, holding me suspended, one arm still around my hips, the other arm slanted across my upper back, fingers curled at my neck, tipping my head down. Then he drove his cock up inside me, hard and deep, as he drove me down on it, impaling me.

Keeping my mouth to his, he kept powering deep at the same time he yanked me down, and I gasped against his lips each beautiful time I took him.

Suddenly he stopped, grinding deep, mouth moving on mine, and asked, "You feel that?"

Oh yeah, I felt it. Definitely.

"Yes, baby."

"That feel real?"

"Yes," I whispered.

"Open your eyes, Kia," he ordered, voice thick, and I opened my eyes, looking into his so close, they felt like they were a part of me. Then he said, "I'm not pretending to feel *anything*."

I felt my eyes get wider.

Ohmigod!

Did that mean—?

"I told you you have me, and, Kia, honey, *you have me.*"

It did.

He loved me.

My limbs tightened around him. I opened my mouth to speak, but he slanted his head and kissed me. Then he fucked me. Then he made me come. Then he came.

And it was the best ever, not because it was the best ever.

But because for the first time in my twenty-eight years, I had fabulous sex with the man I loved…

The man who loved me.

Almost to dreamland, tucked close to Sam, feeling freaking *phenomenal,* Memphis sprawled on her side of the bed, in a voice gruff with oncoming sleep, Sam muttered, "It's good you didn't find a place in Heartmeadow, baby. Now you got nothin' to sort back there and you're just plain home."

My eyes shot open.

Sam fell asleep.

Oh man.

23

YOU'LL DO

Two days later...

I stood at the bathroom basin brushing my teeth while Sam showered, wondering how I got myself in my current mess. This was to say, Sam thinking my declaration of love meant I was moving to North Carolina and then him telling *everyone* I was moving to North Carolina.

And I mean *everyone.*

Yesterday morning, I went downstairs only to be greeted by an excited Maris, who pulled my surprised, uncomprehending body in her arms and cried, "How exciting for the both of you! Setting up house!"

Yes. That was what happened. My wide eyes moved over Maris's shoulder and I saw Sam, who had been downstairs three whole minutes longer than me, was leaning against the counter, sipping coffee and grinning at us indulgently.

He'd obviously shared this news right off the bat.

Maris's embrace was followed by Hap wrapping his arms around me, picking me up off the floor, shaking me half a dozen times and stating, "I hang down here a lot, babe, so I hope you can cook."

I had barely recovered from these when Luci and Celeste arrived and I knew Sam had made a call, I just couldn't fathom *when,* because they arrived and Luci was beside herself with glee. This was evidenced by her racing straight to me, skidding to a halt on her stylish, flat sandals, grabbing my biceps, jumping up and down and shouting, "We're practically neighbors!"

Celeste's response was a little less exuberant but still openly happy.

What could I do?

I went with it.

It got worse.

And how it got worse was, over coffee and Maris's pancake breakfast, while everyone was chatting about how fabulous it was that Sam and I had moved in together (yes, past tense), Sam's phone rang and, for once, he didn't move out of the room to take the call.

No.

Instead, standing by me where I sat on a stool at the kitchen bar, Sam swept my hair off my neck, left his arm around my shoulders and said, "Yeah, Ford, things are still cool. All good. Listen, Kia talked with me last night and she wants you, Essie, Kyle and Gitte to come out for a visit. Can you talk to Kyle and Essie about that? Set somethin' up?" Pause, then, "Right. Whenever you want, we got plenty of room."

Yes, he said, *we got plenty of room.*

We!

Then my lungs froze when he went on to say, "Kia'll need to arrange to have her shit moved here. We might come out and sort it, or we might need you." Pause, then, "Yeah, she's movin' out here." Pause, then on a grin down at me, which meant my father had somehow communicated his utter joy at Sam's statement in the three seconds Sam was silent, "Yeah, Ford, it's all good."

I was blinking up at him, uncertain not only what to do, but also what to feel.

It couldn't be said I was against living in Sam's fabulous beach house with Sam in North Carolina.

It also couldn't be said I wanted to move away from my family and friends in Indiana.

What could be said was that I would have liked to discuss both of these prior to Sam announcing it to his family, my family, and arranging with my father to have my stuff moved.

Shit.

For peace of mind, I decided not to focus on Sam jumping to an erroneous conclusion and then not wasting any time acting on it. Instead, I decided to focus on the fact that Sam wanted me to live with him and wasted no time acting on it.

This was harder to do when we all climbed into vehicles in order to spend the day futzing around Wilmington.

It was harder because I also spent the day taking calls from Mom, Paula, Teri, Missy, Gitte *and* Kyle, all in throes of ecstasy that Sam and I were moving in together. They all knew about it because Dad had shared. They were bummed us moving in together meant me moving to another state, but they definitely felt the upside, considering that included a beach house they could visit.

In fact, during Mom's *second* phone call, she informed me, "Gitte and I have it sussed, honey. How does three weeks sound for you? We'll rent a U-Haul and bring your stuff with us." Before I could answer, she ordered, "Don't answer. Talk to Sam. Call back. But Kyle, Gitte and I are putting in for vacation time today."

Shit again!

Since Maris was leaving the next day, we had a fancy night out at a posh eatery in Kingston. By the time we got home, had after-dinner drinks and conversation, Luci and Celeste went back to Luci's place, Maris upstairs and Hap prepared to crash on the couch, I was exhausted from spending so much effort hiding the fact that I was freaking out.

And I was still freaking out so much, I didn't know how to broach the subject with Sam.

But even if I did, when I hit the bed with Sam already in it, I found Sam was in a different mood. Sam felt like celebrating our future togetherness, not having a chat about it. And he didn't talk me into participating, as such, since the way he *did* talk me into it didn't have words but actions.

So I participated, avidly.

And our celebration lasted a long, *long* time.

Now I was standing in the bathroom, brushing my teeth, dragging.

What *had* been discussed yesterday were today's plans: Sam was taking Maris to the airport by himself so they could have some alone time; I was spending the day with Celeste so she and I could have some alone time; and Hap was spending the day with Luci, then heading back to Fort Bragg.

Which meant maybe tomorrow I could find some time to broach the subject with Sam, and today I had the time to discuss the situation with my sage friend Celeste.

I hung on to this because I was thrilled to bits that I loved a Sam who loved me. But I was terrified at how fast everything was happening.

I kept brushing as the shower went off, and kept brushing but commenced burying the urge to wipe down the fogged mirror in order to watch Sam alight from the shower, when I heard the shower door open.

I felt Sam's arm lock around my waist, his lips touch my neck, then move to my ear where he muttered, "Move over, baby. Need the sink to shave."

"Okay," I muttered through foam, stepped aside and kept brushing.

Sam reached into the medicine cabinet and came out with shaving cream. While he was rubbing it on, I became mesmerized with watching him because, even with all the time we spent together, I'd never seen him shave. And I'd certainly never seen him shave standing at the basin, wearing only a towel around his hips.

Jeez. His jaw was very square.

Since I was mesmerized, I saw his head turn and his lips twitch before he asked, "Jesus, Kia, how long do you brush?"

Oh man.

I was such a dork!

I pulled the brush out of my mouth and covered with "A long time." Then I recommenced brushing.

He grinned at me and commenced shaving, muttering, "Must be why your teeth are so white."

He was wrong. One of the first things I did when Cooter and Vanessa accidentally made me rich instead of making me dead was go to a dentist and have my teeth professionally whitened. I didn't have ugly, yellow teeth, but I found the idea of having your teeth whitened decadent. I always wanted to do it. So when I got my windfall, I did.

Deciding my work on my teeth was done and Sam might think I was a little crazy if I brushed longer *and* stared at him shaving like I wasn't his girlfriend, who was now apparently living with him, but instead a rabid fan who was living the dream of standing in a bathroom with him, his razor and his hips encased in nothing but a towel, I pulled the brush from my mouth and garbled, "Sink."

Sam gave me room. I spit, rinsed, put my toothbrush away and wiped my hands.

Then I muttered, "I'll bring you a cup of coffee," and started out of the bathroom but found myself unmoving and in Sam's arms, looking up at Sam with a shaved neck but jaws and cheeks that were still foamed. In my perpetual freak out at all that was happening, I therefore blurted, "Only you could look supremely hot with shaving cream on your face."

Sam's loose arms went tight as he burst out laughing.

And that was when it hit me, staring up at the man I loved who loved me, standing in his arms in his bathroom, him shaving, me about to go down and get him a cup of coffee, that not only could I do this…

I wanted to.

North Carolina. Indiana. The moon. I didn't care.

Knowing each other a month, a year, a lifetime. I didn't care.

It wasn't too soon.

I loved him. He loved me. And wherever we were, it didn't matter. Just as long as it was a place that had him.

Sam quit laughing, looked down at me and instantly proved that my earth-rocking decision was right by saying, "Well, baby, you look good in your little dresses and your heels, in your shorts, in your nightie, but the best you ever look is in the morning when you roll outta my bed."

See what I mean?

"Stop being sweet in the morning before I've had coffee," I returned. "I don't have the energy to demonstrate my gratitude."

He grinned but ignored me, his face dipped closer and he went on in a low, rougher-than-usual-but-still-velvet voice to finish, "*Especially* a morning after I fucked you hard, I fucked you long and I made you come often. Fuck, baby," his voice went even *more* velvet as his gaze heated, "your eyes are dreamy, your hair's a sexy-as-hell mess and your lips are still swollen." He touched his mouth to mine and whispered, "Beautiful."

Then he got shaving cream all over my face and he did this by kissing me for a really long time.

When he was done, I was breathing hard and Sam was swiping at the shaving cream on my face with his thumb when I decided my only reply could be, "I love you, Sam," so that was what I said.

His thumb swept shaving cream across my jaw as his face got soft, his eyes went warm and he muttered, "Good."

I grinned at him.

He grinned back.

Then he ordered, "Get me some coffee."

"Bossy," I murmured.

He grinned again and gave me a gentle push to the door. I took his direction, nabbed a hand towel on the way and swiped at the shaving cream.

I got myself a cup of coffee and took one up to my man.

I went back downstairs because I'd seen Maris on the deck with Memphis, so I took my coffee out to join her.

Memphis bounced to me, yapping.

Maris turned to me, smiled and called, "Good morning."

"Morning," I called back and asked, "You want time alone or are you good with company?"

"Live alone, honey, so company."

I joined her, sitting in a chair already pulled up next to hers. Memphis joined us by jumping in my lap. I moved my feet to the railing of the deck, my fabulous robe dropped open to expose my legs and Memphis settled in a curl in her momma's lap so I could sip my coffee.

"Got shaving cream on your face," Maris muttered, her sweet, velvet voice vibrating with amusement.

Shit!

I swiped at my face, asking, "Where?"

"Right cheek," she answered, still sounding amused.

I moved my fingers there, encountered Sam's shaving cream and wiped it away. I rubbed my fingers together to get rid of it. Then I started petting my dog.

"That robe sure is pretty," Maris noted.

"Thanks. Luci has one like it and I admired hers, so she took me to the place in Como that sells them."

"They'd be a hit at my shop, but exporting is a pain in the behind. Tried it a couple of times, had to up the prices because of duty, but stuff sat on the rails forever, even in Malibu."

Knowing the cost of this robe, add duty, even in Malibu, I could imagine.

"Hap's out running, by the way," she continued.

"Okay," I replied and took another sip, then told her, "Sam's had a shower and he's shaving. He'll probably be down in a second."

"Right, then I don't have much time."

Oh no.

Surprise attack.

I blinked at the ocean, then turned my head to her, mentally bracing, wondering what was to come.

She didn't tear her eyes from the beach and she didn't waste any time.

"You're not a mother yet, honey, and even if you were, I don't know if you can imagine, but I worried…" she trailed off, kept her eyes glued to the beach, then went on in a quiet voice, "I so worried about my Sammy."

I wasn't sure where this was going. What I was sure of was that I was dying to know just as much as I feared finding out.

"Maris—" I started, and that was when her eyes came to me. They were shimmering with tears so I shut up.

"He had his fun, I know this. He's a man, he would. I also know this because it was up in my face *all the time.* Magazines, even TV. Those women…" She shook her head. "None of them…" She pressed her lips together and looked back at the beach. "After…well, later… well, until a few days ago, I despaired. They…women…it seemed…" She was struggling. She pulled in breath and looked back at me. "It seemed impossible he'd find one even worthwhile, much less…" She pressed her lips together, then finished on a whispered, "*you.*"

Oh God!

Now I felt my eyes shimmering with tears, my body warm all over, and not from the early, summer, North Carolina sun, and I whispered back, "Maris."

"You love Sammy."

I nodded.

"No, honey." She leaned into me. "You love *Sammy.*"

"Yes, Maris, I know exactly what you mean," I told her quietly and I did. I knew what she was saying. I didn't love Sampson Cooper. I loved her Sammy.

This time, she nodded.

Then she said quietly back, "You know I know what was done to you."

"I know," I replied.

"He'll never hurt you, Kia."

I smiled through my wavering tears. "I know."

"I cannot tell you how pleased I am he found you. But meeting you, now I can say I'm pleased you found my Sammy too."

I moved my coffee cup to my other hand, reached out and grabbed hers. I held on tight.

"I can say that too," I shared and grinned. "*Boy*, can I say that."

She gently twisted her hand from mine, leaned into me and placed it on my cheek, saying softly, "We share more than Sammy, honey. I know all about walking right through hell, years of it, and suddenly finding yourself on the other side. Glad it gets to be me who greets you there. But more, I'm glad I can say I raised a man who would take your hand and lead the way."

All right, she was killing me.

I clenched my teeth, sucked in breath and just managed to stop myself from bursting into tears.

Then I muttered, "Jeez, Maris, between your son being sweet and you being sweeter and me not even having a full cup of coffee, if you two don't stop, I'll be a wreck and never be able to face the day."

She chuckled quietly and remarked, "There are worse things."

She was right about that.

"Definitely," I whispered.

She smiled at me. Then she studied me. Finally, she patted my cheek once, dropped her hand and turned back to the view of the beach.

"Do me a favor," she whispered.

"Anything," I whispered back.

"Make him happy."

I sighed before I promised, "You got it."

That was when she sighed and we both fell silent. Thirty seconds later, Memphis yapped, leaped off my lap and bounced to the door. Maris and I looked through our seats and watched Sam approach.

When he arrived, he kissed my upturned lips. I smelled his aftershave and got even warmer. He shifted and kissed his mother's upturned cheek. Then he bent down and lifted up Memphis, who tried to kiss his exposed neck. As usual, he managed to avoid this, but Memphis didn't mind since she was snuggled to his wide chest with one arm and Sam was scratching her neck with his other hand.

"You 'bout ready to go?" Sam asked his mom.

"All packed, honey," she told him and looked at me. "You sure you don't want to join us for breakfast?"

I shook my head. "Thank you, but this is Maris and Sammy time."

Her face got soft and her eyes got warm. I saw that look on another face that day and I smiled into it as she smiled at me and replied, "Thank *you*, honey."

It was then I suspected my face got soft and eyes got warm.

Sam handed me Memphis and told his mom, "I'll go up and get your bag." His eyes came to me. "Be back around two thirty, baby. But if traffic's bad, closer to three."

I nodded.

He bent and touched his mouth to mine again, this time with his hand at my jaw. He finished the lip touch with his fingers doing a light, sweet jaw sweep then turned and strode back into the house.

Maris alighted. I put my coffee cup on the arm of my chair and Memphis and I came up with her so Memphis and I could hug her.

But it was only me who said, "I'm so glad you came. Travel safe and let us know when you get home."

Memphis yapped her farewell.

"Will do, Kia," Maris replied, gave me another hug, Memphis a few head pats then she followed her son into the house.

I looked from the door down to the beach to see Hap and his muscles jogging up to the walkway. I also saw a couple of female walkers watching him go. They were at a distance, but even at a distance, I could tell both of them were hotties. And lastly, I saw Hap was oblivious.

Yeesh. If he didn't pay attention, he'd never find his fine piece of ass.

I decided while drinking more coffee and making Hap breakfast, my next item on the morning's agenda was informing him of this fact.

Then I nabbed my coffee cup and turned to walk into…

I stopped.

I studied the house.

Then I smiled huge and walked into *my home.*

Twenty minutes later…

"So they were hot?" Hap, showered, shaved, sitting at the bar and shoveling in a huge bite of my scrambled eggs, asked after the girls I told him were checking him out at the beach.

"Did you not notice them at all?" I asked back.

He swallowed and grinned at me. "Babe, I'm the hunter, not the hunted."

I'd heard that before, kind of.

So standing at the other side of the bar to him, I rolled my eyes, then rolled them back and surmised aloud, "You're the cat. You want a mouse."

"Word," he replied, and I stifled a giggle.

"Word?" I asked through my self-suffocation.

"Yeah." He took a huge bite of buttered toast, then said through a full mouth, "Word."

"Does anyone say that anymore?" I asked.

"I just did," Hap answered.

I was about to tell him he was a goof when I saw movement on the deck. My eyes went there and I felt them get wide when I watched Skip stomping across the deck to the door.

Uh-oh.

"Uh…Hap, we have company," I announced, beginning to move toward the door that I saw Skip was not going to knock on.

No.

He was coming right in.

Then he came right in and I was halfway across the living area when he stopped, sent daggers from his eyes at Hap, declared, "You do not exist," then his eyes sliced to me. "What's this I hear, you movin' in with Sam?"

What?

"Uh—" I started.

"Luci called me," he shared.

There you go.

"Well—" I started again.

"Know about your windfall, so you got money. Still, Sam's got a fuckload more money than you."

I guessed this was true. Though, I had no clue why he'd come to Sam's and barge right in to inform me of that fact.

"Yes, that's—" I tried and failed again.

"Known each other, what, a month? Who the fuck moves in together after a month?" Skip demanded to know.

"It's been more than a month," I informed him.

"Yeah?" he asked belligerently. "How much more?"

I paused to calculate it, which was a mistake.

"Skip, dude, this is hardly your—" Hap started.

Skip's eyes cut to him and he clipped, "I said, you *do not* exist."

Oh man.

"Skip," I called his attention back to me, but that was as far as I got.

"This is a gold diggin' operation, you fail, you answer *to me*."

Oh my *God*!

Cantankerous character was one thing, but rude and offensive was another.

"Skip," Hap growled, leaving his seat. "That was out of line. What the fuck?"

Skip looked back at Hap and asked, "What'd I say?"

"Your crab shack, your rules," Hap shot back. "But right now, like it or not, you're standin' in *Kia's* house. I exist here and I'm tellin' you to stand the fuck *down*."

Skip assumed a battle stance, which was to say hands up in fists, one foot behind the other, body turned to Hap and he invited, "Make me."

Seriously?

I moved in between them, saying, "Skip, Hap, really. There's no—"

I didn't finish. This was because I saw more movement on the deck and that movement was Celeste running—yes, *running*—toward the door.

I was picking her up and wasn't supposed to be at Luci's place for another hour and a half. I didn't even know how she got here since Luci was driving her everywhere and Celeste didn't have a car. It was my understanding that Luci lived in a beach house down from Sam's, but it was a trek, at least a mile of beach, more if you took the winding coastal road.

What I did know was her running and the look on her face when she got inside did not bode happy tidings.

Memphis felt it instantly and yapped.

"Celeste—" I started, but she cut me off.

"Luci's disappeared."

My chest depressed.

"What?" Hap asked, and Celeste looked to him.

"This morning, she said she was going for a walk on the beach. That was three hours ago. She hasn't come back. I've been up and down the beach. No sign and no one I asked has seen her." Her eyes came to me. "I called you four times. You didn't answer. I found the keys to her car and came here."

My phone was upstairs in my purse in the bedroom.

Shit!

"She take her phone with her?" Hap asked, on the move to his bag, which was sitting in a corner of the living room.

Celeste shook her head. "Left it on the kitchen counter."

"Oh God," I whispered.

"What's goin' on?" Skip asked, looking around the lot of us, eyes stopping on Celeste. "And who're you?"

"I'm—" Celeste started, but I bolted into action.

Darting toward the front door, my eyes on Hap, who was pulling his cell out of the jeans he wore the night before, I said, "Gordo."

"Yeah," Hap said to me.

"Gordo what?" Skip put in.

I ignored him, shoved my feet into the flip-flops I left by the front door and asked Hap, "Where would she go?"

He pressed his lips together and shook his head, looking down to his phone. "This isn't my place, babe. I come down. I crash at Sam's or Luci's. I hang, but I don't know their gigs."

I turned to Skip. "Where would she go?"

"What in the Sam Hill is goin' on?" Skip fired back.

"Luci's not good," I told him.

"Sam, Hap," Hap said into his phone.

"Tell me somethin' I don't know," Skip said to me.

"Celeste is here. Says Luci went for a walk three hours ago, didn't come back," Hap kept talking into his phone.

"Luci's more not good than the normal not good, Skip. We have to find her," I said to Skip, watched his leathery face pale, and I finished, "Fast."

"Would she go to his grave?" Celeste asked quietly.

"He's buried in Arlington," Skip muttered.

"Well, that's out," I whispered, and my eyes went to Hap.

"Right, we're there," Hap said into his phone, dropped it from his ear and looked at me even as he started striding to the front door. "Sam says Luci and Gordo used to spend time in Ruler Bay. It was their spot."

"Let's go," I replied.

"Kia, *ma belle,* you're in your robe," Celeste reminded me.

"I'm covered," I murmured, following Hap out the door.

"Darling, it'll only take—" Celeste's voice followed me.

I stopped, Skip almost ran into me, but my eyes went straight to Celeste.

"I'm fine. Let's go," I stated, turned and rushed behind Hap.

"Coastal road, Hap. Kia's with me. Frenchie's with you," Skip ordered as we all rushed down the walkway.

"Sam's on his way," Hap said to the walkway, not even looking back as his legs moved with wide strides down to the drive.

We hit the vehicles, Celeste moving directly to the passenger side of Hap's SUV, me going straight to the passenger side of a decrepit pickup in which Skip was already at the wheel. I was still swinging in when Skip turned the ignition and I was still closing my door when he started reversing with scary speed, narrowly missing Luci's Corvette in the drive. He cut the wheel severely when he hit road and my body swayed nearly to the seat. He righted the truck, took off; I righted myself, and clicked my seatbelt in place.

"Tell me what more than the normal not good is," Skip ordered on a bark.

"She loves Sam. She likes me. She wants us together and even meddled a little to make that so. Still, Sam and I getting tight, Luci seeing it...Celeste thinks it's making what she lost, already a constant reminder, more intense. She says Luci has dark moments where she can't hide her despair. And Luci told me herself that one day everything is great and the next everything can turn black. So she already wasn't good, Skip, but now she's more than normally not good."

He took a hair-raising turn out to the main road then gunned it as I turned to look at him.

"You know her," I said softly. "Will she do anything crazy?"

"Never seen a love like that, not in my life," Skip replied. My stomach clenched and my heart started hurting.

Still.

"That's not an answer, Skip," I whispered.

His eyes flicked to me and the old pickup increased speed.

To the windshield, he whispered back, "Yep."

That was what I was afraid he was going to say.

"Shit, shit, *fuck*," I hissed. Then I asked, "What's Ruler Bay?"

"Can walk it from Gordo and Luci's place, but it's a ways. On foot, takin' your time, maybe half an hour. Thing is, you gotta climb some rocks and then descend into it. Got a trail, it's not treacherous but enough so it's pretty private. Gordo was home, he ran it nearly every day. He loved it there. Took Luci there all the time. She loved it there too. Far's I know, she hasn't been back, not since he died."

"Is this the only place they'd go?"

"Fuck if I know. Served 'em fries and crab sandwiches. Got drunk with 'em. They didn't whisper their secrets to me."

"What I'm saying is, maybe we should diversify our search," I explained.

"And what I'll say is, if anyone knows where she'd go, it's Sam. First, he and Gordo were like brothers. Nope, strike that. What they had was bigger than blood. Sam stepped in with her when Gordo bit it, and when I say that, I mean big time. They were close before, Sam and Luci, but now they're really friggin' close. Anyone knows where she'd go, it's Sam. So that's where we're goin'."

"Right," I whispered, my thoughts on Luci and his words.

What they had was bigger than blood.

Two brothers Sam lost.

Two.

Shit!

I fell silent.

Skip drove like a demon.

Finally, Skip said, "Nothin' there."

I craned my neck and scanned the coastline, asking, "Can you see the bay?"

"No, woman, what I'm tellin' you is, Sam and Luci are thick as thieves but not that way. Not the way he was with you at the Shack. Fact is, 'fore you, he never brought a woman to the Shack."

Oh wow.

That was news.

My eyes shot to him. "Really?"

"Just don't get fool shit in your head 'bout them. That's all I'm sayin'." He jerked his chin to something and stated, "There's the bay."

I looked back to the coastline to see a short outcropping of rock. It wasn't tall and it was covered with green. You could see the trail running from a small parking lot/pit stop on the road.

Skip swung in as I undid my seatbelt. He barely came to a halt before my door was open and I was out.

"Shit, woman!" Skip shouted, but I took off toward the trailhead, my robe flying out behind me.

About a minute later, I was thinking it was time to join Sam in some kind of workout regime because I had a stitch in my side.

Two minutes after that, I was thanking my lucky stars that the trail was relatively well used and definitely well maintained for I was traversing it easily, even on flip-flops.

Thirty seconds after that, I was heading down and I could see the bay.

Luci was sitting in the sand, knees cocked, elbows to knees, jaw in hands, eyes to the water, the waves rolling toward the shore, licking her ankles.

I kept going flat out.

I was across the beach and five feet away from her when her head jerked to me as her body jumped. She looked up and her mouth dropped open.

"Kia, *cara mia,* what on earth are you doing here?" Her gazed moved down to my middle then back up and she finished, "In your robe?"

I stopped abruptly, sucked in breath and told her, "You've been gone for three hours. Everyone is worried sick."

She blinked up at me and queried, "Has it been three hours?"

"Yes, Luci!" I cried. "Celeste is *freaking out*. We all are."

Her eyes moved beyond me and her brows drew together. "Is that Skip?"

"Yes, it's Skip. He was at the house being cantankerous when Celeste showed *freaking out*."

"Woman! What the hell!" Skip yelled when he arrived.

She gracefully stood, saying, "I'm so sorry, I lost track of time."

"For three hours?" I asked, and she looked back at me.

"I…" She looked to the ocean, then her eyes came again to me. "Yes," she whispered. "For three hours."

I studied her face. I did not at all like what I saw, so I said, "Skip, give us a minute."

"Hell with that, I—"

My eyes sliced to him and I ordered firmly, "Skip, give us *a minute*."

Skip scowled at me. Then he scowled at Luci. Finally, he turned and stomped down the beach toward the trail Hap was running down with Celeste following him some distance behind.

I turned back to Luci and got closer. "Are you okay?"

Her head tilted to the side, her mouth curled into a small smile, but her face suffused with sorrow. The jig was up, the shutters thrown open. No hiding. All of it there for me to see.

And it hurt to witness.

She whispered her answer, "No."

"Luci," I whispered back, moving even closer, my hand reaching out and taking hers.

Her fingers curled tight on mine, but she looked to the sea and kept whispering. "I remember. I remember what it was like to fall in love."

I kept silent, but my heart squeezed because there it was. Watching Sam and me was torture for our Luci.

"Like it was yesterday," she went on softly. "Funny how you can fall so hard but it doesn't hurt. You'd do it again. You'd do it again and again and again. You'd do it forever."

I held her hand and held my peace.

"I thought we had forever," she whispered to the sea.

I swallowed back tears and kept my focus on Luci.

She kept talking quietly. "We used to make love here. In the sand."

Oh God.

God, God, *God.*

"At night, Travis would wake me up and we'd walk in the moonlight, holding hands. No words. Just holding hands. He'd bring me here and make love to me in the sand, under the stars. Then he'd hold me and we'd whisper to each other about nothing. We'd walk back, silent, holding hands. I never slept so well. Those times, after we got home, I slept so well, Kia, safe in the arms of the man who loved me like that. Loved me so much he wanted nothing more than to walk, holding hands in the moonlight, to beauty, create beauty with me, then take me home and hold me while I slept."

I squeezed her hand, inched closer and whispered, "Honey."

Her eyes came to me and her sultry, gorgeous voice was dead when she said, "I'm never going to have that again."

"Oh, Luci, sweetie, you don't know."

"Not with Travis."

Well, she was right about that.

"I'm so sorry," I whispered, because honestly, there was nothing else to say, and seriously, I was.

"I am too," she whispered back, her eyes locked on mine. I watched them get bright as I watched her lip start to quiver. Mine reciprocated and she kept whispering, "I am too. I am very, *very* sorry, Kia."

I saw it and moved right into it when it happened. The sob tearing out of her throat, I wrapped my arms around her and she shoved her face in my neck, her body jerking against mine, wracked with tears.

I held her close, stroked her hair and said not a word as her tears wet my skin. So many of them, they started to slide down my chest and wet my robe. Hearing them, feeling them, I struggled holding back my own. But she needed strength and understanding and I needed to give it to her.

Still, I couldn't stop it—one escaped to slide down my cheek.

"I want that back," she whispered against my neck.

"I'm sorry, sweetie, you can't have it back," I told her gently.

"I know. I know I can't have it back with Travis. But I want it back."

I wasn't following.

Pushing closer, shoving her face deeper in my neck, she said so quietly, I barely heard her over the rushing waves, "I have to let Travis go so I can find it again."

I closed my eyes and held her tighter.

There it was. *Thank you, God,* there it was.

She got there herself.

Thank. You. *God.*

"Yes, Luci, honey, that's what you need to do," I whispered.

She nodded but said no more, nor did she move.

Not until I felt a presence right before I felt a hand on the small of my back. I twisted my neck and tipped back my head to see Sam standing there. I nodded to him, then shifted Luci into his arms. She looked up at him in surprise before her face crumbled again and she did a face-plant in his shirt. Sam's arms went visibly tighter.

I leaned in and kissed the side of her head. Then I reached up and briefly cupped Sam's jaw. I smiled sadly into his intense eyes, dropped my hand and moved away.

I walked down the beach, the wind beating my insanely expensive robe against my body. Celeste, Hap, Maris and Skip were standing at the trailhead. I stopped at their huddle.

"She's worked it through on her own," I announced. "She's letting him go."

Hap closed his eyes and dropped his head. Maris pressed her lips together and turned her face away. Celeste gave me a melancholy smile.

Skip looked me in the eyes and announced, "You'll do."

24

BURNED IN MY BRAIN

It was night, dark, and Memphis and I were hanging on the deck. Memphis on my lap, breathing easy. Me in a chair, sipping an amaretto.

Luci's realization changed our plans for the day. Sam took her back to her house and stayed with her. Skip went wherever Skip had to go. Hap went back to the base. Celeste and I drove Maris to the airport. Then we spent the rest of the day together.

When it got late and there was still no Sam, Celeste got in Luci's Corvette and went to her house. Fifteen minutes later, Celeste texted me with, "All is well. They're talking on the deck. Sam says he'll be home soon."

So I got my dog and my amaretto with a cube of ice, hit Sam's deck, settled in and waited for my man to come home.

Sitting with only Memphis for company, the house empty behind me, watching the moonlight on the waves, it didn't take long for me to come to some realizations myself. The first being that since I met Sam, I had very little of this. Solitude. Time to think. Time to be with me.

And once I realized that, I realized it was by Sam's design. Except for him offering to give me space the next night after the first time we had sex, that offer was never repeated. In fact, neither Maris nor

Sam suggested they have alone time before she went home. That was my idea.

Dad had said it, but I didn't process it then and I didn't understand it now.

Sam and I were inseparable.

I did not question falling in love with him because he was Sam.

And I did not question my decision earlier that day to hook my star to his, to restart my life after Cooter, however that came about, with Sam.

And I no longer questioned that Sam would want to hook his star to mine. We got along great (when we weren't fighting). He was into me. He thought I was beautiful. He liked the way I dressed. We had great sex. I made him laugh. He made me laugh. His friends and mom liked me. My friends and family liked him.

What I questioned was Sam announcing to everyone we were moving in together nearly upon waking the day after he made that mistaken assumption. It was almost as if, in doing so, he was building a barricade I would find it difficult to break through if I decided to go back.

He wasn't trapping me. I had free will; my life was my own. But he was throwing up obstacles, making it difficult, tying me to him.

And I didn't get this.

Sam Cooper *and* Sampson Cooper didn't need to do that with any woman. There was a desperation to it that alarmed me.

A desperation that might come from a man who lost a brother who was a brother bigger than blood, then dealing with that man's wife for over a year and seeing firsthand the devastating loss to a loved one left behind.

No.

That wasn't all.

Seeing it at the same time *feeling* it, for Luci wasn't the only one who'd lost Gordo.

And, thus, I knew Sam loved me, as in *loved* me, for learning about loss by watching it and feeling it, he wasn't taking any chances, he wasn't wasting any time.

This worried me. I didn't want him to feel this loss. I didn't want him to feel this desperation. I didn't want what we had to grow under that cloud. No one could tell the future and we might only have another day together or we might have fifty years. But even if we had only one day, I didn't want Sam living it under a cloud.

But I had no earthly idea how to talk to him because this kind of thing, Sam did not share with me.

On this thought, Memphis's head came up. It jerked to the house and I heard Sam's truck growling into the drive, then the gate swinging closed. I listened to the garage door going up. Memphis jumped down and her claws clicked on the deck as she ran to the porch door to wait for Sam to arrive.

Even with my heavy thoughts, this made me smile. My baby liked my man. Not a surprise. But my man liked my baby.

And that made life all the more sweet.

I heard a yap, twisted in my chair and watched Sam stride through the house I'd left lit softly with a few lamps. He hit the deck, scooped up a bouncing, happy Memphis on the go and came to me.

I tipped my head back, smiling gently at him and waited for his approach and kiss.

He didn't give it to me. On the outside, he rounded the chair beside mine and folded into it, Memphis on his lap. She bounced, trying to lick his face and give him her brand of welcome home.

"Settle, Memphis," Sam ordered firmly but not sharply.

Memphis, somewhat surprisingly, did as she was told.

She was immediately rewarded when Sam's fingers massaged her fur at her neck and his eyes went to the sea.

I was a little troubled he had not greeted me, but I let it go and asked softly, "You okay?"

"Hope to Christ this is a day I will not live again," Sam answered immediately.

That didn't sound good.

"How's Luci?" I ventured.

"Lots of crying, hangin' around while she talked to her folks, more crying and lots of listening to her talk about Gordo."

"She's processing it," I deduced.

"She's processin' the shit outta it. She crammed a year of mourning into a day. She's all over fuckin' processing it."

I pressed my lips together, trying to read his mood and tone. It wasn't frustrated, but it was. He sounded tired. He sounded impatient and over it. The first and the last surprised me.

"Is she coming to any conclusions?" I asked.

"Sellin' her house, movin' back to Italy. It's all about Gordo here. She's got friends, but her life here is her life with him and that's gone. She'll come back and visit, but family and home is not here. Family and home is Italy. She's puttin' the house on the market tomorrow."

Whoa.

"Shouldn't she wait? Think about it awhile? This is a fragile juncture and moving on sudden decisions might not be good," I suggested, and at that, Sam's head turned to me.

"Sudden?"

"Well, yes. Sudden, as in, coming to terms with Gordo dying one day and putting her house on the market the next."

"Nothing sudden about this shit, Kia. He's been dead awhile. It's about fuckin' time she moved on. She's movin' on."

I stared at him and said nothing. This was because I didn't have to try to read his mood and tone. He was frustrated, tired, impatient and over it.

I was shocked.

That was not Sam.

"Wiped," he muttered, got up and moved Memphis to my lap. Without touching me, no kiss, not even meeting my eyes, he went on, "Hittin' it. Got shit to do early so may be gone when you get up. Be back late afternoon, early evening. You don't feel like cookin', text me and on my way home, I'll pick up fried clam platters from Skippy's. Not as good as crab sandwiches. Still can't be beat."

Without another word, a goodnight kiss, or even a gesture, he walked into the house as I watched in stunned silence.

Once he disappeared up the stairs, I twisted back to forward in my seat and looked down at Memphis, who was still looking beyond me to the door. She felt my eyes, her eyes came to me and she yapped.

"Yes, baby, that was weird."

She yapped again and I nodded.

"I didn't like it either."

She whined a little before she settled in my lap.

I pressed my lips together, my mind harking back from now to the first night Sam and I slept together.

He'd never gone to bed without me.

And I'd never gone to bed without him closely following me.

I unpressed my lips when I lifted my amaretto to take a drink.

I swallowed and whispered, "Shit," to the sea.

Memphis concurred with a quiet mini-yap.

Yep. Shit.

I woke up with Sam's mouth at my neck and his hand sliding into my panties.

"Sam," I whispered, and his mouth came to mine.

"No talking," he rumbled, then he made this so by kissing me, his tongue driving into my mouth hard at the same time his finger slid inside me.

I wasn't awake, I wasn't ready and I whimpered with surprise mixed with the usual pleasure.

Sam read it, his finger slid out and hit my clit, pressing, rolling. My whimper this time was again surprised, but now there was far more pleasure. My hips rose up into his hand as his tongue kept driving into my mouth.

Then his lips released mine and his torso twisted. My panties were torn down my legs and Sam rolled, his arm hooking me, taking me with him.

I didn't know what was happening, I still wasn't awake, but I was turned on.

Then I was turned on more when Sam lay back, pulling me up, yanking me over him and maneuvering me to straddling his head.

His hands at my hips tugged me down and he was eating me.

My head fell back and my fingers searched for the headboard to hold on.

He was hungry, *ravenous*. God, he'd never done it like that before, not only in this position but also him being so damn hungry. His hands clenched at my hips, wrenching me down, grinding me into his mouth and tongue.

Oh God. God!

Before I knew it was coming, I came. My head jerking back again, I cried out as it seared through me.

But Sam kept pulling me down, crushing me to his mouth, taking.

Beautiful.

Sublime.

I moaned, whimpered, panted, held the headboard in a death grip feeling it, all of it, loving it, and then orgasm number two soared through me.

Sam pushed me off before I was done and I tried to catch my breath, catch a thought, but found myself on my knees with Sam on his knees behind me, his arms around me. His hand went back between my legs—torture, God, such beautiful torture. I was so sensitive my hips jerked and his other hand plunged up my nightie, his fingers curling around my breast, his thumb rolling my nipple.

"Sam, honey, too much," I protested, but my hips made my words a lie, pressing, seeking. I wanted it, wanted him, wanted more.

Sam's teeth nipped the skin behind my ear and he growled, "No talking."

"Sam—"

His hand between my legs slid away, his arm clamped around my waist, his other hand curled tight at my breast. I felt him move, adjust, then drive up inside me, straight to the root, filling me.

My head again flew back, colliding with his shoulder.

"No…fucking…*talking*," he commanded, deep and low in my ear.

His arms left me, one hand went to the middle of my back, pushing me down so I was chest to mattress. His hands went to my hips, fingers digging deep, and he pulled me sharply back to meet his thrusts, pushing me forward, pulling back, slamming into me, slamming me into him.

Oh God. It was *awesome*. It was *hot*. And it was going to happen again.

Before it could, he pulled out. I moaned my discontent, but he didn't make me wait. He jerked me up, shifted me to facing him and turned us, moving up the bed. My back hit the headboard, he wrapped my legs around his hips, my arms slid around his shoulders and his mouth slammed down on mine as his cock plunged into me.

Again and again, and then he drove deep, grinding hard and groaned in my mouth as my limbs got tight, my third orgasm swept through me and I moaned into his.

I recovered slowly, listening to Sam doing the same, feeling his breaths steadying against my lips, keeping him held close to me, held tight.

Then, even though I didn't say a word, he ordered, "Do not speak."

My heart started beating faster again.

He didn't glide. He didn't take me gently after he took me hard. He stayed buried and his lips didn't leave mine as I stared into his shadowy eyes, which were staring back at me.

"Burned in my brain," he growled, and I swallowed, keeping him held tight to me. "You in those sandals, that dress, sittin' across from me, tryin' to pretend I wasn't there."

At his words, emotion soared through me. A lot. Too much. It felt like my skin couldn't contain it and my limbs spasmed around him.

Sam wasn't done.

"Seein' you sittin' alone that night after dinner, so beautiful, so fuckin' beautiful, speakin' to you only for you to turn and face me and see you had tears in your eyes. Those tears, *Christ*," he bit off the last word on a snarl. "Never in my life...never felt that. I didn't fuckin' know you, but seein' those tears in your eyes fucking undid me."

Oh my God!

"Sam—" I whispered, and his hips ground into mine.

"Do not speak, Kia."

I closed my mouth.

"Burned in my brain," he muttered.

God. What was happening?

"You opening the door to me, wearin' that white dress. You in my arms, tellin' me about your girl with her cardboard cutout. You lyin' beside me, tellin' me about your mom makin' birthdays special. You on the boat, the wind in your hair. You at the table, your head in your hand, your eyes on me. You driving down on my cock after I set you on fire."

He remembered everything. Everything about me. Every moment. Every word.

God, *God* what was happening?

His arms around me got so tight it was difficult to breathe, even as he threatened to tear apart my heart saying, "Should have let you have your breakfast pretending to ignore me."

This wasn't good. This wasn't right. Something was wrong. Something was terribly, terribly wrong.

Sam kept speaking.

"I didn't and now you're mine, Kia. *Mine,*" he declared on another powerful arm squeeze that forced the breath right out of me.

Suddenly his voice gentled, but there was an edge to it that made my heart clutch. A hopelessness. A melancholy.

"Burn us into your brain, baby. Every second, every breath, burn us into your brain."

I tried again, "Honey—"

That was all I got out before one of his hands drove into my hair, fisted and he rumbled, "No, Kia. Say nothing except to promise me."

"We need to—"

His entire massive body pressed mine into the headboard and he growled fiercely, "*Promise me.*"

I stared into his face in the dark, my heart beating, my lungs burning, my stomach hurting, and I was lost. Clueless. I didn't know what to do. What just happened, all he said, he was in the grip of something fierce and ugly and I didn't know how to beat it back or let him know I was at his side to help him fight it.

So I took the only option available to me.

One of my hands slid up his neck to cup the back of his head and my lips brushed his before I left them there and whispered, "I promise you, baby."

His arms got tight again, then his mouth moved down my cheek. He pressed his face in my neck and held me. Even when he pulled out, he kept his face in my neck, my body pressed against the headboard and he kept holding me.

I held him back, then finally, I turned my head and in his ear I whispered, "I need to go clean up."

"No." His head came up. "Tonight, you keep all of me with you. You don't wash any of me away."

"Okay," I said instantly, even as his words tore at my heart.

He pulled me from the headboard, shifting us so we were in our usual positions, Sam on his back, me tucked close to his side, cheek to his shoulder. But this time, his other hand crossed his chest and his fingers drifted through my hair and back and again and again.

I tangled my legs with his and pressed closer.

Then I turned my face to his shoulder, kissed his silken skin and whispered there, "I love you, honey."

His hand settled on my cheek a moment before it went away and he muttered in a normal Sam tone, "Good."

I let out my breath, turned my head and laid my cheek back on his shoulder.

Sam's arm got tighter.

He fell asleep way before me.

Hours later, I woke up alone.

25

LISTEN TO YOUR HEART

One month later...

I was standing at the basin in the bathroom, brushing my teeth, when Sam walked in wearing running clothes. That was to say loose shorts, a loose shirt with the sleeves cut off and running shoes.

He walked behind me, stopped, kissed my shoulder then found my eyes in the mirror.

"Gonna run. Be back before your folks hit the road."

I nodded, still brushing.

He held my eyes.

I tried not to hold my breath.

Then he shocked me when he suddenly whispered, "Love me?"

It took everything I had not to fall to my knees.

As usual, he'd figured me out. He knew I was struggling.

He knew.

I triumphed, pulled the brush out of my mouth and answered, "Yes."

He closed his eyes, but I knew he tried to hide it because his arm went around my belly, his face quickly disappeared in my neck, and against the skin there, he muttered, "Good."

What he did not do was tell me he loved me.

He never told me he loved me.

Never.

His arm gave me a squeeze, he let me go and walked out of the bathroom.

When I lost sight of him, my hand shot out to curl around the basin. I dropped my head and closed my eyes. I held on tight and I held on a long time.

Then, when I felt I could do it, I lifted my head, slid the brush into my mouth and resumed brushing.

The day of Luci's breakthrough everything changed between Sam and me.

None of it—not one thing—was good.

At first, I almost didn't notice. It was just a niggle. But I put that down to his weird mood when he got back from Luci's and the episode when he woke me up in the middle of the night, made love to me then forced that promise.

It was easy not to notice, but I had to admit, I was kind of in denial. Still, Luci was getting her house ready for the market, Celeste was still there and Luci was still processing, talking, working things through.

We also had a short visit from a man called Joe "Cal" Callahan, Sam's security specialist. Like Tanner Layne and Lee Nightingale, Joe Callahan was tall, dark, built and unbelievably gorgeous. He also had a scar on his face that marred his perfect male beauty in a way that was *hot* but also made him more than a little bit scary. But in the short time he was there, although gruff and mostly monosyllabic, he smiled a lot, which made him a bit less scary. He also openly took a phone call from his woman, which became a call where he also spoke to his woman's two daughters during which his face got soft, he smiled even more and he laughed often.

This made him not scary at all.

That was until he traced how my hit man breached his system. This clearly pissed him off. Definitely a man who took his business seriously, had built a reputation and was not fond of that taking a hit. He did not need to make adjustments, considering how the hit man breached his system included the hit man bribing someone at the electric company.

Cal visited this unfortunate electric company employee then returned, announcing firmly, "Situation neutralized."

He gave no further information.

Sam nodded. I shivered.

Needless to say, all of the above took a lot of attention.

But also during it, I noticed that Sam's runs were longer and his stays at the gym were too.

And I further noticed a couple of times when Sam would tell me he had to go meet "a buddy" or had "something to do." He didn't tell me who the buddy was or what he had to do. He'd just go, come back and, like the day after the night of my promise, pretend it didn't happen.

I let this slide and practiced patience, listened to Luci, spent time with Celeste and hoped.

I also kept true to my mission. I didn't shower Sam with attention or change anything about me. I gave him me openly and steadily.

But I told him I loved him often. Not ridiculous amounts but enough.

He never said he loved me back. He liked it, I knew. He made that clear.

But his response was always, "Good."

Then Celeste was gone, Luci's house was on the market and she started to prepare for the big move. I helped. Sam helped.

But Sam's runs kept running long, his workouts kept getting longer and the times he had to see to something or help out a buddy, none of these ever explained, increased in frequency.

I thought about it and decided to stop letting it slide.

If he had to see to something, I asked what.

Sam would say, "Not a big deal, baby. Won't be long."

Then he'd kiss me and he'd be gone.

If he had to help out a buddy, I'd ask who.

And Sam would say, "You don't know him, honey. We're not tight, but he's called a marker. I'll be back soon."

Then he'd kiss me and he'd be gone.

One could not say I had an enormous amount of experience with healthy relationships.

That said, I knew this was simply not right.

But it was worse. He was still Sam—gentlemanly, affectionate, attentive—but something was there, something was on his mind, or there was something between us. I didn't get it, couldn't put my finger on it. The only thing I knew, Sam wouldn't share.

And I was right. He didn't. He acted like nothing was amiss.

I let this slide, practiced patience and continued to hope. I also kept up the steady flow of giving me and sharing my feelings for him.

And to the last, all I ever got back was, "Good."

And that started to hurt.

When Sam was gone, I spent time with Luci. I spent time discovering Kingston. I walked my dog on the beach. I cleaned Sam's house. I went to the grocery store. I did the laundry. I ironed his shirts. I talked to my friends and family on the phone.

But patience wasn't working. I was seeing Sam less and less and I was feeling Sam withdraw more and more.

The time had come for my family to visit and I couldn't let it slide. I couldn't practice patience. I couldn't hope. They'd notice. I knew they would. I had to make something happen. I had to find out what the fuck was going on.

I timed it when I thought it was right. We were in a moment. They were coming few and far between, but it was a moment like it used to be between us. Sam seemed mellow, laid-back...*Sam.*

We were watching a movie on DVD. We'd had a good day out, buying a pullout couch for his office so Gitte and Kyle could sleep there. Sheets. Gifts to give my family. Sam had made me dinner and I'd kept him company in the kitchen, drinking beer, being stupid, making him laugh. He hadn't seen a buddy. He'd only run for an hour. He didn't have something to see to. It was just us all day.

And as we lay on the couch, cuddled together—me with my back to the couch, my front plastered to Sam, my cheek on his chest, my eyes on the movie; Sam with his arm around me, his fingers trailing my hip and waist in random patterns, his eyes on the movie—I took my shot.

"This movie sucks," I announced, and that was not a ploy. It did. It wasn't bad. It was *bad.*

I heard and felt the rumble of his chuckle, his body shaking before he agreed, "It seriously fuckin' does, baby."

I lifted my head from his chest and looked into his smiling, beautiful eyes.

God, I missed that.

God, God, *God*, I missed seeing his eyes smile.

"Sorry," I muttered, because the movie was my choice.

"Punishment: next three flicks we rent, I pick."

"Okay," I whispered, then pushed myself on top of him, reached out to the coffee table, tagged the remote and pointed it at the TV. I hit the button and the action paused. I tossed the remote back on the table and turned back to him. Staying on top of him, I placed my hands on his chest and caught his eyes. "Can we talk instead?"

The guard slammed down.

Oh man. I actually saw it slam…right…*down.*

Both his hands came up and sifted into my hair at the sides, holding it back and he replied, "Better things we could do."

It should be noted that through these nearly three weeks, our sex life didn't suffer.

No. Not at all.

It was better than ever, like that night of the promise—hot, heavy, hard, intense, out of control…but desperate. It was the kind of sex I didn't have to burn in my brain. Sam did it for me. Every touch, every taste, every stroke, I'd never forget. It was beautiful. It was the only thing we shared that made me believe.

Even so…

"I'd rather talk," I told him quietly.

He slid his hands through my hair, down my back and wrapped his arms around me.

Then he invited shortly, "Do it."

Not a good start.

"We're…" I hesitated, then pointed out, "Something's wrong."

"Nothing's wrong, Kia," he replied instantly. So instantly, I blinked.

He couldn't possibly think that.

"Sam, since Luci had her thing on the beach, things have not been the same."

"Everything's fine."

God! Seriously?

"It isn't," I pressed.

"It is."

Was he in denial?

I stared at him.

Then I tried something else.

"You spend a lot of time away and you don't tell me who you're with or what you're doing. That isn't right."

His arms convulsed around me, his eyes got hard and my stomach clutched.

"Don't go there," he warned on a low growl.

Oh man. Not this again.

"Go where?" I asked.

"There" was his one-word answer.

"Sam! Seriously?"

He knifed up. Shifting me so my ass was to the couch, he got up and moved away.

Yes. It was this again.

And I would not stand for it.

I shot to my feet. "Don't walk away from me!" I snapped.

He turned back and clipped, "I told you you got me, you got me. Do not question it. Trust it."

"Okay," I returned. "And you know you've got me. So would you be okay if I took off to do shit you didn't know what I was doing and meet people you didn't know who they were?"

"Fuck no," he replied.

I threw out a hand. "See!"

"You're a woman who's, due to no fault of her own, found herself in a fair amount of trouble. I worry about you, so no, I would not be okay with that. I can take care of myself. If a situation arose, you could not. That said, I trust you and you gotta trust me."

"For how long?" I asked immediately, and his brows shot together.

"What?"

"For how long, Sam? How long do you get to do what you want and be where you are and expect me to trust you before *you* trust *me*?"

"What the fuck does that mean?" he asked on a growl.

"It means, you not sharing tells me you don't trust me."

"That's bullshit," he bit off.

"So now you're telling me how I should feel? Because that's what it feels like, Sam. You keep stuff from me. You keep *you*," I jerked a finger at him, "locked away from me. You don't tell me what you're doing or who you're doing it with. That's how it feels. Like you don't trust me."

"I told you, Kia, you have me, and not five fuckin' seconds ago, I told you to trust that. If this gig is you tellin' me you don't trust that, then *you* don't trust *me*. So fuckin' *trust it*."

I shook my head. "You're lying to yourself and you're lying to me if you believe that. If you expect that to be okay. If you expect that from me. You can't take it all, Sam, and give me only what you want me to have. You cannot have all of me and only give me part of you. That isn't fair."

His torso swung back and he crossed his arms on his chest. "So you're sayin' I'm lyin' and you don't have me."

"Absolutely," I shot back. "If you can stand there and tell me that the last three weeks I've 'had you,'" I lifted my hands and did air quotation marks before dropping them again, "then you are absolutely lying. Something is happening. Something is wrong. And you are shutting me out."

He clamped his mouth shut and a muscle jumped in his cheek.

I waited.

Sam didn't speak.

God! At that very moment he was *shutting me out.*

I fought back tears.

Sam *still* didn't speak.

So I did, and when I did, I changed the subject.

"Tell me about Gordo," I demanded.

His head jerked. It was almost imperceptible, but I saw it.

Then Sam spoke.

"Talk about Gordo enough with Luci, not talkin' about him with you."

I shook my head. "No, I don't want to know about how Luci is processing his loss. I want to know how *you* are."

"Processed it a while ago, sweetheart. Don't need to do that shit again."

He was calling me sweetheart.

Damn.

"You didn't," I said softly.

"Got enough of Gordo buyin' it up in my face, Kia, I do not need more. He bought it. He bought it a while ago. It's done. Can we please, for fuck's sake, let it be *done*?"

"It isn't done," I returned.

"It's done."

"Then what was that that night when you woke me up and made love to me?" I asked. "What was that, Sam? That was far from done."

Sam again shut his mouth and I saw his jaw clench.

He was shutting me out. And looking into his hard features and guarded eyes, I knew I was not getting in.

And that didn't hurt. That killed.

I held his eyes and whispered, "Right." Then I moved toward the kitchen, saying, "I'm taking Memphis for a walk."

"Not alone," he said to my back.

I stopped and turned to him. "What?"

"Aziz and Deaver have been released. You're good, but at night, I do not want you walkin' the beach alone with a King Charles spaniel. Memphis loves you, but someone meant you harm, she couldn't do shit. So at night, you're not walkin' the beach alone."

"I'll be fine," I told him.

"Yeah, you will, seein' as you're not walkin' the beach at night alone."

I stared at him, teeth clenched, tears close. I had to get away from him and I had to do it now.

"Okay," I said quietly. "Then I'm going to the guest bedroom and I'm spending the night there." His jaw clenched again, his eyes flashed, and I hurried on, "And do not do anything macho to piss me off, Sam. I need space and I need to be alone and you're going to give that to me."

Before he could say another word or the look on his face could make me go back on what I said, I turned and ran up the stairs.

I spent the night in the guest bedroom and Sam didn't do anything macho to piss me off. I slept alone. That was, I slept alone for the first time in ages after crying a lot and thinking a lot and neither of them did one fucking thing to help me.

The next morning, eyes still puffy, face blotchy, hair a mess, I struggled downstairs to get coffee at a time when I was certain Sam would be gone.

He wasn't.

He was in his workout clothes, leaning with hips against the counter, coffee mug in his hand.

His eyes came to me immediately and I knew at a glance he'd figured me out. Then again, the puffy eyes and blotchy face and the fact that I probably didn't stifle all my sobs in the pillow the night before gave it away.

His face got soft, his eyes got warm and intense and his mouth said gently, "Bed's not right, you not in it."

"You've slept a lot in that bed without me, Sam. And from what you yourself told me, you've slept with a lot of people in that bed who are not me. So I'm not certain I believe you."

His face lost its softness, his eyes their warmth, but the intensity didn't shift from me when he whispered, "Not cool, baby."

"Maybe not cool, but it's true."

"Do not make this dirty," he warned.

"Right, then, last night, you totally missed how much *this* means to me because I'm willing to play it dirty in hopes of getting something, *anything*, from *you*."

"You have everything from me," he returned quietly.

"That's another lie."

He held my eyes. Then he kept talking quietly. "Right, Kia, honey, then I'll say you've got everything I've got to give."

"That's not enough, Sam. I love you, and when you love someone, you want all of them. I've given you all of me. I'm here. I'm laid bare. Hell, I laid myself bare within days of knowing you. My family is arriving tomorrow, bringing my stuff. I'm living with you, restarting my life, here, *with you*. Now I want all of you."

"Baby, I'm sayin' you gotta take what I can give."

"And honey, *I'm* saying I want *all of you*."

And at that, he was done. I knew this when he pushed away from the counter, twisted, put his mug down then walked toward the stairs to the garage but stopped and turned to me.

"I'm goin' to work out. While I'm gone, Kia, baby, you gotta decide if it's all or nothing. You know where I stand. Your decision."

Then he was gone.

That's right. Without another word or allowing me one, he was gone.

After I heard the growl of his truck fade, the hum of his gate closing stop, I started crying again.

I managed to shower, dress and leave a note. I took Memphis for a walk on the beach. I didn't know if he got back in an hour and a half or three, that was how long I was gone.

Because that was how long it took to make my heartbreaking decision.

When I got back, Sam was dealing with the furniture people who were delivering the sofa. They were pretty psyched and not hiding it that they got to deliver a sofa to Sampson Cooper.

When Memphis and I showed up, Sam turned his back on them, took one look at me, closed his eyes and turned his head slightly to the side.

But I didn't miss the pain that slashed through his features.

Seeing he'd figured me out, seeing his reaction to it, my decision took a direct hit.

His eyes opened, locked on me and they were burning intense. So much, it felt like they burned the air out of my lungs. He walked right up to me, nabbed me by the back of the head, pulled me in and up and laid a hot, wet, heavy one on me.

My decision already on shaky ground, I instantly changed my mind.

Sam lifted his head, his eyes scanned my face and he figured that out too.

His eyes closed again, his fingers convulsed at the back of my head and he dropped his forehead to mine.

Damn, that was sweet.

Yep, I changed my mind.

He opened his eyes, touched his mouth to mine again, then claimed me with an arm around my shoulders, turning back to the furniture guys, who had the couch on the curve toward the stairs and were grinning at us.

"Hope you take no offense, Coop," the mischievous one said, "but your woman is seriously hot."

I sighed.

Sam muttered, "This is not something I've missed."

The men burst out laughing.

I drew in a long breath, held it then released it, relaxing into Sam's side.

Memphis bounced around the living room, yapping and trailing her leash.

I got Sam back that day. Gone were the long runs, workouts and mysterious buddies and errands. This could have had to do with our drama. Or it could have been my family arriving the next day.

But for me and for them, that week, Sam was Sam.

Dad got to toss a ball with Sam on the beach and I was right, he loved it. He was beaming through it and he beamed for days after.

Hap came down and I got my wish of Hap, Luci, Kyle, Gitte, Sam, and I playing three-on-three beach football and I was right, it was wicked fun.

Sam cooked for them and what he made was delicious.

We drank a lot. We ate a lot. We laughed a lot. They got to know Luci. They hilariously met the hard-as-nails Skip. And they got to spend a little time with Hap, who could only come down for the day and then had to go back.

They brought my stuff, which was piled up in the garage, the U-Haul returned. Kyle and Gitte drove straight to Kingston, so did Dad and Mom. Kyle and Gitte only had one week off, but Dad and Mom were taking two, driving back to Tennessee with Kyle and Gitte and spending another week there before Kyle and Gitte were going to drive them home.

It was a good time. It felt nice. That wasn't to say that I didn't catch Mom and Dad both giving me careful looks a couple of times, but I powered through it.

Not to keep them in the dark.

No, I was biding my time, waiting for the right one.

And that time had come.

I finished brushing my teeth, sorted out my hair, tugged on some clothes and went downstairs. I could hear Kyle and Gitte packing in Sam's office. Mom was at the stove, pushing around some sausage patties in a skillet, Memphis at her heels, the smell in the air pure, doggie torture.

Dad was at the bar, drinking coffee.

"Hey, honey, Sam's out running," Mom told me.

"I know, Mom," I replied and went to the cupboard where Sam kept his travel mugs. Then I asked the cupboard, "Dad, will you walk with Memphis and me on the beach?"

I took a mug down, glancing his way to see his eyes were on Mom. They came to me.

Then he said, "Sure, honey."

"Do you want a travel mug of coffee?" I asked.

"I'm nuked up, darlin'. Drink more, we'll be stoppin' every fifteen minutes."

I nodded and sent a small smile to Mom. She sent me one in return.

She knew what this was about. She was curious, but she wasn't upset at being left out. She knew Dad would explain things later.

No hard feelings. This was the way it was.

I was daddy's little girl.

I got my coffee, leashed up Memphis and we walked out to the deck and entered the boarded walk that led down to the beach. When we hit the beach, Dad took my hand and did the hard part.

"Talk to me, Kiakee."

They had to get on the road and I needed quality Dad Time, which might turn into quantity Dad Time, so I didn't delay.

"When we were talking on the phone and I was first telling you about me and Sam, you said something. I mean, what you said was true, but the way you said it, I haven't forgotten."

"What'd I say, honey?" Dad asked.

"You said the word 'inseparable.'" I looked to the side to see him grinning at the beach. "Why are you smiling?"

His hand gave mine a squeeze and he answered, "'Cause, Kiakee, all your life, you reminded me of your mother. You look like her, you act like her. Hell, in a way, you dress like she did when she was young. But then you were with Cooter and you became someone else. I lost you and I lost those bits of you that remind me of your mother."

That sucked. But it was also true.

"Okay," I whispered.

He stopped us and turned to me. "When I met your mom, I couldn't get enough of her."

I felt my breath stall.

He shook his head, a small smile on his mouth as he went on.

"She made me laugh. Christ, Kiakee, never laughed so hard in my life. But married her and got myself a lifetime of laughin' that hard."

This was true as well. Mom and Dad laughed a lot. All my life.

But thinking about it, Dad laughed more. This was because Mom was seriously funny.

I pressed my lips together.

Dad kept talking.

"And she's beautiful. Still is, but back then…" He shook his head again, but his eyes stayed glued to me. "Took my breath away. Sometimes, to this day, I'll lay in bed just to wait for her to wake up. Then she wakes up and looks at me with her beautiful eyes and her wild hair and that pretty mouth a' hers, and I still thank my lucky stars."

Oh my God.

I'd heard that before (kind of).

"Dad," I whispered, moving closer, and his hand dropped mine so his arm could wind around me.

"When we were new, startin' out, no time was enough time with my Essie. Things were different then." He looked in the direction of the house, then back at me. "But, honest to God, I didn't know your granddaddy had a shotgun, I woulda scaled the wall of their house to get to her. I told my buddies the instant I saw her I was gonna marry that girl. And I sure as heck did. I made it so. I stopped at nothin' and I got my Essie. I knew, lookin' at the laughter in her eyes the first time mine fell on hers, she'd make sure I never regretted it. And I'm standin' here right now with you over three decades later and I never did."

I loved that. That was beautiful. I loved that my dad had that.

I dropped my head and pressed the top of it into Dad's chest.

His arm went from around me so his hand could curl around the back of my neck.

And, in my hair, I heard him mutter, "Sam Cooper feels that way about you."

I pulled in breath and lifted my head, Dad's coming up too, and I caught his eyes.

"I'm not sure," I whispered.

"I am," he stated firmly, and I blinked.

"Dad, there are things you don't know. He's…we've…he's holding something back from me."

"What?" Dad asked, and I shook my head.

"I don't know. He won't tell me."

"You talk to him about it?"

I nodded. "Yeah, like, a gazillion times. I tried to play it cool. I tried to be patient. I tried to be gentle. I tried to be nosy. And right before you guys got here, we fought about it."

"What's he say?"

"He doesn't say anything except I have him."

Dad's head tipped slightly to the side and he said quietly, "Kiakee, from what I see, he's not lyin'."

I shook my head. "You don't understand. It's hard to explain, but even Sam kind of admits that he's holding something back. I told him I gave him all of me and I want all of him. He told me he's given me what he has to give, and if it's all or nothing, that's my decision."

"And you stayed," Dad noted.

I shook my head again. "At first, that wasn't my decision. My decision was to call you and tell you not to bring my stuff here, that I was coming home. Then he, well..." I paused, sighed, and continued, "I got back, he figures me out, he knew that was my decision, he kissed me and I changed my mind."

Dad burst out laughing.

I could see the humor, but I still didn't think anything was funny.

"Dad, I'm being serious. This is bothering me, as in *bothering me*," I said softly.

Dad sobered and gave me his eyes.

Then both his hands came to my jaw and he dipped his face close to mine.

"All right, Kiakee, I hate to disappoint you, but what Sam said holds true. That man's got demons, plain to see. And if he's the type of man who wants to keep 'em locked inside, honey, there's nothin' you can do. So there's not anyone who can make that decision but you. If it's all or nothin' for you, then you gotta get out. If you can take what he can give, then stay. And what I'm gonna say next is not gonna help you out a whole lot more."

Great.

Dad kept speaking.

"The man I see with you is a man who is *with you*. That man loves you. He didn't, we'd have words about you movin' in outta wedlock and me and your mom would be in a hotel rather than under the same roof with you and Sam sharin' a bed."

I totally knew Dad was not entirely okay with that.

Dad continued, "He loves you like I love your mom. I see in him what I feel when I look at her. And you can believe that because after Cooter, I would never, honey, *never* say this kinda shit to you if it wasn't what I felt was the God's honest truth."

I knew this last to be true.

Dad wasn't done.

"That said, *my* Kiakee deserves to have it all. She deserves a rich, famous, good-lookin' man who thinks the sun rises and sets in her. She deserves a decent, good, loyal man who thinks the same. Sam is both a' those. But she also deserves to have everything she wants. If she's willin' to give it all, she should expect it in return. And if this doesn't feel right, honey, right there," one of his hands moved to press my chest, "you go with that feelin'. Because my girl is back and she deserves decent, good, loyal, gentle, rich and famous and she always did. But if that's not givin' it all, my girl deserves to find a man who will give all of himself right back to her."

I stared in my dad's eyes.

All he said was beautiful. It was right. It was wise.

But it didn't help me one bit.

Then Dad, being Dad, helped me.

He pressed in at my chest again and whispered, "Listen to that. Always, *always* listen to your heart. It'll guide the way. You'll know, it's enough, it'll tell you. You'll know, it's not enough and never will be, it'll tell you. Listen to your heart, Kiakee. And when the time comes to make the final decision, your heart will lead the way."

In that moment, a moment of blinding clarity, I knew he was *so* right.

Two days before I married Cooter, I couldn't get to sleep because my heart hurt. I didn't get it, not at my age back then. I thought it was nerves and excitement. But two days later, I didn't rush down the aisle, beside myself with glee to be marrying the ex-quarterback of the high school football team.

I did it with uncertainty.

Because my heart was talking to me and I wasn't old enough or wise enough to listen.

Now I was both.

And now I was there. I let Sam kiss me and change my mind, because right now, what I had with him was enough. I didn't need it all.

Tomorrow that might change.

And until the final decision needed to be made, I would burn every moment into my brain, just as I promised. I might not need those memories. But I'd have them all the same.

I wrapped my arms around Dad, held him close, pressed my cheek to his shoulder and whispered, "Thanks, Dad."

Dad's arms around me gave me a squeeze. "Anytime, Kiakee."

Memphis, patient until now, yapped.

I pulled away and looked down at my dog. She jumped a few feet and strained the lead.

"We better walk Memphis," Dad muttered.

"Yeah," I muttered back.

Dad took my hand and the lead out of my other one, which also held my coffee.

When he did, I took a sip.

Then I took a walk on the beach with my dad.

An hour later, Sam still sweaty in his running gear, bags loaded in the car, Sam and I stood in the drive and waved as Kyle backed out.

My family waved back.

We stayed where we were until they were out of sight and I knew Sam hit the button on the remote because the gate started closing.

Now it was only Sam and me.

Oh man.

I felt the tears pool in my eyes, one slid over and trailed down my cheek.

Sam turned into me, and with a hand at my jaw, he tipped my head back so he could look at me.

His eyes moved down my cheek.

Then he whispered, "Seein' that kills me."

Right. There it was. The decision I made just over a week ago was the right one.

It wasn't about Sam's kiss.

It was about Sam giving me beauty just like that.

I closed my eyes and did a face-plant in his sweaty-shirted chest. His arms closed around me.

"You're gonna miss them," he surmised.

I nodded, my face moving against his chest.

"Anytime you wanna go back, baby, you tell me and I'll get you to your family."

"Okay," I whispered, my arms got tight around him and I pressed close.

"Kia, honey, I'm drenched with sweat," Sam told me.

"I don't care," I replied.

That was when his arms got tight. I felt his lips brush my hair. Then he just held me until I pulled away. He turned me to his side, arm around my shoulders, mine around his waist, and with Memphis bouncing at our heels, Sam walked me to the house.

26

DO YOU LOVE ME?

Two and a half weeks later…

I watched Luci take her phone from her ear as I worried my lip with my teeth.

"Well, that's done," she murmured, her eyes sliding away.

We were having lunch in Kingston at Luci's favorite restaurant. It wasn't the first time we did it, but after hearing her end of the phone call where she accepted an offer on her house, I feared it would be one of the last.

"You okay?" I asked quietly, and her eyes slid back to me.

She pulled in a breath, I thought she would speak, but her gaze drifted away again.

"Luci?" I called. She took her time, but she finally looked at me.

"I'm having second thoughts."

I pressed my lips together in order not to shout, *Yippee!*

This was because, since Luci realized she needed to come to terms with the loss of her husband and look to her future, I was never sure about that meaning she needed to move back to Italy.

This was partly selfish. She was my only friend in North Carolina and we'd grown super close.

This was partly because of what Sam told me about her before I'd even met her.

She was, of course, sultry, exotic, glamorous and beautiful.

But she wasn't only the kind of woman who was just as comfortable drinking a beer on a deck as drifting in elegant clothes through posh events. She was actually *more* comfortable drinking beer on a deck than she seemed drifting in elegant clothes through posh events.

Sometimes home wasn't where you grew up. Home was where you were meant to be.

And I sensed Luci was meant to be here.

She'd changed. The sorrow wasn't gone, but it was nowhere near the intensity it used to be. Her smiles were more genuine. Her laughter came more easily. She never tried to fake anything. And she seemed more at peace.

At the very least, I didn't think she should shake up this process by moving to a different country, even if it was the nation of her birth.

"Talk to me," I urged.

She pulled in another breath, then she leaned into me and I was shocked to see it was with excitement.

"Okay, *cara mia*, I…it's hard…" she trailed off, her eyeballs slid to the side, then she looked back at me and declared, "Travis ruined me for other men."

Uh-oh.

Were we back to this?

"Luci, honey—" I began, but she shook her head and her hand darted out to capture mine.

"No, what I mean is…Kia, you know. They, men like that…you can't find just any other man. You have to find a man like *that*."

This was not good.

Carefully and gently, I said, "Luci, there isn't another Travis."

Her head tipped slightly to the side and she replied, "I know, Kia. I mean an American."

I blinked.

"Italian men don't wear baseball caps," she went on.

What?

Baseball caps?

She kept going.

"Or say, 'fuckin' this' or 'bullshit that' or take so much pride in their pickup trucks, you'd think they were their children."

It was then I had to stop myself from laughing.

She wasn't done.

"I mean, Travis wore baseball caps and had a pickup truck, though not as big as Sam's, but I don't need a man who wears a baseball cap or owns a pickup truck. I just mean a man who's *a man.* And I know Italian men or French men or whatever can be men. But only American men can be, well...so...very...*American.*"

I couldn't help it, I started giggling.

She let my hand go and sat back looking adorably disgruntled.

"I wasn't being amusing," she told me.

"Yes you were," I replied. "But I can't say you're wrong. American men are the only men who can be American."

She rolled her eyes.

I kept giggling.

Then I sobered and it was me this time who reached out and grabbed her hand. I held it tight, and when her eyes came to mine, mine locked on hers.

"You don't have to do anything you don't want to do. You don't have to take that offer on your house. You don't have to go home. If you go home, you can come back. You can do whatever you want to do, Luci. Your whole life is in front of you." Then I gave her my dad's advice. "Listen to your heart and find your happiness."

Her face grew uncertain and she asked, "I know that, Kia, but what do *you* think I should do?"

I was learning that Luci needed a lot of advice. She ciphered this and went her own way. But to cipher, she needed input to cipher through and asked for it.

"If I were you, I'd keep that offer, sell the house you shared with Gordo and look for smaller properties here. You already own two homes and can afford it. That way, you have your options open.

If your preference runs to macho American men, you'll find a lot more of them here than you will in Italy, so you need a base from which to launch your offensive."

She grinned.

I let her hand go and sat back.

But Luci, surprisingly, didn't cipher and decided right away. "I will do this. I will call my real estate agent when I get home and set up viewings."

Excellent!

"Good," I murmured.

The waitress came with our bill and we did our usual arguing over who was going to pay for it. I finally convinced her of the truth that it was my turn. I paid and we gathered our purses, left the restaurant and headed to our cars.

Her Corvette was parked in front of my Cherokee and I asked something I'd wanted to know since before I met her.

"What is with your cars?"

Her head snapped to me and the way it did, I realized she wasn't quite there and I'd messed up. I should have been more sensitive. This had something to do with Gordo and she wasn't ready for me to blurt the question like I did.

She looked at her car and her face grew pensive.

God, I was such an idiot.

"Luci, sorry. I shouldn't have asked like that. It wasn't nice."

Her eyes came to me.

"Travis would hate this car." Her gaze moved back to the Corvette. "*I* hate this car. It is not me."

"It's a cool car," I said softly, and she looked back at me. "But you're right, it isn't you."

I didn't know what was her, but she wasn't about flash and dazzle or the need for speed.

She was…well, like me.

"Maybe…" she said quietly, pausing, then, "Maybe I thought if I did something he hated, he'd show up and stop me. He worked hard for his money; he didn't come from it. Although I had it and he made a good salary, the way he grew up, he didn't throw it away. He would dislike me doing it. Clothes, shoes, bags, makeup, things like that he didn't mind." She smiled sadly at me. "They made me pretty and he liked me pretty. They made me happy and he liked me happy. But this," she tilted her head to the car, "was just madness. It would not make him displeased. It would make him angry. And maybe, well, maybe *I* was angry. Angry at him for leaving me. So I wanted to make him angry too." She looked at the car and whispered, "Foolish."

"Understandable," I whispered in reply, and she again looked at me.

Her face changed, and the way it did, my breath caught.

"I love you, Kia Clementine," she said suddenly, and I closed my eyes.

I opened them and moved into her, folding my arms around her and holding her tight.

"Right back at you, Luciana Gordon."

She gave me a squeeze. I returned it.

We broke apart but leaned in and touched cheek to cheek. She got in her car and I hoofed it to the Cherokee and climbed in. I started it up and headed home to Sam.

Then I smiled.

After our blowout three weeks ago, when I almost decided to leave him, Sam changed and stayed changed. We were back. Things were good. No more mysterious outings and long workouts.

Two days ago, we even had a chat about my future. I liked Kingston. I liked clothes. I liked handbags. I liked jewelry. But, although Kingston had some fun shops, it didn't have a cool women's clothing and accessories shop. It didn't even have an uncool one. It was a female clothing and accessories wasteland.

So Sam told me there was a community college close by. I could take business courses, get an associate's degree, but before that, pick his mom's brain and learn from the master. He even suggested we fly out to California and I work with her in her shop for a couple of weeks to see if it was my thing.

I liked this idea. It was something to explore. Something exciting. Something I may or may not be good at. But it was *something*. A direction. A possible future.

As for Sam, although the mysterious outings had disappeared, the private phone calls didn't.

I had chosen to ignore this. They didn't put him in a bad mood that he took out on me or a bad mood at all. They didn't take him away from me for hours on end. And they didn't send him off to do stuff unknown.

He didn't want to share, okay. Maybe one day he would. Maybe he wouldn't and one day it would get to me.

Now it wasn't.

I was going with that.

It was part of Sam and I was accepting what he could give to me since the dark days were gone and we were back to everything he gave me being beauty.

And that was definitely something I could go with.

I drove home, and a couple houses down from ours, I hit the remote for the gate then hit the button for the garage. By the time I was ready to pull in, both were open. I did the button thing again the minute I cleared the gate. I shut the garage door behind me after I turned off the car.

Then I went up the stairs to the kitchen.

I thought I'd hear the game, but I didn't.

And Memphis didn't yap at me.

Hmm.

"Honey! I'm home!" I called, and that was when I heard Memphis yap.

It was coming from upstairs.

But nothing from Sam.

I rounded the stairs and looked through the living room.

No Sam.

"Honey?" I called and got another yap from Memphis. I looked up and saw her at the top of the stairs. She yapped at me again. "Hey, baby," I called as I moved up the stairs.

Memphis yapped her reply.

Three steps from her, I leaned in and she bounced into my arms.

Cuddling her, I was heading toward the office but heard something in the bedroom, so, brows drawing together, I moved there.

I stopped dead in the doorway.

Sam was packing his big black leather duffel. The duffel he used when he went to Italy then went with me to Crete and Indiana.

I didn't get a good feeling about this.

"Sam?" I whispered, my eyes going to him to see his movements were economical, practiced and swift.

He dumped something from the dresser into his bag (what, I didn't care) and his eyes came to me.

"Baby, got a gig I gotta do. I'll be gone three weeks, month, tops."

I froze.

He had a *gig* where he'd be gone for three weeks, a month tops?

What.

The.

Fuck?

"Sorry?" I asked and my voice sounded strangled.

Sam didn't repeat himself. But as he moved to the walk-in, he kept talking.

"I'll text or call to let you know when to expect me home." He disappeared into the walk-in and kept speaking. "But until then, communication will be random and infrequent."

He was suddenly and without notice leaving for three weeks and telling me communication would be random and infrequent.

Was he high?

Seriously?

I forced myself to come unstuck, wandered partially into the room and he came out with a load of jeans and shirts.

"You're leaving for three weeks?" I asked.

He shoved the stuff in without folding it. I already knew this was why his shirts were so wrinkled. I didn't try to break him of this habit before, and for obvious reasons, I didn't mention it now.

"Yeah," he answered.

"You're leaving for three weeks," I repeated as a statement this time.

His eyes came to me but only to skim through me before he looked down at the bed and picked up his passport.

His passport!

Then he repeated, "Yeah," as he shoved it into the back pocket of his jeans.

"You can't be serious," I whispered, and he looked at me, but this time he held my eyes.

"You might wanna take this opportunity to go home," he suggested. "You do, let me know. Just text me or leave a voicemail if I don't pick up. You decide to stay awhile, when I'm done, I'll go to you in Indiana."

He went to the nightstand, picked up his watch and started to strap it on.

This wasn't happening. He didn't seriously think that I could leave him to have lunch with Luci, be gone a few hours, come back and find him packing, taking his passport. All this while telling me he was going to be gone an indefinite amount of time with little to no communication, no understanding of where he was going and what he was going to be doing there and I'd be okay with that.

"Sam, honey, you need to stop a second and give me a little time," I said quietly.

He looked from his watch to me. "Kia, baby, wish I could, but I don't have a little time. Wheels up in an hour and the drive is forty-five minutes. I gotta hit the road."

"Wheels up?" I asked.

"The plane is taking off," he answered.

I sucked in breath and tried to pull in patience with it.

Then I said carefully, "You're telling me you're getting on a plane in an hour, taking off to parts unknown to do deeds unexplained, and for me, this is all at the definition of a moment's notice."

He finished with his watch, eyes still locked on me, and confirmed, "That's what I'm tellin' you."

"And you expect me to accept that," I whispered.

He started to look impatient. "Kia, I told you, I don't have time."

He didn't have time.

He didn't *have time.*

My heart started hurting, like, *a lot.*

"You need to make time." I was still whispering when I gave my warning.

"I cannot do this now," he muttered, definitely impatient. He moved, then bent to his bag and zipped it up.

Memphis in my arms, we watched him go back to the nightstand and tag his phone. We then watched him shove it in his back pocket. We also watched him haul up the bag by the strap and hook it on his shoulder. Finally, we watched him move to us.

I stood immobile as Memphis shook happily in my arms and Sam gave her a head rub. I stayed unmoving as his hand came up, wrapped around my jaw, he tipped my head back and kissed me hard and closed-mouthed.

Then he let me go and moved to the door.

He was leaving.

Just like that. He was leaving.

I moved then.

I turned to face the door and said softly, "I love you, Sam."

He stopped and turned to me. I saw immediately that his face had changed. His features had been guarded, the shutters down, I was shut out.

Now his face was soft, his eyes warm and intense and his lips were tipped up.

He thought he still had me.

But it would be what he would do next that would tip the balance of my heart. He just didn't know he was being tested.

He failed at the first hurdle by whispering, "Good."

Instantly, I asked, "Do you love me?"

The guard rose up, the shutters in his eyes slammed down and my heart split right in two.

He didn't answer.

"Do you love me?" I repeated.

"Go home," he whispered. "Be with your family. I'll be in contact soon's I can."

"Do you love me?" I asked again.

"Soon's I can, baby."

I clenched my teeth so I wouldn't cry.

Maris was wrong.

It had happened.

Sam Cooper had broken my heart.

And Dad was wrong.

My heart didn't guide me.

Not until it was too late.

When I had it under control, I said in a thick voice, "Be safe, honey."

He jerked his chin up.

Then he disappeared.

Memphis yapped.

After long moments, I put my struggling dog down and she ran out the door after Sam as I heard the garage door going up.

I walked woodenly to Sam's office.

I was sitting down at his desk when I heard the garage door going down.

I had the phonebook opened to movers by the time the hum of the gate stopped and I knew it had closed behind him.

Four days later…

The movers arrived late. They were only now just leaving.

I was pressed for time. The car that was taking me to the airport was going to be there in five minutes.

I was packed. Memphis's crate was at the ready with my bags at the door.

I was standing at the kitchen island, staring down at the note I wrote to Sam.

It said:

Sam,

I'm sorry. I can't do this. The answer is all.

I hope you find someone who can accept the beauty you can give how you can give it.

I guess I'm just greedy.

I'll always love you,

Kia

There was so much more to say. Then again, I wished I could find some way to make it shorter. It took four days to get the note to what it was. I didn't have any more time so that would have to do.

I folded it, slipped it into the envelope, licked the flap and sealed it. Then I wrote Sam's name on the front and set it on the island.

I did this deep breathing. I'd cried enough the last four days while avoiding Luci, letting the one call Sam made go to voicemail, making plans and packing. I couldn't afford more tears. I had a trip ahead of me with Memphis in tow, I needed my wits about me and I needed energy. Tears were exhausting.

I turned to Memphis, who was sitting on the floor beside me, unusually silent as she had been for the last four days. She sensed her momma's mood, she sensed her momma didn't want to talk and she was a good dog.

"Before you know it, sweetie, we'll be home," I whispered as I was about to bend to pick her up, but I caught something out of the corner of my eye and focused on it.

Damn.

Skip.

Just like he did the one and only other time he came calling, he barged right up to and through the two front doors.

I bent, picked up Memphis and met him in the living room.

"You and Sam movin'? What's the deal?" he asked by way of greeting.

I had no idea why he was there, but I knew he saw the moving van.

"Sam's not moving. I am," I told him, walking right by him to Memphis's crate.

"Say again?" Skip asked my back.

I turned to him and repeated, "Sam's not moving. I am."

Skip scowled at me, then he looked around the space before his eyes came back to me and he asked, "Where's Sam?"

"I have no idea," I whispered, bent to the crate and gently placed an unresisting Memphis in it.

"Shit." I heard Skip whisper in return. This surprised me. Skip wasn't the kind of man who whispered. So after I hooked the gate on Memphis's crate, I straightened and turned to him. He didn't delay when he caught my eyes. "Is he still doin' that shit?" he asked quietly.

So Skip knew about "that shit."

Whatever.

"I don't know," I answered. "I don't know what he's doing. I don't know where he is. All I know is one minute he was here, the next minute he was gone, off to locations unknown to do stuff unknown."

"Kia—" Skip started, and I shook my head.

"I know you're gruff and rough and speak your mind, but no offense, Skip, this is not the time and this is also none of your business."

"Don't give up on him," Skip said softly, surprising me again with his tone and the intent way he was looking at me.

Seriously, I couldn't do this now. I didn't have the time.

And seriously, I couldn't do this now or ever. I didn't have the strength left to do it.

"Skip, please, this is none of your business."

"I told you, never seen a love like what Gordo had with Luci. I'll also tell you, closest thing to it was how Sam was with you that night at the Shack," Skip replied.

Oh God.

Seriously! I couldn't do this!

"You have to stop, Skip. I can't do this. And you have to go. The car is coming to take me to the airport. It's going to be here soon and I need to secure the house and get Memphis and my bags to the drive."

Skip ignored me totally.

"Didn't think Sam could be like that. Not with anyone."

Suddenly, my hands shot up and I pressed the pads of my fingers to my forehead hard.

Then I jerked them away, twisted them palm out and pressed them toward Skip, begging, "Please, stop. I can't do this."

Skip's leathery face, if it could be believed, got soft (ish).

"That boy's endured a lot," he told me gently.

"I know that," I snapped harshly, scratching at anger in the hopes it would see me through.

"You need to have patience with him. Don't give up. What I saw of him with you, girl, he'll—"

I shook my head again and cut him off. "No, he won't."

His voice got firmer and more insistent. "You have to have patience."

"You don't know!" I cried. "You don't know how it's been."

He went back to soft and gentle when he agreed, "You're right. I don't. I still know you gotta have patience."

I'd had enough.

Really, could you blame me?

"It isn't lost on me he has demons, Skip. I've put it together. A man doesn't leave a professional football career to join the Army when his brother dies unless something is there, something deep, something profound. He has not shared this with me."

I was counting them off, ignoring Skip's soft (ish) face, getting it all out.

"A man does not lose his best friend and look after that man's widow unless the bond between them is so strong, death can't break it. I know this too. He has not shared about this with me either. I've asked. We've fought about it. But that isn't it. There's a big part of his life I have no idea about. He walks away from me to have phone conversations. He leaves to meet people. I ask about this, too, but he doesn't answer."

Skip opened his mouth, likely to repeat I needed to have patience, but I kept right on going to stop him exerting the effort.

"He's determined to keep those demons locked inside him, Skip, and he's determined to keep his secrets. And I know one thing for definite about Sam Cooper: when he's determined to do something, he's going to do it. I tried to live with it. I tried to accept it, but I can't. And the reason I know I can't is, he's gone, Skip. And it is also not lost on me that he's not off on a goodwill mission to bring water, food and medication to drought-stricken areas of Africa. He took his fucking *passport.* And he's somewhere far away doing something dangerous. I know it. I'm not stupid. And I don't have to know everything, but I have to know *something* so I can be prepared. I deserve that. And if he loved me, he'd give me that. Whatever he's doing means something could happen to the man I love and he should love me enough to let me decide if I want to live with that fear."

Skip closed his mouth, settled in and I was grateful because I wasn't quite done.

"And I'll tell you what I would tell him if he'd loved me enough to give me the choice. The answer would be yes. But he should love me enough to allow me to make an informed choice, accept it and to help me learn how to live with it and prepare for the possibility that whatever he's doing may make me Luci. I've given him everything, Skip, and he's given me so much it isn't funny. But he's kept important things locked away. That isn't right. It isn't fair. And it isn't what a healthy relationship is based on. I can't do it. I want it all and he won't give it all. I asked for it and he told me I can't have it. He told me it's my decision and he's right. It is. So I'm making it."

Skip took a step toward me and coaxed, "Wait it out, he'll be back. When he comes back, I'll talk to Hap and we'll have a word with Sam."

That was huge. I knew it. Skip talking to Hap to do that for me.

But I knew Sam. They would fail. If I couldn't break through, they couldn't.

"It won't work," I whispered, shaking my head.

"Woman, let us try," Skip whispered back, and my eyes locked with his.

"You know him, Skip, *you know him.* It won't work."

Skip held my eyes and I let him. This lasted awhile.

I was losing it and felt my lips tremble. Skip's eyes dropped to them then shot back to mine.

"He gets home, I'm gonna kick his ass," he bit off, and I shook my head again.

"Don't. Please. He thinks the world of you and he needs good people around him. You get in the middle of this, Sam won't like it. You're good people, Skip, and he needs you. Just let him be."

Skip visibly clenched his teeth.

A horn honked in the distance.

The car was here.

Shit.

It was time to go.

"I have to go," I told him quietly.

He scowled at me.

Then he muttered, "I'll get your bags."

I swallowed. Skip got my bags. I rushed through the house making sure the back door was locked, all the windows secured, then I rushed back, grabbed my purse, the keys, the padded envelope

I prepared and the remote on the bar. I snatched up Memphis's crate, went to the security panel, punched in the code and hurried out, locking up behind me.

Skip and the driver were loading my luggage in the trunk when I arrived. I greeted the driver and loaded Memphis in the backseat.

Then I turned to Skip.

"Maybe one day I'll come back and have another sandwich," I said on a small smile, knowing this was never, ever going to happen.

Kingston, North Carolina, was a memory for me.

No, it was a dream. Better than a memory, but still, just as unattainable.

"Maybe, after I kick his ass, you will," Skip returned.

"Skip—" I started.

"You do what you gotta do, girl, and I'll do what I gotta do. Life's too short to live with demons and life's too short to miss one second bein' with the ones you love. You gotta go. I see that. I gotta kick that boy's ass when he comes home. I hope you can see that."

This was Skip. I didn't know him very well, but I knew him enough to see that.

I nodded.

Sam wouldn't like that, but whatever. I'd never know. Sam said if it was all or nothing and it was my decision, he meant it.

I leaned in and kissed Skip's cheek.

Skip surprised me again by folding his arms around me and giving me a tight hug.

I hugged him back.

"See you at the Shack," he muttered gruffly in my ear.

I hiccoughed to swallow a sob.

Then, not looking back, I got in the car and gave the driver instructions. He did as he was told, waiting for Skip's pickup to clear the drive, he followed and stopped.

I hit the remote.

The gate closed.

I put the remote and keys in the padded envelope, sealed it, got out and ran to the postbox mounted at the side of the gate. I shoved it through. Then I got back in the car.

I really didn't want to, I really didn't. I needed all my energy, but as the driver drove away, I managed not to look back.

But I didn't manage not to cry.

27

TOUGH

Three weeks and one day later...

I walked on the wet, uneven sidewalks. They were wet, but it wasn't raining.

For once.

I had not noticed London was foggy, but it sure was wet.

As I rushed along the sidewalks, I couldn't shake the feeling I was being watched. It was freaky weird and totally stupid. No one was watching me. But as I went, twice I turned my head to scan my surroundings.

There were a sea of faces, but no one was looking at me.

I rushed because I was late and I rushed because I didn't want to get caught in the rain. I had an umbrella, but I'd moved out of the residential area of Kensington where Celeste and Thomas lived and into the area of Kensington where the sidewalks were rife with people. It was already a struggle negotiating the populated streets. It was a pain in the ass to do it with your umbrella bumping against and catching on everyone else's.

Trust me, I knew this and I'd only been there a week, but I still had plenty of experience.

I left Memphis behind with Mom and Dad and took off.

This was, I knew, because there was a possibility Sam was back in North Carolina and I didn't want him to come after me.

I also didn't want to be in Indiana, thinking he'd come after me when he wouldn't.

He had called in the time I'd been away, done it three times. All three times, I'd let it go to voicemail then deleted his messages without even listening to them, knowing it would undo me (more) if I heard his voice. Especially his voice coming at me not knowing we were over.

I figured with Sam it would be the latter and he wouldn't come after me. He might not like it and I knew he cared about me enough *really* not to like it, but he'd accept my decision.

That hurt. It shouldn't, but it did.

Then again, everything about losing Sam hurt.

Since Sam left me, I struggled with my decision. I wondered if I didn't give it enough time, enough effort, enough patience, my mind consumed with what I might have tried, what I could have done to break through.

But lying in bed every night, tears sliding from my eyes, I knew. I knew that if Sam could see me come home from my long walk on the beach and know I came to the conclusion I came to and still not give me what I needed, he'd accept this. No amount of time, effort and patience was going to give me all of Sam.

I also gave a serious amount of headspace to considering if I should just take Sam as he could give himself to me. This was harder to come to grips with. What he gave would be enough for any woman, much less me, who only had Cooter as a comparison.

But something in my heart was telling me it wouldn't work. Resentment would build. Ugliness would form. I didn't want what Sam and I had to move in that direction. That would hurt worse.

And, bottom line, walking out on your woman to do whatever it was he intended to do without explanation, even minimal…well, that shit was not right.

So there I was, in England with my friends, discovering new things, in the loving company of Celeste and Thomas, trying to mend my heart.

At that moment, I really didn't want to be out on the streets doing what I was going to be doing, but Celeste encouraged me to do so. Then Thomas did.

I was at the Tate Modern museum the day before when I'd met him. We struck up a conversation. He heard my accent, I told him I was in London for a few weeks, he told me he'd lived in London for thirty-three years and then he suggested we should meet for coffee so he could tell me what to see that tourists didn't normally see. Before I knew what was happening, we had plans to meet for coffee the next day.

I wanted to stand him up. But when I told Celeste about it, she encouraged me to go. Then she told Thomas and he encouraged me to go. Since it was Celeste and Thomas, they were wise, they cared about me and I cared about them, I really couldn't say no.

And anyway, I didn't have the strength left to fight them on it. So there I was, going.

When I got to the area he told me the café was, I got a little lost. I was about to give up (and truthfully, I didn't try very hard before deciding to give up) when I saw the café.

Damn.

Right. Whatever. It was just a cup of coffee with a guy I met at a museum. And anyway, I wanted to see the London not many tourists got to see. Even Celeste and Thomas hadn't been living there long enough to show that to me.

I moved inside, and as I did, that feeling came back that I had eyes on me. I looked over my shoulder and again saw nothing but rushing Londoners and clueless-looking tourists.

What was up with me?

I shook it off, turned into the café and saw him.

It hit me I didn't remember his name.

Shit.

Was it Jason? Jacob? Jeremy?

Shit!

He smiled at me, rising from his seat.

Shit.

Okay, just do this.

I smiled back and moved through the café. When I got there, he surprised me by rounding the table then getting in my space. Not *way* in my space, but more than a fifteen-minute conversation in front of a totally weird installation in an internationally-known museum should allow. His hand came to my waist, his head bent in and his lips swept my cheek.

It was then I felt a burning intensity that was totally, *totally* weird. Like two laser beams were searing with pinpoint precision in my back.

I pulled away, moved back instantly, turned and glanced through the busy café.

Nothing.

Seriously, what was the matter with me?

I looked back at Jason/Jacob/Jeremy. That lip sweep was not a cheek touch or even a lip touch. It was more.

I saw the warmth in his eyes as he murmured, "Kia."

Oh hell, he thought this was a date.

Shit!

"Uh…hi," I replied, then made a decision. "I…you…" Damn. What did I say? "Well, I'm so sorry, but I'd agreed to meet you without talking to my friend, Celeste. She made plans for us this afternoon and I don't have much time. You and I didn't exchange numbers so I couldn't call you and I didn't want you sitting here, waiting for me and not knowing what had become of me. I'm so sorry, but I only have a few minutes to have a cup of coffee with you. I hope you don't mind."

Jason/Jacob/Jeremy minded. I could see it in the flash of irritation in his eyes.

Whatever.

I didn't have enough energy for Jason/Jacob/Jeremy's irritation either.

"I'll just run and get a latte," I told him as he was opening his mouth probably to be a gentleman and offer to buy one for me, which would make this friendly meeting into a semi-kinda-date. I dashed to the counter, stood in line and bought a small latte.

I went back to the table and quizzed him about what I should see in London. This lasted fifteen minutes. Several times, he attempted to ask questions about me or steer us in other directions, but I kept him on target. I also sucked back my latte as fast as I could.

After the final sip, I quickly and rudely stood, announcing, "I know this is rude and thank you for giving your time to me. I really appreciate it. But I have to go. I'm so sorry."

I stuck my hand at him and his head jerked to the side. Then he stood, disappointment on his face and his hand closed around mine.

This kind of sucked. Standing there, his warm hand in mine, I noticed his grip was strong. I also noticed he was cute. Blond. A couple of inches taller than me. Nice eyes that were very blue. He dressed well in a layered have-to-be-ready-for-anything London type of way. He was nice as far as I could tell. And he was into me.

I just couldn't go there. Not now. Not for a while. Hopefully someday, but at that moment or in any moment the last month, I wasn't feeling good about that possibility.

And it was then that I got what Luci said about Gordo. Sam ruined me. The problem was, Sam was still breathing, so I figured it was going to be just as hard as it was for Luci to move on. Maybe harder.

Jason/Jacob/Jeremy regained my attention by saying, "It was nice to meet you, Kia."

He got the message. He didn't ask for my number. He didn't ask to meet again. He knew he wasn't getting anywhere.

I debated telling him that the most beautiful, wonderful, sweet, loyal, fabulous man in the world broke my heart just a month ago, so he would get it wasn't him, it was me.

But I decided I probably couldn't do that without bursting into tears, so I figured I should just save him time and get the heck out of there.

"Thank you for having a cup of coffee with me. Take care," I whispered.

Then I smiled, pulled my hand from his warm grasp and got the hell out of there.

Luckily, it still wasn't raining. Nevertheless, I rushed back to Celeste and Thomas's. It was only a ten-minute walk, but I didn't want to get caught in the rain. The wet seemed to hang in the air, waiting, threatening. It could happen any minute.

Celeste and Thomas were away for the day, doing something with the team Thomas oversaw at work and their spouses. So I had the house to myself.

I wasn't good with being alone. Alone made my heart hurt (more) and the thoughts that invaded when I was alone made my head hurt (more), but I was in the mood. I might even call Luci. We had only chatted briefly a couple of times because Luci got just as angry at Sam as Skip was when I called her from Indiana to tell her what was going on and I wasn't in a place to deal with that. Now, maybe, I was strong enough to tell her I wasn't and she could fill me in on what was happening with her.

That would be good. Take my mind off things.

I left the busy sidewalks, moved through the less busy residential section and the feeling came back that someone was watching me. No, it was more than that. It felt like someone was following me. I looked again but couldn't see anything. Then I wondered if I should look at all. If some weird person was following me, maybe I shouldn't let on that I knew they were there.

Maybe I should just get my behind to Celeste and Thomas's, get inside and lock the door.

So I quickened my pace, trying not to look like I was. But by the time I got up the steps to their white Georgian house, I was freaked out. It was silly, no one was following me, that was ridiculous, but I still was freaked out. Totally.

God, I needed to get myself together. I was becoming paranoid.

What was up with that?

I'd reached into my purse and pulled out the keys two doors before Celeste and Thomas's so they were at the ready. But my hands were shaking as I tried to insert the key in the latch. Therefore, I dropped them, squelched an expletive and bent to retrieve them.

When I straightened, my shoulder slammed into something hard.

Oh God, no. Someone *was* following me.

A surprised, small cry escaped my lips and my head twisted just as I felt the keys ripped from my hand. Fear coursed through me. I was preparing to do something defensive (I had no clue what), when my eyes hit Sam.

Sam.

A stony-faced, infuriated Sam.

Oh. My. *God.*

Before I knew it and without a word, the latch was open, the door was open and Sam's big body was crowding me into Celeste and Thomas's entry hall. Sam pushed the door closed behind us, the latch caught, but I didn't even get my mouth open before his long fingers curled around my bicep and he propelled me down the hall and into the first room on the left, the sitting room. He pulled me in, let me go and turned to close the door.

I backed across the room.

He turned back to me and his eyes seared into me.

I stopped dead.

"You're…fucking…*dating*?" he clipped.

Oh shit.

It was *Sam* who was following me.

"No," I whispered.

"Sweetheart, saw you meet him, saw him touch you, saw you drink coffee with him. He crashed and burned, but that was not two friends having a fuckin' *chat*."

Oh man.

He was angry. Really angry.

He was also here.

What was he doing here?

Following me!

Forcing his way into Celeste and Thomas's home and being angry at me!

"What are you doing here?" I asked quietly, unable to make my voice louder, hardly able to catch a thought. Heck, hardly able to *breathe*.

"What am I doing here?" Sam repeated.

"Yes," I said. "What are you doing here?"

"You're here," Sam stated, and there it went.

My breath.

Gone.

It took effort, but I forced oxygen into my lungs and asked cautiously, "Didn't you get my note?"

"Oh yeah," he murmured in a way that sent chills up my spine, his eyes changing in a way that scared the bejeezus out of me. He took a step toward me. "I got your fuckin' *note*."

I stepped back, my entire body trembling. He saw it and stopped.

"I won't hurt you, Kia, and you fuckin' know that," he growled, close to the edge. I knew it by his face, his posture, the energy vibrating off him and his tone.

"No, I don't, Sam, because you already did. You've all but destroyed me but you didn't lift a hand to me to do it."

Yes. That was what I said. It came right out.

His head jerked then he stared at me, the anger shifting clean from his features and I saw him swallow.

I reached inwardly for everything I had, gathered it close, straightened my spine, but still only managed to whisper, "I can't do it. We're over. I can't give everything and get pieces. I can't live with secret phone conversations and you taking off for parts unknown. I loved what we had. I tried to live with it. I thought it was enough. But it wasn't. Living every day with another secret. Knowing the day before there were more. Wondering if the next day will mean you'll walk away from me. Understanding in my heart that you can't trust me with pieces of your life. I know they're dark, but I don't care. I didn't just want your light, your power, your strength. I wanted all of you. I asked for it. I fought for it. But you kept it from me and you did it willingly, knowing I needed it. I'm sorry, Sam. I've made my decision. I thought I could do it, but I was wrong. It's all or nothing."

He didn't speak.

I did.

"I'm sorry." It was my turn to swallow, then I forced out, "You need to leave."

Sam didn't move.

I waited.

He still didn't move. Not a muscle. Not even his eyes leaving me.

God. Really. He had to get out of there. He was killing me.

"Really," I whispered, and the word broke in the middle. Sam closed his eyes the instant he heard it, but I pushed past it, somehow managed to keep my shit together and went on, "Please, Sam, just go."

He opened his eyes and they locked on me, the intensity was there, more than ever before, which was saying something. It was firing his eyes so blazing, it was a wonder the room didn't catch fire.

"Go," I whispered.

Sam didn't move.

I was losing the battle with my emotions. I wasn't strong enough for this. I hadn't had enough time to get to that place and tears filled my eyes.

"Please," I begged brokenly, "just *fucking go*."

I couldn't stop it and a tear slid down my cheek.

Sam watched it go.

Then his eyes shot to mine.

"He died in my arms."

I blinked then I froze. Completely. Head to toe.

Sam kept speaking.

"Bled all over me, his blood so warm, swear to Christ, I actually felt his life draining out, leaking all over me."

Oh God.

He was talking about Gordo.

"Sam—" I whispered.

He cut me off with "Nine words."

He said no more.

"Nine words?" I asked quietly.

"His last words. There were only nine."

I waited, my heart beating hard, not wanting to hear it, *needing* to.

It took some time, but then he gave it to me.

Everything.

"He said, 'Love you, man. Tell my wife I love her.'"

The tears came back and didn't hover. They just fell over and slid down my cheeks, one right after the other.

Sam kept talking.

"Then he died. Said those nine words, then he was gone. Fuckin' watched the light die in his eyes. Just blinked right out. I will never forget that. How he was there, Gordo, my boy, lookin' at me, and not even a second later, just a blink, he was gone for-fuckin'-ever."

"Honey," I whispered.

"Then I had to go tell Luci that shit."

Oh God.

"I did it and watched the light go out in her eyes too."

Oh God!

"Didn't matter to her that his last thought on this earth was that he loved her and he wanted her to know that. All she could feel was that he was gone. All she knew was that she had him, *all of him*, so much, he's in a goddamned chopper, the blood leakin' outta him, and him loving her is the last thing that fills his mind. Then suddenly, in a fuckin' *blink,* all that was gone because he was gone."

"Sam," I said, stepping toward him.

But I stopped when he stepped back.

My heart skipped.

He had never moved away from me.

"Told Felicia too," he declared.

Felicia?

I blinked, then whispered, "Who?"

"Ben's girl. The one I told you about whose friends puked in my car. Only girl he had. They hooked up when he was fifteen, she was fourteen. Got tight fast, stayed tight. She gave herself to him when she was fifteen. He asked her to marry him when she was eighteen. He was focused on his career, his education, givin' her the life she didn't have, the life he didn't have. Thought he had forever to do it. He didn't. He died before he could do it. And it was me who had to tell her he was gone. Three days after we put him in the ground, she overdosed."

My hand flew out and I backed up until I caught a chair, steadied myself and stopped.

Sam watched me move, but he didn't. He just kept talking.

"Found her almost too late. Ma did. Her folks were whackjobs, her entire fuckin' family, dicks and bitches. The lot of them. All she had was us. Ma was worried about her so she went to check on her. Thank Christ she did. Ma called the ambulance and then she called me. Shit was in her system. They nearly didn't get her to the hospital in time. Then it was touch and go if she did damage to her body, her brain. She survived. She came out unscathed. She's married now, has a kid, another one on the way. But every time I see her, every time I speak to her, the last thing she says to me is, 'You know, he's not Ben.' She lives that. Her husband lives it. He's second best to a dead man and he knows it. He tries. He loves her so he tries. Still, I do not see good things."

"I can imagine," I said gently.

Sam kept going like I didn't speak.

"I thought I could take up his work where he left off. I thought, I did what he intended to do, he'd live on. But that shit keeps going. There's always a fuckin' enemy. There's always a fuckin' assignment. Idiots in suits, most of 'em who don't even care enough to expend the energy to walk down the hall, sit in their leather chairs and speak for their people, tellin' men and women where to go, taking them from their families, putting them in danger, getting their legs blown off, making them bleed. That work will never be done. I gave up what I loved doin' to take up Ben's fight and I fuckin' failed."

"You didn't fail," I assured him softly.

"Yeah? We at war?"

I pressed my lips together.

"We're always at war, Kia, even when we're not. I'm trained to kill and I've done it, hand to hand. The light goin' outta Gordo's eyes was not the only light I've seen go out. I've *made* that light go out, with intent, and in the end, I don't fuckin' know *why*."

"To make people safe, honey," I told him.

"Yeah," he whispered. "I held on to that. I held on to the fact that the men at my side, taking my back, were men the caliber you cannot conceive. Honor wears a uniform."

"Yes," I whispered back.

"You have that, you get out, you get lost."

My heart skipped again.

"Lost?" I prompted when he didn't go on.

"Lost. I loved playin' ball, but I never missed the pads and jersey. I fuckin' missed the uniform."

My fingers clenched the chair. "Then why'd you get out, baby?"

"Because I didn't understand what I was doin' anymore. I only knew I respected who I was doin' it with."

That was a good answer.

I was silent.

Sam wasn't.

"They found Gordo first. A unit. Private firm. Buddies of ours. Men we knew. Men we respected. Ex-Rangers, Night Stalkers, SEALs, Green Berets. Gordo recruited me. Pay was huge. Assignments dangerous but worthwhile and infrequent. We were doin' a K and R extraction when he bought it."

"K and R?"

"Kidnap and Ransom. Kid was seventeen. They'd had him for three weeks. We went in, small team, elite, four of us. But intel was faulty. We didn't know that and that was unusual. They had six times our number and they were heavily armed, serious shit, shit no one has but terrorists, drug cartels and militaries. It was a far bigger operation than we thought. By the time we made it to where they were keepin' the kid, we couldn't abort. We got him. He was weak. I was carrying him out. Gordo had my back. He always fuckin' had my back. He was providing cover fire. Then he stopped and I knew why. I got the kid to the chopper and went back for Gordo."

Oh God.

I didn't want to hear this, but more, I didn't want Sam to relive it. I had enough. He didn't need to give me more. Suddenly, I didn't need everything.

"Sam—"

He kept talking, intent on giving it all.

"It was stupid, against all my training, but I couldn't leave him behind. He was my boy. He was Gordo. He wanted me to teach his sons football. I wanted him to stand up with me when I found a woman who was worth it. I got in, I got to him and I did it by killing twelve men. *Twelve.* That's a lot of blood on my hands, but I didn't care. They were filth and he was still breathing. He took three to the back. He had my back, no one had his, and he took three. *For me.*"

The weight he carried, my God, so fucking heavy. How did he bear it?

"Baby—"

"I got him home."

"Sam—"

Suddenly he moved and he did it so fast, his big frame coming at me, my only thought was retreat and I did. Going back, I kept doing it until I hit wall and I hit it hard.

Then Sam's body hit me, pressing me in. His hands came to my jaw and his fingers dug in, his face in my face so close, the world melted away and it was only him and me.

"'Love you, man. Tell my wife I love her,'" he whispered.

That haunted him.

It haunted him.

Gordo was haunting him.

The tears formed and slid down my cheeks again as my hands lifted and fisted in his shirt.

"Baby—" I started.

"'Love you, man. Tell my wife I love her.'"

"Sam—"

"Felicia, broken. Luci, broken. I didn't want to break you."

Oh God!

I went up on my toes as my hands slid up to his neck, fingers curling around and digging deep.

"Honey, let me—"

"He had that in his death. Ben, no doubt, no *fuckin'* doubt, thought about Felicia in his final moments. I can take that. Fuck, I buy it, I *want* that. My last thoughts on this earth to be of you. But they didn't know. They had no fuckin' clue what they left behind. I knew. I lived that shit twice. And I was not going to do that to you."

"Please, Sam. I—"

"I love you, Kia."

My breath left me and I stared. I wasn't breathing, but my eyes were still forming tears and they were falling.

Sam's thumbs slipped through them, but his eyes didn't leave mine when he semi-repeated, "I love you, baby."

"Sam," I breathed, then said no more. I had no words to say. I couldn't even think.

I could only feel.

And what I felt felt fucking *great.*

"You cannot leave me," he whispered, his hands tightening on my face as he repeated, "You cannot leave me."

"Okay," I whispered back, my hands tightening too.

He either didn't hear me or decided to ignore me because he continued.

"You walked into that dining room, baby, and you know, the minute I saw you, I wanted to fuck you. Two days later, I saw you outside havin' a drink, and even before you looked at me with tears in your eyes, just when I saw you sittin' there, I was annoyed, thought you were playin' games, and I didn't care. Just you sittin' there, I knew it was you."

He knew it was me.

Me.

I closed my eyes.

"Look at me," Sam ordered quietly, and I opened them. "Weeks after that, Kia, I saw you standing in my kitchen, writing a grocery list. Doing nothing, just writing a grocery list. But you'd just made me laugh, and just like you, you made me do it hard. That shit with Gordo, with Luci, losin' Ben, Felicia tryin' to off herself, that shit's too much, it wears you down. I hadn't laughed like that in months, not since Gordo died, and in that moment, you in the kitchen, I realized I did it all the time with you. There were times before, a lot of them, I'd look at you and feel your pull, so strong. I wanted to fight it, deny it, but I couldn't, you wouldn't let me, and I didn't get it. But seein' you standing in my kitchen, effortlessly beautiful, writing a fuckin' grocery list after you made me laugh like that, I knew what it was. I got it. I knew it was more. I knew that wasn't an offer. That was a promise. Even with all the shit goin' down with you, shit that would wear any other woman down, it didn't with you and you gave me that from the beginning. And it hit me then that was what my life would be like if I lived the whole of it with you. And I knew I couldn't live without you."

Oh. My. God.

He couldn't live without me.

His face got close. "You cannot leave me. You can't. I can't live without you."

He couldn't live without me.

He was in hell, just like me.

And just like he did for me, I showed him heaven.

"Sam," I whispered, melting into him, "I said okay."

"Never," he returned immediately.

"Sorry?"

"Promise you will never leave me."

"Sam, honey, I love you."

"But you left me."

"Right, because *you* left *me*. But now you're back and you just gave me all of you. I needed it. You came all the way to England and gave it to me, so now that I have you, all of you, I promise you, honey, I will never leave you."

He stared at me and I let him.

Then he said, "You went on a date."

Oh man.

"It wasn't a date," I told him.

"Looked like a date," he told me.

"Well, it wasn't. We had coffee. I was only there fifteen minutes. That's not a date."

"So who was he?"

"Some guy I met at a museum. He was nice, friendly, asked me for coffee so he could tell me what parts of London I should see. He's from here."

"It was a date."

I felt my eyes narrow and snapped, "Sam! He was just being friendly!"

"To you, because you're clueless about bein' beautiful. To him, he wanted in there."

He was, of course, right.

But…

Seriously?

We just had a month of separation and an emotionally charged drama and we were here?

I took my hands from his neck and planted them on my hips.

"Honestly? I see you for the first time in a month. I think we're over. My heart is broken. I cry myself to sleep every…single…*freaking* night, knowing I'll never have all of you. Wanting all of you so much it hurts to breathe and knowing even what you gave me will be better than what I could get from *anybody*. Worried that I made a huge mistake but knowing in my heart that I couldn't live with the secrets. Then you come back, give me all of you, *then* you give me shit about some stupid guy who means nothing to me. So much of nothing, I didn't even remember his name. A guy who I will never again *see*, instead of, oh…I don't know," I said the last sarcastically, "maybe kissing me?"

Sam glared at me.

Then his gaze shifted over my features, his face went soft, his eyes went warm, his lips twitched and his hands slid back into my hair.

"You didn't remember his name?" he asked.

"No," I snapped.

His lips twitched again.

Seriously!

"You want me to kiss you, baby?" he whispered.

It was my turn to glare at him and I returned, "I did. Now I'm thinking, not so much."

His lip twitch turned into a smile as his hands in my hair tilted my head one way, his head slanted the other and his lips muttered against mine, "Tough."

He kissed me.

It was heaven.

Naked, lying next to a naked Sam in his huge, posh hotel room, my cheek to his shoulder, I was drawing random patterns on his chest with my fingertips while my eyes watched.

Sam was drawing random patterns on my hip, but I doubted his eyes were watching.

After Sam kissed me, he dragged me out of the house, down the street and he hailed a cab. He shoved me in it, told the driver his hotel and ordered me to text Celeste to let her know I wouldn't be home until the next morning. *Late* the next morning. And when I went there, it was only to pick up my stuff.

I texted Celeste. The taxi took us to Sam's hotel then Sam dragged me out of the cab and up to his room.

The door barely closed before he was kissing me. Half my clothes were gone before we got to the bed.

And there we stayed for hours as Sam welcomed me home and I returned the favor.

Now was now.

And I was watching my hand move on his fantastic chest, thinking a year ago I had nothing and now I had everything.

Everything.

And I wasn't talking about millions of dollars, a ridiculously expensive robe and a beach house.

All that could be gone and the man who was lying beside me all that was left and I'd still be a girl with everything.

On this thought, Sam's voice came to me.

"You want it all?"

I stopped drawing, lifted my head and looked at him to see his eyes on me.

They were sober.

All he gave me before, he wasn't done.

Oh man.

Well, the only answer to his question was affirmative.

I wanted it all. The dark, the light, the good, the bad, the laughter, the fights.

All of it.

When it came to Sam, I was greedy that way.

So I lifted up, shifted and settled down mostly on his chest, my gaze never leaving his.

"Yes," I whispered.

"I'm in a situation."

Great. He was not an ex-commando, he was a current one.

This could mean anything.

"What situation?" I asked carefully.

"Got a dead best friend, a dead brother and now, lyin' on me, a woman who's worth it. I don't need the money so I don't need the work. It's time to leave the unit."

Thank you, God.

I didn't verbalize this thought, or say, get up and dance around the room.

I just nodded.

"So what do I do?" Sam asked.

When he said no more, I asked back, "Is this an essay question or are you going to give me multiple choice?"

He grinned, then both his arms wrapped around me and he pulled me full on him.

I left a hand at the warmth of his chest but wrapped my other one around his neck, my thumb moving lazily against the stubble of his square jaw and he spoke.

"Three offers from three different networks. They've been on the table awhile. They know the others are gunnin' for me and they keep pushin' it. I thought they'd back down, but they haven't. They think I'm playin' hardball so they keep offerin' more shit. Now the pay is off the charts."

"Networks?"

"Television networks. Sports shows. One offer is to join a panel, Sunday game banter. One is for my own show, once a week for the football season…talk about football, have guests, shit like that. One is to be the man on the field and in the locker room, interview coaches and players."

For your average man, your not-so-average man and your seriously cool man, all of these sounded awesome.

But I could not see Sam doing any of them. In fact, it kinda weirded me out in a bad way just to think about it.

This must have been written on my face because Sam's arms got tight around me and he burst out laughing.

I watched.

I missed that.

And he loved it that I gave him that.

I missed it so much and I knew he loved it so much that it actually hurt having it back. It wasn't a beautiful pain, it was just pain.

I wasted a month of our lives and it hurt.

It wasn't stupid. I followed my heart and it led Sam back to me, all of him.

Still, it hurt.

Sam stopped laughing and his eyes focused back on me when he explained, "Your face, honey, says exactly what I keep thinkin'."

"Okay, so A, B and C are out. Is there a D?" I asked.

"Got an offer to be the Defensive Coordinator for an NFL team. Again, pay is good, but it doesn't have to be. I got all that I need, and if I didn't, my woman is loaded."

That got him a grin.

Sam grinned back.

"Well, that sounds like you like the idea better, but you're obviously not doing cartwheels about it," I noted.

Sam's grin got bigger as he told me, "Never did a cartwheel in my life."

"Mental cartwheels," I explained.

"Never did those either."

"Sam!" I snapped, slapping his chest. "You know what I mean."

"Yeah," he kept grinning, then his face grew thoughtful. "They're dumpin' the guy they got. He's performing, it's politics. The head coach doesn't like him and the head coach is *not* performing. Thinks he's competition and he'd be right. Higher-ups aren't smart enough to see the head coach is talkin' them into dumpin' the only talent they have on the coaching squad. I do not need that shit in my life."

"No, you don't," I agreed. "Is there possibly a choice F?"

That was when Sam's face grew even more thoughtful.

"Talked to Tanner," he said, and I thought I knew where he was going. Sam was thinking about becoming a private investigator, which would be cool…*ish.* It also might continue to be dangerous, which was something I wasn't a big fan of.

"And?"

"His boys play ball. Their coach just got heaved. Physically abused his son right on the field, then did some other crazy shit and now he's in prison."

Whoa.

"College?" I asked.

"High school," he answered, and I blinked.

"High school?" I queried. "A high school in Indiana?"

I didn't know what to think about this. Would we sell the beach house?

I didn't want to sell the beach house.

"No, baby, they promoted from within. Those boys are already training. That's not an option."

My face dipped closer to his and I said softly, "It would be an option for Sampson Cooper. Any high school program would consider you for their coach. They'd freaking love it."

"I use my name and celebrity without anything to prove I got what it takes, the coaching squad won't love it, and if I don't have a decent team loyal to me at my back, the boys pay."

I was confused.

"So this isn't option F?"

"I told you that because it gave me the idea. The Kingston Wildcats' coach retired last season after twenty years. They hired a new guy out of Texas. Their training has started too. When I got home two days ago, found you gone, took off to find you. But while I was home, one thing I did learn 'cause Skip talked to Hap, Hap made some inquiries and Skip, Hap and Luci were waitin' for me at the beach house when I got home."

Uh-oh.

Sam went on.

"Hap and Luci were itchin' to lay into me, plain to see, but they didn't get in a word. Skip chewed me out, then after I told all of them to take a hike, they didn't. I left them on the deck, found your note, made my own decision. They all followed me in. I told them I had shit to see to. They got it, cooled off and *then* Skip shared that the new coach was already caught helpin' kids to get juiced, so he's out on his ass. The team has no coach. The old guy came outta retirement to take up the reins again and he loves the game, but when you make a decision that it's the end, it's the end. His heart isn't in it. He wants to be fishin'."

I decided it was best to process the Skip/Hap/Luci drama at a later date and asked, "So do you want to coach a high school football team?"

"My degree is in education and I never used it."

I smiled at him. "So you want to coach a high school football team."

He stared at me.

Then he said quietly, "That's when it's exciting. The boys are young. They know what they're doin', but they still got a lot to learn. They're hungry. College, part of 'em is hard, part of 'em is soft and greedy. It's about the game just as much as it's about tail, and if you're good, money. My coach in high school was the shit. He taught me early that I should always focus on the game." He smiled, then continued, "That's not to say I didn't take my share of tail and wasn't glad to get the money. But all the way to the pros, it was about the game, the team, winning. Having that served me well when I enlisted. I already understood team. I understood focus. I understood doing what it takes to win."

"So coach high school football."

His arms gave me a squeeze and his face got serious.

"Baby, this is it. This is us, you and me. That's the future. You wanna tie yourself to a high school football coach?"

All right.

That pissed me right…the fuck…off.

And Sam saw it or felt it or both.

"Kia?" he called.

"You know, it sucks you're big, tall, strong and fast, because I'd like to get a punch in right about now and I figure you have the skills to deflect it."

His brows drew together. "Come again?"

"Sam," I hissed, my face getting super close to his, "if you told me you had a burning desire to clean toilets, sure, that would kinda freak me out, but if that's what you wanted to do, I would not care. Be a janitor. Be a high school football coach. Have your own network talk show. Build Zen gardens. I don't care. If this is it, you and me, that's all I need. Just as long as I'm me and you're Sam and we're happy. What you just asked is about Sampson Cooper and I'm not in love with *him*."

"That wasn't what I asked."

"Yes it was."

He stared at me.

Then he grinned.

Then he muttered, "Fuck, it was."

I rolled my eyes.

Sam rolled me to my back with him on top of me.

"You're cool with me being a janitor?" he asked.

I rolled my eyes again.

Sam's body shaking with laughter shook mine and I rolled my eyes back to him.

In all seriousness, I answered, “Yes.”

Sam’s laughter died.

And, with warm intensity in his eyes, he whispered, “Fuck, I love you.”

My anger died and my arms slid around him.

I smiled at him.

Then I whispered back, “Good.”

EPILOGUE

Heaven

One year later...
"Hey, Mrs. Cooper!" I heard shouted and I looked up from the tray of sliced tomatoes, onions and lettuce leaves I was arranging to the front door.

Three of Sam's boys were crowded there, grinning at me.

"Yo," I replied.

Their grins got bigger. They knew me and thought I was a dork. In fact, Demaine, who was standing there, was brash and hilarious and, at the barbeque Sam and I had for the boys at the end of last season, told Sam right out, "Your woman is hot, Coach, but she's a total dork."

Sam had burst out laughing and replied, "You are not wrong."

I didn't take offense. My husband thought I was hot so I figured I was allowed to be a dork.

I gave them a half wave. They gave me chin lifts and moved out to the crowded deck.

This year's barbeque was preseason as Sam decreed from here on out it would be. Preseason barbeque at our house, postseason party at Skippy's Crab Shack. Team building. No parents. No girlfriends. Only coaches, boys and me.

Considering last year Sam grilled hamburgers (that I made), hot dogs (that Sam "prepared" by expending the effort of slicing open the package with a knife) and brats (again with Sam and a knife), and I did everything else, I disregarded Sam's "team and Mrs. Cooper only" rule and called in reinforcements.

That was why Maris, Mom, Dad, Luci, Hap and Skip were there.

Well, I didn't call Skip. He just showed as Skip was wont to do randomly and with relative frequency but always in a bad mood about something, though it usually (and luckily) wasn't about Sam or me. He currently wasn't doing anything but drinking our beer and being surly, but whatever. The kids thought he was a stitch mainly because he was.

My eyes scanned the deck and I smiled to myself.

Then my eyes dropped to what my hands were doing and I caught sight of my wedding rings.

My smile got huge.

Sam was Sam, always, and to everyone who even slightly knew him.

But my wedding rings were the wedding rings worn by the wife of Sampson Cooper.

It was safe to say Sam did not fuck around when he bought me my wedding rings. The solitaire was enormous, set high, its platinum band embedded with smaller diamonds. The wedding band also was set with diamonds. It was not borderline ostentatious. It just was.

I loved it.

Obviously, Sam and I got married.

Sam wore a tux, a dove-gray vest that looked hot on him, no tie or shoes, the hems of his trousers folded up over his ankles. He looked beautiful.

I wore a Massimo wedding gown that *way* beat the shit out of the gown I wore to marry Cooter. I also was barefoot.

I knew I looked fantastic mainly because Sam told me so repeatedly that day as well as after that day. In fact, he reminisced about "how fuckin' gorgeous" I looked while studying our framed wedding picture just yesterday.

We tied the knot on the anniversary of the day we met and had breakfast. We did it on the beach in front of Sam's house. We did it with only close family and friends in attendance. And we managed to do it without the media catching on.

After it was over, Sam's agent released a photo of us to the paper. Then Sam released his agent. He didn't need him anymore. Sam had made his decision. He no longer had a public life. No more guest appearances on sports shows. No more anything. He had other things to occupy his time.

And he was loving it.

And because my husband was loving it, I loved it more.

Even before Sam and I got back from England, as ever, when Sam made a decision, Sam didn't mess around. He called the president of the school board in Kingston and told him he was interested in coaching the Wildcats. As I guessed, they were all over it. When Sam and I got back, Sam dove in. The old head coach stayed involved for half the season and then (gratefully, seriously, Sam was not wrong, he was all about fishing) bowed out.

This caused a furor not only in Kingston but nationwide. America *adored* the idea of Sampson Cooper moving from being a national hero to being a high school football coach. They thought it was awesome. They thought it was cool. They thought it showed exactly the kind of man he was. No network television. No big man stunts. It wasn't about keeping his celebrity. It was about doing whatever the hell he wanted to do. It was pure Sam.

They were right.

However, this meant there was intense scrutiny on the Wildcats once they entered the season.

They lost their first four games, the first two soundly, and Sam and the boys took those hits very publicly, very widely and, surprisingly, viciously.

I was terrified. The sniggering tone of the commentary was not at all to my liking, as it wouldn't be. I worried for Sam and I also worried about his boys, who were not used to that kind of attention.

Sam didn't react at all. He was focused. And he managed to keep his boys focused.

After that, they didn't lose a single game. Not one. And in the end, they kicked ass.

It. Was. *Awesome*!

Unfortunately, the early losses meant they didn't see postseason play.

I had a feeling they would this year.

Incidentally, watching Sam coach and his boys play, I learned to love football.

But only the high school kind.

At the end of the football season, the School Board approached Sam with the offer to be the school's Athletic Director. The old coach held that position too and they had yet to fill it.

Sam took it. It meant more time, more money (not that that mattered) and it was something he enjoyed.

Therefore, we were at the school all the time.

Yes, *we*.

Sam did his gig alone with his boys at practice, but I came to all of his games. I also went with Sam to all the other sporting events at the school. Girls volleyball, track, girls and boys basketball, baseball, softball, wrestling. We even went to away games, matches and meets. Sam was serious about the job, was hands on and he paid attention.

I'd never been into sports, but high school athletics was something else. It was about heart. It was about team and school spirit. It was totally amazing.

So I became queen of Kingston athletics to Sam's king. In other words, the Booster Club approached me to become their chair. I took it on and I was all about bake sales, setting up carnivals and planning all-you-can-eat spaghetti dinners. The kids needed equipment, decent uniforms, stuff like that and there was never enough money. So a bunch of parents and I went about raising money.

I found I had a knack for it. But not only that, it was all kinds of fun.

This wasn't to say I didn't investigate the idea of opening a shop in Kingston. I looked into this. I even went out to California for a week with Luci and hung with Maris at her ultra-awesome shop in Malibu.

And I didn't like it much.

It just was not for me.

Luci *loved* it.

So *she* opened a shop in Kingston.

Obviously, considering her fashion connections and good taste, it was a hit. And I helped her out, working part-time, which mostly meant hanging out with Luci, gossiping, giggling, trying on (and often, taking home) gorgeous clothes and sometimes waiting on customers or tidying racks and shelves.

But mostly I spent my time cleaning the house, grocery shopping, cooking when Sam wasn't in the mood (my man did most of the cooking, what could I say? He liked it and he was good at it), taking my dog for walks, going to sporting events with Sam and arranging fundraisers so the kids in the sports program could have kickass shit.

I was particularly pleased with the volleyball outfits the girls would have this year. They were top of the line, the brand Olympians wore. They cost a blooming fortune, but the carnival made a killing. And they were worth every penny. Freaking phenomenal. The girls were in fits of glee.

See? Told you I had a knack for it.

Sam had also taken on another project, something he shared with me in bed one night not long after we got home from England. It was something he shared with me he'd been kicking around for years, even before he quit playing pro ball.

He wanted to do a summer football camp for underprivileged boys like the boys he'd grown up with, like the boy he used to be. A minimal number of slots, the boys had to apply, but they wouldn't pay, not even for travel. Three weeks of training and not just in football. It would be a kind of football boot camp. Part sports training, part military training. It wasn't just going to be about physical fitness and learning to play the game. It was about dedication, loyalty, team, honor, reaching inside and finding that part of you that you could latch on to to pull yourself out of the circumstances life thrust you in and find something better.

I loved this idea. Loved it enough that I gave three million dollars to help endow it. Sam put in the rest. Then he recruited buddies in the game as well as buddies from the military who not only helped process the applications to select which boys would get to go, but also to run the camp.

And last July, using Kingston High as their base, Sam and a bunch of NFL and Army badasses inaugurated the Sampson and Kia Cooper Football Camp. I was against my name being added, but Sam did it anyway.

There it was. Sam made a decision, acted on it, and really, there wasn't anything to complain about. So I didn't.

This also caused an outpouring of love for Sam and the men who gave their time. Sam ignored it. The NFL players involved didn't and their agents got them a lot of play in the media for it. This was good, seeing as donations started coming in. So Sam and I started a fund, got not-for-profit status and we got so much money, next year, we were going to be able to take twice as many boys. Not to mention, younger NFL players heard about it, dug the idea and approached Sam about being involved.

It was cool.

This also, since I managed the administrative part of it, took my time.

I finished with the tray, picked it up and took it out to the deck. There were tables set up against the screened porch, all groaning with food. I'd learned last year that high school football players really didn't care if the potato salad, macaroni salad and brownies were homemade. They'd eat anything, lots of it and think it was the bomb.

So, except for forming a gazillion hamburger patties, slicing veggies and laying stuff out, the work was done. In other words, it wasn't as much work as last year.

I didn't tell Sam this. If he knew, I might not be able to call in reinforcements next year and I liked our beach house filled with family.

I put the tray down and turned my eyes to Sam, who was standing with Hap and a couple of his boys at the grill. My gaze moved to one of the boys because he had Memphis in his arms, a Memphis who was wriggling and licking.

Memphis, not that it was a surprise, totally loved Sam's team. She also liked to go to the games with me. This meant she could run around the field after the games were over, chasing the boys while they played with her.

Memphis's version of heaven.

The boy holding my dog, Wes, was a senior. He was an excellent running back. He had a steady girl. And he clearly didn't care that liking a King Charles spaniel might mean a hit to his street cred. Then again, none of the boys did. This was likely because Sam didn't and his kids, every one, thought he walked on water.

He couldn't walk on water. But he could do everything else.

I grinned at Wes then my eyes moved to Sam to see his on me.

So I grinned at him.

I watched his face get soft and his eyes get warm and intense.

Then he grinned back.

Beautiful.

Never, not ever, would I get used to his beauty. I knew this and this made me happy.

I felt fingers clamp on my arm and my head turned to see Luci had hold of me. She looked serious, she looked kind of pissed and she looked like she was on a mission.

Oh man.

I suspected this was going to happen.

And I suspected this because, three weeks ago, something happened.

What, I did not know.

What I did know was that Hap had been down for the weekend and stayed with Luci at her new place, which was only ten houses away from Sam's and my place. We'd all gone to Skip's (incidentally, after what went down with Luci, then with Sam and me, Skip had lifted the ban on Hap having his ass at a picnic table at the Shack, which was a relief since we spent a lot of time at the Shack). We'd all had a sandwich and accompanied this by having a few drinks. We'd then moved the party to Luci's. Sam and I left and then, well…something happened.

I just didn't know what.

But I suspected.

Luci didn't share. Hap didn't share. But before whatever it was went down, Hap came most weekends. After what went down, he stopped. He also mostly stopped communicating. As did Luci. They were avoiding Sam and me.

Then Luci came by our house the weekend after. Hap was supposed to be there, but he'd called Sam to say he wasn't coming. For some reason, when Luci heard this, she got pissed.

But she still didn't share.

The next weekend, the same. Hap didn't make plans to come. Luci called me, found out there was no Hap and I heard her voice get tight over the phone.

Now, with the barbeque, Hap couldn't avoid coming. He also couldn't avoid Luci. Though, he was doing a bang-up job trying, even though she was right there.

When she arrived, it wasn't lost on me she'd made an effort on her appearance. And for Luci, this meant her sexy, sultry, exotic beauty was off the charts. Heck, I'd seen some of Sam's boys running into each other, the deck railing and furniture because they were mesmerized by her beauty.

Hap was immune.

And, obviously, Luci didn't like this.

As for me, I had a bad feeling about it.

"I need to speak with you," she hissed, then didn't give me the chance to tear free and run screaming to the beach. She pulled me to the side walkway and down to the drive. There she stopped us and wasted not a second before ordering, "Okay, I need you to go back up there and find some way to bring Hap down to me."

Uh-oh.

"What?" I asked. "Why?"

"Something happened," she announced.

Oh man.

"I think I got that, sweetie," I told her quietly. "For a year, Hap's down every weekend. For the last three weeks, we don't see him and barely hear from him, and this is all after we left him with you. What went down?"

Again, she wasted not a second and informed me bluntly, "I made a pass at him."

I blinked.

Okay, I was thinking that was what happened or something akin to that, but for some reason, having this assumption confirmed threw me for a loop.

"What?" I asked.

"You and Sam left, Hap and I kept drinking, then we drank more. We were laughing and talking, but he wasn't *doing anything*," she griped. Definitely griped. All sexy, sultry, deep-throated, Italian-accented griping. It was cute coming from Luci. It still threw me.

"What do you mean, 'doing anything?'" I asked.

"He wasn't hitting on me!" she snapped.

There it was.

This was bad. I knew it. This was definitely bad.

"So, you did," I whispered, worried.

"Of course I did. I learned not to play games. Not to waste time. So I kissed him."

Oh man.

"What did he do?" I asked.

"He kissed me back, of course."

I blinked again.

That wasn't what I expected to hear. I expected Hap would deflect her pass and he was avoiding her in an effort to keep deflecting it.

Clearly, I was wrong.

"Seriously?" I queried, and her brows shot together.

"Yes, *seriously*. Of course, *seriously*. It was a good kiss!"

Oh man!

"How good?" I asked.

"So good he picked me up, carried me inside, put me on the couch, joined me there and we did more than kiss. *A lot more*."

Oh man!

"Luci—" I started, but she kept talking.

"And that was good too. *Very good*. Unbelievably *good*. Then, when it was getting *amazingly* good and close to *phenomenally* good, suddenly, out of nowhere, he stops, gets to his feet, mutters, 'Luce, so sorry, so fuckin' sorry,' and *he leaves*!"

Exasperated, she threw her hands up on the last two words.

I got closer and grabbed both of them.

Then I did the only thing I could do.

I gave it to her straight.

"Honey, Hap…" I shook my head. "You can't go there."

"Why?" she snapped.

"Because he's Hap," I explained, but obviously this was not enough of an explanation.

I knew this when she snapped again, "So?"

"He was tight with Gordo," I reminded her.

She nodded her head sharply and repeated a curt, "So?"

I shook my head gently and kept explaining, "So, to Hap, no matter what, you're Gordo's and always will be."

"Travis is dead," she returned shortly, and I sucked in breath.

She yanked her hands from mine, took a step away and dragged the fingers of one through her thick hair.

Then she locked her eyes on me.

"I know," she told me. "I know how it is with these men. But he feels it, I know he does. It started a while ago, months ago. *Months*, Kia. He made me laugh. He always made me laugh, but suddenly, the sadness was gone and he made me *laugh*. And I saw the way he would look at me. And I liked it, *cara mia*. Not just noticing a man's attention, but noticing the attention of a man who could make me laugh like that."

I'd heard that before, in a way.

"Honey—" I began again, only to be cut off again.

"And he's handsome."

She was right about that. Hap was beyond muscle-bound, but that didn't mean he wasn't very good-looking. He was. Totally.

Luci wasn't done.

"And he is who he is. You take him how he is. He's rough around the edges and that's all he'll ever be. He knows who he is and he isn't going to change for anybody. I like that. And I like that, even being like that, he senses things about me. The laughter and that, just *that,* when I noticed he senses me, that was when he wasn't just Hap anymore. He was *Hap.* And rough or not, his eyes would be gentle and his tone would be gentle if he sensed I needed that. And it was beautiful. This man, so coarse, who could also be so unbelievably *gentle.*"

Yes, I'd noticed that too. Hap being gentle with Luci.

And I'd also noticed its beauty.

"Sweetie," I said carefully, "he may feel things for you, but you know these guys. They're about honor and he would be dishonoring Gordo's memory if he took anything anywhere with you. He won't do it." I got closer to her again and whispered, "He'll never do it and he's probably struggling with what happened. I hate to say this to you, but it's the truth. You need to back off and let this be. It'll only be hard on him, hard on you and you might lose what he can give you if you—"

"That's stupid," she interrupted me to hiss. "He has one life. I have one life. Why would you not explore something that might mean happiness? There is no reason. I won't accept there is. And I do not believe, not for one second, that the man I fell in love with and married, who died way too young, would not encourage both his friend *and* me to find happiness, even if it meant with each other."

Well, I had to admit, she had a point there.

Her voice changed, got soft, pleading, "Please, Kia, go and bring him to me."

I bit my lip.

It was Luci who then caught my hand, and when she did, she squeezed.

"This is not a tryst," she whispered. "This is not for fun. He's my friend too and I love him. I would not do this to him, myself, or the memory of my husband if this didn't *mean something to me.*"

I believed her. Looking at her, it was impossible not to believe.

But it was more.

She was in love with George "Hap" Cunningham.

"Oh, honey," I whispered back.

I saw bright fill her eyes and she continued, "It isn't the same. It wasn't what I had with Travis. It didn't hit me like a bullet. It snuck up on me. But I go to bed thinking about him and I wake up thinking about him. Now, for months, I've been waiting breathlessly for the weekend to come, for *Hap* to come. And these last three weeks, not having even a little of him, it *hurt, cara mia.* It was a new kind of pain, but I knew feeling that pain, being separated from him, not knowing what he's thinking, worried about him…I know he means something to me. I know it's worth trying. And I know, as a woman knows, the way he kissed me, touched me, that he goes to sleep and wakes up thinking of me too. So I must try. Life doesn't give you *two* chances to feel that strongly about *two* men and I cannot waste life, Kia. *I cannot.*" Her hand squeezed mine and she finished, "You know this just the same as me."

Boy, did I.

Shit.

Shit!

"I'll go get him."

Yep. That was me.

Shit!

She smiled a trembling smile. She was relieved I agreed. But that tremble was something else. The beautiful, ex-supermodel Luciana was worried a man would deny her.

I was worried about the same thing.

Shit.

"Be right back," I whispered.

"Okay," she whispered back.

I gave her hand a squeeze.

Then I let her go, turned and walked up the walkway.

I didn't want to do this, and when you didn't want to do something you had to do, you did it fast and got it out of the way. So that was what I did.

And anyway, Luci was waiting.

I walked right to the deck, right to the grill, and therefore, right to Hap.

But also right to my husband.

Eek!

"Can you come with me a sec?" I asked Hap, looking in his eyes and ignoring my husband's eyes on me.

"No," Hap answered instantly.

He saw me leave with Luci.

"Hap—"

"Don't go there, babe," Hap said quietly. It wasn't mean. It was just quiet.

And, unfortunately, firm.

"What's goin' on?" Sam asked, and I looked at him.

"Nothin'," Hap muttered. "I'm gonna go to the beach and pass the ball with the boys."

"No you're not, Hap. You're gonna come with me," I told him, and his eyes came back to me.

"Kia, babe, I said no."

"And I say you owe her this," I returned, then got close. "I get you, honey. I get the war you're waging within, but there's a woman waiting for you. She cares about you. You care about her. And even just as friends, after what happened, you owe her this."

Hap glared at me.

Sam semi-repeated, "What the fuck is goin' on?"

I ignored my husband and endured Hap's glare.

Hap muttered, "Fuck," and stomped around me toward the walkway.

I started to follow him.

"Kia, baby," Sam called.

I looked over my shoulder and called back, "Explain in a minute, honey."

Sam looked displeased.

I ignored that (kind of) and hurried after Hap.

I caught up halfway down the walkway, and I knew I was right to agree to Luci's demand when I saw her standing in the drive, wearing her heart right on her sleeve.

Oh God. I hoped this worked out right, however that right would be.

"Luce, babe, this is not—" Hap started immediately when he stopped three feet from her, but I put my hand up and interrupted.

"Nope, no," I stated, then looked between a stony-faced Hap and an unhappy, visibly scared Luci. "Ground rules," I declared and looked at Luci. "I love you. *He* loves you." I jerked a thumb at Hap. "Sam loves you. And Sam told me once that no matter how beautiful you are, Luci, and how *Luci* you are, he would never go there. Never. Because of Gordo. And he meant it, sweetie. It wasn't an option. And if that's what Hap tells you now, you need to deal with it, process it and accept it. For Hap. And then you have to find it inside you to move on with him in your life the way he used to be."

The tears started shimmering in her eyes again, and when she opened her mouth to speak, I turned to Hap.

"And you," I began. "You only have this life and the woman who's standing here right now goes to bed thinking of you. She wakes up thinking of you. She thinks you're handsome, a good kisser, gentle and you make her laugh. Travis Gordon was a good man and I know you loved him. But do not do something right now that you're going to regret for the rest of your life because you're intent on honoring the memory of a dead man. Or because you might be worried about what your buddies might think. Regret is the worst feeling you can feel and that would be compounded knowing the decision you're about to make will make someone you love feel the same for the rest of hers."

Hap stared at me, face still stony, jaw still hard, but his eyes were heated and I knew I got in there.

Just a little bit.

My work was done.

"All right," I finished. "This conversation is between the two of you. Have it. Make your decisions based on that and that alone. Whatever happens next, nothing changes for anyone else except you two." I sucked in breath, then ordered, "Commence."

Without looking at either of them, I walked away.

I saw Sam standing at the top of the walkway, arms crossed on his chest, feet planted, eyes on me, face a little bit scary.

I got close to him and instantly tried to push him to the deck.

"What the fuck?" he asked, staying planted, solid, not budging an inch.

I gave up and told him, "Luci and Hap need some privacy."

Sam's more-than-a-little-bit-scary eyes tipped down to me.

"Again, baby, what...the...*fuck*?"

"Sam—" I started.

"Talk," he bit off.

"They're in love," I whispered, and Sam blinked.

Then he declared, "They are fuckin' not."

Oh man.

"Yes, honey, they are."

"They are not."

"Sam!" I snapped.

"Hap would not do that to Gordo," Sam announced.

"Sometimes, shit happens," I said gently.

"Hap…would not…do that…to Gordo," Sam stated definitively.

I sucked in breath.

Then I whispered, "Gordo's not here, honey."

Sam scowled at me, then his eyes cut down the walk. I turned to stand by his side and started biting my lip.

Hap had his arms crossed on his chest, legs planted just like Sam, making it appear like Sam was right.

Luci was looking beautiful and gorgeously beseeching, leaning into Hap, her fingers curled on his forearm, making me hope Luci could pull this off.

Hap shook his head.

Okay, shit, maybe Luci couldn't pull this off.

Luci leaned closer and said something.

Hap's body went visibly still and he shook his head again.

Crap.

Even from a distance, I saw a tear fall from Luci's eye as she said something else.

Oh God.

Hap shook his head again.

Oh God!

Luci stared at him. Then she nodded and stepped away. My heart squeezed as she studied him a half a second, turned on her foot and *ran away*.

"Fuck," Sam whispered.

I stopped breathing.

Hap didn't move.

I forced myself to breathe.

Hap still didn't move.

I stopped myself from finding something to pick up and throw at him.

Hap dropped his head and looked at his feet.

"Fuck," Sam repeated, still whispering.

"Go after her," I whispered to a Hap who couldn't hear me, but I didn't care. "Go, go, go, go, *go after her*," I kept whispering, ending by doing it fiercely.

Hap didn't move.

Not for a while.

Finally, he lifted his head and stared at where Luci last was seen.

That was when my breath started coming fast.

He started walking that way.

I pressed my lips together and locked my body to stop myself from jumping up and down and shouting with glee.

"Fuck," Sam whispered again.

Hap disappeared around the house.

I turned to my husband and lifted my finger to his face.

"Whatever comes of this, you'll accept it," I ordered.

His hand shot up, his fingers wrapping around my entire hand, including the finger I was wagging in his face, and he pulled it down and pressed it to his chest.

He studied me. I glared at him.

His lips twitched and he muttered, "Bossy."

There it was. He was giving in. For me and for his friends.

Thank you, God.

I grinned and leaned into him.

And I made a decision.

So I leaned further into him and wrapped my arm around his waist. He let my hand go so he could wrap both his arms around me. My freed hand went up to curl around his neck.

"Right, so, drama that could mean good or bad things to the Cooper household. We won't know until that plays out." I jerked my head back to indicate the walkway. "So, now, you want something that could only mean good things to the Cooper Household?"

Sam's brows drew together.

"Baby, seriously? You're askin' that shit?"

I grinned and decided, "I'll take that as a yes."

"After bad drama, good drama, or uncertain drama, I'm all for learnin' anything that means good things for the Cooper Household," he pointed out the obvious, making it clear he was irritated yet amused he was pointing out the obvious.

"Right then. I'm pregnant."

Yes, that's what I said and that's how I said it. I just blurted it out.

Sam's body froze solid and he simply stared at me.

I kept blurting.

"I know we haven't been trying long." And this was true. We'd been trying for six weeks but "trying" in Sam World meant he expended a lot of effort. Not that I was complaining. "But either you have strong swimmers or my womb is exceptionally welcoming or both, because the deed is done. I took three pregnancy tests, then the doctor confirmed it. And I will tell you now, if it's not a boy, I'm gonna be pissed. I'm sure I'll be happy with a girl if that's what she is when she gets here. But right now, I want a boy you can teach how to play football so Memphis and I can sit on the deck and watch you two toss the ball around on the beach."

Sam remained unmoving and staring at me.

I kept babbling.

"The one after this can be a girl," I allowed.

Sam continued to stand there, immobile, and staring at me.

"Hello, Sampson Cooper?" I called. "Your wife, Kia Cooper, is talking to you."

Sam moved then. He let me go, grabbed my hand and dragged me to the deck.

Once there, Sam stopped us both and shouted, "Yo! Attention!" Everyone—family, coaches, Skip and the boys who were not on the beach—looked at Sam. And Sam, just like Sam, didn't hesitate to share private news very publicly and he did this by announcing, "Kia's havin' my baby."

"*Ohmigod!*" I heard Maris screech.

She could say that again.

Jeez, my husband.

"*Oh, my sweet baby!*" I heard Mom shriek.

"Well, all right!" I heard Skip shout.

Dad just stared at me, head tipped to the side, mouth smiling, eyes dancing. Happy.

The boys and coaches hooted and clapped.

Sam let my hand go, curled an arm around my shoulders then he curled me into him and his other arm locked around me. I tipped my head back, smiling at him. But when I saw his face, my smile died.

My husband was beautiful. My husband was gentle, protective and loving. My husband was funny, but he thought I was funnier. My husband gave me everything.

And I returned the gesture.

But until that moment, I didn't realize I had more to give.

Nor did I know when I gave it, how he would feel.

But I knew, looking in his eyes.

I knew it because I felt it in me.

We thought we already had heaven.

We didn't.

Now we did.

He bent his head and kissed me, hard, wet, deep, thorough and long. He did it through more cheering, more hoots, some of his boys shouting lurid encouragement and a loud, ongoing ovation.

I didn't really hear it.

Neither did he.

Yes, it was that good of a kiss.

Then again, with Sam, it always was.

No matter how many he gave me.

And I knew they always would be.

"Hey, did I wake you?" I whispered into the phone.

It was night. Our guests were gone. The house was clean. Our family members were in their beds. We had not heard word from Hap or Luci (which I decided meant good things, but Sam refused to discuss it through the thirteen times I tried). And I was lying on Sam's chest, Sam's arms around me, my cell to my ear, Sam's eyes on me.

"Yes, *ma belle*, but that's okay. Is everything all right?" Celeste asked, sounding sleepy.

"Yes, I just…well, we told everyone today. You weren't here and you're part of the everyone who needs to know and I couldn't wait until you were awake, so, well…" I pulled in a breath. "Celeste, honey, I'm pregnant."

Silence.

"Celeste?" I called.

More silence.

Then I heard a soft, delicate sob.

Yeesh. Only Celeste could make crying sound pretty.

Then I heard, "Kia?"

That was Thomas.

"Hey, Thomas, I'm sorry to wake you both. Is Celeste okay?"

"Not really. She's crying in my arms. Are *you* okay?"

"Uh…yeah. I just told her Sam and I are going to have a baby."

Again silence.

Oh man.

"Thomas?" I called.

"Give me a moment, my love," he whispered, voice thick.

Oh man!

I looked to Sam as tears filled my eyes. His face got soft and his arms gave me a squeeze.

I smiled at him, then turned my head, rested my cheek on his chest and waited.

Finally, Thomas said quietly, "We're happy for you Kia. You and Sam. Very happy."

"Thank you, Thomas. We are too."

"What did I say?" Thomas asked.

"Sorry?" I asked back.

"I would assume, at this very moment, you, my beautiful Kia, are content in the knowledge you've done very well. I would further assume your husband is not too far away and he's feeling much the same thing. Except, perhaps, more."

I closed my eyes, but the tears still escaped, wetting Sam's skin. His hand slid up and cupped the back of my head as his other arm got tight and stayed that way.

That would be a yes. Thomas assumed right.

I didn't answer, but I knew Thomas heard my not-nearly-as-pretty sob.

And I knew this when he whispered, "Told you so."

I sobbed louder.

Sam slid the phone from my hand. I wrapped my arm around him tight and listened to him murmur into my phone. And I listened to it clatter on the nightstand.

Both Sam's arms were back around me, pulling me up his chest. He rolled me to my back, him on top and one hand went to my face to wipe away my tears.

"We have good friends," I told him.

"Yeah, we do," Sam agreed. His eyes coming to mine, he whispered, "Wish Ben was here today."

Tears filled my eyes again, my hand lifted to cup his cheek and I whispered back, "I do too."

He kept going. "Gordo too."

I nodded and swallowed.

Sam's eyes held mine.

Still whispering, eyes intense, he said, "Love you, baby."

He loved me. *Me.* All that was him loved all that was me.

"Love you too, honey."

I watched my husband smile.

I closed my eyes because he kissed me.

Then he made love to me.

After that, I fell asleep in the arms of a powerful man, content in the knowledge that I did very well…

And he did too.

Two and a half years later…

Coming home from his work managing the dining room in an exclusive hotel on *Lago di Como*, Paolo Garibaldi opened his postbox and saw the padded envelope inside.

He smiled. Then he grabbed it, hurried into his apartment building, up the stairs and through his door. He didn't take his shoes off his aching feet. He didn't pour himself a much-needed glass of full-bodied red Italian wine. He didn't do anything he normally did.

He tore into the envelope.

He pulled out the piece of paper, unfolded it and saw, like always, she'd had her message translated.

He set that aside for later.

He was eager to see.

So he pulled out the item wrapped in bubble wrap, deciding, as he always did, he would save the wrap. When they came to visit, his grandchildren loved popping those bubbles.

Carefully (so as not to pop too many of the bubbles), he tore the tape away. When he was done, he had the back facing him so he turned it to its front.

Then he smiled.

"*Bellissimo. Sempre,*" he whispered.

He allowed himself a moment to study it and he did this closely. Then he moved through his apartment to the shelf. Adjusting the items already on it to make room, he pulled out the arm and set his new piece at the end.

He stepped back and looked.

The first item was larger than the others. The frame silver and heavy. Sampson Cooper in his well-cut tuxedo, standing tall, strong and handsome on a beach, the waves of the ocean crashing in behind him as he held his brand-new wife, who was wearing a stunning (Italian designed and made, so of course it would be stunning) wedding gown. He was facing the camera full-on and holding his new wife in both arms, her front tucked close to the side of his. The new Mrs. Cooper had her arms wrapped around her new husband's middle and she was looking over her shoulder, the wind catching her magnificent hair, the skirt of her angelic gown, and she was beaming.

The next was a smaller frame, wooden but lovely. Sampson Cooper sitting upright in a hospital bed, his beautiful Kia in a hospital gown, resting back against his chest, a tiny bundle held in her arms. Sampson looked happy and proud. Kia looked happy and tired. The baby just looked tiny.

The next in another silver frame, a beautifully decorated Christmas tree in the background, a dark-headed baby on the floor in his jammies in front of a heap of jumbled presents, half-crawling, half-on his belly, being licked on his baby-laughing face by a little brown-and-white dog.

The next in a black lacquered frame, the photo black-and-white, Sampson Cooper walking down the side of an American football field. Held to his chest, sleeping head resting on his shoulder, was his little son. Held to his side—arm around her shoulders, hers around his waist—was his wife. There were boys in uniform and football pads in the background. Sampson was looking down at Kia. He was not smiling. His face seemed serious, intent, but nevertheless, *content.* Kia, head tipped way back, was looking at Sampson. She was smiling. She was also very, *very* pregnant.

And the last, the most recent, in another lovely wooden frame were Sampson and Kia Cooper standing in front of a white-painted wooden railing. The small dog was sitting by Sampson's feet, probably panting but looking like she was grinning. Sampson was wearing jeans and a shirt and holding a dark-headed toddler straddled to his hip in one arm. His other arm was around his wife's shoulders, holding her close. Kia had one arm wrapped around her husband's waist. Her head was bent to the side, resting on his broad shoulder. She was wearing a sundress and her skin was tan. Her hair, again, was blowing in the wind. In her other arm she held another little bundle, closely and protectively.

Except for the infant and the toddler (but, as noted, also the dog), they were all smiling, beautiful and big at the camera.

The infant appeared to be sleeping.

The toddler, Benjamin Travis, appeared to be laughing.

Paolo went to the letter.

It began (in Italian, of course):

Dearest Paolo,

Talia Celeste has arrived! And she's perfect!

The *perfetta* was underlined. Twice.

Seeing it and reading one of Kia's frequent letters, all the way through, Paolo smiled.

His wife, Talia, rest her soul, always told him he was a hopeless romantic.

This wasn't a complaint. Her life was not long, but he did his best to fill it with romance.

Then, when she was gone, he had to find other ways to act out these tendencies.

Sometimes they didn't work.

Paolo's eyes went to the shelf, and, again, he smiled.

And he smiled, because sometimes they did.

Spectacularly.

He had never been to America. He didn't know what North Carolina was like.

But from those pictures, it looked like heaven.

45934650R00350

Made in the USA
Lexington, KY
20 July 2019